B *...* **SH**

by

Bill Rogers

CATON

Published in 2013 by Caton Books

First Edition

Published by Caton Books

Paperback ISBN: 978-1-909856-17-2

Cover Design by Dragonfruit

Design & Layout: Commercial Campaigns

Proofreader: Sarah Cheeseman

Dedication

This book is dedicated to the Memory of WPC Nicola
Hughes and WPC Fiona Bone of Greater Manchester Police,
whose lives were taken in the line of duty
on 18th September 2012

Backwash – aftermath, wake, consequence, effect, result, upshot, outcome, event, issue. A phenomenon that follows and is caused by some previous phenomenon (Thesaurus)

Backwash – the water that rolls back down a beach after a wave has broken (Wikipedia)

Chapter 1

The fingers of his right hand danced a tarantella with the mouse.

Scroll, click, click.

Scroll, click, click.

His left hand hovered expectantly above the keyboard.

Lee was in his element. Today had brought a score of bites and a handful caught, hook, line and sinker.

Scroll, click, click.

He paused, read the comment twice, the second time to savour, and laughed out loud. Literally. None of that LOL nonsense. What had started as a nibble had become a record catch. The index finger and thumb of each hand flew into action. Their cadence rose and fell in time to the rush of words tumbling from his brain. A flush of heat welled in his chest, and spread towards his face and groin. He began to sweat.

There were footsteps on the stairs.

He signed off with his customary barb, clicked *Home* and leaned back in his eBay-bargain, tension-sprung, task chair.

'Hi, Mum.'

Nell Bottomley closed the door with her bum and struggled down the narrow hallway, her carrier bags bouncing off the walls. She shouldered open the kitchen door, dumped the bags on the floor and collapsed onto the pinewood bench.

Her hair, forehead and collar were soaking wet. Beads of sweat dripped onto the tabletop and trickled down the front of her blouse. It had been a hot and humid day. Unseasonably hot. She'd had to stand on the number twenty-two in the middle of rush hour, squashed between a massive, fat, stinking bastard who couldn't be arsed to wash, and some foreign woman who stank of garlic, and God knows what. There were plenty of kids on the bus, most of them with one parent or another, but not one of them offered her a seat. There was no respect any more. The world was going to the dogs. She wiped the sweat from her eyes with the back of her hand. Gone to the dogs, more like.

She bent, rummaged in one of the bags and took out a bottle of vodka. She examined it for a moment. It wasn't the real deal. Couldn't be, not at that price. Lee said it was probably made by a load of East European illegals in a disused factory somewhere in Gorton. He said it would make her blind. Send her mad. Kill her. That's why she'd promised to stop. Truth was she couldn't. Didn't want to. Was past caring.

She unscrewed the top and lifted it to her lips. An hour in the freezer would make it tolerable. She couldn't wait that long. Closing her eyes, she tipped her head back and poured.

The bitter watery liquid flooded her mouth and gushed down her gullet like a stream of burning petrol. Her stomach heaved, forcing her to clamp her hand across her mouth as the reflux hit the back of her throat, bringing with it the taste of ethanol and raw potatoes. She clung to the tabletop and lowered the bottle to her side. She looked at the label again. Searching for something about other uses. Like paint stripper.

Sighing, she screwed the top back on the bottle, dragged the bench over to the wall cupboard beside the fridge and hid the bottle inside the ceramic pasta jar on the top shelf. She pushed the bench back and went to the sink, where she gulped two mouthfuls of cold water, splashed her face and dabbed it dry with a dirty tea towel.

She stood for a moment, catching her breath, listening to the silence. There was something missing. The irritating tapping that accompanied Lee's every waking moment. She shook her head. Probably playing with himself, instead of that bloody computer. Mind you, if he didn't have that, what the hell would he do with himself all day? She rooted in the bags till she found the treat she had bought him, and headed for the stairs.

His door was open, but she knew from bitter experience to warn him that she was there.

'Lee darling, I'm home. Can I come in?'

She nudged the door open with her elbow, and stepped tentatively forward.

'Look what I've brought you.'

Her scream was heard two streets away. Nobody reported hearing the sound of her body hitting the floor.

Chapter 2

Caton drummed his fingers on the dashboard in sheer frustration. Just three point one miles the satnav said, from Central Park to the address in Abbey Hey. Estimated journey time, six minutes forty-seven seconds. Clearly no allowance was made for a Manchester rush hour on a Friday in mid-autumn.

Even with his blues and twos announcing a pressing engagement, it had already taken him ten minutes, and he was still half a mile away, on the railway bridge on Cornwall Street. A wide load and a container lorry had decided to cross the bridge at the same time from opposite directions. Neither was giving way. Even if one of the drivers had been prepared to, the traffic was backed up solid. He cursed, switched off the siren and the flashing blue lights, and climbed out of the car. If you wanted a job doing, best do it yourself.

Five minutes later he was back in the car, sweating cobs, thankful his uniform days were far behind him. Five times he'd received a mouthful of abuse before they'd clocked his warrant card. In two cases, that had simply made it worse.

He switched his blues and twos on again and set off, gaining speed as drivers pulled onto the kerb or mounted the pavement. Estimated time of arrival, one minute. Probably why the traffic was slowing down up ahead. Either they were rubbernecking the crime scene, or there was already a diversion in place.

Suspicious death, the dispatcher had said. One witness in shock. Paramedic in attendance. No suspect on scene. Forensic physician and crime scene manager on their way. He hoped they'd have better luck with the traffic.

A police van was broadside across the street. Beyond it Caton could see a BMW paramedic saloon parked at the kerb. There was a handful of women and some kids huddled in the doorways of the terraces.

He switched off the siren and lights, mounted the pavement, eased past the van, and pulled up behind the ambulance. A uniformed officer stood on the step of a neat red-brick two-up-two-down. Caton locked the car and went, warrant card in hand, to meet him.

Relief flooded the young man's face. Fresh out of training school by the looks of it.

'I'm Constable Byrne,' he blurted. 'I'm glad you're here, sir.'

'Okay, son,' said Caton. 'Take a deep breath, and take your time. Where are we up to?'

Where did that come from? he asked himself. *Son*, and I'm only forty-one myself.

Byrne rattled through it as though he had been going over and over it in his head. Rehearsing for just this moment.

'Victim, deceased, in the back bedroom upstairs. Male, twenty-four years of age, name of Lee Bottomley. Discovered by his mother, Nell, at approximately five twenty. She'd just come home from work. She's in the front room with my partner, Sergeant Green, and the paramedic. She's in shock, but otherwise unharmed. The house is clear. No sign of intruders. There are no obvious hazards. The back door was unlocked, as was the yard gate into the back alley, so I bolted them both to secure the scene, then parked the van across the road to secure the front of the property. We didn't touch anything.'

'Apart from the handles and bolts on the back door and the gate.'

Byrne held up his hands encased in a pair of black leather gloves.

Caton nodded. 'Witnesses?'

'None apart from the mother. Haven't started door-to-door though, obviously.'

It was a textbook handover. Straight out of the manual. And the fact that he had a sergeant riding shotgun confirmed it. Give me a probationer every time, Caton thought. Keen, alert and bang up to date. Just as long as they didn't freeze when it really mattered.

'How did he die?' he said. 'In your opinion.'

Byrne's face fell.

'Badly, sir. Bludgeoned if you ask me, and cut.'

'Not self-inflicted then?'

'Not unless he was a contortionist.'

'Right. Shift that van so the rest of the team can get as close as possible. Then get some crime scene tape.'

He pointed to a lamp post and three black iron downspouts.

'Tie it to those. Then do the same at the back. Anyone wanting access to the houses within the perimeter uses their own back doors, and the part of the alley not sealed off.'

'Yes, sir.'

'And, Byrne.'

'Yes, sir?'

'Well done.'

His reply was drowned out by the wail of a siren as Gordon Holmes' titanium Mondeo swung into the street and screeched to a halt behind the police van.

Cursing, Holmes backed up and squeezed past the van, just as Caton had done.

Caton watched as Gordon hauled his solid frame out from behind the wheel, and Joanne Stuart made a far more dignified exit from the other side. Any time now she'd be taking her competency-based interviews for promotion to inspector. She was ready, but he would be sorry to lose her to another team.

'What have we got, boss?' said Gordon Holmes.

Caton was aware of the woman two doors down watching them intently, ear-wigging. If she'd ever worked in one of the mills round here back in the day, she could probably lip-read.

'DB,' he said. 'WM. SUS.'

Dead body, white male, suspicious death.

'187?' said Holmes. He sounded hopeful.

Caton smiled. Gordon must be the only detective in the UK who insisted on using the old California Penal Code number for murder. A legacy of his addiction to Dirty Harry films.

Two more cars were waved through the cordon set up by PC Byrne between his repositioned van and the house. Jack Benson, the Senior Crime Scene Investigator, was in the first, and Carol Tompkins, Force Forensic Physician, in the second.

'Great,' said Gordon. 'Now we've finally got a doctor and a crime scene manager we can get going.'

They headed for their cars to kit up.

All five of them stood by the bright-red solid-wood front door. In their white and blue Tyvek protective suits they were distinctly out of place. Would have looked more at home in an operating theatre, Caton often thought. Jack Benson was studying the diagram PC Byrne had sketched out for them.

'Straight into the hallway,' he said. 'Stairs on the left. Door on the right leads into the front room. End of the hall opens out into the kitchen. Top of the stairs is the toilet and bathroom. Next to that, the back bedroom where the victim is. Opposite is the door into the front bedroom. Yard out back. Nice and uncomplicated.'

He folded the sketch and placed it at the back of his notebook.

'Too cramped for all of us to go up at once. I suggest that I lead the way, followed by DCI Caton and Dr Tompkins.'

He registered Gordon's snort of disapproval.

'DI Holmes and DS Stuart could talk to the witnesses, and then change places with me and the doc when we've finished.'

'Good idea,' said Caton, pre-empting further discussion.

The door was wide open. They stood outside, Benson in the centre, Caton on his left, Carol Tompkins on his right. Eight feet away, Lee Bottomley was slumped forward over his desk. His head and shoulders were covered in blood that was already matting his hair. The computer monitor lay drunkenly on one side. The LCD screen had been smashed to smithereens. A slimy black liquid leached from the bottom right-hand corner onto the desk. The computer stack down by the young man's side had been destroyed.

'Hazardous substances,' declared Benson, making a note. 'Lead, copper, mercury, bromine, just for starters. Forensics are going to love this.'

He studied the beige carpet and noted the dirt, the scuff marks, and the fragments of metal and plastic from the broken equipment. He took a pack of small cards from his pocket, folded the first one in half and placed it beside the outside of his right foot. Then he stepped forward with his left, placed another card beside the inside edge of his foot and stepped forward again. Two cards later he was level with the body, and two feet to the left, just beyond the ugly stain where the blood had pooled.

He took a deep breath, surveyed the scene before him, made some notes and then retraced his steps, careful to plant each foot beside the corresponding card.

'Right,' he said. 'You first, sir. In my footprints. No touching.'

He didn't need to say it, but he always did. Force of habit.

Caton did as he was told. He found himself breathing in deeply, just as Benson had done. He held it for a moment and let it out slowly. Byrne had been right. It wasn't pretty.

The back of the young man's skull had been crushed. So badly that it had caved in, exposing grey matter. It was difficult to tell, but it looked as though his nose and cheekbone had been broken by the force with which his face had struck the keyboard. Not that that explained the damage the keyboard had sustained across its entire length. Nor did it explain the injuries to his hands that lay face down on the desk. The tip of every finger appeared to have been smashed by a blunt object. No, that wasn't true, he told himself. The index finger of the right hand had been severed at the first knuckle. And something else was missing. Although he wasn't sure what.

He had seen all he needed to see. The photographs and the video would fill in any gaps. He retraced his steps as Benson had done.

'Okay, Doc,' he said grimly, 'he's all yours.'

They watched as Carol Tompkins went through the motions. She checked for a carotid pulse. Crouched, switched on a mini Maglite torch and lifted his left eyelid. She took non-contact readings of his surface temperature using the digital infrared thermometer Benson handed to her. Then she stood, exhaled and checked her watch.

'I gather the paramedic confirmed death?'

'That's right,' said Benson.

'Then I shall check the timing and certify accordingly. The deceased is warm and flaccid, with a surface temperature that indicates, ceteris paribus, that death occurred within the past three hours.'

Ceteris paribus. All things remaining constant. Caton sighed. Whatever else had happened in this room, nothing had remained equal. Nor would they ever be the same again. Not for the victim, nor for his mother.

'Could it have been as recent as within the past hour then?' he asked.

'Probably closer to my earliest estimate.'

'More like three hours then?'

She studied the desktop, and the stain on the carpet by the victim's feet.

'I'd say that was also supported by the extent to which the blood has congealed, wouldn't you, Mr Benson?'

She backed up carefully, her size five and half shoes, wrapped in their protective paper covering, placed meticulously beside the markers.

'There's nothing more for me to do here that your team can't handle,' she told Benson. 'I'm on-call in the morning, but you'll need a Home Office pathologist for this one. Professor Flatman is back tomorrow, so you'll probably get him.' She grimaced. 'Frankly, he's welcome to it.'

Chapter 3

'She's in pieces, I'm afraid.'

Sergeant Jan Green eased the regulation cap over the barely visible hairnet encasing her jet-black bun, and pulled the peak down firmly at the front.

'The drink isn't helping.'

She saw Caton's eyebrows rise.

'Slurred speech, cloudy eyes, metallic breath. My money's on vodka or Bacardi. Possibly gin. Not just because of what she saw either. Regular drinker.'

Caton looked beyond her into the meagre room. Nell Bottomley lay slumped on a red faux leather sofa. Her legs were raised above her head upon two cushions. The hand with which she held a sodden tissue to her nose was shaking. A paramedic in his late forties sat beside her, studying a blood pressure cuff fastened to her left arm.

'She had a vasovagal faint about five minutes ago.' The sergeant explained. 'Nothing serious.'

'Has she told you anything?'

'Her son was in his room when she left to go shopping at about two o'clock this afternoon. When she got back there was nothing out of place. The house was quieter than usual.'

She checked her pocket notebook.

'Normally she can hear the sound of him typing on his keyboard. She went up to his room, found him like that and fainted. When she came round, she crawled downstairs, called 999 on her pay-as-you-go and waited for us to arrive.'

She slipped the elasticated band marked POLICE around her notebook and placed it in a zipped trouser pocket.

'I reckon she topped up on alcohol between then and PC Byrne and me arriving. Can't say I blame her. No sign of a bottle, though.'

'He did well, PC Byrne,' he told her.

She smiled. 'I know. He's a good lad. Wet behind the ears, but a quick learner. By the way, did he tell you the kitchen door and the gate onto the back alley were both unlocked when we arrived?'

'Yes.'

'Apparently she never locks them during the day. No need, she said. Could be how the perpetrators got in.'

'Perpetrators, not perpetrator?'

'Single or plural. It's for you to find out which.'

He nodded towards the woman on the sofa. 'How long before she's going to make any sense?'

She shrugged. 'How long is a piece of string? Not this side of the Nine O'Clock News, I wouldn't think.'

'I'll see if they can find a bed for her at the RMI,' he said. 'And get a family liaison officer to sit with her.'

'Good idea. Can I go now, sir? Check that Byrne is alright? I'll keep an eye on the PCOs while I'm about it.'

'Of course.'

She patted her trouser pocket. 'I'll get this typed up and over to you as soon as possible, sir. Central Park Divisional Headquarters, is it?'

'I'd appreciate that. Number One, Major Incident Room. And it's Tom.'

She flashed him a smile. She had a dimple in each cheek.

'Roger that, sir.'

He watched her squeeze past the Police Community Support Officer manning the front door and disappear into the street. He made a mental note of her name. Maybe she'd fancy a transfer to the Serious Crime Division. It paid to talent spot, especially with DS Stuart due to go before the Promotion Board.

It took five minutes for the paramedic to confirm that they had found a bed for Mrs Bottomley at St Mary's, so that she could be checked over properly and kept under observation overnight. Caton suspected they were doing him a favour, because under normal circumstances there was no way she would be admitted. He was mightily relieved, because it would give Jack Benson and his SOCOs a free hand. Speaking of which, standing here in the hall he was making it nigh on impossible for them to get past with all their gear. He backed into the front room to allow the photographer to squeeze through, and then exited into the street.

Joanne Stuart was in earnest conversation with the officer keeping the crime log. DI Holmes was struggling out of his protective suit.

'Poor kid,' he said. 'Someone had it in for him.'

Gordon was right, as ever. This was no random act of mindless violence. This was pathological rage executed with purpose. The mangled hands and severed fingers were testament to that. Nothing had been desecrated apart from the computer, the keyboard, the young man himself and his mother's memories. He doubted that she would ever be able to look at a photograph of her son, or a home video, even think of him, without seeing that battered bloody head, broken face and mutilated body.

It would be some time before any of his team, him included, hardened as they were, stopped having flashbacks of that scene. Experience told him that surprising though it might be to others, the photographs that would shortly find their way into the murder book and onto the walls of the Incident Room would help. Replacing the need the brain seemed to have to revisit the scene with an impersonal two-dimensional artefact that was a puzzle to be solved, rather than an aberration of which sense had to be made.

They watched as the paramedic guided Nell Bottomley over the step and into the rear of the ambulance.

'If she was a boozer before,' said Holmes, reading Caton's thoughts, 'God knows what she'll be like after this.'

Joanne Stuart joined them.

'Where are we up to?' said Caton.

'Initial door-to-door interviews are under way,' she replied. 'Mixture of PCSOs and uniformed officers. Nothing so far, but the mother's closest thing to a confidante lives four doors down. I've asked the officer to get as much detail from her as possible. Including the whereabouts of any family relatives; there's a sister in Droylsden apparently. Also any disputes or problems involving the Bottomleys that she knows of.'

'CCTV?'

'According to the community PCSO, the nearest are on the industrial estates, Wright Robinson Specialist Academy College, Ashton Old Road and on the A57.'

Caton grimaced. 'Not a lot of use to us until we know what we're looking for.'

'What happened,' said Holmes, 'to, *You're never more than ten metres from a camera*?'

'Google Earth had their vans down here a couple of months ago,' she said, more in hope than expectation. 'Apparently, you can walk the whole area at street level online in virtual reality.'

'What are the odds that the perpetrators were casing the house just as their video van went past?' Gordon replied. 'A billion to one?'

'It'll be useful for our investigation, though,' Caton reflected. 'To be able to remotely visit the area in detail from the Incident Room.'

It was something they had never done before. He couldn't understand why not. He looked up and down the narrow row of solid red-brick terraced houses, with satellite dishes sprouting from the walls, *For Sale* and *To Let* signs on one in four, and barely six or seven private cars in the entire street. When he was growing up streets like this still had a sense of community. Doors were left unlocked, neighbours popped in and out of each other's homes, everyone knew everybody else's business. Not any more. He doubted the door-to-door would turn up anything, unless they came across a busybody who spent her life peering out from behind net curtains.

'It's going to be a long evening, and a longer night,' he told them. 'I'm going home to change. I'll see you in an hour.'

Chapter 4

He was in the shower when he thought he heard the front door open and close. It was closely followed by Kate's voice telling him that she was home. She sounded particularly chirpy. What was it she'd said that she was doing that day? He turned off the water, reached for the towel and began to dry his hair. That was it. She was going to present her paper to the entire faculty: *US Women Serial Killers: Challenging Our Stereotypes.* She'd almost ruined a good night's sleep by insisting on reading it out loud in bed. He'd been really impressed, said as much, and was accused of being patronising. It was bad enough getting that right at work without having to tread a tightrope at home as well.

The door opened and there she stood, smiling broadly.

'Well hallo, handsome,' she said, accompanying it with a worryingly authentic impression of a lascivious leer. 'I see you've started without me. Hang on, and I'll fix us a couple of drinks, whip my things off, and come and join you.'

Before he could stop her, she had disappeared into the bedroom. He rapidly dried himself, grabbed his robe from the back of the bedroom door and stepped into the open-plan lounge just as she emerged from the kitchen area carrying a Bombay Sapphire gin and tonic for him, and a J2O for herself.

Her face fell.

'Oh, Tom, I was serious you know?'

'How did it go?' he asked, hoping to gain a few brownie points before he dropped the inevitable bombshell. 'Your paper?'

She beamed. 'Brilliantly, as it happens. The students lapped it up, and I got the distinct impression that Professor Stewart-Baker was really impressed. How was your day?'

Before he could find the right words, she'd read the expression on his face. Her own was crestfallen.

'Oh no, Tom! It's Friday. Don't tell me you've got a major incident?'

'A murder, I'm afraid. I only came home for a shower and a change.'

She placed the drinks down on the coffee table and turned, hands on hips, to face him.

'You were going to check the suit sizes for your best man and the ushers so we could get them ordered.'

'Don't worry, I'll do a group email before I go back in. We've got plenty of time.'

She wasn't impressed.

'Three weeks tomorrow, Tom. That's not plenty of time.'

'What's left to do?' he asked, playing the innocent. 'The venue is sorted. The church, taxis, and flowers and photos, the catering. I've arranged the honeymoon – and don't ask. I've told you, it's a surprise.'

She raised her eyebrows. 'That's what worries me.'

'Why?'

'You took me to see Cold Play in Sheffield, only to discover that it had been cancelled the day before. Then there was the surprise party for my thirtieth birthday, for which you were the only one not to turn up.'

'That's not fair. An officer was fatally stabbed, and I was on-call.'

'You'd better not be on-call for our wedding.'

'As if.'

She made a passable attempt at a snort, scooped up her glass and headed for the kitchen.

'I picked up a Chinese *Dine In for 2* at M&S,' she told him. 'I'll put yours in a carrier bag; you can shove it in the microwave when you've got a moment. Less the bottle of wine, obviously. I'll console myself with that, and a couple of episodes of *Anger Management*.'

He picked up his glass.

'What's Charlie Sheen got that I haven't?'

'He's always there when I need him,' she replied. 'Just a click away. That reminds me. You'd better have this wrapped up by three p.m. next Sunday. That's when I've booked our first session with Father Brendan at the Sacred Heart.'

He shook his head and downed half of his drink. Kate had been baptised and raised as a Catholic, he Church of England. She had lapsed, as had he, but she was insistent that she wanted their children to experience the same moral code. Getting married in church meant them attending instruction. It was a compromise he was willing to make, but it wasn't going to be easy. His parents' deaths, when the numbness had receded, had left him agnostic at best. Then there was the history of abuse in both churches, and the manner in which they had both failed to deal with it. He suddenly realised that she had been watching him, arms folded.

'I know what you're doing,' she said. 'You're talking yourself out of it. You've changed your mind.'

'I haven't, Kate,' he said. 'Honestly. It's just I have my reservations.'

'It's not just the church, that has problems' she told

him, 'it's any male-dominated community that demands absolute obedience.'

He sat down wearily on the sofa. He hadn't wanted this, not now, when he was going to have to go straight out again.

'I know that,' he said. 'I still believe in what it was, is, that Jesus stands for. Just not the rituals and the man-made laws. You don't have to join up to the whole thing to do that, surely?'

She came and sat down beside him, her hand on his knee.

'I know,' she said. 'But it's easier when you're part of a faith community. It helps a child to see that they're not alone.'

'And their schools have better turned-out pupils, and better results.'

She removed her hand.

'That's not fair. That's not why I want to do this.'

'I know,' he conceded. He put an arm around her shoulder and pulled her towards him. 'I don't suppose it'll be that hard.'

She placed a hand against his chest and wriggled free.

'You'd better get dressed,' she told him. 'I'll put your dinner in a bag.'

He watched her walk into the kitchen dining area. The baby was showing now. What was it, four and a half months? He still didn't know if it was a boy or a girl. Didn't want to know. Just so long as it was healthy, and Kate too.

Ten minutes later, he was ready to leave. She handed him a Tesco carrier bag.

'Dim Sum starter, beef in black bean sauce, egg fried rice. I've kept the raspberry panna cotta. You can have it tomorrow night, assuming they'll allow you a Sunday night in with your wife?'

He held up the bag.

'I thought you said it was from M&S.'

She grinned. 'It is. But I wouldn't want Gordon thinking you'd developed airs and graces living with me.'

He bent to kiss her, but she skipped away.

'What time do you think you'll be back?' she said. 'No, don't answer that. Silly question.'

'There's a limit to what we're likely to find out tonight. Unless it turns out there's a witness who saw something really helpful, or CrimeStoppers comes up trumps, we'll have to wait on the post mortem, and the results of the CCTV trawl. Once we've done an initial analysis and put a plan of action in place, I'll send them home. Better to have a clear head, and an early start in the morning.'

'In that case I might wait up, and you can have the wine tomorrow.'

She patted her bump.

'I was only joking about finishing it myself,' she said. 'Obviously.'

She moved closer, stood on tiptoe and kissed him on the lips.

'Now beggar off,' she said. 'Do what you have to do, and don't ring me if it's going to be after midnight. Just text.'

Chapter 5

Gordon Holmes entered the Incident Room and called for silence.

'The first briefing for Operation Janus will begin in two minutes, at nineteen thirty hours precisely,' he announced.

'Janus?' muttered someone crouched over a keyboard, his head hidden behind the monitor screen. 'Where did that come from?'

'The GMP computer, you wally. Randomly generated,' said DS Carter.

'Does it have any relevance to the case?' the voice persisted.

'Don't tell me DC Woods is back on the Force,' said Holmes, causing muted laughter around the room.

There were those who felt sorry for their disgraced colleague, but many more who were embarrassed for DS Joanne Stuart whose safety Woods had compromised.

Holmes walked across to the offender's desk.

'Well, well, if it isn't the new boy. What the hell do you think *random* means, Detective Constable Hulme?'

Jimmy Hulme was unabashed.

'It's just that Janus was the Roman God of doors and gates,' he replied. 'He had two faces; one looking forwards and one looking back, because a door can let you out, or let you in.'

Holmes pointed to the door to the corridor, through which Caton had just entered.

'I may not be two-faced,' he said, 'but I can let you out of that one any time you like, and there's no saying I'll let you back in again.'

'Is there a problem, DI Holmes?' said Caton, striding to the front of the room.

'No, boss. Just a lesson in philately.'

'Don't you mean philology?' said Joanne Stuart.

Holmes smiled broadly. 'No. I was *stamping* my authority.'

Even Jimmy Hulme joined in the laughter. Caton waited for it to die down.

'Operation Janus,' he said. 'We have been tasked to investigate the brutal murder of a young man, in his bedroom, in the middle of the afternoon. Not a laughing matter.'

The room was silent. Heads turned instinctively towards the crime scene photos already posted on a Perspex board. It didn't need the post-mortem report to transform this suspicious death into a murder inquiry.

Now that he had their full attention, Caton ran through the facts. Some of the team made notes on paper, others directly into tablet computers. All were listening intently. At times like this, when all his team was in the zone, Caton felt you could cut the atmosphere with a knife. When he had finished, he turned to his senior crime scene investigator.

'What do we have so far from Jack?'

Benson stood and turned to face the room.

'Apart from the victim, and his IT equipment, including his mobile phone, nothing else appears to have been touched. As far as we can tell, nothing of obvious value has been taken, nor was there a lot in the house. We'll need the mother to confirm that in due course. There was no sign of the murder weapon, or as is more likely in this case, weapons; one to deal the blow to the head, the other to sever the digits from each hand.'

Heads turned again, briefly.

'We have already established that the victim never allowed anyone into his room, apart from his mother. We have so far only recovered fingerprints relating to two persons. One we already know belongs to the mother. At this stage we are assuming that the others belong to the victim.'

'You've managed to take and match the mother's fingerprints already?' said Caton, knowing from bitter experience how long it normally took.

'Don't ask,' said Benson with a hint of a smile.

'What about footprints?

'Now there we may have been lucky. It looks like the house hasn't been cleaned in years, so there's plenty of dust to hold good impressions. We have some complete and partials in the bedroom, and on the stairs carpet. Problem is eliminating those made by the mother, and the PC who found the body. However…' He paused for effect.

It was a habit Benson had developed lately, but it didn't bother Caton because it meant that people tended to listen even more intently.

'Indications are that the perpetrators entered via the rear of the property. There are traces of dirt in the prints we have in the kitchen, on the stairs and in the bedroom. Since the PC didn't go back upstairs after he'd been down the backyard, we can safely assume they are not his.'

'How do we know the perps came in through the kitchen?' asked DS Carter. 'What's to say the victim didn't answer the front door and let them in himself?'

'We don't know that he didn't,' Benson replied.

'But if they were strangers, it's unlikely he'd have taken them upstairs and let them into his room, and if they were known to him, wouldn't you think he'd know if they intended him harm?'

'My missus was known to me, but I didn't know she was going to slash my clothes and take me for all I was worth,' someone declared.

'Serves you right for playing away,' Holmes told him.

'It's a fair point, though,' said Caton as the laughter faded. 'The injuries this young man received were delivered with anger and rage. This was not a random attack. It was personal. Even if his perpetrators were not known to him, he was certainly known to them.'

'Unless the perpetrators were covered from head to foot in protective clothing, there will be DNA evidence at this scene,' said Benson. 'Trouble is, just like the footprints, we'll need bodies to match them to.'

'You get the evidence,' said Holmes, 'we'll get the bodies.'

Caton hoped the certainty with which his deputy investigating officer had said those words would prove to be justified.

'Thank you, Jack,' he said. 'DS Stuart, where are we up to with local CCTV and Automatic Number Plate Recognition footage?'

'There's good news and bad news, sir,' she said.

In public she still preferred the formality of sir, just as he tended not to use her first name. Shortly after the Bluebell Hollow investigation, rumours of an unprofessional relationship between them had circulated. To anyone who knew them it was patently absurd, as evidenced by the fact that she was in a civil partnership with Abbie, and he was engaged to Kate. But someone had had it in for them. Probably the former DC Dave Woods.

'Give me the good news first,' he said.

'Well,' she began, 'that information from the neighbourhood PCSOs that there were no CCTV cameras on the estate turns out not to be the case. There's an old guy at number 17, that's three doors down from the victim's house and on the other side of the road, who's been having a spate of harassment. Graffiti on his walls and windows, stuff shoved through his letter box.' She grimaced. 'Condoms, dog muck and such like. He didn't think the council or the police were taking it seriously enough, so he got his son-in-law to set up surveillance cameras.'

'You're joking!' said Gordon Holmes.

She shook her head and consulted her notes.

'It's a two-camera vandal-proof system. They can see up to forty feet in complete darkness, and three times that in daylight. The digital video recorder that came with them has two hundred and fifty gigabytes of hard disk, capable of recording up to six weeks of continuous video. His son-in-law got it on eBay for a hundred and sixty quid.'

'How long has he had it running?' asked Caton.

'For the past three weeks.'

'And the victim's house is within their range?'

'Absolutely. Each camera has an eighty-degree angle of view. The one which is angled up the street covers the front of the victim's house and a couple of metres further up the road.'

'So, anybody approaching the house…'

'Will be on those tapes. The cameras have been configured to record only when they detect movement within the picture.'

'How did we find out about this?'

'The old boy volunteered it when he found out what had happened.'

'And the bad news is?' said Caton.

'That so far nothing significant has emerged from those tapes. What is clear, is that nobody approached the front of the house between the victim's mother leaving at two p.m., and her returning to find him dead.'

'That's significant in itself,' Caton pointed out. 'It means that the perpetrator, or perpetrators, must have entered from the rear, just as we suspected.'

Mutters of agreement rippled around the room.

'The other bad news,' she said, 'is that there are no cameras anywhere along the back of the properties or where that alley meets the adjoining streets. Nothing, in fact, until you get to the A57, a mile away, or further down Abbey Hey Lane.'

'Can you put up the map of the immediate area, Douggie?' Caton asked.

The response was almost immediate, suggesting that Douggie Wallace, the Resident Intelligence Officer, had been one step ahead of him. The image on the interactive whiteboard was more than just the pinpoint two-dimensional Google map. There was also the Google Earth satellite image, with street-level options that allowed them to walk through the entire area with pinpoint clarity. There were even photographs that users had posted of the surrounding area. A boon for law enforcement agencies in Caton's opinion, but equally of use to those with less honourable motives.

Caton put himself in the place of the perpetrator. If he were to turn right out of the victim's property, the alley would take him onto busy Abbey Hey Lane where there were cameras, and lots of people. Turn left, however, and it brought you out at a fifty-metre strip of grassland that led down to a ramshackle industrial estate, and the banks of Gorton Lower Reservoir. From there it was possible to continue left under the cover of trees behind Wright Robinson

Specialist College, all the way along the bank of Gorton Upper Reservoir, to cross the narrow strip between the reservoirs beyond where there was plenty of woodland cover. At this point there was a choice between Denton golf course, or the former Fallowfield railway line all the way to Staylbridge, four miles away. In the opposite direction it would lead them undetected, other than by the occasional dog walker or fitness fanatic, all the way to Sale Water Park, or Old Trafford, depending on which branch they decided to take. Six miles or more in either case, with innumerable opportunities to leave the path and disappear into surrounding streets and industrial premises. The rest of the team were making the same computations.

'If he had a mountain bike he could have been miles away in a matter of minutes,' said Gordon Holmes.

'Or if he went across the reservoirs and had a car waiting on the other side,' DS Stuart observed.

'And if there was more than one of them they could have each gone in a different direction,' said DS Carter. 'Make it more difficult to spot them.'

'They only needed to have worn a baseball cap and cycled with their heads down,' said Jack Benson, 'and no one's going to see their faces. If they were cycling reasonably fast there's not much chance anyone's going to remember what they were wearing either.'

Caton knew they were right.

'Be that as it may,' he said, 'I still want that CCTV and ANPR footage. And I'll get the Press Office to prepare an appeal asking anyone who was in the vicinity of the crime scene, and in particular on the old Fallowfield line, on or around the reservoirs, and the golf course, between thirteen thirty and seventeen hundred hours today, to contact us.'

Douggie Wallace raised his hand.

'When you say *us*, boss, do you actually mean this team?'

Caton knew what he was getting at. He might have been lucky to get his old team back, but there was no way he had enough officers to answer the flood of calls that might come in.

'This isn't something we can filter through CrimeStoppers,' he said, 'but I take your point. I'll see if I can get us some extra bodies drafted in to staff the phones. I'd like you, Douggie, to draw up a list of questions they'll need to use as a checklist.'

'What if we don't get the bodies?' said the intelligence officer.

'We'll cross that bridge when we come to it.' He turned back to the map. 'Can you bring up the street-level view,' he said, 'and take us down the alley and out to the point where the lane splits by the reservoirs?'

'There's no coverage of any of the alleys,' said Wallace. 'No way would they have been able to get their video van down there, even supposing people were interested.'

'We're interested,' Holmes said.

Wallace ignored him.

'But I can take us down the street parallel to the alley, to the point where it emerges.'

They watched in silence as the camera panned down the street, past the solid wooden door of the victim's house, past the occasional white-painted frontage, incongruous among the rows of dark red Accrington brick. Past *For Sale* and *To Let* signs, and walls sprouting satellite dishes. Wallace paused the camera for a moment and homed in on one particular house.

'There are the cameras DS Stuart was referring to,' he said.

A pair of dark grey pods, the size of tennis balls, a metre apart, had been concealed beneath the eaves. Their presence was even less obvious because of the decorative row of scalloped bricks that the builders had added to the entire street, and into which the cameras had been cunningly nested.

'No wonder the neighbourhood team didn't spot them,' DS Carter remarked.

'Perhaps the perpetrators did, which is why they came in through the back?' said DC Hulme.

'This is all conjecture,' Caton reminded them. 'We don't know for certain what happened. Let's not turn our hypotheses into assumptions just yet.'

The camera continued its journey to the end of the street and turned left. It paused for a moment, swivelled through one hundred and eighty degrees, and focused in on the alley. A pair of closed black metal gates, approximately seven feet high, spanned the gap.

'They're only locked at night,' said DS Stuart. 'And they were definitely open today, I checked. Same with the ginnels that run off the street into the alley.'

The camera panned out and tracked down the street between an iron-railed public green space and children's park on one side, and the side wall of the end-of-terrace properties. When it reached the bottom, where the road terminated, and a tree-lined tarmac path led off through a gate towards the reservoirs, it stopped.

'That's as far as we can go in this view,' Wallace told them.

It had left Caton none the wiser, except to strengthen his gut feeling that this was the route the perpetrators would have used. He held out little hope of accurate and useful sightings, let alone comprehensive descriptions of the killer, or killers.

This had been too well planned, despite the intensity of the attack. What he needed was a motive of some kind. The clue to that he felt certain lay in the manner of the death, the mutilation and the smashed equipment. And that meant finding out all there was to know about the victim. Every last detail of his life.

Ged, the Office Manager, appeared at his shoulder. The out-of-character blush on her cheeks and neck suggested that she was embarrassed to be interrupting his briefing. She needn't have worried. As far as Caton was concerned she was as important as any member of his team, and always would be.

'Excuse me, sir,' she said, 'but the victim's aunt is downstairs asking to speak to whoever's in charge of the investigation.'

'His aunt?'

'Yes, sir. His mother's sister. Apparently, after two uniformed officers let her know what had happened she went straight to the hospital to find that her sister had been sedated. She told the family liaison officer who's sitting by the bed that she wanted to speak to whoever was in charge of the case. The officer sent for a squad car. The sister's in interview room two right now. I thought you should know.'

Chapter 6

She looked nothing like her sister. They shared snub noses and a sallow complexion, but there the likeness ended. Where Nell Bottomley was short, thin and gaunt, with hollow watery eyes, sunken cheeks and straggly hair dyed blonde, her sister was a good eight inches taller, six stone heavier, with dark brown eyes and a shock of curly-permed brown hair that framed a fleshy face the size of a watermelon.

'Mrs Duggan,' said Caton. 'My name is Detective Chief Inspector Caton; this is my colleague, Detective Inspector Holmes. I would like to offer you my sincere condolences, and…'

She stopped pacing the room like a caged lion and cut him off mid-sentence.

'Sod your condolences!' she said. 'What I want to know is what you're doing about it?'

Caton pointed to the chair.

'If you'd like to sit down, I'll be happy to tell you.'

For a moment it looked as though she was going to tell him where to put his chair, or worse, put it there herself. Then she thought better of it, took a deep breath and sat down.

Gordon Holmes appeared mesmerised by the way her chest had swelled as she breathed in, and then by the way her backside hung over the edges of the chair. Caton tugged at his jacket and nodded towards the other chair. When his deputy was seated, Caton started again.

'As I was saying, Mrs Duggan, I would like to offer you my sincere condolences, and assure you that we are doing everything we can to catch the person, or persons, who did this to your nephew. We *will* catch them, I promise you.'

She responded with a grunt.

'You're telling me you haven't the faintest idea who did it, but you're definitely going to catch them. Am I right?'

'This investigation is only a few hours old,' Caton began, but she cut him off yet again.

'I am right, aren't I?' Another snort.

Beside him Caton could feel Gordon Holmes preparing to pitch in and put her firmly in her place. He placed a hand on Gordon's arm to stop him.

'Yes, Mrs Duggan,' he said, 'you are perfectly correct. We don't have the faintest idea who entered you sister's home and brutally murdered your nephew. But we *will* catch that person. To do that we need all the help we can get. I assume that's why you came here, to help us find his killer?'

She took a deep breath between clenched teeth, sucking in her cheeks in the process. It looked as though her face had imploded.

'Course I am. Why else would I be here?'

Caton could tell that she was one of those people who ordinarily wouldn't be seen dead helping the police. The only way that she could come to terms with doing so was to be combative. But the wind had gone out of her sails.

'Thank you,' he said. 'I have officers gathering and examining evidence from the scene, but right now we desperately need to find out all we can about your nephew. Anything you can tell us about him, anything at all, would be invaluable.'

Furrows appeared in the folds of skin on her forehead.

'Our Lee?' she said. 'He was a loner. Always has been. A bit weird really, but he was as good as a carer to our Nell.'

'Carer?' said Caton. 'In what way does your sister need a carer?'

Her eyes searched his to see if he was being serious.

'Have you seen her?'

Caton nodded.

She sat back and folded her arms across her generous bosom.

'Well then. She lives out of a bottle. Half the time she's no idea what she's doing. Nearly burnt the house down twice. If Lee hadn't been there she would have done. He either cooked their meals or went down the Chinese for takeaways. He did what little housework got done. Helped her up the stairs when she was too pissed to do it herself. Covered her with a blanket on the sofa if she was too far gone. Made sure she didn't choke on her own vomit.' She sniffed. 'God knows what she's gonna do without him.'

For the first time he had a sense that she was acknowledging her own loss.

'Did Lee have any enemies, Mrs Duggan?' he said.

More furrows, and raised eyebrows.

'Enemies?'

'Enemies.'

She shook her head slowly. 'Not that I know of. He was harmless really. He was bullied at every school he went to, except his last one. And he's always been the butt of jokes and tricks – you know how cruel kids can be round here. Nothing like this, though.'

'Why was he bullied?'

'Why is anybody bullied? Because he wasn't into

football, and going round in a gang. He worked hard at school and kept himself to himself. Always had his head in a book, glasses on the end of his nose. Bit of a nerd, I suppose.'

'You said he'd been bullied at every school except his last one. Why not at his last one?'

'First off, it wasn't a school, it was Manchester College. My Alfie went there at the same time. He reckoned it was because Lee was amazin' with computers. He could fix anythin'. The other students used to come to him for help. Bit of a geek Lee was, Alfie said. Apparently, at college that was a good thing.'

'Tell me about his father,' said Caton.

She pulled a face that would have graced the world gurning championship.

'Useless good-for-nothing loafer. She's better off without him. All he did was sponge off her. And he's the reason she got into drink in the first place.'

'Where is he now?'

'God knows. Last I heard he'd shacked up with some other poor cow in Salford. Got her pregnant, and then when her brothers came round to sort him out he buggered off out of there too. Good job he did. There's no telling what they'd have done to him.'

'When was this?'

'Couple of years ago.'

'Did he maintain contact with his son?'

'Never paid any maintenance, never wanted any contact.' She thought about it. 'Last time he saw our Lee was at his third birthday party. That's when she threw him out. He turned up when it was almost over. Pissed as usual. Tried to cut the cake with her hair straighteners. Thought it was an electric carving knife.'

'An absent father, then?'

'Absent? Don't make me laugh. He was never there in the first place. Physically, emotionally or mentally.

She'd have been better off with a turkey baster.'

'You didn't like him, then?' said Holmes, earning a frown from his boss.

'Can you tell us a bit more about Lee?' said Caton. 'What were his interests?'

'Interest, more like. Just his computer. Played with it all day. First thing you heard when you walked in the house was tippy tappy, tippy tappy on that bloody keyboard.'

Her voice faltered and her eyes began to well up. She dabbed at them with the corner of her blouse. Caton handed her a tissue from the box on the table. She took it, blew her nose and crumpled it in her hand

'I told him he'd be better off getting a synthesiser, then he could make a bit of money down the club.'

Caton looked at his deputy and sat back. Gordon Holmes leaned forward.

'Talking of money,' he said, 'did Lee have a job at all?'

She shook her head again. 'Not what you'd call a proper job. He applied for a few when he left college, but he never got past the interview. It's one thing being clever with computers, another being good with people.'

'So he was on benefits?'

'Him and his mum both. Mind you, he made some money on the side repairing people's computers, unblocking mobile phones, that sort of thing.' She gave a wry smile. 'I wouldn't have told anyone if he'd still been alive. But now…'

Her voice tailed off as she reached for another tissue and pretended to blow her nose. She crumpled it up and put both balls of tissue on the table.

'I suppose our Nell's gonna have to come and stay with me for a while,' she said. 'Can't have her going back there. Not till you've caught them.'

'That would be a great help,' Caton told her. 'My officers will still be gathering evidence from the house for a day or two. I'd like to send a family liaison officer to stay with her during the day, if that's alright with you?'

He steeled himself for her objections. They never materialised.

'My old man is going to go mad,' she said. 'We haven't got room to swing a cat. Alfie can go and stay with his mates for a while, I suppose. He'll be glad of it. So will I to tell the truth. Out of sight, out of mind.'

Chapter 7

With less than five hours' sleep apiece, and a frustrating morning briefing behind them, Caton and Holmes had endured the mental torment of Professor Flatman's post mortem examination of Lee Bottomley. It was not enough that they had to witness the gruesome procedure and the delight which he took in it, they also had to suffer his pompous, ponderous, patronising explanations. It was a relief when he finally arrived at his concluding summary.

'I know you've been taking notes, gentlemen, and that you'll be wanting my report yesterday, which isn't going to happen, obviously, so I'll give you the headlines one last time. Ready?'

Caton chewed his cheek. Beside him Gordon was rubbing his chin furiously. They had been ready for over an hour. Flatman smiled as though enjoying a private joke.

'Jolly good.'

He sat on a stool and turned to face the screen on which a series of images appeared each time he pointed the remote.

'So, the blows to the skull are what killed him. As a result of the first blow, here, he suffered a traumatic intracranial injury, with coup and contrecoup damage to the parietal lobe, here, and the frontal lobe, here, respectively. This would not have killed him immediately, but it would have rendered him unconscious, could well have done within forty-eight hours or so. There was, however, a second blow at the base of the skull, here, which shattered the cervical vertebrae C1 and C2, and crushed and severed the spinal column. It was this injury that caused his death. The regulation of his heart, and his breathing, would have ceased. Given his other injuries, death would have been more or less instantaneous.'

He turned to face them.

'Cold comfort for his mother, but preferable to her dwelling on the fact that he might have suffered.'

He swivelled back to the screen. An image appeared of grey and black flecks that, magnified thousands of times, looked like metal shavings.

'Both injuries were caused by the same blunt instrument. Smooth curved metal, specks of black paint, some oil and grease. Possibly a tyre lever. But then it could have been any number of things you might find in a garage or a mechanic's toolkit. The blows to the back of the hands were almost certainly delivered using the same instrument that stove his skull in.'

'And the laceration?' said Gordon Holmes.

The pathologist looked over his shoulder and gave him a wintry stare.

'*Cut*, Detective Inspector, cut. The term laceration is reserved for a torn or jagged wound. Usually caused by a collision, a fall of some kind, or a blow. In this instance the blows to the back of the hands, to which I have just referred, were what I would term lacerations. I'd have thought you'd have picked up that distinction by now?'

Holmes was about respond when the toe of Caton's shoe caught him just above the ankle.

'Ow!' he complained, bending to rub his shin. 'That

hurt. You could have lacerated it.'

Professor Flatman smiled benignly. 'You see,' he said, 'you do remember. As for the *cut* that severed the index finger of his right hand, I'm fairly confident that was made with a pair of bypass secateurs.'

'Secateurs? You mean pruning shears?' said Holmes.

'If I'd meant pruning shears, or hand shears, or anvil shears, or parrot-beak shears, I would have said so,' Flatman replied testily.

Holmes saw Caton's foot hovering, and remained silent.

'What's special about bypass pruners, Professor?' asked Caton.

'They consist of two blades that pass each other, just like a pair of scissors. One of the blades will always be curved. Generally, it will be concave. The other blade can either be concave, convex or straight, just so long as it passes the first blade.'

He turned towards DI Holmes as though explaining to a simpleton.

'Hence the term by-pass.'

He turned back to Caton.

'Although we have only the stump of the finger, I am fairly confident that if and when you recover the missing piece, the surface of the bone will show a reciprocal cut, typical of bypass secateurs, at an angle to that on the attached digit.'

'How,' said Gordon Holmes, after moving out of range of Caton's foot, 'can you be sure it wasn't one of the other kind?'

The pathologist was torn between ignoring him and taking yet another opportunity to display his erudition. The desire to present won hands down.

'Because anvil secateurs have only one blade, which closes onto a flat surface. They would have crushed the finger rather than leaving a clean cut. The parrot-beak secateurs have two concave blades which would not have had sufficient force to sever bone. They are best suited for exceptionally narrow stems, or for cutting herbs, for example.'

'Secateurs – easy to come by and to slip in the pocket,' Caton observed.

'Exactly so,' said Flatman. 'I always carry a pair in a little holster when I am in the garden.'

Holmes took another step backwards.

'Where were you, Professor,' he said, 'yesterday afternoon, between the hours of thirteen thirty and fifteen hundred?'

'I told you he had a sense of humour,' said Holmes as they made their way back to Central Park Divisional HQ.

'It was touch and go there for a moment,' said Caton. 'I keep telling you, you'd better hope these smart comments don't come back to bite you next time you're the SIO.'

'No chance while you're so intent on working on cases yourself instead of putting your feet up in the office like chief inspectors are supposed to do.'

This was the first time that Gordon had intimated any frustration at acting as his deputy senior investigating officer. Not that Gordon hadn't led some major investigations in the past few years. It was just that they had been few and far between. Unwilling to take his eyes off the road for more than a second, Caton glanced at his deputy. The traffic on Princess Parkway was moving swiftly for a change. He wondered if there was a fire engine ahead of them for whom the lights were automatically staying on green in sequence.

'Come on, Gordon,' he said, pulling over into the

nearside lane to let a marked police car, lights flashing, speed past towards Moss Side, 'you know that isn't going to happen. The only reason I've resisted all the pressure to go for promotion to superintendent is because I'd miss the action, and hate the politics and the paperwork. Anyway, I thought you enjoyed being part of the team?'

Holmes reached for the lever beneath his seat and eased it back so that he could stretch out his feet. It also meant the boss would have to turn his head to look at him. Caton wondered if that was deliberate. If he wanted to avoid eye contact.

'It's a great team,' Holmes replied. 'The best. I love being part of it, you know that. And I know where you're coming from about promotion. I don't want it either. Same reasons as you.'

He made a sound that hovered between a grunt and a chuckle.

'Mind you, Marilyn won't be happy until I'm Chief Constable. It's the pension she's thinking about, not me.'

'I'm not saying you couldn't make Super,' said Caton. 'Because you could, and you'd do a better job than some of the fast-track flummeries we've got at present. But you'd hate it. It would probably see you in an early grave, before you had time to draw your pension.'

'Do me a favour, boss,' Holmes replied, 'tell that to the wife.'

As they approached the Moss Lane crossroads Caton eased to a halt, his eyes on the rear-view mirror as a large white van thundered towards them, seemingly oblivious to the fact that the lights ahead had changed to red. He pressed his brake pedal, and simultaneously flipped the switch that operated the flashing blue lights. Holmes sat bolt upright and braced himself. With a screech of brakes the van fishtailed, straightened up and slid to a standstill inches from their rear bumper.

Holmes grabbed the door handle and unclipped his seatbelt.

'Leave it, Gordon,' said Caton, staring at the pale face reflected in his rear-view mirror. 'He's had a bloody good shock.'

'He's not the only one!' Holmes proclaimed, turning to stare at the unfortunate driver in a way that could only be interpreted as a desire to cause serious harm.

Caton gazed through his side window at the carpet of wild flowers sown by the City Council in the field across from the Royal Brewery. There was a time when he could have named most of the yellow, blue, pink and purple heads bending in the slipstream of traffic thundering by. Now he could only recall the common poppy, whose blood-red blooms adorned year-round the war memorials and cenotaphs.

Another field of flowers filled his mind's eye. On a roadside verge seven miles away, in Hattersley. A thousand or more bouquets. Among them, a child's posy of wild flowers. A public outpouring of grief for two female colleagues, senselessly murdered. His feelings were still raw, as they were for everyone in the Force. He felt sad and angry that it would have taken just a fraction of the respect for law and order that their deaths had surfaced to prevent them happening in the first place.

A horn sounded from somewhere behind the van.

'Boss!'

He turned, saw that the lights had changed, and set off.

'Penny for them, boss?' said Holmes. 'You were well away there.'

Caton knew that it would help to talk about it. But not to Gordon. He was a hell fire and damnation advocate. In his view even hanging would be too good for the perpetrator still awaiting trial. There were times, and this was one of them, when Caton found it hard to disagree.

When it was clear a reply was not forthcoming, Holmes settled back in his seat.

'Alright then,' he said. 'Answer me one question.'

'Go on,' Caton replied.

'What's a flummery?'

Chapter 8

'Nothing from the cameras,' said Joanne Stuart. 'But sightings of people on the various paths and tracks have started to trickle in from the door-to-doors and CrimeStoppers.'

'Any of interest?' Caton asked.

She swivelled round to face the monitor and pulled up a document. It was a list in table form.

'I've started to categorise them by location, time, description and likelihood,' she said. 'That way, we begin to get a picture of who was where at any one time, and what direction they were travelling in.'

'What are your criteria for likelihood?'

She frowned. 'They're not very scientific, I'm afraid. I've ruled as unlikely anyone who was obviously too old or infirm, with a dog, or travelling in the wrong direction – that's towards the scene rather than away from it at the critical time.'

'Why with a dog?'

She half turned to face him.

'Because there weren't any pets in that house. A dog would have left traces. There weren't any.'

'They could have left it tied to the gate at the bottom of the yard?'

'True, but then the dog would have slowed them down. Maybe barked. Drawn attention to them?'

'Fair enough,' he said. 'What about *likely*?'

'The reverse really. Young enough, fit enough, travelling to or away from the scene during the relevant periods. Described as suspicious by the witness.'

'Maybe your criteria aren't scientific, but they are logical. So, what have you got so far?'

'In the main, more or less what we'd expect. People taking short cuts on foot or on their bikes, walking their dogs, pupils in uniform going home having stayed late at school.

'Any of those pupils old enough to have done it?'

She raised her eyebrows. 'What's *old enough* these days?'

'Good question. But you know what I mean.'

'All of them were teenagers. A couple were more like students. Sixteen to nineteen years of age. None of them struck any of the callers as being suspicious. Dawdling, most of them. The only one on a bike was loaded down with a gym bag, a sandwich box and a rucksack. Not the sort of things you'd take to a murder. I've started plotting them on Google Earth.'

She clicked the Blue Earth icon at the foot of the screen. Up jumped a map centred on the Bottomleys' house. A series of numbered yellow pins marked each of the sightings. He counted four on tracks across the golf course, another seven on the paths skirting the reservoirs and more than double that number on the broad tarmac stretch of the old Fallowfield railway line.

Caton craned forward to look over her shoulder.

'Which are in your most likely category?'

Her mouse moved over one of the pins on the golf course. She left clicked twice on number 7 on the golf course, and the camera zoomed in. He could see now that it wasn't a track at all, it was Cornhill Lane. She consulted the table.

'Number 7, presumed to be a man, cycling at speed towards the motorway.'

Caton checked the map. For just under six hundred metres the lane wound its way across the golf course, past three farms and ended abruptly at the foot of an embankment bordering the M60.

'Why presumed to be?'

'Because he was wearing a parka, had the hood up, and she only got a glimpse of him.'

'She?'

'The farmer's wife. She was crossing this yard.'

A parka, with the hood up, in early October, on an unseasonably warm afternoon. He could see why she'd put him down as suspicious. Assuming he was a he.

'Where was he going?'

It was a rhetorical question. There were just three possibilities: one of the remaining farms, or the motorway.

'If whoever it was tried to cross the motorway,' she said, 'with or without the bike, they'd have been spotted by the cameras.'

She was right. There was an overhead gantry on the southbound carriageway less than a hundred metres north of where the cyclist would have emerged, and another one further south.

'The bike wasn't dumped at the foot of the embankment,' she added. 'I got the locals to check.'

'Someone could have found it and ridden off with it.'

'True. Of course, he could always have turned left and used this footpath.'

She zoomed in and followed the thin line between the foot of the embankment and the golf course until it reached King's Road.

It didn't make sense, he decided. If that had been his

destination, he needn't have crossed the reservoirs and the golf course at all. He could have used the Fallowfield line, or any one of the paths behind the college.

'Unlikely, though,' she said, mirroring his thoughts. 'He'd have been spotted by golfers for sure, and no one has rung in, yet. DC Hulme is checking the farms to see if he ended up there.'

'What about the others?' he said.

She went through them in turn.

'Youth jogging along this track behind Wright Robbie High School, away from the scene just before five p.m.'

'It's a college now,' said DS Carter, joining them.

'Same difference,' she replied. 'The caller had him down as suspicious because he wasn't dressed for running. He was wearing trainers alright, but he was in jeans and an anorak. And guess what?'

'The hood was up,' said Caton.

'And his head was down. Like he didn't want to be recognised.'

'Age?'

'Fifteen to twenty? She couldn't be sure.'

She moved the mouse to the left, halting about a mile along the disused railway line.

'Number 3. A pair of youths. IC1 and IC3. About seventeen or eighteen years of age, according to the witnesses. Three people mentioned them. One white Caucasian, the other black: African or African-Caribbean heritage.'

'What was special about them?'

'It looked like they were arguing. Although one witness said he thought they were joshing around. Pushing each other in the middle of the path. Forcing people to walk round them.'

'Seems unlikely,' said Caton. 'Drawing attention to themselves like that?'

'Villains falling out?' observed Carter.

'That's what I wondered,' said Joanne Stuart. 'There was one other thing, though.'

'Go on.'

'They were wearing hoodies, and…'

'Their hoods were up!' chorused Caton and Carter.

'Close,' she said, grinning. 'One of them – the IC1 – had his up. The other one didn't. They left the path and turned left onto Kenwood Road.'

'That's an industrial estate,' said Carter. 'What would they be doing on there?'

Caton watched as she changed to street view and led them between the warehouses, repair shops and wholesale units. It was a good question. They wouldn't be going to work at that time of day, especially on a Friday.

'What this?' he asked as she came back out into aerial view.

'Start of the housing estates,' she replied. 'Terraces, then semis, and then some really nice detached. I suppose they could have been heading for any of those.'

'What time was this?' he asked.

'First sighting at four fifty p.m. heading west.'

Well within the timescale for someone heading away from the house after killing Lee Bottomley. It just didn't feel right somehow.

'Any others?'

'No, that's it. But it's early days yet. You know how long it takes for some people to bother to get in touch.'

He did. There had been one case where a vital witness didn't come forward until an innocent man had been in jail for fourteen years.

'So there was nothing suspicious in the alleyways, or on the streets approaching the crime scene?'

She shook her head, causing her neat brown bob to sway from side to side.

'No, boss, sorry.'

'Not your fault,' he said. 'That's a good set-up you've got there, DS Stuart. And remember, I never shoot the messenger.'

'He might not shoot them,' Nick Carter observed wryly when Caton was out of hearing, 'but he has been known to give them a good bollocking.'

Chapter 9

'It's a soft, sweet pudding that's normally made using stewed fruit, thickened with cornflower.'

'What is?' said Caton, wondering if Gordon Holmes had finally flipped.

'A flummery.'

'I didn't know that.' Caton signalled right and turned onto Alan Turing Way.

'Not a lot of people do. I Googled it.'

'Not on GMP time I hope?'

'My mother always said that you shouldn't use words you don't know the meaning of.'

'Did she ever tell you it was a bad idea to wind up your superiors?'

His DI chuckled. 'I was the apple of her eye. She never thought anyone could be my superior.'

'That explains it,' said Caton.

'What?'

'Everything. In particular, the fact you never admit you're wrong.'

'That's not true!' He sounded genuinely wounded by the insinuation.

They drove in companionable silence past the imposing bulk of the Etihad Stadium and the gentle silvered curve of the National Cycling Centre, gleaming in the early morning sun. Caton was delighted that it would remain the home of Britain's elite cycling despite London, with its own velodrome, having just hosted the most successful Olympic and Paralympic Games in history. It was only right in his view, given that all those dozens of cycling gold medals won in Beijing, and London, had been made in Manchester. And hadn't the City Council demonstrated its commitment further by helping to fund the 24-million-pound National BMX Centre right next door? It made a change to see loyalty and commitment being rewarded.

He crossed Ashton New Road, then Ashton Old Road, and turned left into Whitworth Street.

'Where did you say we were going, boss?' said Holmes.

'Given that his mother is still under sedation, I thought we'd try the next best place to find out more about our victim. Manchester College. The Openshaw Campus. Lee Bottomley was a student there. He left two years ago.'

Holmes rubbed his chin.

'So he'd have been what, twenty-two when he left?'

'I guess so.'

'That's what's wrong with this generation. Perpetual students, the lot of them.'

'That's because they can't get a job,' Caton told him. 'We are in a recession, or hadn't you noticed?'

Holmes snorted. 'That's only an excuse. They're too bloody idle if you ask me.'

'I didn't,' said Caton, turning right into Clayton Lane and immediate right onto the access road to the main car park.

He parked up in a visitor bay, and the two of them climbed out. Holmes looked around and whistled approvingly.

'This is smart,' he said. 'Even posher than Central Park.'

It was difficult to disagree. Modern red and grey brick buildings nestled among immaculately mown green lawns. A vast white canopy appeared to float like a horizontal sail above the polished white stone steps of an outdoor performance space, much like the one in Castlefield. They approached the main building between two large rectangular pools of water, on the banks of one of which a pair of mallard ducks stood watching a heron, statue-like among the reeds. Small groups of students lounged on the grass, and couples occupied the stylish concrete benches by the water.

'More like a university than a college,' Holmes observed. 'What do they study here?'

'What you'd expect,' said Caton, who had done his homework before setting off. 'Employment-related mainly. Business and computing, and IT courses, media, drama, fashion. Most of them all the way up to and including degree level. You can even do an online Master's in Business Administration degree. So you were right in a way. As good as a university.'

'Better, if you ask me,' Holmes replied. 'More like a University of Life. I wouldn't mind our Jimmy coming here.'

'How's he doing these days?' said Caton. It was only a couple of years ago that he had been wagging school, and causing Gordon and Marilyn stress that had started to affect his DI's performance.

Gordon stopped and looked out across the water at a couple canoodling.

'Alright, as far as I can tell. At least he's talking to us these days in a more or less civilised fashion, instead of all that grunting and surly silences.'

'He takes his GCSEs this year, doesn't he?' said Caton.

Holmes turned to look at him and smiled.

'That's right. Fancy you remembering that.'

It paid to remember the little things about your team. Caton had learnt the hard way that morale and loyalty were about more than pats on the back.

Through the automatic glass doors, the concourse opened out ahead of them. Black steel girders, a flat glass roof and a broad suspended wall of polished wood the colour of mahogany led the eye down the atrium to three huge signs proclaiming *Media Centre*, *Library*, and *Lecture*. Halfway down they stopped at the Reception desk. Caton showed his warrant card.

'Mr Lawrence Raymond. He's expecting us.'

She pointed to one of the low-cut brown leather chairs on the other side of the concourse.

'He's waiting for you over there.'

A youngish man, late thirties, of African-Caribbean heritage, rose from his chair and came to greet them. Of athletic build, he stood head and shoulders above them both.

'He's on *my* team,' whispered Holmes.

'What is it you do, Mr Raymond?' said Caton once they had settled themselves into their chairs in the office to which he had taken them, attached to a very impressive IT suite.

Raymond ran a hand across his tightly coiled hair as he leaned back comfortably in his chair.

'I am a senior lecturer in computing and information technology. I teach on the BTEC Diploma courses and other higher professional qualifications. I also act as a tutor and course manager on our offender learning programmes.'

'Offender learning?' said Holmes, immediately alert.

Caton tried to catch his colleague's eye. He knew what Gordon would be thinking. The assumptions he would already be making.

'That's right,' said the lecturer. 'We are the leading

provider for offender learning throughout the UK. We have over three thousand staff working in Her Majesty's prisons, immigration removal centres, private sector run prisons, approved premises, and within the community.'

It was obviously something of which he felt immensely proud.

Holmes looked sceptical. 'Learning to offend more successfully,' he said, 'is what prison does in my book. What do you do that's different?'

Caton frowned at him, but Lawrence Raymond had heard it all before and took it in his stride.

'That's the point, Mr Holmes,' he replied. 'We are trying to break that upward spiral. By helping them to acquire worthwhile knowledge, to develop appropriate work-based skills, and skills for life, including anger management, effective communication and coping skills. Did you know, for example, that eighty per cent of prisoners have the writing skills of an eleven year old? And most of these students have poor emotional intelligence. It explains how they ended up falling foul of the law. Why they are in custody. We try to fill that vacuum. Above all, we aim to improve their employability, and to develop progression pathways for them. In doing so we are helping to bring down reoffending rates. And it appears to be working. Overall crime is falling. Reoffending by juveniles serving custodial sentences is down by over fourteen per cent.'

It all sounded admirable to Caton. Except for the bit about falling foul of the law. It made the police, and the courts, sound like rogue poachers setting traps for the innocent and unwary.

'Lee Bottomley wasn't on an offender programme surely?' he said.

Raymond shook his head. 'No, not at all. I was just

responding to Detective Inspector Holmes's question, that's all.'

'But he could have worked alongside some of these offenders?' Holmes persisted.

'Only once they'd moved out of specific programmes targeted at offenders. And isn't that true for all of us, Inspector, that we may be working with ex-offenders without ever knowing it? And with supposedly law-abiding people who regularly offend without ever getting caught? Like drink drivers, and people who break the speed limits?'

Before his DI could respond, Caton said firmly, 'Perhaps we should concentrate on what Lee Bottomley actually studied here, and with whom, and what kind of person he was, rather than whether or not he may have rubbed shoulders with an offender.'

To his credit, Lawrence Raymond appeared relieved to be moving away from that particular subject. Holmes, on the other hand, looked distinctly miffed at what he saw as a put-down.

'Lee Bottomley was actually very bright,' said Raymond. 'We didn't just go on his GCSE results, we gave him an initial assessment – a skills and knowledge test – as a result of which we put him straight onto the BTEC Diploma course.'

'What did that involve?' said Caton.

'Using IT to present information, an introduction to computer systems, website development, customising applications software, database and spreadsheet software, graphics and so on. Actually, he was well ahead on almost all of that.'

'Is that what he left with, a BETC Diploma?'

'No, that was just for starters. He went on to the IT Technician course.'

'What did that cover?'

'It's for anyone who wants to work in IT

networking and computer repairs. And he didn't stop there. By the time he left…' He consulted a file on his monitor. '…he was twenty-two years old by the way, he knew just about everything there was to know about using, maintaining and developing IT networks, servers, routers, security systems and dealing with threats. And much, much more.'

'If he was that good,' said Gordon Holmes, 'how come he didn't have job?'

Raymond sighed and shook his head.

'It takes more than practical competence and creativity, I'm afraid. Poor Lee was able to communicate very effectively through a computer, but not face-to-face.'

'What was that down to, confidence, self-esteem?' asked Caton.

'Neither,' the lecturer replied. He noted the surprise on both of their faces. 'I know, that sounds daft, but it's true. He was well aware of his ability when it came to information technology and computing, and he did not lack confidence in tackling work-related challenges. If anything, his problem was that he not only had no interest in sharing his knowledge, or discussing his work with anybody else, but he was also rather disdainful of other people's ability. Not just his fellow students either, but his lecturers as well.'

'I can think of a few people like that,' muttered Holmes.

Caton glanced at him to see if, given their earlier conversation, this remark was meant for him. Gordon made it easy for him.

'Not you, boss. I was thinking of some of those on the fifth floor.'

'Don't kid yourself,' Caton replied. 'They don't even know who you are.'

Holmes grimaced. 'That's not going to boost my self-esteem, is it?' he said.

Raymond Lawrence leant forward.

'That's exactly the kind of exchange in which Lee Bottomley would never have taken part. He stayed aloof, in a kind of self-imposed bubble. I did manage to get him some interviews, one in particular with Fujitsu just over the road. They take quite a few of our students.'

'But not Lee?'

'No. He passed his practical test with flying colours, but he never got past the interview. The feedback I received was that they couldn't decide if he had a serious communication problem or was simply arrogant.'

'Which do you think it was?'

He sat back and thought about it.

'Probably both. Either way, he gave the impression of being disinterested in anything other than the task in hand, and even then his responses were monosyllabic.'

'Yes and no?' said Holmes.

'And why and when,' said the lecturer. 'Occasionally he amazed us all with two words.'

'Which were?'

Lawrence smiled. "S*o what?*"

'Nice person,' observed Holmes.

'Actually, I don't think he was being deliberately offensive or ignorant, I just don't think he cared about anyone else. Like I said, it was as though he was in his own little bubble.'

'Did he make any enemies among the other students?' asked Caton.

'Not that I was aware of. I think I would have picked up on it if he had. They quickly came to regard him as odd and left him to his own devices. Unless they needed his expertise, of course.'

'Did he have a Facebook page?' asked Gordon Holmes, much to Caton's surprise.

'No, he didn't. At least not in his own name.'

'How do you know?' said Caton.

Lawrence Raymond looked a little sheepish.

'I checked. I was just curious to see if he communicated better in a virtual space.'

'Don't you think that was odd, for someone his age who was into computers like that?'

'Not really. The clue's in the name – social network. You've got to remember, he wasn't sociable at all.'

'He helped other students with their work, though?'

'Sometimes, but he did that not for friendship but because it got them off his back. He got rid of viruses for them, boosted their memory and security settings, that kind of thing. And he did repairs sometimes, but they paid him for it.'

'Do you know what he did with the money?'

He appeared surprised by the question. He thought about it for a moment or two, then shrugged.

'I'm sorry, Mr Caton, I haven't the faintest idea. You could try Ali Bukhari.'

'Ali Bukhari?'

'He's one of the few students on Lee Bottomley's course who is still at the college. I say still, he's actually come back to do the BSc Creative Media Management course at our St John's Centre.'

'St John's? That's in Spinningfields, isn't it?' said Caton, trying to remember if he had enough change for the parking round there.

'Yes,' replied Raymond. He wheeled his chair back and stood up. 'But you're in luck. He's on location today, just behind us, at The Monastery.'

Chapter 10

'It's not a monastery at all,' Caton told him as they pulled up in the car park between the waste ground and the boundary fence. 'It's the Church and Friary of St Francis. Designed by Pugin, and built by the friars themselves during the 1860s. They served Gorton from here for the next one hundred and twenty years.'

'*Served* how exactly?'

The emphasis on 'served' reflected the scepticism with which Gordon Holmes regarded every faith known to man.

Caton engaged the handbrake and released his seat belt.

'That's uncalled for,' he said. 'They ran three schools, a youth club, a choir and a brass band, numerous football teams, and worked with the poor and the elderly. Will that do for you?'

They crossed the car park and the front of the wall enclosing the cloistered garden, and stood before the four wooden doors and soaring buttresses of the Gothic red-brick, stone and Welsh slate church.

'Back in 1997, when it was declared one of the most endangered buildings in the world and given World Monument status, they nicknamed this Manchester's Taj Mahal.'

Holmes regarded the grotesque gargoyles staring back at him from the ledges beside each door.

'Doesn't do it for me,' he muttered. 'Anyway, how come you know so much about this place?'

'Two reasons,' Caton replied. 'I came here with Manchester Grammar School on a local history trip in the early eighties, just before the friars left.'

He started up the steps, closely followed by his DI.

'Two reasons, you said?'

'Kate and I are getting married here in two and a half weeks' time,' he replied, without breaking stride. 'You should read your invitation.'

Even Holmes had to admit that the inside was impressive. Beneath the ribbed vault of the ceiling, the nave was set out for a wedding. Soft pink lights illuminated the towering stone pillars, the choir, altar and the apse. Without warning, the light changed to blue, mottled with purple where the pointed arches reached the first and second storeys. It was like a vast film set for a gothic movie.

'I think I'll come to this wedding after all, boss,' he said. 'What theme are you having? Vampires or Cinderella?'

Caton was already moving away towards the group of five people standing in the west transept. A young man had a large video camera hefted on his shoulder. Another held a boom mike towards a young woman standing two metres in front of them. Beside the cameraman stood a third man with a clipboard in his hands.

'Ali Bukhari?' Caton called out as he approached them.

His voice seemed to swell and deepen as it bounced from the walls up into the roof space. They turned as one, making no attempt to hide their annoyance.

'Do you mind? We're trying to make a documentary

here,' complained the girl, flicking her auburn curls into place, as though he had somehow disturbed them too.

'It's alright, Gemma,' said the man with the clipboard. 'Take five.'

'Take five? Do they still say that?' said Holmes, joining them.

Caton held out his warrant card.

'Detective Chief Inspector Caton. Can I have a word, Mr Bukhari?'

The lights changed to pink again.

'The others will be in the café,' the student told him. 'We could always go over to the offices.'

'It'll be fine here,' said Caton, indicating the nearest table.

The three of them sat down, their chairs slightly away from the table itself, careful not to disturb the place settings. Caton studied the young man. Medium height, medium build, short black hair, intelligent yet wary eyes. He looked older than he had expected. Late twenties. Of Pakistani or Northern Indian heritage, he guessed. Not that it was relevant. Just a policeman's instinctive need to commit a face to memory.

'I'd like to ask you about Lee Bottomley.'

The student nodded. 'Mr Raymond told me to expect you.'

By way of explanation, he glanced at the mobile phone sitting on the clipboard balanced across his knees.

'It was terrible what happened to Lee.' He moistened his lips with the tip of his tongue. A bead of sweat glistened above his upper lip. 'I'm not sure how I can help you, though.'

'What *did* happen to Lee?' said Caton.

Bukhari looked from one to the other of them in turn, searching their faces for a clue. None was forthcoming.

'He was murdered, wasn't he?'

'What makes you think that, Ali?' said Holmes.

The fact that it wasn't Caton who had replied seemed to throw him.

'I … I … it was in the papers, wasn't it? And on the television?'

'*Death was suspicious*, were the exact words I think you'll find,' said Caton.

'So it could have been suicide,' said Holmes. 'What made you think it was murder?'

'I just assumed. You do, don't you?'

'I think it's a little more that, Mr Bukhari,' said Caton.

He waited, watching the man wilt under their scrutiny. He knew Holmes would know better than to fill the vacuum they had created. Eventually, he cracked.

'It's all round college,' he said. 'It's what everyone is saying. He was battered … and … and cut.'

The detectives looked at each other. None of this detail had been given to the press. But then the mother knew, and her sister presumably. And the paramedic. And these days you couldn't be certain that it hadn't leaked from the mortuary, or even from inside the force. You only had to look at the Leveson Inquiry into the phone hacking scandal. Caton decided to cut him some slack.

'Fair enough, Mr Bukhari. We're not here to go into any of that. What we would really like to know is what kind of person Lee was.'

His shoulders slumped and the tension seeped from his face. He leant back in his chair and looked up at the roof high above them, gathering his thoughts. It was close to a minute before he brought his head level with Caton's.

'It's difficult,' he began. 'Partly because I think it is

always difficult to talk honestly of the dead. We're tempted to make allowances for them that we might not have done during their lifetime. But also because Lee was an enigma.'

'An enigma?' said Holmes.

'A mystery, a riddle,' the student responded.

Holmes leant forward, and found his belt had become entangled with a large silk bow on the back of his chair. He tugged himself free.

'I know what it means!' he growled. 'We're waiting for you to elucidate.'

'What I meant,' said Bukhari, 'is that I don't think any of us ever got to see the real Lee. He was a proper loner. A self-imposed outsider. Never made any attempt at conversation; never joined in with any activities outside of lessons; never came to any of our social events. End of term do's, student rag week, that sort of thing. And he had an edge to him.'

'Edge, what kind of edge?'

'Well, he had a really high opinion of himself, not that it wasn't deserved. He was bright, clever, verging on brilliant when it came to anything to do with computers. But he knew it. It wasn't just arrogance either. He didn't show off, not really, but he had a way of making people feel small.'

'We've been led to believe that he helped other students with their work sometimes,' said Caton. 'For money?'

'That's true. But only because they pestered him. It was a way of getting rid of them. As for the money, that was only for technical stuff; unblocking phones, repairing their hardware, getting rid of viruses. Things they would have had to pay for anyway. Only he did it cheaper and faster.'

'Do you know what he spent the money on?' asked Caton.

He looked surprised by the question.

'I've no idea. He didn't confide in me. He didn't confide in anyone.'

'Did he ever buy new equipment? New clothes? Did he have a car, a bike, a scooter?'

He shook his head. 'If he did, he never brought them to college. He used the college computers. Saved his own work on USBs and portable disk drives.'

'How did he get to college?'

'Search me. I only ever saw him on foot. It was only just over a mile. He probably walked. I would've done.'

Holmes raised his eyebrows. Caton leant forward and scrutinised the young man's face.

'How do you know it's only just over a mile?'

Bukhari blushed, and looked uncomfortable under their gaze.

'His address, it was in the papers, on the TV.'

'Where do you live, Mr Bukhari?'

'Cheetham.'

'As in Cheetham Hill?'

He nodded uncomfortably.

'How well do you know Abbey Hey?'

He squirmed on his seat.

'I don't.'

'So how come you know the exact distance between this college and the home of Lee Bottomley?'

He bowed his head and mumbled something.

'Speak up!' said Holmes.

He raised his head.

'When I saw the report on TV, I decided to look it up on Google Earth.'

Gordon Holmes snorted. 'Why?'

'I was curious, that's all.' He shuffled his feet across the polished white stone floor. 'I bet I wasn't the only one.'

'Just to be clear,' said Caton, 'did Lee have any friends at all?'

'No.'

'Enemies?'

He had to think about that.

'No,' he said at last. 'Don't get me wrong, nobody liked him. But I don't think anybody had reason to hate him either.'

'Just one last question, Mr Bukhari,' said Caton. 'Then you can get back to your filming. If you had to describe Lee Bottomley in one word, what would it be?'

The student folded his arms, rested his chin on the fist of his right hand and stared down at his feet. So intense was his demeanour that Caton found his eyes drawn towards the man's shoes in case there was something significant about them. Eventually, Bukhari sighed and looked up.

'I was tempted to say aloof, but that says nothing about what was going on under his skin. Then I thought angry. But now I come to think about it, even that isn't quite right. Bitter, that's what he was. Bitter. Like nobody appreciated him, and it was him against the world.'

'So much for speaking well of the dead,' said Holmes.

The lights had changed to green, and a pattern of trees had been projected onto the floor. Holmes deliberately stepped from leaf to leaf as they wove their way between the tables.

'What about him checking the murder scene out on Google Earth?' he continued. 'What's that then, the new rubbernecking?'

'I bet you never stepped on the cracks on the pavement when you were a child,' said Caton.

Holmes chuckled. 'I still don't. Never been eaten by bears either!'

Chapter 11

They were back in Gorton, at the home of Lee Bottomley's aunt. The small terraced house looked sad and drab in the glare of the midday sun.

'Is the mother home do you think?' asked Holmes.

'Well, she's been released from hospital, and this was the only place she was supposed to come back to.'

The door opened, and the family liaison officer stepped aside to let them in.

'She's not in very good shape, I'm afraid,' she said. 'Go gently with her.'

'I don't know any other way,' said Holmes.

Caton hoped he was going to behave himself.

Nell Bottomley sat on the sofa, dabbing her eyes with a soggy tissue. Her sister stood in the doorway to the tiny kitchen, a cigarette in her mouth. She removed the cigarette and pulled a face.

'You're not going to get anything out of her,' she said.

'A glass of water would be nice, Mrs Duggan,' said Caton. 'And a cup of tea for DI Holmes; milk, one sugar. Don't worry, we'll be fine on our own with your sister.'

She scowled, flicked ash into the palm of her hand and turned away.

Caton sat down on the sofa opposite Nell Bottomley. The family liaison officer joined him.

Gordon Holmes leaned against the kitchen doorframe trying to look inconspicuous. It didn't work.

'I'm very sorry to have to intrude on your grief, Mrs Bottomley,' said Caton, 'but if we're going to catch your son's killer we need to find out as much as we can about Lee.'

She looked up wearily. Her eyes were bloodshot. He noticed a tremor to her hands. Probably withdrawal, he surmised, as much as grief.

'Ask Marilyn,' she said. 'I can't do this.'

The liaison officer reached out and took her hand.

'Yes you can, Nell,' she coaxed. 'For Lee's sake.'

For a moment it looked as though she was not going to respond, but then she reached out with her free hand, took another tissue from a box of Kleenex on the coffee table, blew her nose loudly, and gently placed the crumpled tissue on a pile that had colonised one corner of the sofa.

'He was a good boy,' she whispered. 'Really caring.'

She sniffed, and wiped her nose with the back of her hand.

'He didn't deserve to die … like that.'

It looked as though she was going to burst into tears until the FLO squeezed her hand tightly.

'In what way was he a good boy, Nell?' Caton asked kindly.

'He just was,' she said. 'Good. As a child I used to say he was as good as gold.' She looked at each of them in turn, as though imploring them to believe her. 'He never lied, or got into fights at school, or gave me cheek. He did his homework without being made to. He ran errands for me and his nan. He was a good boy.'

She reached for another tissue.

Caton waited for her to finish blowing her nose.

'Did Lee have any friends, Mrs Bottomley?'

'No, he didn't,' her sister answered for her as she thrust a glass of water into Caton's hand and a mug of thick brown tea in Gordon Holmes' direction. 'Not then, not ever. He was a born loner was Lee.'

'Thank you, Mrs Duggan,' said Caton. 'I was asking your sister.'

She folded her arms in a sulk and leant against the opposite side of the doorframe to Gordon Holmes. The room was beginning to feel claustrophobic to Caton; he wondered how it must feel to Nell Bottomley.

'He was caring, too,' she said, ignoring his question. 'Cared for me. Made sure I took my medicine. Cooked my meals, or went down the chippy or the takeaway. Who's going to do that for me now?'

She began to whimper like a puppy. A low, broken, sobbing sound.

'Now look what you've gone and done,' said the sister, storming back into the kitchen.

Holmes slurped his tea, pulled a face and plonked the mug down on the table. Caton settled back and waited patiently for the sobs to subside.

Another tissue joined the pile.

'Are you okay to carry on, Mrs Bottomley?' he said.

'Nell?' said the female FLO, squeezing her hand in encouragement.

She looked him in the eyes and shook her head slowly from side to side. Her answer surprised them all.

'No, Mr Caton, he didn't have any friends. I used to worry about that when he was little, but as he grew older I could see it didn't matter to him, so why should it to me?'

'How about enemies?'

'Enemies?' She seemed stunned by the question.

'Was there anyone he might have upset? Someone who might have been angry with him?'

She looked at her free hand, as though suddenly aware of her trembling fingers. She eased her other hand free from the grip of the FLO and tucked them both beneath her thighs as though that might still them.

'How could he upset anyone?' she asked nobody in particular. 'He was a good boy.'

'That was a waste of time,' said Holmes as Caton turned his Skoda onto Pottery Lane.

'Not entirely. She confirmed what everybody else said about him, that he had neither friends nor enemies.'

'Well, somebody had it in for him.'

Caton turned the air conditioning to low, causing the fan to kick in and a blast of cold air to assail them both. His colleague let out a yelp and turned the knob on his side to twenty degrees, which forced Caton to adjust his to fifteen degrees.

'For heaven's sake, Gordon,' he said. 'It's like an oven in here.'

'It may be to you,' Holmes retorted, 'but I'm cold-blooded.'

'That explains your reptilian brain.'

'Cheers, boss. I take that as a compliment.'

Caton frowned. 'Don't,' he said.

His DI turned the knob up another notch, reached under his chair and eased it back so that he could stretch his legs out even further.

'There was something we forgot to ask,' he said.

Caton glanced across at him, then back at the road ahead.

'Go on.'

'What he did with the money he made.'

Caton chewed his lip. Gordon was right. They'd asked everyone but the mother.

'He can't have made that much,' he replied. 'And he was unemployed, remember. My guess is that what little he had left over went on his computer. Upgrades, software, that sort of thing.'

'Even so, we should have asked her.'

'What was the name of the FLO?'

'DC Kent. Sally Kent. Bit of a looker. I'm surprised you didn't remember her name. Not like you, boss.'

Gordon was right. He never forgot names; he prided himself on the fact. But then so much was going on at the moment, what with the wedding, and the prospect of losing DS Stuart, and the case itself.

'When we get back,' he said, 'I want you to give DC Kent a ring. Get her to find out what the mother has to say. And tell her well done, from me.'

'Will do, boss.'

As they drew level with the former site of Heatherwick's *B of the Bang* sculpture, dismantled for safety reasons three years previously, Gordon Holmes pulled his chair forward and sat bolt upright.

'Take the next right,' he said, his voice urgent, as though their lives depended on it.

Caton glanced at him. 'Gibbon Street?'

'That's it.'

Alongside the East Stand of the Etihad, Caton checked his mirror, indicated right, pulled into the outside lane and waited for a gap in the steady flow of traffic heading south on Alan Turing Way. There was nothing down there other than Philips Park, and row after row of apartments built for, and since, the Commonwealth Games.

'Where are we going?

His DI grinned. 'McDonalds,' he said. 'I don't know about you, but I'm starving.'

Chapter 12

It was eight thirty p.m., and the fourth Operation Janus team review was coming to a close. The flood of calls to CrimeStoppers, and their own dedicated line, had become a trickle.

'We still have a couple of hundred to follow up,' Benson told them, 'but none of them looks promising. We're trawling Twitter as well, just in case someone shares something they're not telling us.'

'I hope you're tracking any vitriolic comments about the victim,' said Caton. 'It's not beyond the realms of possibility that the perpetrator might give vent to his or her spleen on one or other social network.'

'Absolutely,' he replied. 'Although I'd have expected the prison sentences handed down in the past few months, to idiots posting hateful and abusive comments about the dead, to have stemmed the flow.'

'I wouldn't count on it,' said Caton. 'The clue is in your description of them, *idiots*.'

His gut told him otherwise. The perpetrators may have taken risks, but it was increasingly looking as though they had been calculated. He turned to DS Stuart.

'Any luck in identifying any of the people in your most likely category?'

'Good news and bad news again, sir,' she said. 'The

good news is that we finally tracked down the two hoodies who'd been having a go at each other shortly before they disappeared into the Kenwood Estate. The neighbourhood team from Stockport Division thought they recognised them, went round to the pad where they hang out and picked them up.'

'Picked them up, or questioned them?'

She smiled broadly. 'Both. Plus arrested and charged. They caught them packaging cannabis, ready to sell it on. Naturally they're delighted. Unfortunately, it seems they had nothing to do with our victim. When they were spotted by our witnesses, they were coming back from a sales trip round Openshaw and Gorton. They were arguing about how to split their ill-gotten gains. When they cut through the industrial estate they were on their way to the station.'

'Station?'

'The railway station. Reddish North, en route back to Bredbury.'

'Bredbury?'

He was beginning sound like an echo.

'I know,' she said. 'That's what I thought. The millionaire footballer and stockbroker belt? What we have here is a couple of middle-class chancers hoping to make their first million on the backs of the working classes.'

'Their mummies and daddies are not going to be well pleased,' said Holmes.

'Neither am I,' said Caton. 'What's the bad news?'

'We got nowhere with the guy on the mountain bike who disappeared near the motorway, and nothing new on any other sightings.'

'Nothing from the door-to-doors either,' Carter informed him, rather more cheerfully than the situation warranted.

He looked around the room.

'So, basically we still have nothing to go on at all.'

It wasn't a question.

'What do you want us to do, boss?' said Gordon Holmes.

'That's easy,' he replied. 'In direct contradiction to the First Rule of Holes, I want you…'

They chorused as one.

'To keep digging!'

'I hope you're not thinking of staying up all night.'

Kate watched him swirl the red wine around in his glass. He had only been home a couple of hours, but in all that time he had seemed distracted. Even now, watching Homeland on the television, it was clear that he was taking nothing in. He hadn't registered a word she'd said.

'Tom!'

He turned, surprised by the sharpness of her tone, and had to hold the glass with both hands to stop it spilling.

'Sorry?' he said.

'I know it's a difficult case,' Kate said, 'but it is Saturday night, Tom. You've only had four and a half hours sleep in the past thirty-eight. They'll ring you if anything comes up.'

He looked at his watch. It was just thirty hours since he had been called to the house in Abbey Hey. Early days in a murder investigation, yet it already felt as though the trail had gone cold. Not that it had ever been hot, or even lukewarm come to that. She was right, though. There was nothing more he could do until all the evidence had been sifted and the forensics report arrived. It was unlucky that it had happened late on a Friday. It was bad enough getting a priority rush analysis when some of it was done in-house and the rest at Euxton. Much harder now that the Forensic Science Service centre had been closed and the work farmed out further afield. He had nothing against privatisation in theory, it was the practice that worried him.

'You're right,' he said. 'I'm sorry, I was miles away.'

She came and sat beside him, her hand on his knee.

'I was reminding you that we have an appointment in the morning.'

Conscious of her eyes on his, he fought to keep his expression neutral.

'Of course. Father Brennan.'

She squeezed his knee, hard.

'Brendan,' she said. 'Father Brendan.'

'I knew that,' he said. 'I was just teasing.'

'Liar.'

She took the glass from his hands and placed it on the coffee table.

'You've already had too much of that,' she said. 'I want you clear-headed for tomorrow.'

Her left hand curled around his shoulders, drawing his lips towards hers. The other hand slid sinuously along the inside of his thigh.

'And for tonight.'

'What about the baby?' he said, instantly aware that it was a foolish thing to say. Not least because it hadn't been an issue before.

She pulled back a little and smiled.

'Don't worry,' she said, 'I'll be gentle with you.'

Chapter 13

'And now let us move on to your duties towards each other.'

Caton surreptitiously pressed his arm against his side and moved it forward to ease back the sleeve of his sweater. He checked that Father Brendan was looking down at his papers, and sneaked a look at his watch. They had only been here ten minutes, and his eyes were already beginning to glaze over.

'Conjugal love,' the priest continued, 'the love you express for each other in your marital bed, will only grow strong and mature if it follows God's decree, rather than simply depending on human sexual attraction and physical release.'

This was the part that Caton had been dreading most of all. He was tempted to ask what the hell the priest knew about all this, but Kate was staring directly at him, and he didn't need to be a mind-reader to know what she was thinking. In any case, now he came to think about it, the confessional had probably revealed a damn sight more information over the years than the Kama Sutra.

'What, then, are God's ordinances in this matter? Firstly, the duties of the husband.'

Caton steeled himself.

'The husband is the head of the family. He is the

king of this little kingdom. The provider and supporter of his wife and child.'

Now it was Kate that was staring at the priest. The look on her face hovered between incredulity and outright hostility. Caton was starting to enjoy himself.

'St Paul makes this clear in his letter to the Ephesians: "Let wives be subject to their husbands," he says, "because a husband is the head of the wife, just as Christ is head of…"'

He was rudely interrupted by the fierce ringtone of Caton's mobile phone.

'I'm sorry,' he said, reaching for his jacket. 'I asked them not to ring unless it was urgent.'

'Oh, Tom!' Kate exclaimed. 'I asked you to switch it off.'

'It's alright, Kate,' said Father Brendan, in a practised conciliatory tone. 'I understand. Tom has an important job.'

It was Gordon Holmes.

'I'm sorry, boss,' he said. 'I know you said not to disturb you, but this can't wait. We've got another one. I'm there now. Male. Similar age. Same MO. In the Green Quarter.'

'Text me the address,' Tom told him. 'I'm on my way.'

As he stood, he began to apologise. The priest held up his hand.

'No need, Tom. We can do this again.'

'I'm sorry, Kate,' Tom said. 'You know how it is.'

'Just go,' she said.

As he opened the door, Father Brendan called after him,

'I'll say a prayer for you, Detective Chief Inspector.'

'With all due respect, Father,' he replied, 'I'd save your prayers for the victim and his family.'

The Green Quarter. He had checked it out with Kate when they were looking for an apartment to share together. A self-proclaimed urban oasis squeezed into the triangle of land bounded by Cheetham Hill Road, Wince Brook and Red Bank. Ten apartment blocks replete with Poggenphol kitchens and Siemens appliances, a state of the art health studio, business accommodation and the Park Hotel. At its centre, a one-hundred-metre-long lawned and tree-lined avenue, and a channel of rippling water that terminated in a pool from which spurted six twelve-foot-high jets of water.

They had both been tempted by its proximity to the city centre, the Manchester Arena and Victoria Station, he to the National Museum of Football, and she to Harvey Nicks and Selfridges. On the other hand, for both of them, Her Majesty's Prison Manchester – formerly Strangeways – was just a little too close for comfort. Several of the apartment blocks had been under construction the last time he was here. As he parked up, he wondered how it would look now that it was finished.

'It's on the fourteenth floor,' said the uniformed officer as he filled in Caton's details on the crime scene attendance log. 'You'll have to take the stairs, I'm afraid, sir. The lift has been sealed for forensic examination.'

He was young and keen, trying hard to find just the right balance between excitement and a sombre acknowledgement of the gravity of the situation. This was probably his first suspicious death. Caton barely remembered how that felt. On his birthday before last Kate had told him that forty was the new thirty. He was beginning to wonder if that was true.

As he climbed the stairs, he tried to sense the soul of the building. In the foyer he had noted that the majority of the postboxes had neither names nor numbers on them. His assumption that it was largely unoccupied was reinforced by the silence, the lack of any kind of adornment and the chill emanating from the smooth, polished concrete walls. It was not the kind of place he would want to come home to of an evening.

By the time he was halfway up he had become conscious of each breath and a creeping tightness in the thighs. It seemed to be getting colder, which was strange. On the fells the temperature dropped one degree for every 300 feet you climbed. But here, inside, surely hot air rose?

With one floor to go, his breathing had become laboured and his calves were burning. This is ridiculous, he told himself. With all the last-minute preparations for the wedding, and mounting paperwork on the back of the forthcoming inspection, it was four weeks since he'd been to the Y Club, but surely his fitness couldn't have plummeted that fast? He promised himself that as soon as they got back from the honeymoon he'd return to the three times a week schedule.

He paused on the landing and stared out of the floor-to-ceiling window. The weather had turned suddenly, as it often did in autumn. The sky was leaden; what few clouds there were reflected like puffs of pewter in the platinum-coloured mirror tiles of the facing apartment block, and in the shifting shadowy grey channel of water that was Wince Brook. Not yet forty shades, but heading that way.

Revived, he took the remaining steps two at a time and pulled open the fire doors onto the corridor. Five doors down, another uniformed officer stood guard opposite an open door, from which Gordon Holmes' voice resounded.

'Why not?!'

Caton held up his warrant card for the constable, slipped on the blue Tyvek suit he had been carrying and crossed the threshold. The first thing that struck him was that the large lounge he had entered was empty. Not a stick of furniture anywhere. A thin green plastic duckboard led towards a second room.

'Why not what, DI Holmes?' he said.

Holmes appeared in the doorway.

'Finally,' he said, without a hint of his usual humour. 'What kept you, boss?'

Caton joined him.

'Why not what, Gordon?' he repeated.

'Why not lift his head and see if there's anything under it?' replied Jack Benson, turning to face them.

'His head?' said Caton, beginning to envisage all manner of scenarios.

The Crime Scene Manager stepped to one side.

'See for yourself.'

In the centre of the room, four metres from where Caton stood, a man knelt, head down, with his backside raised. Between his feet was a wooden stool padded with green leather. His hands were stretched out in front of him as though reaching in vain for the black and steel-blue computer table lying on its side close to the windows.

The manner in which the man lay reminded Caton of the yoga child's pose that Kate had once shown him when his back was troubling him.

'I was telling DI Holmes not to touch anything until the cameraman has finished,' said Benson, gesturing for Holmes to get back onto the portable walkway he had taken such care to lay down.

'Where is he?' said Holmes as he reluctantly complied. 'Come to that, where's the doctor? We haven't even had the victim certified as dead.'

'There doesn't seem to be much doubt about that,' said Caton. 'Where *is* the doctor, Jack?'

'Carol Tompkins is on her way,' he replied. 'She was due half an hour ago, but she was coming from Hyde and got stuck on the M60 somewhere between Death Valley and the Middleton turn-off.'

'On a Sunday?'

'City are playing at home. Lunchtime kick-off.'

Caton turned his attention to the victim. He moved closer. It was obvious what had led Gordon to link this death with that of Lee Bottomley. The back of the victim's head was matted with blood, some of which had run down the right side of his face, over his shoulders, and had pooled on the bare asphalt floor. The tips of every finger had been smashed. The top of the right index finger had been severed.

'Where have I seen a table like that before?' he asked, pointing to the contraption lying on its side like the skeleton of a naked robot.

'Schools, colleges, offices,' said Benson. 'It's a monitor lift table, with locking castors and a slot for the computer stack.'

'They had some in the IT room next to that Raymond Lawrence's office at the college yesterday,' Holmes reminded him.

That was it. On the end of an adjustable arm, the LCD monitor screen protruded drunkenly from a square hole in the centre of the console. The screen was cracked but, unlike the victim, had not bled out. The keyboard tray must have snapped on impact and come apart from the platform for the mouse. The computer stack housing was empty.

'Any sign of the computer and the keyboard?' he asked.

'The keyboard's over there.'

He followed Benson's outstretched arm to the far

right-hand corner of the room, where a jumble of black plastic lay along the base of the wall where it met the window.

'No sign of the computer,' said Holmes. 'Must have taken it with them.'

'Could they have thrown it out of the window?' said Caton.

'See for yourself. The windows are all closed, and in any case, they only open six inches. It's a safety feature.'

'What about the other rooms?'

'The same, and this apartment doesn't have a balcony. Probably why it's one of the ones that hasn't been sold.'

Caton pointed to a bulge in the back pocket of the victim's jeans.

'That could be his wallet.' He held up his gloved hand. 'Time is of the essence, Jack. Just a quick look. I'll put it back for the photos.'

The Crime Scene Manager shook his head.

'Go on then,' he said.

Up close, telltale black leather edges confirmed his suspicion. As he bent, he caught a rank smell of urine and voided bowels that caused him to gag. Knowing that it was part of an ancient sensory warning system made no difference; it happened every time. The jeans strained tightly against the wallet, and forced him to place his gloved left hand on the man's un-bloodied shoulder to tug it free. He stood up and studied the contents. A Costa Coffee loyalty card stamped four times, a receipt from a newsagent on Cheetham Hill, another from MicroDirect online sales, an out-of-date student union card from Sheffield University, a Manchester Libraries card, a Visa card, a business card for TechWays Computer Repair Service, two twenty-pound notes, one ten and one five-pound note.

'Not a mugging then,' Holmes observed.

'Spencer Miles-Cowper, with a W,' said Caton holding up the student ID card. 'According to this and his library card. Different name on the credit card, though.' He read it again. 'C N Brooker. Perhaps he stole it.'

He placed them back in the wallet. It proved even more difficult to squeeze into the pocket of the jeans than it had been to extricate it.

'If he's got a credit card, cash and a double-barrelled name, what's he doing squatting in an empty apartment?' Holmes wondered.

'Do we know for a fact that he was squatting?' said Caton.

'There's a toothbrush and toothpaste, a razor and a towel in the wet room,' said Benson. 'And a stack of empty takeaway cartons in the kitchen. And the toilet's not been flushed.'

'And there's a sleeping bag and a pillow in one of the bedrooms,' added Holmes. 'QED.'

'I wish you'd stop saying that,' said Caton. 'We both know you don't know what it means.'

'I will, if you stop using double negatives,' said Holmes. 'And I think you'll find it's *What has to be demonstrated*.'

'*Which had* to be demonstrated,' said Benson, who was looking intently at the body.

They both stared at him.

'Don't be so picky,' said Holmes.

'Picky? Sounds like my cue,' said a woman's voice from the doorway. 'Is it okay for me to enter the inner sanctum, Mr Benson?'

'There isn't room for all of us on the walkway,' said Caton. 'Gordon, I suggest you and I change places with Dr Tompkins.'

They waited in the doorway, watching her go

about her work with a professional detachment that had long since ceased to surprise either of them.

'Point of entry?' said Caton.

Holmes nodded towards the front door to the apartment.

'Unless they had wings.'

'Was it open?'

'The door was ajar, and the lock had been engaged. As though they wanted him to be found.'

'Who did find him?'

'Don't laugh. Security. Which consists of one man and his dog who tour each floor once every twenty-four hours.'

Caton thought that reasonable. It was more than the apartments got where he and Kate now lived. But then they were all occupied. No squatters or vandals to worry about.

'Any disturbance to the scene?'

'Only foot and paw prints. He reckons he didn't touch a thing.'

'Point of exit?'

'Take your pick. Lift or stairs. There's no CCTV in the lift, but there is in the foyer. I've already asked for the tapes. However, if it was me, I'd have gone past the reception to the Lower Ground and used the fire exit to get out at the back. Not least because there's no CCTV round the back either.'

'From the expression on your face,' said Caton, 'you're going to tell me that's what they did.'

Holmes shook his head.

'Sorry, boss, wish I could. Apparently, the fire doors are self-closing. To stop people re-entering the building, or looters getting in. There's no way of knowing whether they did or they didn't. Not until we've seen those tapes.'

'What does that leave us with?' said Caton, as

much to himself as to his DI. 'Articles removed from the scene by the perpetrators?'

Holmes rubbed his chin with the palm of his left hand. It was a habit Caton no longer found annoying.

'Computer stack. Not a laptop, since he was using a separate keyboard. Possibly a mobile phone. Printer? Unlikely, since there's only one mains lead. Oh yes, and it looks like the mouse is missing.'

'That's what I was missing,' said Caton. 'The mouse. Both here and in the first victim's room.'

'That's why I asked Benson if I could lift his head up. See if it's under there.'

'It isn't,' said Carol Tompkins. She stood up, arched her back and stretched her arms. 'Why can't people die on their feet for a change? Or propped up against the wall? Make my job a damn sight easier.'

Chapter 14

'You've been hanging around Major Incidents too long,' Caton told her. 'You've started picking up some of Gordon's bad habits.'

The hood of her Tyvek had slipped forward, threatening to cover her eyes. She nudged it higher on her forehead.

'Don't kid yourself,' she said. 'The first two years in Med' School taught me all I needed to know about gallows humour.'

'What's the verdict, Doc?' said Holmes.

Her lips curled into the hint of a smile.

'I'm tempted to say he's dead, Detective Inspector, but I expect that even you have worked that out by now.'

'Nice to have it confirmed, though,' he replied.

She stared down at the body.

'He received a blow to the back of the head with a blunt instrument. He may then have fallen forward of his own volition, but it's more likely that his head was gripped, and smashed several times into the floor and or the keyboard.'

'How can you tell?' said Caton.

'By the degree and extent of the damage to his face. His forehead has lacerations, his nose is broken. Those injuries could well have occurred as the result of a single impact. But both cheekbones are fractured. That would require his head to have been angled in a different direction for each injury. So, at least two, and probably three, sites of impact.'

'And his hands?' prompted Holmes.

This time there was no smile. The look she gave him reminded Caton of Professor Flatman, the Home Office Pathologist, except that his was a more or less permanent expression.

'I was coming to that,' she replied, 'if I hadn't had to deal with the interruptions.'

'Whoops!' said Holmes, not the least bit chastened.

She shook her head and continued.

'The middle and distal phalanges of both hands have been shattered by blows from a blunt instrument. The distal phalange of the right digitus secundus has been severed at the joint.'

'The same injuries sustained by Lee Bottomley,' said Caton.

'Except that this appears to have been a slightly more sustained attack,' she said. 'There are more injuries to the hands, and those to the face are new.'

'Chummy's beginning to lose control,' Holmes speculated.

They both stared at him.

'Chummy?' said Caton. 'You've been watching too many B movies from the 1950s.'

He looked around the room, trying to recreate the events in his head. The perpetrator had entered through the door from the corridor. He or she, or they, had either entered unobserved and crept up on the unsuspecting victim, or he had let them in. If the latter, it was likely they would be known to him. If not, they would have had to force their way in and drag him to his chair, where they then attacked him. That didn't seem likely. Whichever it was, the force of the blow propelled him forward, his outstretched arms dragging the keyboard to the floor and pushing the computer table away. Would that have been sufficient to upend it and leave it that far away from the body? He doubted it. Then they gripped his head, probably by his hair, which was shoulder-length, and smashed it into the keyboard several times. Then they would have smashed his hands and severed the finger. The computer stack was then removed from its shelf. When they left they took the stack and the computer mouse with them, pulling the door to behind them, but leaving it on the latch.

'How did they get in?' he said.

His DI rubbed his chin with his gloved hand.

'Either he let them in or the door was on the latch, like the security guard found it.'

'Come to that, how did our victim get in?'

'A third of the apartments are unoccupied,' said Holmes. 'Perhaps it was left unlocked by the cleaners, or the building management?'

'Or maintenance staff,' added Carol Tompkins.

'Add that to the list, Gordon,' said Caton. 'We need to know. And find out if there are any more squatters in this building.'

'Excuse me, sir!'

DC Jimmy Hulme stood in the main doorway, shifting his weight nervously from one foot to the other. Caton gestured for him to join them.

'Stay on the path!' Benson called out.

Caton looked down at his feet. It was the first time he had seen duckboards this thin before.

'Neat, isn't it?' said the Crime Scene Manager. 'My idea. It's really for garden paths, but I've attached non-slip pads to the bottom to preserve evidence on smooth, shiny indoor surfaces. D'you think it'll catch on?'

'What is it, DC Hulme?' said Gordon Holmes.

'A patrol car from Collyhurst nick was called out to an incident at nine thirty a.m. A motorist reported a computer landing in the road just metres ahead of him. Another couple of seconds and the patrol reckon it would have smashed through the windscreen and stove his head in.'

The young detective constable sounded breathless. Presumably he'd jogged all the way up the stairs. Caton knew how he felt.

'How soon after it happened did they get there?' he asked.

'Five minutes.'

'Collyhurst nick is only a minute away,' observed Holmes.

'They didn't come from the station, they were in Crumpsall, at the hospital.'

'That fits with the approximate time of death,' said Carol Tompkins.

Caton turned to look at her.

'Which is?'

'More than an hour, less than five hours. I'll be able to narrow it down for you when I've done the calculations.'

Caton checked his watch. 'So, between five a.m. and ten a.m.?'

She nodded. 'I'd say much nearer to ten o'clock than five o'clock, but don't quote me on that.'

'Given the window openings are all restricted, how the hell did they lob it out of the building?' Holmes wondered.

'The patrol asked themselves the same question,' said DC Hulme. 'The driver said he got out of the car and stepped onto the pavement. He reckons he looked up to see where it'd come from, but all the windows were closed.'

'That leaves the roof,' said Caton. 'Too heavy and

conspicuous to take with them. Dropped from a great height would be the best way to destroy it.'

'Especially if you want to make a point,' said Holmes. 'Bit risky, though, in broad daylight. Good way to draw attention to yourself.'

'Not that many people about early on a Sunday morning,' Caton reminded him. 'And if it is the same person who killed Lee Bottomley, they don't seem to be particularly risk adverse.'

'You think they want to be caught?'

'I'm not saying that, only that either their planning is meticulous or they are completely driven by their task, to the exclusion of all else.'

'In which case, they've been lucky so far, sir,' said Jimmy Hulme tentatively.

Gordon Holmes grunted. Caton gave his DI a warning look.

'Exactly, DC Hulme,' he said. 'What made the patrol contact us?'

'They heard about our call-out, and put two and two together.'

'I hope they've preserved the remains,' said Jack Benson.

'Yes, sir,' said Hulme.

'You don't have to call Benson sir,' said Holmes. 'He answers to Jack.'

The young DC looked embarrassed.

'A little civility wouldn't go amiss around here,' said Caton, giving Gordon another look.

'Hear, hear!' chorused Benson and Tompkins.

There was a shout from the outer room.

'That's my camera team,' said Benson. 'It's going to get crowded in here.'

'I'm away,' said the doctor.

'We'll get out of your hair too,' said Caton. 'We'll start by having a look at that roof.'

'Watch where you're walking, and don't touch anything!' Benson shouted after them.

They located the door on the sixteenth floor, just two floors up from the apartment. It was a fire exit, and consequently unlocked.

'Not bothered about people jumping off the roof then,' Holmes observed. 'Only out of the windows.'

'I assume it's for evacuation by helicopter if the stairwells are blocked or engulfed by fire,' said Caton. 'They wouldn't be able to use a spiral chute this high up.'

The roof was bare except for three rows of a score or more solar panels, and a small wind turbine spinning rapidly in the breeze. A gentle curvature to the otherwise flat roof facilitated drainage into gutters, which ran beneath metre-high walls along all four sides.

'It must have been thrown from over there,' Holmes said, pointing to the south-east side.

They walked across together, searching the ground for anything that might have been left by the perpetrator. Nothing stood out on the dull grey surface. They stopped at the edge and looked over the wall. A marked police car, its unique identification number emblazoned on the roof, was parked almost immediately below them. A police motorcycle was parked diagonally across the centre of the street to the north of the building, and at the south-west end, by the entrance to the tunnel under the disused railway line where Red Bank joined Aspin Lane, stood a uniformed officer.

'Looks like they've closed the street off,' said Holmes. 'Like closing the stable doors when the horse has bolted.'

'At least they've preserved the evidence,' said Caton.

'All they'll have needed was a shovel and a carrier bag,' said his DI.

Caton tried to put himself in the place of the perpetrator. It would have taken less than a minute and a half to climb the two flights of stairs, cross the roof, hurl the computer stack off the roof and return to the lift. Another minute to reach the Lower Ground floor, out through the fire exit and away. It would have taken longer than that for anyone from the street to run round to the entrance of the building to report the incident. Not that anyone had.

He took a moment to take in the view. To the south it seemed as though he had only to take a few steps across the rooftops to enter the square mile that was the heart of his city. A mile and a half to the north-west stood the twin skyscrapers housing the Force Headquarters and the Divisional Headquarters.

Turning counter-clockwise, he came upon the star-shaped mass of the prison, with its central panopticon hub and the soaring red-brick ventilation tower, mirrored just a quarter of a mile closer by the famous Boddingtons chimney, the last vestige of the much-lamented brewery and the 'Cream of Manchester'.

Gordon Holmes followed his gaze.

'Only a matter of time,' he said, 'before we have the bastard that did this locked up in there.'

Caton slowly raised his head, scanning across Salford and the snake-like course of the River Irwell until he reached the gleaming white mast pointing skywards like a giant lightning conductor on the summit of Winter Hill,. Two deaths in three days. Time was something they did not have.

Chapter 15

'Spencer Miles-Cowper, with a *W*.'

Douggie Wallace rotated the screen through twenty degrees so they could all see.

'No criminal record, but he's on the Missing Persons list!'

'When was he reported missing?' asked Caton.

'Two years ago. By his mother. He was supposed to be studying computer science here at Manchester University. Suddenly, he stopped going to lectures, tutorials, the lot. When they finally checked on him, his room was empty. Well, that's to say his books and his bed were still there, but his clothes, his laptop and his personal possessions were gone.'

'What else does the file say?'

'Not a lot. They ran the usual checks, but decided there were no suspicious circumstances, so the impression I get is that it went on the back-burner.'

'Meaning?'

'No active searches, just relying on the system being triggered when he was picked up for some misdemeanour or other.'

'Or found murdered,' said Caton.

'The parents have been notified by the Met. They're coming up on the train, but, given it's a Sunday, it'll be teatime before they get here.'

'What's teatime?' grumbled DS Carter as he filled

a bottle at the water dispenser.

'There must be a record on that MisPers file of friends or fellow students who were contacted after he went missing,' said Caton. 'Print off the details, and see if you can find out where they are now. And I know it's a Sunday, but see if you can find out who his course tutor was, and any other staff who might have known him well. Oh, and check this out.'

He handed him the credit card in the name of C N Brooker. It was in a security-sealed clear evidence bag.

'I need to know if it's been reported stolen. If not, I need to know where we can get hold of the owner.'

Wallace took his biro from behind his ear, and filled in his name and the time on the chain of evidence list printed on the front.

'What order do you want me to do all this in?' he asked.

Caton knew he had a point. They were all equally important and equally time-consuming, and Douggie Wallace was a crime intelligence analyst, not a detective. At this stage in an investigation there was a danger things would start to race away from you. It was time to put his foot on the ball.

'Fair enough,' he said, acknowledging the unspoken plea. He raised his voice to fill the room. 'Does anyone know if DI Holmes is back from the crime scene yet?'

'He's just phoned in, sir,' responded Ged, the Office Manager. 'He should be with us in about ten minutes.'

'Right, everyone,' he said, 'slow down time. Task allocation meeting, in here, fifteen minutes.'

'Just so you're all clear,' Caton began, 'the crime scene from which DI Holmes has just returned is linked by modus operandi to that of our first victim,

Lee Bottomley. Consequently, it will now form part of Operation Janus. As Deputy SIO, DI Holmes is the Action Allocator for both strands of this operation, and Ged as Office Manager will maintain the action log. In extremis, in the absence from the Incident Room of both DI Holmes and me, and assuming that we can't immediately be contacted, urgent decisions regarding actions will be taken by the most senior officer in situ. Any questions? No? In that case, over to you, DI Holmes.'

There were very few occasions when he reverted to this formal approach, but he'd always found that it helped to get the attention of every member of the team when it really mattered. Gordon Holmes stepped forward.

'Right,' he said. 'Douggie, you follow up the MisPers information first. Then follow up that credit card found in the victim's wallet. Was it lost, stolen or cloned? DS Stuart, you carry on analysing, and cross-reference the witness statements.'

He paused dramatically and looked around the room.

'At least what we're laughingly calling witness statements, since so far nobody seems to have heard or seen anything. DS Carter, passive data collection. We need something from the CCTV in and around that building. We're working on the hypothesis that the perpetrator, or perpetrators, may have used the Lower Ground fire exit to leave the building at the rear. The question is, how did they get into the building in the first place?'

Not recognising it as a rhetorical question, Detective Constable Hulme raised his hand. For once Caton's deputy showed remarkable tolerance.

'Yes, DC Hulme?'

'Maybe they disguised themselves, or hid their faces. Maybe an accomplice let them in through the fire doors?'

Caton could tell that the rest of the team were resisting the temptation to clap ironically, as they might have done with DC Woods in the past. He knew that they would only give their new colleague so much rope before someone hung him out to dry. It was a tough call whether to embarrass him by warning him to temper his enthusiasm, or let him find out the hard way, as the rest of them had done.

'Thank you, DC Hulme,' said Gordon Holmes. 'So there you have it, DC Carter. Anyone entering the building whose features are hidden, by a scarf, a hat, a hoodie, whatever, or who for whatever reason can't easily be identified, I want them tracked back on all of the approaches to the building. And, if they left it, where they went.'

He checked his notes.

'This brings me to you, DC Hulme. You'd better see what information you can dig up about his parents. Quick as you can. DCI Caton will need that before he takes them to the mortuary to identify the body. Then you can get on to the university for a list of staff and students who were most closely connected with our victim during his time there.'

He turned towards the right-hand wall on which was pinned a list headed *Fast Track Menu*.

'Let's see,' he said, scanning down the twelve bulleted points. 'What have I missed? *Scene Forensics, Crime Scene Assessment* and *Post Mortems*; that's down to Jack Benson. He'll give us updates as the data comes in. Which leaves the following for DCI Caton and me: *Media, Possible Motives, Identify Suspects* and *Significant Witness Interviews*, starting with the parents of Mr Spencer Miles-Cowper.'

He looked at Caton.

'Over to you, boss.'

'Thank you, Gordon,' said Caton. 'There is just one more task, however. I'd like you to liaise with the Press Office on the next release. You'll also have to do a short television appearance, including an appeal for witnesses.'

There were muted oohs and aahs around the room that added to his deputy's evident embarrassment. Caton was unrepentant. It wasn't a case of cold feet on his part; it was something Gordon would have to get used to if he was ever going to get the promotion Marilyn believed he deserved. And to be fair, she was right. Not just because of the boost it would give to his pension, but because he was a better detective and a better team manager than he realised.

'And finally…'

He reached towards the desk behind him and grasped, and then held up high above his head, a hand-held tablet computer.

'Ged will issue every non-office-based member of this team with one of these.'

This time the oohs and aahs were accompanied by cheers and applause.

'Don't get carried away,' he said. 'It's only a trial at this stage, so don't bugger it up, or the headmaster will confiscate them. Here are the rules. Number one, they're exclusively for work only. So no games, random surfing of the Net, checking the latest football scores, booking holidays, Tweeting, Facebooking, blogging your Diary of a Super Cop, and no porn. Same as your desktop PCs, any misuse will be regarded as gross misconduct, and may lead to suspension and eventual dismissal.'

That wiped the grins off some faces at least.

'Secondly, whilst we will be able to share all of our

own internally generated data, including forensic reports, witness statements, etc., you will not have access to the Police National Computer, or HOLMES2. Thirdly, these are the most secure tablets available, with additional firewall software, password protection and data encryption. But, just as with paper-based files and data keys, they do not leave your possession, and you lose them at your peril. If you do, you will be charged for their replacement and disciplined. I'm sure I don't need to remind you that the Force was recently fined £150,000 for the loss of highly sensitive data relating to serious crime investigations that was stored on a memory stick and stolen from the home of an officer in another team.'

He looked around the room to make sure they were all listening to him.

'And last but not least, you should know that these tablets are traceable via wireless and satellite tracking.'

'So no flogging them down the market,' quipped Jimmy Hulme.

Nobody laughed.

Caton checked the Arrivals Board. The Virgin train carrying the Miles-Cowpers was on time and due in fifteen minutes. He carried his Styrofoam cup of coffee to a table and sat down. It was still too hot to drink, so he removed the lid, opened his tablet and entered the password. There was a message waiting for him from DC Hulme. He opened the attachment. It began with the father's entry in Who's Who.

MILES-COWPER, Herbert James, OBE. BSc.Econ (Hons); MBA. Chief Investment Manager, USRTB Global Investment Bank Since 2005; b 24 December 1956; s of late Jasper Miles, and the late Hermione Cowper; m 1989, Harriet Winter. Son, Spencer. Edu: Old Swinford Hospital;

London School of Economics; Cranfield University; Address: The Vault, Lower Village Road, Sunninghill, Surrey; Clubs: City of London Club.

Then there was some additional information he appeared to have trawled from news reports on the Internet:

A lifelong member of the Conservative Party, he was awarded his OBE following staunch support for Margaret Thatcher during the election campaign of 1987 that led to her third term in power. Since the banking crisis and subsequent recession he has been outspoken in defence of the banking system, bankers in general and investment bankers in particular. Came in for much criticism for insisting on retaining his bonus every year for the past three years, despite the historical mis-selling of Payment Protection Policies by his bank, and heavy losses in the property market. None of which he claimed he had any personal responsibility for.

His notes on the wife were brief.

Harriet Cowper. Daughter of Frank and Ethel Winter. Father a butcher, mother a teacher. Met at LSE. Brief relationship. Met again in 1989 at a party. She was working for a major retail store as a manager in the accounts department. Married later that year. NB. Spencer born just five months after they were married!

Caton tried the coffee again and found it bearable. When he had that conversation with DC Hulme he would have to remember to tell him not to pepper his reports with NBs and exclamation marks. He scanned the piece on the son. It was equally scant.

Sent to same school as his father. Left at 14. Query expelled? Sent to local comprehensive: Charters School. Did well – straight As and A*s at GCSE and A Level. Went to

Man Uni to read Computer Science. Dropped out in his second year there. Reported missing.

There were five jpeg files attached. He opened each of them in turn. One was of the parents on their wedding day. Two were of the father, taken to accompany the newspaper articles Hulme had referred to, and two were of the son taken from his cached Facebook page. As far as Caton could tell they were both of his time at the university. Each showed him with a group of male students, all grinning or holding outlandish poses. Judging from the number of pint glasses in evidence, drink seemed to be involved.

The impression he gained of Miles-Cowper senior was of a supremely confident person. His wife seemed far less self-assured, especially given that this was a wedding photo. He found that strange, given that she was head and shoulders taller than her husband. Maybe, he reflected, it was the bump that was already showing through the layers of white embroidered silk. The bump that now lay on a stainless steel shelf in the mortuary refrigerator.

He looked closer at the photographs of Spencer. The boy took after his mother. It wasn't so much his looks as the fact that he didn't seem to belong in either group. His glass was raised in both photos, but the grin on his face lacked authenticity. It was hesitant, uncomfortable, embarrassed even. Just like his mother's.

He closed the applications down, logged out and finished his coffee.

Chapter 16

It was impossible to miss them. Him marching down the platform like Bilbo Baggins, his little legs going nineteen to the dozen; her, ten years younger, struggling to keep up despite her greater stride, pulling a large case on wheels behind her.

For a moment Caton feared that the man would cannon straight into him, but at the last second he braked sharply and thrust out his hand.

'Miles-Cowper, Bertie; that's my wife, Hermione. You must be Caton?'

Caton shook his hand and found it squeezed in a vice-like grip. No sooner had it been released than Miles-Cowper grasped his elbow with his left hand and started to steer him towards the exit.

'Keep up, Mani!' he shouted over his shoulder.

The only Manis Caton could recall were a Greek peninsular, an Iranian prophet and the bass guitarist of Stone Roses. He pulled his arm free and waited for her to join them.

'Can I give you a hand?' he asked.

She smiled wanly and shook her head. Her mascara was smudged, and there were telltale streaks on her cheeks.

'Thank you, I'll manage.'

'Course she can,' said her husband. 'Had years of practice.'

Caton wondered if the perpetrator hadn't got the wrong man. He could cheerfully have killed him himself.

'Allow me,' he said, taking hold of the handle and easing the case from her grasp. 'My car's this way.'

He took them beyond the glass partition wall at the end of the platform, across the concourse and down the escalator into the undercroft. All the while the husband kept up a litany of complaints, peppered with expletives, about the extended travel time, diversions caused by essential work on the line and the limited First Class service on a Sunday. Not a word about his son. It went a long way to explaining his wife's demeanour. Caton wondered why on earth she had agreed to marry him. Then he remembered the bump in the wedding photograph.

While the Miles-Cowpers settled themselves into the car, Caton had called Joanne Stuart, and told her to hand over the task of analysing the witness statements to another member of the team and to meet them at the mortuary. He sensed that they would get nothing from the victim's mother so long as her husband was there. Everything about their demeanour in the car had strengthened that belief. Sitting here, in the viewing suite of the mortuary in the Clinical Sciences Centre, he knew for certain that he was right.

'I'll do it,' said Miles-Cowper. 'No need to bother my wife.' It was as though she simply wasn't there.

'I want to see him too,' she said, so quietly that Caton had to strain to hear her.

'I have to warn you,' said Caton, 'that if it is your son, I am afraid that his face has sustained significant damage. Your husband's formal identification will suffice.'

'I don't care,' she whispered. 'I need to see him.'

'Speak up, woman!' said her husband. 'So Mr Caton can hear you.'

'I can hear your wife perfectly well, thank you,' said Caton. 'If your wife wants to stay, she has every right to do so. What is more, experience suggests that it will help her to come to terms with your son's death if she does have a chance to say goodbye.'

Miles-Cowper made a bubbling sound deep in his throat, like a blocked drain.

'Let's get on with it then,' he said.

The two of them stood and approached the window. The pathology technologist peeled back the sterile evidence sheet until the head and torso were revealed. Caton was relieved that the hands were still hidden, and that from this distance, and given the time spent in the zero-degree cabinet, the facial injuries were less evident. The father stared at the body for the space of three heartbeats, and then turned away.

'That's him,' he said.

His voice was emotionless. Matter of fact. He could have been responding to the photograph of a celebrity in a quiz down the local pub. But Caton sensed a powerful feeling being held in check.

The wife was still staring intently at the body on the gurney.

'Mrs Miles-Cowper?' said DS Stuart gently.

Slowly she nodded her head.

'Yes,' she whispered. 'This is Spencer ... my son.'

'Are you both sure?' said Caton.

'Of course we're sure,' said the father brusquely. 'There's the tattoo on his shoulder, just as I described it. Now, are we done here?'

He turned to go. His wife remained rooted to the spot.

'Hermione,' he snapped.

'I need to be with him,' she said. She half turned in Caton's direction. 'Can I touch him please? To say goodbye?'

'I'm sorry, Mrs Miles-Cowper,' said Caton. 'I'm afraid I can't let you do that. Not until after the post mortem.'

She clenched her fingers tightly. A shudder seemed to run through her body, ending with a heartbreaking sob.

'Mani!' said the husband.

She took a deep breath, and gradually let it out.

'Can I just sit here with my son?' she said.

'Of course,' said Caton. 'But you will have as long as you need when Spencer's body has been released. And then he will look as you would wish to remember him.'

He had to lean closer to hear her reply.

'I can see him the day he was born. The day he broke his leg jumping from a tree in the garden. In his uniform the day he started big school. I remember the last time I saw him. I don't need a make-up artist to help me remember my son. I just need to be with him.'

There was such strength in her tone that it took Caton by surprise.

'Your husband and I will wait for you outside,' he said. 'DC Stuart will sit with you, just a few rows back. Take as long as you need.'

The family waiting room for bereaved relatives was occupied. Caton took him through to the adjoining counselling room.

'Don't worry,' he said, 'DC Stuart will know where to find us when your wife is ready to join us.'

'Better settle down then,' he said, slumping on a chair and folding his arms. 'Could be in for a long wait.'

Not worried at all then, thought Caton. However

lonely the poor woman must have been living with this excuse for a husband, how much worse it was going to be without her son.

'I've arranged for a family liaison officer to join you while you're here in Manchester,' he said. 'And when you decide to return home, I can make a referral for you both to the Homicide Service and Cruse Bereavement Counselling in your area.'

This brought forth yet another snort.

'Don't bother,' said Miles-Cowper. 'Don't need any of that. Well capable of managing it myself.'

'And your wife?'

'I'll take care of my wife. I suggest you concentrate on finding the person responsible for murdering our son.'

Caton let it go. There was no point in arguing with someone like this. When the time came he would make the referral on behalf of Mrs Miles-Cowper, then she could decide for herself whether or not she wanted to take it up. There was no need for her husband to know.

'The advantage of having someone from Family Liaison,' he said, 'is that he or she can liaise with me, with the mortuary and with the coroner's staff on your behalf.'

'I'd prefer to do that myself,' he replied. 'Talk to the organ grinder, not the monkey.'

Talk was not something Miles-Cowper did. Nor did he converse. Pester and bully were the adjectives Caton had in mind. He decided it was time to skip the touchy feely approach.

'Very well,' he said. 'How would you describe your relationship with your son, Mr Miles-Cowper?

That hit the mark. It was clear that he was surprised by the question. It took him a moment or two to gather his thoughts, during which Caton sensed that he was actually asking himself the question, and having difficulty arriving at an answer. When he did decide to reply, Caton was prepared for him to pretend to be affronted, but at the last second he fell back on sarcasm.

'As a father and son relationship,' he said. 'Why, what did you expect?'

'As you had so helpfully pointed out, this is a murder investigation,' said Caton calmly. 'So I had at the very least expected an honest response.'

Miles-Cowper briefly held his gaze, like a silver back gorilla attempting to dominate a rival, and then slowly dropped his head in an unconsciously submissive gesture. It was a response that Caton had seen a thousand times from over-confident criminals and hostile witnesses. There came a point when cold, hard reality struck home and pretence flew out of the window.

'We didn't get on,' he said. 'We never did.'

His words were ponderous, heavy with an emotion Caton was unable to identify. It was neither guilt nor remorse, but something akin.

'Why do you think that was?' he asked.

'I don't know. He fought me all the way. Even as a child.' He shook his head. 'No, that's not true. He didn't fight at all. If he'd stood up for himself, fought his corner, I could have respected that. It was the dumb insolence that got to me. He would just stand there and stare at me. If I lost it, started shouting at him, he'd curl up in a ball until she pulled me away.' He looked up. 'I didn't hit him. Never once did I hit him.'

Caton believed him. If the way he spoke to his wife was anything to go by, he didn't need to resort to physical violence; his voice was a lethal weapon.

'He was a solitary child. Head in his books, or more

often gazing at a screen. Spoke in monosyllables long before he became a teenager. I paid for him to go to my old school, you know?'

Caton nodded.

'Thought it would do him good, and give us both a break from each other. It didn't, of course. Didn't stick up for himself there either. Got bullied. Found sly ways to get his own back. Made him even more unpopular. Got himself thrown out.'

'Why was that?'

'Took a hand drill from the design and technology workshop, drilled a hole in the wooden partition wall that separated the dormitory from the matron's room and used it to spy on her. Stupid fool got caught.'

It spoke volumes that getting caught was the greater sin.

'What happened when he told you he was dropping out of university?' said Caton.

Miles-Cowper's demeanour changed instantly from disappointment to anger. He leapt from his chair, arms by his side, fists clenched. Caton revised his judgment about the man not being capable of physical violence.

'Dropped out?!' he yelled. 'What do you mean, dropped out? When did he drop out?'

Disappointment. That's what it was. All his life his son had been a disappointment to him. He had thought the manner of his death was the final humiliation. Now here was another. It didn't matter that his son was dead, only that he had been a failure, a disappointment.

The door opened, held back by DS Stuart to allow Mrs Miles-Cowper to enter the room. Her husband stabbed his finger at her.

'Did you know?'

Her face changed to a whiter shade of pale as she

shrank back from him. Caton stood between them.
   'Mr Miles-Cowper,' he said, 'sit down!'

Chapter 17

Joanne Stuart sat with the wife in the family room, leaving her husband to kick his heels next door. Caton was in the corridor, taking a phone call from Douggie Wallace.

'Some good news, boss,' he was told. 'The credit card wasn't stolen, and I found out where you can get hold of the owner.'

Caton sensed from his tone that this wasn't good news at all.

'Spit it out,' he said.

'The mortuary.'

'The mortuary?'

'That's where you'll find him. The victim, Spencer Miles-Cowper, applied for it in person. It's his.'

'He used a false identity?'

'He cloned one. There is a C N Brooker. Charles Neil Brooker to be precise. Alive and well, living in Chorlton.'

'And he's never had his card stolen?'

'Nope. Somehow Spencer Miles-Cowper got hold of enough of his personal details to apply for a credit card online.'

'How did he manage that? I thought they verified your computer address, sent confirmation emails and sent the card and pin code separately to your home address.'

'I don't know, but I'm prepared to bet that the answer lies somewhere in what remains of his computer. I checked the date he took it out. Two months after he'd slipped out of sight. So he had enough to live on presumably, until he took on a new identity.'

'Stole,' said Caton. 'Stole a new identity. But he'll have needed to pay off his old card, and still survive for those two months.'

'That wouldn't have cost him much, given he was squatting.'

'He'll have needed to eat. So where did he get the money from?'

'Me. He got it from me.'

Hermione Miles-Cooper dabbed her eyes with a tissue from the ubiquitous box on the coffee table. She had once been a beautiful woman, he decided. Still was beneath the grief-stricken face and worry lines. The immaculate clothes and expensive accessories aside, there was an inner beauty just waiting to be released.

'We were in regular contact. Then, this summer, he came back up here to Manchester early, in July, even though he had hinted that he was unhappy with the course, and with university life in general. Then, just as he was about to start back, he told me that he was dropping out. He didn't want his father to know. He knew that he would go ballistic. He wasn't bothered for himself, only that he would take it out on me.'

She dabbed her eyes again and screwed up the tissue, as though resolved to get a grip on herself.

'He told me not to worry. He said he'd got a great idea on how to build up a business. A niche in the market, he called it. He just needed some time and space.'

'And money,' said Caton.

She cast her eyes down and nodded. When she looked up, a little confidence had returned.

'Of course he needed money. You do when you start up a business. It's called investment.'

They could see that she was only trying to fool herself, and failing.

'So what was this business he was developing?'

'I don't know. Something to do with computers. It was all over my head.' Her eyes lit up briefly. 'Anyway, whatever it was he must have succeeded, because he stopped asking me for money two months ago.'

Caton handed her one of his contact cards. On the back he had written the website addresses for the Victim Support Homicide Service and Cruse Bereavement Counselling.

'One or other of these organisations will contact you,' he said. 'They will do so in complete confidence. Your husband need never know, although I have a feeling he would benefit from their support just as much as I am certain you will.'

'Thank you.'

She looked around for a wastepaper bin, found it and dropped the tissue in. Then she took the card and placed it in the wallet compartment of her handbag.

'You can also ring me at any time,' he said, hoping he wouldn't regret it.

As she searched his face, her lips formed a fragile smile. He thought it a giant step forward.

'I'll try not to,' she said. 'You'll be so busy.'

'We won't rest until we find out what happened to your son,' he assured her. 'Not even the wedding will get in the way.'

He had no idea where that had come from. His brain had taken over and he had simply spoken his mind. She immediately picked up on his embarrassment.

'You're getting married?' she said.

This time the smile was broad.

'At the end of the week,' he said. 'But it won't affect this investigation, I promise. My team will…'

She raised her hand, cutting him off mid-sentence.

'I know you'll do your best. I wouldn't want this to mar your happiness. This time should be the most precious in your life. Are you going on honeymoon?'

'To Venice. Just ten days.'

'Take my advice. Don't take your mobile phones. Don't give anyone the address. Forget this case. Your attention should be only on one another. With luck, you'll never have an opportunity like this again.'

In all of this there was so much self-reflection, Caton realised. He could imagine what her honeymoon must have been like. The self-important, misogynist husband. The young wife besotted with her powerful, successful bridegroom. The constant phone calls, messages and inattention. The gradual dawning that this was what married life with Bertie was going to involve.

'Thank you,' he said, 'I will. And I promise we'll get whoever took your son from you.'

She reached out, placed her hand on his arm and squeezed gently.

'Of course you will.'

'So, Bank of Mum,' said Joanne Stuart as they headed back to base. 'No surprises there. Do you think she'll be alright?'

'I doubt she's been alright since she married him,' Caton replied. 'I'm going to arrange for Family Liaison to keep an eye on them regardless of what her husband wants, and I've already made a referral to Victim Support. Their Homicide Team will contact her without her husband knowing.'

'What a bastard,' she said with a vehemence that surprised him. 'No wonder he and the son never got on. What d'you think she'll do now?'

The hoardings on Hyde Road, immediately opposite the Apollo, heralded the coming of the Christmas markets in just five weeks' time. Was it his imagination or did they seem to come round earlier every year? Was it really three years since Kate had been held captive on the Town Hall roof?

'Boss, are you alright?'

He shook his head. 'Sorry, I was miles away.'

'I hope not,' she said. 'You are driving.'

He tightened his grip on the steering wheel.

'What were you saying?'

'Mrs Miles-Cowper. What d'you think she'll do now?'

He thought about all the women he had known who had endured loveless marriages for the sake of their children and, as soon as the last of them had left the nest, had walked away. He had glimpsed an inner strength in her during their last conversation. With Spencer gone he could see no reason why she would stick with Albert Miles-Cowper, and every reason why she should not.

'She'll be fine,' he said. 'When the dust settles, he'll be the loser. Trust me.'

They soldiered on late into the evening. It was obvious by nine p.m. that there was nothing more they could do that night. It was DS Carter's turn to hold the fort as night detective, just in case something came up. He would carry on with the analysis of the CCTV footage, and take naps as necessary.

'Everyone else, back here at seven fifteen a.m.,' said Caton. 'Bright-eyed…'

'And bushy tailed,' shouted DC Jimmy Hulme.

He seemed surprised but not the slightest bit embarrassed that he was the only one to assume that the boss was looking for a chorus.

Kate tucked her feet under her bottom and leaned back into the cushions.

'So,' she said, 'if I've got this right, you have a father who is an outwardly successful banker, but at home he is a sexist, overbearing, dominant perfectionist. A wife who was forced to sacrifice her career to raise their son, and slave for her husband. The son retreats into himself, and his computer, the one thing where he excels and over which he has control. This interest and expertise his father doesn't rate, despite the fact that he must have relied on computer technology to accumulate his considerable wealth. Sent away to boarding school, the son unsurprisingly rebels and gets himself thrown out. Repeating the pattern, he drops out of university, this time with a mysterious and hopeful business plan. Within months his body is discovered, battered and mutilated, among the shattered remains of his computer.

'If you ever think of moonlighting,' he said, 'you could always write the blurbs for detective novels.'

'If I was going to moonlight,' she replied, smoothing her hands provocatively over the swell of her breasts, across her taut stomach and down the front of her thighs, 'I can think of far more lucrative ways.'

He started to move closer, but she placed both hands in the centre of his chest.

'Down, boy,' she said. 'The honeymoon's a week away.'

'Come on,' he said, placing his hands over hers. 'Athletes have to train for the big race.'

She raised both eyebrows. 'Is that how you see it? A race? What are you training for, a sprint or a marathon?'

He curled his fingers through hers.

'I was thinking multi-event, over a number of days.'

'Would that include riding?' she said.

'And wrestling.'

'Mmm.' She did not resist as he pulled her towards him. 'What exactly does the training involve?'

She allowed him a single searching kiss, and then pushed him gently away.

'Not with this staring up at us,' she said, indicating his newly acquired tablet glowing portentously on the top of the coffee table. 'Do you want an answer or not?'

'Go on then,' he said, sitting up and plumping a cushion behind him.

'Make yourself comfortable why don't you?'

'Am I supposed to sound disappointed that you stopped when we were just getting going, or grateful that you're helping me on this case?' he said. 'I'm damned if I do, and damned if I don't.'

She laughed. 'You'll have to get used to that when we're married,' she said. 'Now, where was I? Oh yes. Given the years of anger, frustration and resentment that must have festered in that young man, I would suggest that he had embarked on some criminal or anti-social enterprise, and that was what got him killed.'

'Someone could have stolen his idea, or his application software, or been involved in whatever he and Lee Bottomley, our first victim, were planning, and then killed them both to reap the benefits themselves.'

'It's possible.'

'But you don't think so?'

'No. For a start, you don't have any connection between the two victims, other than the manner of their deaths.'

'Not yet, but we will.'

'Of course you will. It's inevitable that the two are connected. The question is how?'

She picked up his tablet and studied the crime scene photos one by one, swiping them from right to left with slow deliberation.

'The damage to the computer and the keyboard, that might fit your theory, but the injuries to his hands, and in particular the mutilation, they speak to me of rage. Controlled rage, but rage nonetheless.'

She put the tablet back down on the coffee table.

'Didn't you say the computer mouse was missing from both crime scenes?'

'That's right.'

'I don't suppose they would have held any data?'

It was an interesting thought. Not something any of his team had suggested.

'I've seen a computer mouse with a USB attachment for flash drives, but never one where the memory was inside the mouse itself.'

'If not that, then it only leaves the possibility that they were trophies. No murderer is going to take something from the crime scene unless it has a utilitarian value, or an emotional one. Judging by these photos, I'd say it was an emotional one.'

'We're looking for a sociopath?'

'Come on, Tom, keep up,' she said with more than a hint of disappointment in her voice. 'That goes without saying. What you have here is a sociopath whose personality disorder is manifested in criminally aggressive behaviour, without a shred of remorse. Ergo…'

'A psychopath. I know.'

'Then why didn't you say so?'

'I was looking for a second opinion.'

'When it comes to psychopaths, mine is the first and most qualified opinion,' she reminded him. 'And don't you forget it.'

'I won't.'

He leaned forward and flipped the cover across the front of the tablet, sending it to sleep. Tired though he was, sleep was the last thing on his mind.

'Now,' he said, turning to face her, 'where were we?'

Chapter 18

Monday morning, eight a.m. The hot weather had broken, and a customary autumnal drizzle had greeted the team as they joined the first wave of rush-hour commuters into the city. There was so little progress to report in relation to either of the victims that the briefing was already over. Caton asked Jack Benson to stay behind for a word before he headed out to supervise the scenes of crime officers.

'Nothing at all? Are you sure?' he said.

'His computer was smashed to smithereens,' said Jack Benson. 'They knew what they were doing chucking it off the roof. The tecchies say there's no chance of recovering any data whatsoever.'

Caton stared at the photos of the two battered faces on the whiteboard.

'I was banking on that to make the connection between our victims.'

'Smithereens,' said DC Hulme, 'apropos nothing at all. 'From the Irish, *smiodar*, for fragments, and *een*, for little, as in *coleen*.'

Alerted by the silence, he looked up from his computer and saw them staring at him.

'It was a quiz question,' he said. 'I'm a member of a pub team.'

They turned back to the whiteboard.

'Somebody loves him then,' muttered Holmes.

'Cut him some slack,' said Caton. 'He's still learning.'

'We don't have time for slow learners,' his deputy replied.

Caton smiled. 'We had time for you.'

'The door-to-doors have been worse than useless,' said Holmes, changing the subject.

Caton didn't agree. 'Not completely. We've established that he's been staying there for over two months. That he was seen with someone several times in the downstairs bar at The Angel.'

'The Angel?' said Holmes, who thought he knew just about every pub within three miles of the city centre.

'In Angel Street. Used to be The Beer House.'

'The Beer House!' exclaimed Holmes wistfully. 'What a pub that was. The only place to match it was Tommy Ducks; I don't suppose you ever ventured in there, boss, with you being a City supporter?'

'Some of the tables at Tommy Ducks were glass-topped coffins,' said DC Hulme. 'One even had a skeleton in it. I don't think anyone ever found out if it was real or not.'

They turned to stare at him again. Misinterpreting their response and encouraged by their apparent interest, he ploughed on.

'Did you know that on their first visit to the pub, women were invited to remove their knickers and pin them to the ceiling? A group of feminists raided the pub to take them down – not their own knickers obviously – but they got rebuffed. The knickers were still there when the brewery demolished it overnight in February 1993, despite the City Council having put a preservation order on it.'

As one, they turned back to face the whiteboard.

'If he keeps this up I'm going to pin *him* to the

ceiling,' said Holmes.

'Unfortunately, the descriptions of his companion are far too hazy to do a photo fit,' Caton reflected. 'Male, twenties to thirties, mid height, medium build, not sure about the hair colour, never saw his face.'

'It could have been victim number one,' said Benson.

'True,' said Holmes. 'But then again, it could have been DC Hulme!'

Caton sat down on the edge of the desk behind him.

'It's all we've got, until the rest of the forensics come back from both crime scenes. Even if we get lucky with trace evidence, we'll need suspects to match it to. You and I are going to the university to talk to his tutors and any students who are still there.'

'I hope we have better luck than we did with Bottomley,' said Holmes.

'And I want someone to go to The Angel with photos of both victims. Assuming they knew each other, it's possible they met there. We also need to know if any of the staff or regulars can come up with a description for the man Spencer Miles-Cowper was seen with.'

'I'm happy to do that,' offered DC Hulme.

Gordon Holmes's derisive snort put Caton in mind of their second victim's father. It also helped him to make up his mind.

'Good idea,' he said. 'DI Holmes will brief you.'

They parked at the Commonwealth Games Aquatics Centre, stepped out onto the Oxford Road pavement teeming with students and walked the couple of hundred yards down to the slatted red-brick box that was the Kilburn Building. A sign saying *Access to Computer Science Building* directed them up a winding metal staircase. On the first-floor platform Holmes nudged Caton's arm and pointed diagonally across the road. A banner attached to the side of the Manchester Museum's Café Muse proclaimed: *Lindow Man. A Bog Body Mystery.*

'Give me one of those any day,' he quipped. 'No witnesses to interview, and the perpetrator's long dead.'

Caton shook his head and started up the second flight.

'Not a lot of call for detectives then,' he said.

'How long is he going to keep us waiting?' Holmes demanded.

They had been sitting in the cramped office for over ten minutes. It seemed that flashing a police identity and warrant card no longer guaranteed an instant response. Apart from the chairs in which they were sitting, the room contained a large computer desk, a task chair and three bookcases. Every surface, other than the coffee table, was strewn with piles of books and papers. There was barely room for their feet.

'Professor Stroner is in the middle of a supervisory session with a postgraduate student,' his secretary had informed them. 'He shouldn't be more than five minutes.'

She handed them some leaflets on the Centre, and promised to return with drinks.

Holmes held up one of the leaflets. 'Have you seen this? That Alan Turing has a building named after him as well as a road. Now I know why. Says here he worked on radar during the war, and then at Bletchley Park breaking the German Enigma Code.'

'He also helped to design the first ever computer programme, and designed the world's first commercial computer,' Caton told him. 'Most people regard him as the father of computer science and artificial intelligence. Not that he lived to reap the benefits.'

Holmes put the leaflet down.

'How so?'

Caton sighed and put his own leaflet down.

'You won't find it in there,' he said. 'He was gay at a time when it was still illegal to engage in homosexual acts. He was arrested in 1952 and given the choice of a lengthy prison sentence or chemical castration.'

'Bloody hell! What did he decide?'

'He agreed to be treated with female hormones. Two years later, just before his 42nd birthday, he was found dead. Cyanide poisoning.'

'Suicide?'

'That's what the inquest determined. His mother and some of his friends and colleagues believed that it was accidental.'

'Either way, he didn't deserve that.'

'I agree. So do most right-minded people. There was a big Internet campaign on his behalf a few years ago that led to Gordon Brown apologising as Prime Minister on behalf of the government for the appalling way he was treated. As we speak, there's a private members Bill, and also an e-petition, pushing for an official pardon.'

Holmes rubbed his chin thoughtfully.

'Bit late for that.'

He tried to change the cross of his feet and found a stack of files blocking his way.

'So much for a paper-free world,' he complained.

The door opened and in came a tall man in his mid-forties, followed by the secretary carrying a tray on which were two cups of coffee and a beaker of hot water.

The man waited for her to place the tray on the coffee table and retire.

'David Stroner,' he said breezily. 'Sorry to have kept you.'

He shook hands with each of them, moved some papers from the seat of his chair onto the desk and plonked himself down. He was almost entirely bald apart from the sides of his head, where the hair was cropped close. His nose was pronounced, his jaw firm and his green and hazel eyes bright and searching. He reminded Caton of the Star Trek character Jean Luc-Picard. He looked too young to be a professor, but then he'd read somewhere that most computer experts were over the hill at thirty. Stroner steepled his fingers and reclined in his chair. The armrests and the neck rest adjusted automatically to cradle his body. I wouldn't mind one of those, thought Caton. Fat chance.

'Shirley said you wanted to talk about Spencer Miles-Cowper. What's he done?'

'What makes you think he's done something?' said Holmes.

Caton saw the man's pupils dilate as he computed the possibilities, faster even than his state-of-the-art computers.

'If he hasn't, then he must be a victim of some kind?'

'I didn't say he hadn't,' Holmes replied. 'I was wondering what had made you assume that he had.'

'When two detectives turn up out of the blue wanting to know about a former student who disappeared without a by your leave, wouldn't it be reasonable to conclude that he must have done something?'

'That aside,' Holmes pressed, 'would you be surprised to learn that he had been involved in something nefarious?'

His eyebrows arched. 'Nefarious? I haven't heard that word in a while.'

He swivelled his chair from side to side as he decided how to respond. When the chair stopped, he folded his arms across his chest and deliberately addressed himself to Caton. It was a trivial, petty attempt to marginalise the junior of the two. It didn't go unnoticed.

'Let's say I wouldn't be surprised,' he said. 'Not that I was aware of his being involved in anything *nefarious* while he was here. It was just that he was difficult to read. Secretive. Not a team player. He also had a remarkable talent for programming, and was an exceptionally creative thinker. Attributes that might well come in handy in a criminal enterprise.'

'You know a lot about that sort of thing, do you, Mr Stroner?' said Caton.

The word *Professor* began to form on Stroner's lips, but he must have thought better of it.

'Cybercrime is *the* crime of both the present and the future, Detective Chief Inspector,' he said. 'As with most learning at the frontiers of human knowledge – physics, chemistry, biology – computer science can be used as a tool for good or for evil. Of itself it is just that, a tool. The hands that take and use it are what determine the impact it will have. Whether for the common good, or for personal greed. Students come here to study from all around the world. I believe that the majority will leave here better equipped to help make their country, and our Global Village, a happier, wealthier, more secure place. I am not so naive as to think that none of them will use that knowledge and skill to spread disharmony, or to exploit others.'

Caton thought it a good response, even if it did sound like something taken from one of the papers on his desk. Written for some symposium or other.

'And where on that continuum would you place Spencer Miles-Cowper?' he asked.

'On the cusp. Although, as I indicated in my earlier response, I wouldn't have been surprised to learn that he had strayed from the straight and narrow.'

Caton leaned forward.

'Are you aware, Dr Stroner,' he said, tossing him a partially redemptive designation, 'that you have consistently referred to Miles in the past tense? Is there a reason for that?'

The question took him by surprise.

'No, I wasn't,' he replied. 'But it's hardly surprising since I was talking about my past experience of him, before he dropped out.'

'Would you be surprised to hear that yesterday morning Miles Spencer-Cowper was found dead?'

His chair sprung into the upright position, catapulting him to within a few feet of Caton's face. He rested his hands on the armrests and eased himself back.

'My God!'

He smoothed his thighs with the palms of his hands as though the action would somehow render this news more palatable.

'That body, the one they found in the Green Quarter, it was Miles?'

'That's correct.'

'But it said on the news that it hadn't been identified.'

'Well it has now,' said Holmes.

'Dead? How?'

He searched their faces, but neither detective responded.

'Not suicide surely?' He shook his head. 'No, not suicide.'

'What makes you so sure?' said Caton.

He joined his hands right up to the roots of his fingers. It was clear that he had been affected by the news.

'Sadly, every university has the occasional suicide. Hardly surprising given that we, for example, have thirty-nine thousand students on the largest single campus university in the UK. Most of them young people, many away from home for the first time. None of those suicides I recall were anything like Miles.'

'In what way were they different?'

'Whilst as many as five per cent of students seriously contemplate suicide, those who go through with it tend to have some history of mental ill-health. They are also likely to substance abuse. Most will feel lonely, isolated and completely worthless. They may have had plans fall through, relationship plans or otherwise. They will feel totally overwhelmed. The act of taking their own life may be the last and only thing over which they have control.'

'Miles exhibited none of those characteristics?'

'None. They weren't in his nature. Okay, he was solitary and secretive, as I said, but he was also tough and resilient. It was as though he had purpose, a mission, something to prove perhaps. Nothing was going to stand in his way.'

'Well, you were right about that at least,' said Caton. 'He didn't commit suicide. He was murdered.'

Chapter 19

'What did his course involve?' said Caton. 'What exactly was he studying?'

Stroner picked up his mug and took a sip; it was tepid. He put it back down on the tray.

'I can get you a course leaflet.'

'That would be helpful. But in the meantime, just give us a rough outline please.'

'The core consists of artificial intelligence, computer science, computer systems engineering, distributed computing and software engineering programs. Students are able to concentrate their studies on one or more aspects that particularly interest them.'

'Such as?'

'Computing for business applications, Internet computing, computer science with business and management, and computer science and mathematics.'

'So Miles-Cowper would have been able to write software programs, know his way around the hardware, that sort of thing?' said Holmes.

Stroner turned to look at him. He shook his head, expressing disappointment. As he might with a student he'd thought capable of better.

'Spencer was able to do all that before he started the course. This is a research-intensive university, Detective Inspector. We are equipping our students to change the world.'

'How?'

He swivelled his chair and bent down to rifle through a stack of papers. He pulled one out and handed it to Caton.

'This is a list of the destinations of last year's graduates and postgraduates.'

Caton speed-read the list. The vast majority went straight into employment. A surprising number – mainly the postgraduates – were shown as self-employed consultants. The industries represented were impressive: Aerospace, Healthcare, Nuclear Power, Gas and Oil, Engineering and Construction, Investment Banking, Automotives, Films, TV, Media and Gaming, Computer and IT, and several Government departments including Defence, GCHQ and the Home Office. Their roles included Network Administrator, Software and Applications Developer, Technical Consultant, and Development Engineer.

Caton handed the list to Holmes.

'Very impressive,' he said. 'Did Spencer show a particular interest in one area of his course?'

Stroner pursed his lips. 'My role is to deliver lectures to a large number of students at any one time. To prepare online seminars and learning materials, and to work face-to-face in the supervision of postgraduate students studying for Masters and PhDs. That's when I'm not carrying out my own research and writing papers. I don't spend much time with individual undergraduates.'

'And yet you seem to have quite definite opinions about this student. For example, that he was…' He looked down at the notes he had been taking. '*Not likely to commit suicide. Secretive. Not a team player. A remarkable talent for programming. Exceptionally creative thinker*.' Caton looked up. 'Given what you say about how your time is spent, how is it that you know so much about this particular undergraduate?'

'I was about to say,' Stroner replied, 'that Spencer was an exception to the rule.' He sounded affronted by Caton's interruption. 'The quality of his work brought him to my attention early on. I kept an eye out for his assignments. Discussed them with his personal tutor. When he dropped out, we went over his work to see if there might be some connection with his leaving.'

'And was there?'

He shook his head. 'Not that we could see.'

'What did his work involve?'

It was another of those occasions when he felt that he was drawing blood from a stone.

'His coursework was not different to anyone else's, other than the fact that it was of a consistently high standard. It was the creative work, work that he was doing on the side, as a personal pursuit you could say, that stood out.'

'Which involved?'

'Internet security. An examination of the methodology used by Internet hackers, and the counter-measures employed by the designers of security systems for the Internet, and for supposedly closed information technology systems.' He paused. 'I know what you're thinking, Detective Chief Inspector,' he said.

'That's very clever of you, sir,' said Holmes. 'Is that part of the course, telepathy?'

Stroner swivelled his chair so that his back was towards him.

'You are hypothesising, Mr Caton, that Spencer may have been involved in a hacking experiment, and come across something so important and dangerous that it led to his being murdered.'

'That is one possibility, surely?'

'A possibility, I grant you, but a remote possibility. Large organisations don't murder people who hack into their systems, they prosecute them. You only have to look at the US Government.'

'I doubt that criminal organisations rely on legal recourse,' said Caton. 'In our experience they tend to use more immediate, certain and final solutions.'

'I wouldn't know anything about that,' said Stroner.

'How do you know about Miles-Cowper's interest in these matters?'

'Because of the articles he accessed from our library, and our digital library. Because of his files stored on our file servers.'

'Do you still have copies of those files?'

'Of course. He is still a registered student at this university … until now, of course. I can arrange for you to have copies to take with you. Would you prefer paper or digital copies?'

'Digital,' said Caton. He held up his notebook and biro. 'These are only for first-hand notes. We find they are less susceptible to alteration. Their one advantage over modern technology.'

Stroner crossed his arms and leant back in his chair.

'Always assuming,' he replied, 'that what is written down is actually what was said.'

'Cheeky sod!' said Holmes as they left the building.

'He had a point, though,' said Caton. 'If you're going to falsify the evidence, best to do it from the outset.'

'Can I quote you on that, boss?' said Holmes cheerfully. 'Here's another one, though. What if our victim had come up with something revolutionary? Something that could make its inventor millions? Like Facebook, or Google, or Microsoft Windows?'

'If he had, that would be billions or trillions,' said Caton.

'And somebody – another student, Stroner even – found out and wanted it for themselves?'

'So Miles-Cowper dropped out to concentrate on developing it in secret.'

'And whoever it was tracked him down, and stole it.'

It was exactly what Kate had suggested.

'So where,' said Caton, 'did victim number one, Lee Bottomley, come in? We haven't found anything to connect them.'

'Doesn't mean they weren't connected. Maybe they tortured Bottomley to get him to tell them where Miles-Cowper was hiding out.'

'It doesn't explain why they mutilated Miles-Cowper's hands, and severed his finger.'

'To get him to hand over the stuff he'd been working on.'

'It would have been on his computer, surely? Why did they smash it up instead of just taking it, or the hard drive?'

'Maybe he kept a copy on a data key, or a flash drive. Maybe he'd hidden it somewhere. In Dropbox or in the Cloud?'

Caton was seriously impressed. Not so much with Gordon's line of reasoning, which had always been evident; it explained why he was a detective inspector. The surprise was his sudden expertise in computer know-how. Gordon saw the look of surprise on his face and grinned. He took his hand from his pocket and held up the USB flash drive they had been handed by Stroner's secretary.

'There's this,' he said. 'And that Sunday Okowu-Bello case. That reporter guy. You thought I wasn't paying attention, didn't you? Anyway, we've got all that at home now. Marilyn's gone computer nerd on me. Does half her shopping and all of our banking online. Scares the hell out of me.'

'It's something to think about,' said Caton. 'Your theory.'

They carried on walking in silence, mulling it over.

'D'you reckon it was a good thing what Turing and those others did?' said Holmes.

'What's that got to do with it?' said Caton.

'Nothing. But you're the one who told us that sometimes it's best to stop concentrating on something. Just let your brain work away at it in the background while you think about something else. That's what you said.'

'Fair enough.'

'So what d'you think; was it a good thing what they did?'

'Like what? Cracking the Enigma Code, and helping to win the war. Inventing the computer?'

'The computer, obviously. Look at all the problems it's caused.'

'Such as?'

'For a start, it's ruined the art of conversation. Nobody talks to anybody any more, they're all too busy texting and tweeting, and whatever else they do on their phones.'

'What they're doing, Gordon, is communicating. If anything, young people have more conversations than we ever did, not less.'

'Yeah, but not face-to-face. And what are they texting about? Where they are, what they're doing right this minute, like brushing their teeth, drinking a coffee, going to the loo.'

'What did you talk about when you were their age? Proust, the meaning of life, or was it just football and Top of the Pops?'

Holmes was undaunted.

'And what about the kids? Stuck in front of one screen or another from before they can walk. No wonder we're becoming a nation of overweight zombies.'

Caton thought he had a point, but he wasn't going to admit it. It didn't do to encourage Gordon when he was on his bandwagon, and there was always the danger that he would claim him as a fellow traveller.

'What about all the advances it's brought about in every aspect of human life, including science and medicine?' he replied. 'Not to mention how it's speeded up criminal investigations.'

'Anyway,' said Holmes as they approached the car, 'looks like someone's decided to put a stop to it.'

Caton stopped in his tracks.

'Is that what you think this is about? A one-man crusade against computer technology?'

Gordon was already climbing into the car with a smug grin on his face. It was clear that he didn't think anything of the sort. He was just winding him up, as usual. But that didn't mean he was wrong. If there was one thing that Caton had learned in this job, it was that life was stranger than fiction.

Chapter 20

Jack Benson stuck his head around the fabric-covered partition.

'Sorry to intrude, boss,' he said, 'but I've got the initial forensics report on the Lee Bottomley crime scene.'

Caton gestured for him to sit down.

'No need to apologise, Jack, I just hope you've got some good news.'

'I wouldn't go that far, but we've got a starter for ten.'

He handed the file over.

'I'll send a digital copy to your tablet as soon as you've read it.'

Caton turned the cover, skipped the contents list and went straight to the findings.

'While I do,' he said, 'give me the headlines.'

'One set of fingerprints, found in various locations, almost certainly belonging to one of the perpetrators.'

'How do you know?' said Caton.

'They were found on the back of his chair, and on fragments of the broken computer. There were even two bloodstained prints, one on the keyboard, the other on the door jamb.'

'You said *one* of the perpetrators?'

'That's because there were also smudged prints that they reckon were made by gloved fingers, so no possibility of identifying them. If you read on you'll find there were four different sets of hairs found, other than the victim's; three on his clothing, and one adhered to the keyboard.'

'Adhered?'

'With blood. One of the hairs on the clothing belonged to his mother, another to the sergeant who responded to the call and a third to her constable.'

Caton nodded. 'Constable Byrne.'

'The remaining hair is unidentified, as is the one on the keyboard. Those two hairs do not match each other.'

'Two people,' said Caton. 'It doesn't mean that either hair belongs to a perpetrator.'

'Be handy if they did, though. Checking their DNA with the database will take another couple of days, as will DNA analysis of the other trace evidence found.'

'Such as?'

'Saliva stains, skin flakes and urine.'

Caton looked up. 'Urine?'

Straight-faced, Benson nodded. 'Looks like someone other than the victim peed in his pants.'

'Or her pants.'

'Or her pants. A small pool, behind and to the right of the victim's chair. I spotted it when I was setting up the walkway.'

'Somebody unaccustomed to violence?'

'Or who wasn't expecting to witness it.'

'It says here there was also a viable footprint,' Caton noted.

'Two footprints. One left foot, the other right. The left one was behind the victim, to the left, pointing forwards. The right one was between the victim's chair and the door to the landing, going out. That one had traces of blood in it. There were others, thanks to the fact Mrs Bottomley doesn't keep her house clean, but not as clear as those two. Mind you, given it was only a two-dimensional impression, we had to use an electrostatic lifter.'

Caton understood the process. A voltage passed across a thin conductive film caused the particles that made up the impression to jump onto the black base, reproducing it exactly.

'Both belonged to the same person,' said Caton, reading out loud. 'Size seven trainers, popular make, heels disproportionately worn on the right outside heel edge, and the medial forefoot indicating significant over-pronation. Estimated weight of wearer, between fifty and fifty-eight kilograms.' He looked up. 'How can they be that precise?'

'You'd be surprised how much the technology has come on. Retrieval performance analysis, enhanced by three-dimensional imagining, checked against a growing database...'

Caton held up one hand. He didn't need to know how to do it, only that it was reliable. That it would hold up in court. He had reached the end of the findings. All that remained was a statement of the additional tests available, subject to approval of funding, and those that were pending. And a series of technical and scientific references.

He closed the file and placed it on his desk.

'So,' he said, 'initial indications are that we're looking for two perpetrators. One who was either very careless or who came not intending to kill, and someone else who took the trouble to wear gloves, but was scared enough to wet himself.'

'Or herself,' Benson reminded him. 'We'll know which it is by the end of the day. It's a simple test using Radioimmunoassay to test for the presence of hormones. I wish I could get you the DNA analyses as quickly, but you did want a full analysis, and I did warn you that would take longer.'

Caton knew what Benson was driving at. The cost seemed to rise exponentially with each new level of testing. He'd already been warned by Helen Gates, his Chief Superintendent, about the cost of over-analysis, but he wasn't going to risk waiting to see what might or might not be needed, and then discover months down the line that the original samples had been lost, mislaid, corrupted or the chain of evidence broken.

'Where are we up to with the forensic computer analysis report?' he said.

Benson shrugged. 'I have to be honest, boss. You saw what was left of his gear; it was a right mess. I spoke with Jenny Soames over at the High Tech Crime Unit half an hour ago, and she's not holding out much hope. Mind you, if anyone can find a needle in that particular haystack she can. It's been complicated by what's left of the computer from the second crime scene.'

'How so?'

'Because they've had to set up two separate audit trails for both sets of computer-based electronic evidence from each crime scene. That's two different chain of evidence trails for the physical evidence, and two separate audit trails for the electronic data, assuming they can retrieve any. That really slows it down, but anything less and if they do come up with anything we can use, the defence team will challenge it, and the way the courts are these days it'll be thrown out.'

Caton understood. There was the recent case of the serial perpetrator who led the senior investigator to the grave of his second victim, only to have his confession discounted on the basis that he had not been cautioned with regard to the second offence, and their conversation took place out in the open, not in an interview room. Net result, he was found guilty of the first murder, but not of the second. No closure for the victim's parents, and censure for the detective for ignoring Code C of the Police and Criminal Evidence Code of Practice. Caton had always regarded himself as a right-thinking liberal and champion of human rights. His fellow officers regarded him as a stickler when it came to both PACE and political correctness. With murderers having their confessions discounted, and the Home Secretary having to fight for over a decade to have terrorists extradited, even he was beginning to think that things had gone too far.

'Tell them I need to know what was on those computers,' he said. 'I don't care what it costs.'

Benson rose to join him.

'I've already told her,' he said.

'What did she say?'

'She pointed to a sign on her wall. It says: *Miracles we do at once. The impossible takes a little longer.*'

'I'll settle for that,' he said.

Inquiries continued into the background of both victims. Fellow students of Spencer Miles-Cowper were interviewed by members of the team. The files containing everything he had saved on the faculty computers was still being pored over by people who could make sense of it. Nothing useful had emerged. It was early in the evening that the first crumb of comfort came Caton's way.

'You'll need to come over to my monitor, boss,' DS Carter told him. 'It could be nothing, but I'd like your opinion.'

Caton pulled a chair up alongside Carter and stared at the screen.

'This guy here,' said Carter, pointing at the figure in a navy hoodie top over blue jeans.

He had entered through the glass doors of the

building in which Miles-Cowper had been found, and was crossing the foyer. The hood was up, the face hidden. His gait was all they had to go on, but that alone supported Carter's contention. It was almost certainly a male. Caton had been in those lifts. There had been at least nine inches clearance for his own head. Allowing for the way this person was hunched, possibly to further conceal his face, maybe even trying to disguise his height, it meant that he was between five foot six and five foot nine.

'What time is this?' said Caton.

Carter pointed to the digital counter at the bottom of the screen. It was eight fifty-nine a.m. and counting. The lift doors slid open.

'Can you freeze it there?' said Caton. 'Now, can you zoom in on his shoes?'

'They're not trainers, if that was what you were wondering,' said Carter. 'They're black leather, like you'd wear to the office, and from the thickness of the soles I'm willing to bet they're flat and smooth.'

Caton knew what he was thinking. If this was one of the perpetrators, it would explain why only one set of retrievable footprints had been found.

Carter zoomed out and pressed play. The doors began to close.

'Watch this,' he said.

The lift descended. In the box above the doors, the letters LG appeared.

'Lower Ground floor,' said Carter.

'Where the fire exit is located.'

'Exactly.'

Fifty seconds passed, and then the lift began to move again. Upwards. It stopped on the sixteenth floor.

'Two floors above the victim's apartment,' said Carter.

Caton nodded. 'They could have been checking out the roof, or trying to muddy the waters for anyone checking the CCTV.'

Carter pressed fast forward, and then play.

'This is the lift coming down again, six minutes later.'

Caton watched the doors open. Out stepped a woman, mid-thirties, shoulder-length hair, dressed for the office. She had a handbag in her left hand and a designer satchel slung from her left shoulder. She glanced at her watch, and scurried across the foyer and out through the door.

'Late for work,' Carter observed.

He pressed pause and sat back in his chair, waiting for the boss's reaction.

'When did the hoodie come back down?' said Caton.

'He didn't. Or to be precise, I can't tell you.'

'Precise is good,' said Caton pointedly. 'Why can't you tell?'

'Because he never emerged from either lift. So, assuming he's not still in the building, he must have either used the stairs – the stairwell is round the corner, so it's not visible from either camera position – or he carried on all the way down to the Lower Ground and let himself out through the fire exit, together with whoever it was we're assuming he let in.'

'And the fire exit doors are self-closing, so we've no way of knowing if that's what happened.'

'Nope.'

'Right,' said Caton. 'We'll need a still photo of our friend with the hood. I'll have it shown to everyone in those apartments who has already been interviewed, and posters put in all of the other buildings in the Green Quarter. Someone must have passed him, seen where he came from.'

'I can tell you that,' said Carter, swivelling back to face the monitor and gripping the mouse.

Caton was about ask why the hell he hadn't told him straight away when a new sequence started to play. It was the same figure, hooded, head bowed, hands thrust in the pockets of jeans. His pace was inconsistent. The first thirty metres or so were covered with shuffling steps, as though he was reluctant to reach his destination. He paused, took his left hand out of his pocket, appeared to stare at his wrist and then thrust his hand back into his pocket. Now he was moving faster, with the swaggering gait that so many young men seemed to adopt when trying to impress. He reached a junction between the main street he was on and a tarmac path between two apartment buildings. He paused again, drew his shoulders back as though stiffening his resolve and turned left onto the path. To Caton's annoyance, the sequence stopped.

'Hang on, boss,' said Carter. 'I need to select a different tape.'

There was no sign of a tape or a tape recorder. Either it was an anachronistic term wrongly applied, or the tape footage had been transferred to a disk or some other digital equivalent. Caton didn't care, so long as the chain of evidence was secure.

'Here we go.'

Carter pressed play.

This time the suspect was captured from the rear as he hurried down the path and up the steps into the foyer of the victim's apartment block.

'Timings fit. It's definitely him,' said Carter. 'He comes up Lord Street from Red Bank, turns left down Hornbeam Way and then left into the apartments. I'll show you.'

He pulled up Google Earth, showed Caton the aerial satellite view and then switched to street view.

He traced the route the suspect had taken in 3D and colour all the way to the foyer.

'This where the first CCTV was,' he said, indicating a globe surveillance camera on the side of a factory building halfway up Lord Street. 'This is the second directional camera on the post at the top of Hornbeam Way, and the others are on each subsequent post. By a process of deduction he must have used the tunnel under the disused railway line at Red Bank to cross into Lord Street. Probably left the same way. Came out the back of the building with his accomplice. Hugged the pavement to stay out of range of the cameras trained on the gates of the units under the railway arches, then into Roger Street, and then away into one of the industrial estates. Jumped in a car, and off and away. There are no cameras down there, so long as you steer clear of the better-protected warehouses. I checked. Nothing till you get to Rochdale Road. We could try all of the traffic cameras on the main routes for that period, but it'll be a needle in a haystack job. And we don't even know if he used a car.'

'Do it,' said Caton. 'Just do it.'

Chapter 21

'I don't know how you do it.'

Caton licked his fingers clean, savouring the final vestiges of virgin olive, black balsamic and vermillion chorizo oil.

'It's easy,' Kate told him as she carried their plates to the dishwasher. 'Cook the onion and garlic in olive oil for a couple of minutes, add the chorizo, cook for another five. Add the butter beans, tomatoes and paprika. Reduce the heat, cover and cook.'

'How long for?' he said.

'Twenty minutes. Then remove the lid, thicken with a bit of flour or cornflour if you want to, then serve with crusty bread and a nice Rioja. If your partner has a dodgy palate he's likely to want some salt, pepper and balsamic vinegar on the table. Take it from me, it doesn't need it.'

He took a sip of his wine and rolled it around his tongue, savouring the fresh, peppery berry taste, with a hint of vanilla.

'Thirty minutes from start to finish. Like I said, I don't know how you do it.'

'I just told you,' she said. 'Next time it's your turn.'

Caton would be happy to oblige. He enjoyed cooking, even more so now that he had someone else to cook for, and to share it with.

'That wasn't what I meant,' he said. 'I meant

juggling work and cooking, doing our laundry, keeping this place clean and doing the lion's share of organising the wedding.'

She brought two bowls of apple pie and crème fraiche to the table and plonked his in front of him.

'Good of you to notice,' she said. 'It was something I was going to mention after the honeymoon, but since you've brought it up.'

He picked up his spoon, sliced into the crisp golden double crust and the soft juicy flesh of the apple beneath, and topped it with a little of the crème fraiche.

'I'm sure it can wait,' he said.

Two hours later they had agreed when he was going to pick up the dress suits for the ushers and the best man from the Trafford Centre, and he had promised to pack his case for the honeymoon when he got home from work the following day. Then they watched two episodes of *State of the Nation* back to back, and went to bed. Fifteen minutes of Elmore Leonard's *Djibouti* on his Kindle, and Hilary Mantel's *Bring Up The Bodies* on hers, and they switched off the lights.

An hour into a blissfully deep sleep, plagued by neither his recurrent nightmare nor thoughts of Operation Janus, he was woken by the phone. It was Gordon Holmes.

'Sorry, boss,' he said. 'It's official. We have a serial killer on our hands.'

Hoping not to disturb Kate, Caton carefully turned back the duvet, slid his legs out of bed and went to sit on the dressing table stool.

'Where?' he said.

Gordon gave him an address in Hulme.

'It's a shared student house. Jack Benson's organising another team of SOCOs to attend. Doesn't want to leave us open to accusations of cross-contamination. I'm already here.'

'I hope you're using a new Tyvek suit and overshoes then,' said Caton, rubbing the sleep from his eyes.

'You say that every time,' Gordon complained.

'I wonder why. Can you get a car to pick me up? I had a couple of drinks during dinner.'

His clothes were laid out ready in the spare bedroom. It was a procedure he always followed during fast-moving investigations. He placed the phone on the dressing table and crossed to the door, which by design was left slightly open. As he opened it wider, he heard Kate turn over.

'See you when I see you,' she mumbled. 'Call me.'

This, he reflected, was happening too often. Far too often than was good for either of them or their relationship.

Caton parked his car, suited up and then paused for a moment to take in the surroundings. This habit of his was about more than just visualisation, the storing of mental photographs and maps. It was also about the creation of narratives. What might have happened here. And especially about sensing the scene as it must have felt and seemed, and even smelt to the victim, and to the perpetrator.

He'd tried explaining it once to Gordon Holmes. In the end he found the best way to describe it was to get him to listen to the lyrics of *Walking In My Shoes* by Dépêche Mode. Not that the things he did were going to come close to telling him about what the perpetrator had put the victim through, or the reason why, or why it had happened in this place, and at this time. But it helped, in ways he was unable to put into words.

This was the last in a row of 1980s terraced houses on the northern edge of Hulme, in the shadow of two towering blocks of flats. As a boy, Caton had watched them building these houses, designed to replace and replicate the Victorian terraces that had stood here. To try to retain the sense of community that the older residents had valued so much. Opinions were fiercely divided on how far this social experiment had succeeded.

The house was in fact two that had been merged to provide a better rental opportunity for gregarious students. Dark stained fences, hip high, surrounded neatly tended gardens. Slender street lamps directed pools of muted sodium light onto the pavement, spilling into the road and over parked cars. The stairwells on the twelve-storey-high St Thomas' tower were lit up like parallel airport runway lights. Closer still, St George's flats were in total darkness. Several streets away, the forlorn howl of a dog made its presence felt above the gentle hum of the traffic on the *This Is Manchester* roundabout, where Chester Road met the Mancunian Way. An orange glow above the horizon, just visible between the flats, the only clue that the city centre was just half a mile away. There was a distinctive reek of damp leaves, and the faint sulphurous smell of diesel fumes.

Until this year, Caton's entire life had been played out within one and a half square miles of this place. Standing here, watching the ghost-like shapes of SOCO walking up the path with their equipment, their breath clouding the chill night air, he realised that it no longer felt like home. A wave of sadness welled up, and just as quickly ebbed away. He shivered, pulled up the hood of his Tyvek suit and headed for the door.

The body lay face down on the floor between an overturned office chair and the bed.

The room was crowded. A Scenes of Crime Officer was placing 'FINGERPRINTS. DO NOT TOUCH' labels on the desk and the shattered computer equipment. The photographer was removing her last few tent-like photo evidence markers. There was barely room for him to see.

'Can you give us minute?' he said.

He stepped aside as the two SOCOs left the room and waited on the landing.

Caton could now see the familiar concave mess of matted hair on the back of his head, the mangled fingers, the missing digit and the pooling blood.

'His name is Imran Qureshi,' said Holmes. 'He's a second-year student, *was* a second-year student, studying medicine at Man U.'

Caton had followed a succession of fluorescent yellow first-responder markers from the hallway, up the stairs and along the landing.

'He was attacked downstairs?' he said.

'His nose was broken. That's where all the blood downstairs is from. I'm guessing either he opened the door or was followed straight in, was hit in the face and then dragged up here. That's when they smashed his skull in, and did that to his hands.'

The blood looked fresh, and smelt recent. More abattoir than copper pennies.

'When was the body discovered?'

Holmes pushed back his elasticated sleeve.

'An hour ago. Three of his housemates found him. They reckon he was still warm. Paramedic was first on the scene. He concurs. Dead less than hour, he said. I've requested a forensic pathologist. We'll know more then.'

Caton doubted it. The longer the lapsed time between death and examination, the wider the parameters would be for the time of death. He was happy to go with the paramedic's assessment.

He studied the scene. The room was the size of a small double bedroom. A single bed lay along the wall to his left. The bed was made, and there was a rolled prayer mat lying diagonally across it. Beside the bed was a small locker with an alarm clock, a table lamp and a crumpled tissue. On the wall above the bed was a single poster. It depicted what Caton took to be a tree. Two broad brown brushstrokes formed the split trunk, surrounded by two concentric circles of green leaves. The outer leaves were smaller than those forming the inner circle. On the back wall was a slim pinewood wardrobe. The desk had been placed beneath the window. The curtains were closed. An all-in-one computer lay shattered into pieces across the desk, along with its keyboard and printer. Several books and sheaves of papers, some bloodstained, littered the floor. The cover of one of the books was red, embossed with gold lettering. He leant closer. As he suspected, it was a copy of the Qur'an. All of the drawers were open and had been ransacked.

'It's a 21-inch iMac,' said Holmes, sounding far more knowledgeable than either of them knew him to be. 'Wouldn't come cheap, not for a student.'

Caton studied it more closely. His attention was caught by a different-coloured evidence marker adhered to what was left of the silver-coloured rear of the screen. He stepped around the body, careful to stay on the designated path, noting as he did so that at least one more team had adopted Douggie Wallace's little invention. He leaned closer. There was a piece of white adhesive tape just beneath the marker. It had writing on it, in biro. He had to bend and twist his head sideways to read it.

'Happy Mondays,' Holmes informed him. 'It says *happymondays*. All lower case.'

Caton straightened up.

'You could have told me. Saved me the trouble.'

'Must've been a fan,' said Holmes. 'Probably went to see them at the Nynex Arena in May.'

Their fourth reincarnation. Caton was there at the Hacienda in '86. The night they lost The Battle of the Bands on votes but Tony Wilson still named them as the winners. One quirk of fate, and their fortunes had changed forever. Just as tonight had Imran Quereshi's.

'Where are these housemates?' he said.

Chapter 22

They were waiting in the shared kitchen. Two female students sitting together on a pine bench; a young man standing by the sink, staring out of the window into the inky darkness beyond. There were four mugs of coffee on the table. Those in front of the girls were almost empty. The one belonging to the man was untouched. The fourth belonged to a uniformed officer seated opposite the girls, her back towards the door. She looked over her shoulder and jumped up, spilling coffee on the table.

'I'm sorry, sir!'

She looked around for something to wipe it up with.

'It's fine,' he said, taking the mug from her hand and placing it on the table.

One of the girls stood, picked up a cloth from the draining board and proceeded to mop up the spill.

'This is Becky Stamford,' said the policewoman. Then she pointed to the other female student. 'This is Delima Tengu, and that is Adam Davis. There is one more student living here.' She consulted her notebook.

'Jama Gambu,' said Becky Stamford. 'He's staying with a friend in Fallowfield tonight. Won't be back till tomorrow evening.'

'Mr Gambu is South African,' said the WPC, eager to redeem herself. 'He is currently studying aeronautical engineering.' She held up her notebook. 'I have the address, sir.'

The tension in the room was palpable. Caton pulled out the bench on his side of the table.

'Let's all sit down, shall we?'

It was a larger kitchen than he had expected. Much larger than the student kitchens he had inhabited. Two rooms had obviously been knocked into one. The victim's bedroom had been substantial too. Four study bedrooms, two bathrooms, a lounge and this kitchen; that was his guess. Not bad for four students.

Becky Stamford sat down again. Gordon Holmes took out his notebook and leaned against the door jamb. Unsure of what was expected, the WPC hovered beside him.

'And your name is?' said Caton.

'Joyce Wells,' she said. He half expected her to add her rank and number.

'Please, come and join us,' he said. 'You seem to be the only person here who knows everybody.'

She came and sat beside him, leaving more than elbow room between them.

The young man was still staring out of the window, as though there was something there he could not quite believe.

'You too, Adam,' said Caton. 'Come and sit down, please.'

Both girls were ashen. Even the one called Delima, whose skin was naturally dark. Thai, Burmese or Malay, he guessed. But when Adam Davis reluctantly turned and came to sit beside the girls, Caton was shocked. The young man's face was as white as chalk, as though every drop of blood had drained from it. His eyes, sunk into their sockets, stared blankly at the wall opposite. These were some of the hallmarks of shock.

'Are you alright, Adam?' he said.

The young man was slow to respond, but when he did, he nodded his head slowly several times. His eyes continued to stare into space.

'DI Holmes,' said Caton. 'If the paramedic's still around, can you get him to come in here? If not, I'd like him to come back and check these young people over. And I've a few questions for him.'

Gordon Holmes hesitated. He looked pointedly at the WPC. Caton shook his head, and sent him on his way.

'Now' he said, 'I know this has been a great shock for all of you, and the last thing you need right now is to have to answer a load of questions. But you are all intelligent people. You know that the sooner we have answers, the quicker we are going to be able to catch whoever did that to Imran.'

He gave them take-up time. The girls looked at each other, and then slowly nodded in unison.

'Good. We'll get started as soon as I'm sure you're well enough to do this.'

Gordon Holmes arrived on cue. With him was a female paramedic, a similar age to himself.

'This is Jenny Brookes,' said Holmes. 'The first responder had the sense to ask her to make a statement and hang on till you said it was okay for her to go.'

Caton got up and took her into the hallway.

'I'd like you to check them all for shock,' he said. 'But it's the lad I'm really concerned about. I don't want him keeling over on me.'

'I wouldn't blame him if he did,' she said. 'I'm surprised the girls are holding up this well. After all, they were the ones that found his body. I'm not even sure he went upstairs.'

Grim-faced, she headed for the kitchen. Caton

wondered why the lad had taken it so badly. Particularly if he hadn't been in that room. Perhaps Imran had been a good friend. Or more than just a friend.

Three minutes later, she was back.

'They're all fine,' she said. 'Well, that's not strictly true. They're badly shaken, but over the worst of it. Certainly well enough to answer your questions.'

'Including the lad?'

'Him too.' She frowned. 'I know he looks bad, but his pulse and his blood pressure are fine. I think it's more what's going on up here…' She tapped her head. '…than a physical reaction. You see that sometimes. People chewing over "what if?" and "if only" and "it could've been me," in their minds.'

Caton knew exactly what she meant. 'And feeling guilty when they don't need to?'

She smiled bleakly. 'That too. Especially that. Am I alright to go now? This won't be my last call-out tonight.'

'Of course, and thanks.'

'You're welcome.'

He watched her walk down the hallway, through the open doorway and into the chill night air. He had no idea how she did it. It was bad enough what he and Gordon had to contend with. But to start every day knowing with absolute certainty that there would horrendous accidents, tragic deaths and brutal injuries inflicted by one human on another to face. Not merely to observe and report, but the awesome responsibility to treat them, and often to fight to save their lives. It was more than any policeman on a daily basis had to do. He felt an overwhelming sense of respect for her, and her colleagues. It was a perfect antidote for self-pity.

'Ready when you are, boss.'

Gordon stood by the kitchen.

'I'm coming,' he said.

Adam Davis sat alongside Becky Stamford, his legs angled awkwardly away from her. A little colour had returned to his cheeks, and his eyes met Caton's briefly, before looking back down at the tabletop. Caton sat down and considered his options. Gently does it, he decided.

'Let's start with how you came to live together,' he said.

The two girls looked at each other and then at Adam, who was still avoiding them. Becky Stamford took on the role of spokesperson.

'Delima, Imran and me, we all started Med' School together. Delima and me, we hit it off straight away.'

'I'm from Malaysia,' said softly spoken Delima. 'Becky was a great help to me. A new country, a different culture. She showed me the ropes.'

'By the time it came to finding accommodation for our second year,' Becky continued, 'Delima and Adam had started seeing a lot of each other. We agreed to rent a house together. We needed two other students to share the rent for this place. We approached Imran, who jumped at it. Jama was the first person to answer our advert in the Student Union.'

'He's very funny, and gentle,' said Delima.

'Polite, and house-proud,' said Becky.

They looked at each other and smiled.

'We didn't look any further.'

'How did you and Adam meet?' he asked.

She looked tentatively at Adam, giving him the chance to answer. It was clear that he was not going to.

'We met in a bar,' she said. 'I was with some of the med students; Adam was with some of his mates. He asked me if I'd liked to go and listen to a band at the Thirsty Scholar. It went on from there.'

He thought he detected a blush.

'You know how it is,' she said.

Caton did. It was how he met his first wife. Also a medical student here at the university. He hoped their relationship would last a lot longer. Based on her boyfriend's performance so far, he doubted it.

'I need to know where each of you was this evening,' he said. 'Starting with you, Becky.'

'That's easy,' she said. 'Imran, Delima and me, we all had lectures this morning and clinical scenarios this afternoon. Delima and I got back here at about five o'clock. Imran had forgotten something. He arrived back here about ten to six?'

She looked at Delima, who nodded vigorously.

'What about you, Adam?' said Caton.

He lifted his head slowly, and when he did reply, his eyes remained focused on the table.

'I didn't have any lectures till eleven this morning. Then I had some coursework to do. I did some at uni.'

'What are you studying?'

'Sociology and Criminology.'

'The Williamson Building?' said Caton.

Taken by surprise, the student looked up and found himself looking straight into Caton's eyes.

'It's where I did my Criminology,' explained Caton. 'A long time ago.'

There was a flicker of recognition in Adam's eyes, and something else Caton couldn't identify, before the student tore them away and stared instead at the back of his hands.

'Then I came home to do the rest.'

'What time was that?'

'About three o'clock.'

'So you were here when Becky and Delima arrived home?'

He nodded.

'And then what happened?'

'We had something to eat about seven o'clock,' said Becky. 'All except for Imran. He tends to make his own meals.'

'He was the only vegetarian among us,' said Delima.

She was the first, Caton noted, to use the past tense in relation to their deceased housemate.

'It was my turn tonight. I made a prawn curry.'

Becky nodded her head, and placed her hand over Delima's.

'It was really good,' she said.

These banal and seemingly irrelevant exchanges were a sign that the girls at least were beginning to come to terms with what had happened.

'Then we decided to go out for a drink,' said Becky. 'Imran said he'd come too.'

She saw the lift of his eyebrows.

'Not alcohol. He came for the company. And the non-alcoholic cocktails.' She smiled thinly. 'To be honest, I quite like some of those myself.'

'Where did you go?'

'To Alibi, on Oxford Road, near the Circus. They have a good sports bar, and loads of screens. There was a Champions League match on. We were there till ten thirty, then we went down to the Thirsty Scholar.'

It was good choice, Caton reflected. Tucked under the viaduct arches by Oxford Station, it had been a favourite haunt for almost two decades, and was still one of the best free live band venues in the city, with great beers and decent food. A bit pricey for students maybe, but he'd considered it for his stag-do.

'What time did you leave?'

'Imran left first,' she replied. 'About eleven o'clock. He said he had some work to finish. The rest of us, about three quarters of an hour later.'

That sounded about right. Pushing midnight with two miles to walk. It would have taken them about forty minutes, a bit longer if they were chatting. Now for the hard part.

'What happened when you arrived back here?'

Becky gripped Delima's hand. The Malaysian student placed her other hand on top of Becky's and squeezed tightly.

'The door was locked,' said Becky. 'I was first in. The light was on, and I could see bloodstains on the floor in the hall. Delima was in next. We could see them on the stairs too. I called Imran's name, then we both did. When he didn't reply, we both ran up the stairs.'

Her eyes began to fill with tears. Delima's were welling up as well. Becky wiped her eyes with the back of her free hand and gulped a breath.

'His door was open. We could see him lying on the floor. I went to help him … then I saw … his head … the blood … his hands.'

Her voice caught in her throat and she began to sob. Delima put her arm around her shoulder and began to cry.

'What were you doing all this time, Adam?' said Caton.

He lifted his head. There were tears in his eyes too.

'I waited down here,' he said, 'in case he was somewhere else in the house. When the girls screamed, I got my mobile phone out and rang for an ambulance.'

'Not the police?'

He shook his head slowly.

'I didn't know we'd need them till Delima told me what had happened.'

'What *had* happened?'

He looked flustered.

'I don't know, do I? I meant that it didn't look like an accident.'

'What did it look like?'

His head dropped again.

'I don't know. I never saw his body.'

'Do any of you know of anyone who could have done this to your friend?'

They shook their heads almost in unison. Didn't even need to think about it.

'He didn't have any enemies,' said Delima. 'Only friends.'

Caton decided it was as much as they could manage for now. He'd get Joanne Stuart to talk to them again in the morning.

'I'm afraid you won't be able to stay here tonight,' he said. 'Probably for several nights. Do you all have somewhere you can stay?'

'You can both stay at my mum and dad's house,' said Becky. 'I know they won't mind.' She turned to Caton. 'They live in Turton, north of Bolton. It's only forty minutes away.'

'Not in rush hour,' muttered Gordon Holmes.

'That's fine,' said Caton. 'Get together everything you need. Except for your computers and tablets, I'm afraid. I know how important they are to you. We'll let you have those back as soon as possible, I promise. Let WPC Wells know where you'll be staying. And give her your mobile numbers. She'll also contact the University Counselling Service first thing in the morning. Can you do that, Joyce?'

'Of course, sir.'

She looked surprised by his use of her first name, and pleased that he had given her these tasks to do.

'Just one last question,' he said. 'How is it that Imran, a devout Muslim, is sharing this accommodation with two girls?'

'We worked it out,' said Delima. 'Jama is a Muslim too. Not as devout as Imran, though. Imran, Jama and Adam sleep on this side of the house, Delima and I sleep next door. We have separate bathrooms too.'

To Caton's surprise, Adam Davis raised his head and spoke, but so quietly that he had to strain to hear him.

'I don't think Imran was as devout as people thought he was.'

Chapter 23

'Ironic really,' said Holmes.

Caton paused by the passenger door of Gordon's Mondeo, one hand on the roof.

'What is?'

'Happy Mondays.'

Caton knew what was coming, and knew that he couldn't stop it. He opened the door and started to get in.

'Not this week it wasn't,' said Gordon. 'Not for Imran.'

He grunted as he bent to get in the car.

'Are you alright, Gordon?' said Caton as he buckled his seat belt.

'Just a bit of indigestion,' he replied, turning on the ignition.

Caton wasn't convinced. He had been piling weight on recently. It was more than just middle-age spread.

'You should get it checked out.'

'I will,' he said, easing his way around the line of emergency vehicles. 'When I get a minute. When people stop killing each other.'

When they were through the roundabout and on to the Mancunian Way, he glanced across at Caton.

'What do you think then?'

'What about?' said Caton.

'Adam Davis.'

Caton nodded. 'You noticed then?'

'Course I noticed. I'm a detective. It's what I'm paid to do. First off, he let the girls go up the stairs on their own. It was almost like he knew what they'd find. Secondly, he couldn't look anyone in the eyes. Not even his supposed girlfriend. Thirdly, when you asked him what the hell he meant about the victim not being as devout as people thought he was, he was unable to elaborate.' He snorted. 'Unwilling, more like.'

'What are you saying?'

'What you're thinking. That he's hiding something.'

'You're not just a detective then,' said Caton. 'You're a mind-reader too.'

He opened the glovebox and found half a roll of strong mints where he knew they would be, among the crumpled greasy burger wrappers.

'No wonder you're getting fat,' he said.

Gordon grunted. 'What happened to political correctness all of a sudden?'

'I wasn't being abusive; it was an expression of concern from a friend.' He held up the mints. 'D'you want one?'

Gordon shook his head. 'No thanks, I'm cutting down.'

Caton took a mint, popped it in his mouth and put the roll back in the glovebox.

'There was something else,' he said. 'Adam Davis spends a lot of time in the Williamson Building.'

'So?'

'It's next door but one to the Kilburn Building.'

'Where victim number two hung out?'

'Exactly. They could easily have bumped into each other.'

'But didn't Miles-Cowper drop out before Qureshi started?'

'True, but students have been known to revisit their alma mater, use the library. Especially if the university hadn't cancelled his student cards.'

'He said he didn't recognise the photos of either victim you showed him on your tablet; none of them did.'

'I know. And what was it Stroner said? There are over thirty-nine thousand students at the university.'

'It's a coincidence, though. We don't like coincidences.'

He slowed down on Pin Mill Brow and pulled over to allow an ambulance to speed past.

'We're going to need a profiler,' he said.

'I know.'

There were two good reasons they couldn't use Kate. Even if it had been possible, there were only four days to the wedding; she'd have gone ballistic. Aside from that, there was a conflict of interest; the two of them were in a relationship, cohabiting. Any defence team would have a field day.

'I'll see if Professor Stewart-Baker is available,' he said. 'Failing that, we'll have to take whoever the Home Office put forward.'

Forensic profiling had had its ups and downs in recent years. He knew how important it was to find one you could work with. More importantly, one the Crown Prosecution Service trusted.

'I feel sorry for the plod,' said Gordon, speeding up again.

'Why?' said Caton. 'And you know I don't like you calling them that. They get enough of that from the general public.'

'Having to tramp up and down those tower blocks taking statements. My idea of a nightmare.'

'What happened to Lee Bottomley, Miles Spencer-Cowper and Imran Qureshi,' Caton replied. 'That's my idea of a nightmare. Their parents too.'

'Imran's parents are going to want a quick funeral,' said Holmes. 'With him being a Muslim. That's going to prove tricky.'

'That's the least of our worries.'

'How long do you think it'll take them to fly over here?' said Holmes as he drew up at the barrier to the Divisional Headquarters car park.

'Not long,' said Caton coolly. 'They live in Blackburn.'

In the event, it proved much less difficult than either of them had imagined. The victim's father, Muhammad, and his mother, Fatima, were accompanied to the mortuary by Imran's uncle, a doctor in general practice, and their local Imam, both of whom were well acquainted with the protocols surrounding sudden and violent deaths.

'The Coroner will require a post mortem,' the uncle explained. 'Your consent is not required. If you wish, I can represent you at the examination; they cannot refuse.'

'Yes! Yes!' said Muhammad. 'You must be there. You can see that Imran's body is respected. That it is bathed.'

It was plain that he had no concept of what the post mortem would involve. Given the parents' all too evident grief, none of them felt inclined to explain.

'Then there will an inquest,' the uncle continued.

'When? When will it be?' Muhammad demanded. 'When can we bury our son?'

Knowing the answer, but unwilling to impart it, the brother-in-law looked to Caton to provide it.

'The inquest will open shortly after the post

mortem,' he said. 'By the end of this week. However, under the circumstances it is likely to be adjourned until our investigation is completed. I'm sorry, but I am afraid you will have to be patient.'

The wife clung to her husband. Turning to his brother-in-law, Muhammad began to shout in Punjabi. The Imam placed a hand on his arm and spoke to him calmly in Arabic. The doctor saw Caton's quizzical look and translated for his benefit.

'For those who patiently persevere, there is the attainment of the final home. Gardens of perpetual bliss, they shall enter there, as well as the righteous among their forefathers, their spouses and their offspring. It is from the Qur'an.'

Fine words, Caton reflected. He hoped that they came true. There would precious little bliss on this Earth for Muhammad and Fatima. Not now.

Chapter 24

'You have to do this press conference, Tom,' Detective Chief Superintendent Gates told him. 'No ifs or buts. I'm not covering your back on this one, not on my own. The press are tired of hearing my voice, and Derek's certainly not going to do it.'

Caton wasn't in the least surprised. Derek Hadfield had been trying to keep a low profile ever since he'd made the mistake of cosying up to the now disgraced former Commissioner for Police and Crime. And, confounding everyone else's expectation, Gordon Holmes had made a good fist of the last conference. That had involved two deaths, and an appeal for witnesses. This one would be another matter entirely.

'I understand, Helen,' he said. 'I half expected it. On a related matter, I need to bring in a Home Office approved forensic profiler.'

'You can't use Kate,' she said, sounding as though she feared he might.

'Of course not. I'm going for Stewart-Baker, if he's available.'

'Fine. But he's going to need more to go on than you've got so far, so you'd better get a move on.'

'I'm on my way,' he said.

'I'm not talking about the press conference!' she called after him. 'I'm talking about Operation Janus!'

He waved a hand in acknowledgment as he

disappeared into the corridor where the lifts were situated.

'Detective Chief Inspector, can you confirm that this recent death is connected to those of Lee Bottomley and Spencer Miles-Cowper?'

The press room was packed. There were video cameras everywhere; it was one of the disadvantages of having Media City on the doorstep.

'There are some similarities between them.'

'Such as?' pressed the BBC reporter.

'They are all young men, of a similar age.'

'Is this a gay hate crime?' shouted someone from one of the tabloids.

'There is nothing whatsoever to indicate that,' he said firmly, eager to knock it on the head. 'To the best of our knowledge, none of the victims was gay.'

'Were they all killed in the same way?' asked the woman from Granada News.

'There are some similarities.'

'Like the mutilations?'

Many of those present turned to see where it had come from. It was Larry Hymer from the MEN, the region's largest newspaper. It was pointless Caton wondering where he'd got the information from; the permutations were endless.

'I am unable to comment on details in an ongoing investigation,' he said.

'Unable, or unwilling?'

'Unable,' said Helen Gates, leaning in towards the microphone. 'Next question?'

'Three deaths in five days,' said Hymer. 'Are you treating these as serial killings?'

'I don't think trying to label this investigation in that way is helpful,' said Caton more calmly than he felt.

'Will you be calling on the services of a forensic profiler?' the reporter persisted.

Helen Gates placed her hand over the mike and whispered in Caton's ear.

'I am unable to comment,' said Caton.

'Seems to me there's precious little you *can* comment on!' shouted the red-top reporter.

The laughter it provoked spurred Caton into action. He placed both hands on the table and raised his voice.

'I know,' he said, 'that you and your organisations will be as eager as we are to bring this investigation to a speedy conclusion, for the sake of the grieving families of these three young men, and for the safety of the public as a whole. The best way you can assist in that is to publish our appeal to members of the public to come forward with any information, however small, that might help us to apprehend the perpetrators. You have each been given a copy of that appeal, and the information we are seeking. We will leave you with the telephone numbers which people can call in complete confidence. Thank you for coming; thank you for your cooperation.'

He stood and turned to go, leaving a surprised Helen Gates and the Force Press Officer to scramble to their feet and follow him. On the screen behind them, in six-inch-high fonts, appeared the CrimeStoppers details.

'Carry on like this and you'll be in line for Assistant Chief Constable,' Helen Gates told him.

'Over my dead body,' he replied.

'That can be arranged,' she said. 'If you don't get this sorted fast.'

There was an excited buzz in the Incident Room. He felt it the minute he walked through the door. Gordon

Holmes, Douggie Wallace, Joanne Stuart and Nick Carter stood in front of the whiteboards. DC Hulme was standing behind them, listening in.

'What's going on?' said Caton, joining them.

Gordon turned, his face lit up by a wide grin.

'Jenny Soames, over at the High Tech Crime Unit, came up trumps, boss. I said she would.'

'How did she manage it?'

'They hadn't damaged Bottomley's hard drive as much as they, or she, thought. They should have taken it with them.'

'What was on it?'

'Have you ever heard of trolls, boss?' asked Nick Carter.

'Cave dwellers, the supernatural beings in Norse mythology who also pop up in *The Lord of the Rings*, or those equally mischievous individuals on the Internet?'

'The latter,' said Gordon Holmes. 'That's what victim number one was doing on his computer.'

'Lee Bottomley was an Internet troll?'

'Obsessively. On social media, Twitter and other people's blogs.'

'And worse,' said Joanne Stuart, 'he was also into kiddie porn.'

'Child pornography?'

The implications raced around his brain faster than the speed of sound.

'We've alerted CEOPS. They're going to liaise with Jenny Soames, and with you, boss,' said Douggie Wallace.

Caton stared the photograph of Lee Bottomley. The carer on whom his mother had depended. Her perfect boy. If Caton had learned one thing in this job it was that you never really knew anyone. They all had their secrets, himself included.

'It gives us motive,' he said. 'If the others were engaged in either of those activities it would provide the connection between them too.'

'It would explain why nobody had ever seen them together,' said DC Hulme. 'They wouldn't need to meet up. They'd probably prefer not to. You can be anonymous online. That's the whole point of it.'

Ten minutes earlier Caton had been feeling depressed. Now he was on a high. It was something he loved about being part of Major Incidents. The surprises, the flashes of inspiration, the roller-coaster ride. But his instinct, nurtured by experience, was to remain cautious.

'It's a start,' he said. 'We need to know more about his email contacts, and the websites he frequented. We need to know if any of them were visited by either of the other victims. And we need to know who he might have rubbed up the wrong way. So badly that they wanted to kill him.'

'Do you want us to keep digging into the backgrounds of the other victims, boss?' said Gordon Holmes.

It was, Caton realised, more a gentle reminder than a question.

'Absolutely. In the meantime I'm going to chase up that profiler.'

The group quickly dispersed, returning to their desks with renewed enthusiasm. Caton remained staring at the faces of the three victims. Trolling, and child pornography. He thought he could detect the potential for that in two of the faces staring back at him. Imran Qureshi he was less sure about.

Chapter 25

'It is a credible theory.'

Professor Stewart-Baker leaned back in his reclining task chair, steepled his fingers and stared at his favourite spot on the ceiling.

It was a little over two years since Caton had sat in this room during the hunt for the Bluebell Hollow killer. The black that had been predominant in the mass of tight wiry curls on the forensic profiler's head had been all but replaced by grey. The creases on his high forehead and broad temples had deepened, as had the smile lines around his mouth. The patterned cardigan had been replaced by a grey-twist crew neck jumper with brown shoulder and elbow patches. He wore military chinos the colour of caramel, over tan wedge brogues. Caton smiled to himself. The professor was still bang on trend. Catching sight of it from the corner of his eye, and misreading it completely, Stewart-Baker sat up and swivelled in his chair.

'You don't agree, Tom?'

'No, I mean yes,' said Caton. 'I was miles away. Of course I agree.'

'Well, try to keep up. My time is precious, as I am sure is yours.'

He leaned back again, interlocked his fingers and placed them behind his head.

'Do you know where the word troll comes from?' he said.

Caton had been on the Web and believed he did, but thought it better not to admit the fact.

'I'm not absolutely certain,' he said.

Stewart-Baker smiled knowingly. 'Good answer,' he said. 'We have the old Norse word used to describe mythological creatures hell-bent on mischievousness; the Middle German, English and French use of the word to denote rolling about, or wandering; and the Old French verb *troller*, which is generally held to be a hunting term. All of these of course could apply to the modern Internet troll, but perhaps the most apposite is the modern English use of the verb *to troll*, which describes a method of fishing that involves slowly towing a baited hook, or lure, behind a fishing vessel.'

He swivelled his chair and looked directly at Caton.

'You see the connection?'

'Of course,' said Caton. 'As I understand it, the modern-day troll trawls the Internet seeking victims to bait with contradictory or unsavoury comments on their social network pages and blogs. The more vulnerable and sensitive the victim, the better. When a victim takes the bait by responding, the troll becomes increasingly abusive, causing more and more anxiety and stress. When the troll becomes bored, or the victim gives in, he or she wanders off in search of another victim.'

'Precisely,' said the professor. 'Like all bullying, it's about power. Many victims of cyber bullying experience anger, rage and, ultimately, powerlessness. The troll, on the other hand, gets off on this. His own sense of power is fed by the increasing desperation of the victim. The best advice to anyone pursued by a troll, or trolls – like sharks, they frequently hunt in packs – is to ignore them. Of course, that's easier said than done.'

'And you think it's possible that a victim could become so enraged that they might kill the troll?'

Stewart-Baker sat up and folded his arms.

'Bearing in mind what I said about victims experiencing powerlessness, I would have thought that extremely unlikely. They would also need to have the means to track down whoever it was that was trolling them.'

'Unlikely, but not impossible.'

'As I said, it's a credible theory. It would, however, have taken something extreme to trigger such a reaction, and the victim of the trolling would have to already possess the capacity to react in that way.'

He picked up the photographs of the victims that Caton had brought with him and studied them.

'And to follow it through with such ferocity and ruthlessness…'

'It would take someone with a serious personality disorder,' said Caton. 'A sociopath, a psychopath?'

'Precisely.'

'That doesn't sound like the kind of person who would take the bait in the first place, let alone allow himself to become a victim,' said Caton.

Stewart-Baker shuffled the photographs together and handed them back.

'That's why I don't think your killer is a victim of the trolls,' he said. 'I think you may well be looking for someone acting on their behalf.'

'On their behalf?'

He nodded. 'Most probably, without their knowledge.'

Caton sat looking at the uppermost photograph. The one of Lee Bottomley.

'We believe there is more than one perpetrator,' he said.

'It's not unknown for psychopaths to work in tandem. And there will have been many victims of the trolls. In the same way that trolls form partnerships, why not those who set out to hunt them down?'

'Like small sharks being stalked by larger ones?'

'A good analogy.'

'Is there anything you can tell me about the perpetrators?' said Caton.

Stewart-Baker folded his arms again and stared at the ceiling.

'About their antecedent behaviours? I don't think so. This is neither your archetypal mass murderer nor you typical serial killer. Not that there is such a thing, but you know what I mean. As to the typology of your three victims, and the perpetrators' chosen method…'

He held out his hand for the photographs, looked at them briefly and then handed them back.

'This bears all of the hallmarks of revenge killing. Particularly now that you have reason to believe the victims' computers, and by extension their fingers, were the architects of their own demise.'

'Forensic evidence suggests that one of the perpetrators is a woman,' said Caton.

Stewart-Baker thought about that for a moment. Then he sat up and looked directly at Caton.

'You know the most commonly accepted typology for serial killers who are male?'

Caton nodded. He had studied the work of Kelleher and Kelleher some years ago, and had occasion to revisit it during the Bojangles and Bluebell Hollow investigations. The *Visionaries* claimed to be driven by divine or psychic messages, or an alter ego. *Missionaries*, like Bojangles, believed that they had a duty to cleanse society. Although in his case there had also been an element of revenge. *Hedonists*, the most common male serial killer, were driven by the pleasure, often sexual, that the hunt, the capture and the killing gave them. The remaining type, the *Power Seekers*, killed for excitement, and above all for the sense of power over the victim that they gained. The more extreme the violence they exercised, the greater their sense of power.

'Of course you do,' said the profiler. 'When it comes to female serial killers, however, it is rather more complicated.'

He stood up and walked across to a bookcase beside the door. He reached down to the second from bottom bookshelf and selected a hardback book. He took it back to his seat and held the cover up for Caton to see. The background was blood-red. On it was superimposed the shadowy figure of a woman clothed in black. The title was unambiguous: *Murder Most Rare. The Female Serial Killer. By Michael D Kelleher and C L Kelleher.*

'Same people,' said the profiler. 'It may appear sensationalist, something from the tabloids, but it's based on good, solid academic research.'

He started to flick through the pages, talking as he did so.

'When it comes to women, even though violence and killing by the fairer sex is definitely increasing, there's a lot less to go on. Two reasons: there are less of them, about two thirds less, and they tend not to get caught.'

'Why is that?' said Caton. 'Their not getting caught?'

'Because, unlike the men, they tend not to draw attention to themselves. They are also less likely to have a criminal record. And their modus operandi tends to be less dramatic, less evident.'

'Such as?'

'Drug overdose, poison, smothering with a pillow. The victim is usually known to them, and often a member of their family or close circle of friends.'

'In those cases, aren't they often referred to as Black Widows?'

Stewart-Baker peered over the top of the book.

'So you've read this?'

'No. But I've heard the expression used in that context.'

'Hmm,' said the professor, burying his head back in the book. 'Money tends to be a much more common motivation for these women. The remainder are more or less evenly spread among similar motivations to their male counterparts: control, thrill sex, enjoyment, feelings of inadequacy.'

'And Munchausen Syndrome by proxy?' said Caton.

The profiler lowered the book and looked thoughtful.

'I'm not sure that should be included in this typology,' he said. 'Not as a blanket category. The Kellehers include those mothers and other carers who knowingly cause the death of those in their care in their *Angel's of Mercy* typology, but only where they have killed multiple victims, and had the intent to do so.'

He returned to the book.

'This brings us to the most relevant group for your current investigation. Those who kill for revenge; appropriately named, *Revenge Killers*.' He chuckled at his own pedantry. 'Quite common among female killers, although less so among serial killers. According to this tome, there is something about the psychology of revenge that does not lend itself easily to repetition. I agree. Revenge killing is often explosive, cathartic and leaves the killer remorseful. With women it tends to be a crime of passion.' He smiled. 'Think *Fatal Attraction*. Serial revenge killing, especially as in your case where there is little or no cooling-off period between the murders, indicates a deeper, sinister, obsessive motivation that I believe must feed on the killings themselves.'

Caton looked at his notes.

'How common would it be for such killers to work in teams?' he said.

'Very common, especially in the case of a woman. It is estimated that at least a third of all female serial killers have worked in teams. Most often as part of a male–female partnership, but also in family teams, and all-female teams.'

He held up the book.

'According to the authors, so long as a perpetrator takes part in the enterprise that results in a murder, she should be classified as a team killer even if she does not carry out the killing itself.'

'The law would agree with that,' said Caton. He checked his notes again. 'Two final questions. Number one, what kind of people are we looking for?'

Professor Lawrence Stewart-Baker closed the book and placed it on his desk.

'I don't need to go over all of the characteristics commonly attributed to serial killers with you, Tom,' he said. 'We've been there before. What I would say is that in this case, you may be looking for both of the classifications identified by Holmes and Holmes in 2009: a disorganised, asocial offender, and an organised social offender.'

'What makes you say that?'

'The fact that whilst the killings appear to have been meticulously planned – in terms of tracking down the victims, arriving and departing unseen, displaying the bodies in a particular way, the specific, almost ritual mutilation – from what you tell me, the actual killings themselves show a complete disregard for covering their tracks. The bodies were sure to be found quickly. Fingerprints and footprints were left at the scene.'

'Only one set, as far as we can tell.'

'Precisely my point. One of them – assuming it was two, and not more – taking the trouble to wear gloves, the other not. Your second question is?'

'What ages are they likely to be?'

'As to the age of the female, if she is part of a family team she is likely to be young. Late teens, perhaps. If not, or if both of the perpetrators are female, then in her mid-twenties to thirties. If the partner is a male, he will possibly be older. Think Paul and Karla Bernardo, Fred and Rosemary West, Ian Brady and Myra Hindley. But who knows?'

He ran the fingers of both hands through his hair as though rearranging it. It was a hint of vanity that Caton had never noticed before.

'Interestingly,' he continued, 'teams of either sex are much more likely to use guns and knives than individuals.'

Caton wrote it all down.

The professor looked at his watch, scooted the chair away from his desk, stretched his legs and stood up.

'Are we done?' he said. 'I've got a meeting with the Faculty.'

Caton stood and held out his hand.

'Thank you, Lawrence,' he said. 'You have no idea how helpful that's been.'

'I think I do,' said the profiler, with a twinkle in his eyes. 'And it's Larry. Except in court.'

He started to open the door, and then paused.

'One other thing you should know,' he said. 'The

average number of victims killed by serial teams ranges from nine to fifteen. I'm afraid, Tom, that your perpetrators may have some way to go.'

Another six to twelve victims! Thank God, Caton reflected as he walked to his car, that neither Larry Hymer nor the rest of the media pack had found that out. He zapped the alarm, opened the door and climbed in. It was only a matter of time, though. Half an hour on the Internet, and some bright spark would make the connection. He turned left out of the Manchester Metropolitan University Campus, then third left onto tree-lined Wilmslow Road and headed for Kingsway.

What concerned him more were the lives that were still in jeopardy, and the fact that even with all this knowledge, they were still no closer to finding a single suspect.

Chapter 26

When Ged informed him that Assistant Chief Constable Martin Hadfield, Head of Crime, would be sitting in on the briefing, Caton had thought his day couldn't get any worse. He was wrong.

Having received further confirmation from forensics that at least two people were involved, and provided the team with a succinct summary of Professor Stewart-Baker's opinions, Caton issued a warning.

'I want everyone to be clear about this,' he said. 'We are assuming that all three victims were engaged in trolling on the Internet. We have no evidence to support that. Nor do we have any evidence that any of them other than victim number one – Lee Bottomley – had downloaded child pornography, or that the three of them knew each other. It may be a reasonable assumption that they were engaged in a common enterprise, and it would provide us with a motive, but let's not get carried away. We follow the evidence. So I want you to keep open minds, and treat every scrap of information we receive with the same diligence, whether it fits our assumptions or not. Any questions?'

He scanned the faces in front of him. Every one of them looked serious, and thoughtful. He only hoped he hadn't pricked the bubble of optimism and the sense of energy that had met him when he arrived back from the university.

'Nobody? Good. Let's get to it then.'

Martin Hadfield gestured for Caton to join him in the corridor. He waited until the door had swung to behind them.

'Well done, Tom,' he said in the patronising tone that had become his trademark since he'd moved up a floor. 'I thought you should know that I intend to inform the press that the victims had been trolling.'

He raised his hand, pre-empting Caton's protest.

'I believe that it could help to flush out the perpetrators and, equally importantly, I believe that we have a duty to warn other trolls to be on their guard.'

Caton dug his fingernails into the palms of his hands. He had met some incompetent people in this job, but very few of them had the ability to consistently provoke such feelings of anger and frustration.

'I don't think that's a very good idea, sir,' he began.

Hadfield cut him off. 'You said yourself,' he responded, 'that we should expect more killings. I can't accept that. Our priority is to protect the public first, catch the villains second.'

'I appreciate that, sir,' said Caton, determined not to inflame the situation. 'Have you considered, however, that it might have the reverse effect? That it might actually enrage the perpetrators further, and lead them to step up their operation?'

Hadfield's face reddened. He stuck a finger under his collar in an attempt to loosen it.

'Step up!' he barked. 'Step up? They committed three murders in four days. How much faster do you think they can possibly go?'

Caton could see that logic wasn't going to get him anywhere.

'As Senior Investigating Officer,' he said, 'I want to make it clear that I am unhappy with this proposal.'

Hadfield thrust his face close to Caton's. Given that he was considerably shorter, it was a foolish thing to do. He had to tilt his head upwards and the already constrictive collar tightened, turning his face the colour of beetroot.

'Duly noted,' he croaked. 'And as Assistant Chief Constable, Head of Crime, *I* want to make it clear that I am bloody well going ahead with it!'

He turned smartly on his heels and marched off down the corridor, the sound of his footsteps ringing around the open stairwell and out into the atrium. Caton wondered how many other people had heard this exchange of views.

Much to Caton's dismay, Hadfield lost no time in carrying out his promise. It was Gordon who came to tell him.

'Have you seen this, boss?' he said, rounding the screen surrounding Caton's work space with a printout in his hand. 'Makes a mockery of your little speech.'

Caton read with mounting incredulity. It was a press release from the Communications Branch.

Police have reason to believe that the three young men, whose deaths in separate incidents in Manchester during the past week are being treated as murder, were engaged in the practice of trolling on social network sites. We are therefore appealing to anyone who may have been a victim of this trolling, or who may have information regarding these three men, to contact the police. You can do this by contacting members of your neighbourhood policing team, by calling 101, or by ringing CrimeStoppers on 0800 555 111.

'Made sure his own name wasn't on it,' Holmes pointed out.

Caton didn't need to be reminded. Everyone would assume that it was his doing.

'Lunatic,' he said. 'Not only has he removed any element of surprise we may have had, but this will probably unleash a frenzy of media speculation, not to mention thousands of completely unrelated phone calls from the public ringing up to complain about every snippet of abuse on the Internet. It's a nightmare.'

'It's worse than that,' said Gordon cheerily. 'Were you aware that ACC Hadfield is one of the Force's approved tweeters?'

Caton put the note down and got up out of his chair. He could feel the veins in his neck pulsing.

'Please tell me you're joking.'

Gordon shook his head. 'Sorry, boss.' He pointed to Caton's computer screen. 'You'll find him on there, *@gmpolice*. If you take my advice, you might want to sit down first. I'll be back in a tick.'

Caton knew of the existence of the GMP Twitter feed, but was not a follower, and had never had occasion to visit it. He sat back down and typed the address into his search engine. If anything, on account of its brevity, the tweet was far worse than the press release. The only positive was that, knowingly or otherwise, Hadfield had included his initials.

@_MJH:@gmpolice Murder victims may have been Internet trolls. Police appeal for help in tracking down those whom they targeted.

Not content with compounding all of the mistakes inherent in the paper version, he had now made it look as though any targets of trolling by Bottomley, and potentially by the other murdered young men, were in some way culpable themselves, and by implication potential suspects. There was no way they were going to want to come forward now. They were more likely to do everything they could to avoid discovery. As for the perpetrators themselves, forewarned was forearmed.

Caton cursed, exited and thumped the desk with his fist. It was a futile gesture. Worse still, his hand hurt like hell. A head peered over the top of the screen.

'Are you alright, boss?'

Gordon Holmes had returned; he had Jack Benson with him.

'Tell him, Jack,' he said, grinning. 'Make his day.'

Benson handed Caton a sheet of paper. It was a report from the Forensic Service.

'They found two matches in Qureshi's room,' he said. 'One of them was identical to the set found at both of the previous crime scenes. The second belonged to Adam Davis.'

Caton stopped reading and looked up.

'Adam Davis? What's unusual about that? They both lived in the same house.'

Benson pointed to the report.

'Read on,' he said. 'They were all over the keyboard, the modem and the iMac.'

Understanding dawned and Caton smiled.

'And,' he said, 'Imran Qureshi's password was stuck on the back of his computer for all to see.'

He stood up, took his jacket from the back of the chair and shrugged it on.

'Do we know where he is?'

Gordon's grin widened. 'That's the funny thing,' he said. 'He's waiting downstairs. He asked for you.'

Chapter 27

'I'm sorry,' he muttered.

It looked as though he had just rolled out of bed after a sleepless night. His hair was messed and greasy, the stubble on his face anything but designer, his eyes red-rimmed and bleary.

'What for, Adam?' said Caton.

The student rested his elbows on the table and cradled his face in the palms of his hands.

'I didn't mean this to happen.'

'You'll have to speak up,' said Gordon Holmes. 'For the tape.'

Caton placed a hand on Gordon's arm, warning him to back off. This was not the time for good cop, bad cop.

'What didn't you mean to happen, Adam?' he said.

His head rocked back and forth, his fingers scraping through the stubble like pine on sandpaper.

'Delima saw it on the Web. Why Imran was killed.'

'Because he was trolling?'

There was a long pause before he answered. 'Only he wasn't.'

'He wasn't?'

The rocking stopped. He took a deep breath as though gathering himself, then let it out like a sigh. He looked up and stared straight into Caton's eyes.

'It was me. I was the troll.'

'Whose computer were you using?'

'Imran's.'

'Why?'

'So if there was a problem, it couldn't be tracked back to me.'

Nobody spoke. They were all reflecting on the manner in which that simple, naive decision had come back to haunt him. And Imran.

His eyes began to fill with tears and he lowered his head. There was no doubting Davis' remorse, Caton decided, or the fact that his life would never be the same again.

'How did you get access to his computer?' said Caton at last.

He brushed his eyes with the back of his hand.

'Sometimes he never logged out. When he did, I used his password. It was on the back of his screen.'

'*Happymondays,*' said Gordon Holmes.

He looked up as though surprised that they knew; his expression changed as he realised that he shouldn't have been. He nodded his head slowly.

'How did you avoid Imran knowing that you had been using his computer?' said Caton.

'I created a pseudonym account on all the social network sites, and any other sites I had to sign into. Then, when I'd finished each time, I deleted all the files I'd created or downloaded, and cleared the browser history.'

'And Imran never suspected?'

He shook his head again.

'For the tape please.'

'No, I don't think he ever suspected.'

'What I don't understand,' said Gordon Holmes, 'is how come, if you'd set up this pseudonym, whatever it was you were doing led the killers to Imran?'

Adam Davis jerked backwards as though he had been slapped across the face. He didn't need reminding that his housemate's horrific death had been his fault.

'I don't know,' he said despairingly. 'I don't know.'

Caton gave him a moment to recover his composure, as much as he was going to, and then said, 'When you were trolling, did you engage with any other trolls?'

Davis looked confused.

'Engage?'

'Did you wind up your victims together?' said Holmes, trying to be helpful. 'Did you hunt in a pack?'

Much to Caton's surprise, it seemed to have the desired effect. A glimmer of understanding flickered in the student's eyes. Caton waited, letting him process it.

'It wasn't like that,' he said.

'What wasn't it like?' said Caton.

'It wasn't organised. Not like *he's* implying.'

'Detective Inspector Holmes,' said Caton, 'was not implying anything. He was asking a question. I repeat, what wasn't it like?'

He managed to look chastened. He probably was.

'There were other people doing it, yeah, but it wasn't planned. Not like a conspiracy.'

'These other people, did you ever meet any of them, face-to-face?'

He shook his head.

'For the tape.'

'No, I never met any of them.'

Caton opened the folder on the table in front of him and slid two photographs across the table.

'I'm going to ask you again. Have you seen either of these two men before?'

Davis shook his head.

'Only in the papers, and on the television,' he said. 'And the last time you showed them to me.'

'Don't start getting cocky!' said Holmes.

'I wasn't,' he replied. 'I was just stating a fact.'

'Presumably you trolled more than one person?' said Caton.

He nodded. Then remembered the tape.

'Yes.'

'How many?'

He shifted uneasily in his seat.

'I don't know.'

'A handful? A dozen? A hundred?'

'I hadn't been doing it long. Ten, maybe fifteen.'

'And how many of those were being trolled by the same group of people?'

He thought about it.

'I don't know. A handful, maybe.'

Holmes surprised Caton for a second time.

'Were there any websites where you all met up?' he asked.

Davis looked down at the tabletop as though wondering how to reply. When he looked up, there was resignation in his voice.

'Just the one,' he said.

'You might want to revisit some of your answers,' said Gordon Holmes. 'Sounds like a wolf pack to me.'

They left him making a list of all of the social network sites he had visited, the pseudonyms of any trolls with whom he had attacked people on those sites, and the names of as many victims as he could remember. Then he was going to get access to a computer to show them online. It would be a long night.

'Looks like that press release paid off after all.'

Caton refused to take the bait.

'Using Twitter and the Internet was a masterstroke,' Gordon continued.

Caton still didn't rise to the bait.

'You going to apologise to Mr Hadfield then, boss?' said Holmes.

Caton grimaced. 'In your dreams!'

'We can't charge him with anything, can we?' said Holmes. 'Withholding information maybe, but since he doesn't even know the perpetrators, he can't really be seen as an accessory. Then there's the Data Protection Act, but that wouldn't apply. And he is cooperating.'

'You're forgetting the 1990 Computer Misuse Act,' said Caton. 'He's guilty of gaining unauthorised access to computer material, and with intent to commit further offences. That's two criminal offences for a start.'

Holmes nodded sagely. 'What's that, a fine, or up to twelve months in prison? It's a bloody good job you cautioned him.'

'Then there are the actual offences,' Caton continued. 'It depends on what his trolling consisted of, but we could be looking at using a public communication network to send an offensive, indecent, obscene or menacing message or matter. If recent sentences are anything to go by, he could get anything from community service and a supervision order, up to eighteen months in prison for that. Put the two together…'

'And he'll have plenty of time to study for his degree in Criminology on the inside. Poor sod.'

'Don't feel sorry for him,' said Caton. 'Imran Qureshi is the one who paid the ultimate price for his stupidity. I reckon he'll see two years inside as getting off lightly. I know I would.'

'Why do you think he waived the right to a solicitor? Because he's been studying Criminology, and a bit of law?'

'It's more likely to have been because he was so ashamed of what he'd done.'

'Well, he's getting one now,' said Holmes, 'whether he likes it or not. Just so long as they understand that he's agreed to cooperate. '

Caton nodded. 'And that other people's lives depend on it.'

Chapter 28

'I wonder who came up with this as a name?' said Gordon Holmes, holding up the list that Adam Davis had provided.

He placed it in the middle of the desk so that the three of them could see it.

'*Flammatory.com*,' Douggie Wallace read out loud.

'What's that then?' said Holmes. 'A place where they inflame people?'

Wallace entered the name into the search engine.

'Here we go,' he said. 'Not a bad guess. It stands for *flaming* and *factory*. Flaming is a term for online activity that's intended to get people fired up. It's what trolls do; they use abuse, misdirection and personal insults to hijack a conversation and wind people up.'

He scrolled down the page.

'Basically this is a social network set up by a troll who wanted his website and blog to be private, and visible only to users he invites to join his network. It looks like they use coded messages to direct one another to sites they can mass troll.'

'This is the pseudonym that Davis claims he was using,' said Caton, pointing to the list. 'These other ones are names of people he remembers being part of his regular conversations. Are any of them on there?'

Wallace moved the mouse around the screen at a

bewildering pace. The cursor hovered over the name *adjarlam666*.

'Here you go,' he said. 'This is Adam Davis, if he's telling you the truth.'

Caton and Holmes leaned closer to the screen.

'I can see the *adam* bit,' said Holmes. 'What's the *jarl* got to do with anything?'

'It's a common name for trolls on a number of war-gaming sites,' Wallace replied. 'In Norse mythology he was son of the God Rig. And before you ask, yes, I am a bit of a Warcraft aficionado.'

'That's one word for it,' said Holmes.

'It also stands for Japan Amateur Radio League,' said DC Hulme, who had suddenly appeared at Caton's shoulder. 'And the 666 is…'

'The Number of the Beast!' said Holmes fiercely. 'From the Book of Revelations.'

Caton smiled to himself. Gordon must have remembered it from the blood-red graffiti on the wall in the underground tunnels beneath the Great Northern Warehouse during what he had nicknamed the Secret Santa investigation.

'Believed by many to refer to the Emperor Nero,' continued DC Hulme, as ever oblivious to the wake he was creating. 'Because the transliteration of his name from Greek into the language of the Book of Revelations – Hebrew – gives the value 666.'

Holmes rounded on him.

'And this is helpful how exactly?'

Hulme shrugged. 'Things like that,' he said, 'you never know if they're going to be relevant in advance, do you?'

'And I bet this is Lee Bottomley's handle,' said Douggie Wallace, mercifully directing them back to the screen. '*Ingimárr#Bot*.'

'*Bot*, I got,' said Gordon Holmes, parading his

literary dexterity. 'What's with the *Ingimárr*?'

Wallace worked his magic, then pointed at the screen.

'*Ing* was the Norse God of fertility, and *maar* or *maerr* means famous.'

'Neither of which,' Holmes declared, 'could be said of Lee Bottomley.'

'He is now,' said Caton. 'Famous, that is. What about these other names? Can you find out who they are? They could be the next victims.'

'Sorry, boss,' Wallace replied. 'That's way beyond me. You need to talk to the Cyber Crimes Unit.'

'Come on in,' she said, holding open the door.

He tried surreptitiously to read her name from the security tag suspended precariously on her chest, a trap for the unwary.

'Detective Sergeant Jenny Soames,' she said, saving him the trouble. 'And the small print says forensic computer investigator, and Internet analyst.'

He felt his face redden, but she seemed not to have noticed. She closed the door behind him.

'It's not much, Detective Chief Inspector, but it is home.'

'Tom,' he said.

'Jenny,' she replied, gesturing to a vacant chair.

It was a small office. Four computer terminals, each with its own desk, phone and task chair. Pinboards and whiteboards lined the walls. He assumed the printers would be somewhere close by. Not what he'd expected of a regional e-crime hub.

'You're lucky,' she told him. 'My two DCs are running some training at Sedgley Park, so we've got the place to ourselves.'

She sat down beside him and swivelled her chair so that they were facing each other. Her seat was adjusted several inches lower than his, and still her feet only just reached the floor. Holmes would probably have described her as stocky, but from the way she moved, Caton knew that beneath her light-grey business suit and crisp white shirt, she had a naturally muscular body. Her face also exuded strength, with a wide forehead, pronounced cheekbones, angular jaw and a square chin. Her hazel eyes were fiercely intelligent. The whole appearance was softened, however, by textured curls of chestnut hair.

'What exactly is it you do here?' he asked.

She smiled. 'You're wondering how a tiny office, with just a DS and two DCs, could possibly be described as a regional e-crime hub.'

He began to reply, but she brushed his protestations aside.

'It's alright, everybody does. But there's a lot more to us than what you see. Like everything these days our strength lies in networking. There are four hubs: the Metropolitan Police Central e-Crime Unit; one in the East Midlands; one in Yorkshire and Humberside; and us here in the North West. We work together, and with the Child Exploitation and Online Protection Unit, and call on private sector experts as necessary. And we also have links to the intelligence agencies.'

'Does that include the Government Communication Headquarters in Cheltenham?'

'Especially GCHQ. And now that the National Crime Agency is up and running we have links through them to Europol, the FBI and other international agencies.'

'You still haven't told me what it is you do.'

She raised both arms as if in prayer, and adopted the tone beloved of corporate publicists.

'We are the front line in the battle against cybercrime.' She grinned. 'And before you ask me, that includes cyber-based terrorism, computer intrusions that threaten the UK's essential infrastructures, espionage, large-scale identity theft and major cyber fraud. Although, to be strictly accurate, in the hubs we tend to concentrate on specifically criminal activities, leaving the terrorist stuff to the intelligence agencies.'

'It sounds like a tall order.'

'We've been allocated £30 million over four years for the hubs, and the rest of the agencies have got £320 million.'

'I've no idea whether that's a lot or not,' said Caton.

She pursed her lips. 'Put it this way. Over £600 million pounds a year was being spent in the UK on anti-virus measures and cleaning up after the effects of cyber attacks of one kind or another. Finally they're giving us the means to catch and punish the perpetrators.'

'It sounds,' said Caton, 'as though your brief might be too high powered to cover the specifics of my investigation.'

'Strictly speaking,' she replied, 'the activities your victims appear to have been engaging in wouldn't fall into the serious cybercrime category, but if it led to their deaths, I'm hardly going to quibble, am I?'

She swivelled round to take a folder from the desk top and turned back to face him. She flipped it open and scanned it to refresh her memory.

'It's beginning to look,' she said, 'as though your three victims acted in common, in that the first and third at least, and presumably the second, were members of the same social network, *flammatory.com*. This suggests that others on the same network could be potential victims. We need to get their Web host to warn them. There are another five trolls who are UK-based; I suggest we prioritise those. The rest are from all over the world: the States, Eastern Europe, Spain, Australia.'

'How many?'

'Twelve, apart from the UK ones.'

She took a copy of her notes from the file, placed it in another folder and passed it to him.

'Your man Wallace did a good job by the way. He'd done a lot of the donkey work. Saved us hours, as it turns out.'

Caton speed-read the file. It was impressive how much she had achieved in less than two hours. The time it had taken him to brief Helen Gates and get over here.

'We are working,' he said, 'on the assumption that the killers were people targeted by these trolls. How on earth do we track them all down?'

She frowned and folded her arms. Neither of which filled him with confidence.

'It's going to be difficult,' she said, 'but not impossible. The major social media sites they have been using to find and troll their victims have all blocked *flammatory.com*. They've also been busy deleting the worst of their posts as a result of complaints, removing your evidence in the process.'

'What about the Internet service provider who hosts *flammatory.com*? Surely they can tell you?'

'The host is in the Ukraine. They won't cooperate. We'd have to subpoena them to get them to divulge the owner of *flammatory.com*, his legal identity and UIP address.'

'Can you do that?'

'We've already contacted Europol and they've promised to put pressure on the country's Ministry of Internal Affairs. I have to warn you, though, it's not likely to be a priority for them. They're up to their ears in fraud, child pornography and trafficking.'

Caton closed the file and placed it on the desk in front of him.

'What if we start from the other end? If we can just work out how the perpetrators tracked down our victims, wouldn't that lead us back to them?'

She shook her head. 'My guess is that somehow they got hold of the email address of one of the trolls. It would only need one of them to get careless and divulge it somewhere – possibly on their own website. But that wouldn't help you.'

'Why not?'

She unfolded her arms, turned to face her monitor and typed away at the keyboard. Seconds later, she swivelled the monitor so that he could see the flow chart on the screen.

'Let me show you one of the tricks we use,' she said. 'This is from our training manual.'

Using her mouse, she guided him through the chart with the cursor.

'If we tried to hack into the account of a suspect or perpetrator using our networked police computers like this one, we'd leave a bloody great digital footprint that anyone with a modicum of IT skills could spot. So, we do what the hackers do. We use special software to create a pseudonym account. One that hides our real IP address.'

'IP address?'

'Every device connected to the Internet is given a unique number known as an Internet Protocol address, consisting of four numbers separated by full stops. It identifies your Web host and location. It's how we track down people using the Internet to commit crime. It's one of the ways that private companies track down people committing copyright theft by illegally downloading music, videos, books.'

'How does hiding your IP address help you to identify them?'

She moved the cursor on.

'Once we're in, we can explore their social media sites and contacts. We can even befriend them. The odds are we'll find email addresses. Then we can use something called a Reverse email finder to reveal details of the sender. It's commonly available on the Web.'

'You think that's what the perpetrators have done?'

'Probably.'

'So what we need to do is identify who our victims had been targeting. And you can investigate them in the way you've described?'

She nodded. 'In theory. But from what I can tell, *flammatory.com* had been targeting hundreds of innocent people. The list of names Wallace sent me is a start. If you can narrow them down any further, let me know.'

She glanced at her watch, slid her chair back and stood up.

'I'm sorry, Tom, but I've got to get over to Sedgley Park to do the wind-up session in the Sir David Wilmot Suite.'

Caton picked up his copy of the file, got to his feet and found himself towering over her.

'Thanks, Jenny,' he said. 'You've been a great help.'

She opened the door.

'Good luck,' she replied. 'You're going to need it.'

Chapter 29

As he exited the building, Caton switched on his BlackBerry. He had two text messages. One from DI Holmes, the other from Kate. Equally brief. Equally urgent. *Ring Me!*

He started with Gordon.

'Boss,' his deputy began, 'it's Imran Qureshi's father, Muhammad. He's downstairs, and he won't go away.'

'What does he want?'

'His son's belongings. Specifically his copy of the Qur'an.'

'You've explained that the coroner won't release the body until the inquest has been reopened?'

'His brother explained all that to him. In the meantime he says he wants his holy book. He doesn't trust us with it.'

'Is there something I'm not getting, Gordon?' said Caton. 'Do you think he's trying to hide evidence?'

'No, boss. I had DC Hulme check it out. Apparently, when the owner dies his copy of the Qur'an either has to be burnt or buried. His dad intends to wrap it in a cloth, and when his son is finally buried he's going to bury it close by, where it can't be trampled on.'

'Have we had a good look at that Qur'an? Are we sure we haven't missed something?'

'Seriously, boss, it's just a book. There's no special marks in it. No bits of paper. Nothing.'

'It's obviously not "just a book" to his father.'

'He says his Uncle Hazrat is a famous Islamic scholar. He told him he has to retrieve the book and see that it is treated with respect. That's all there is to it.'

Caton could hear the exasperation mounting in Gordon's voice.

'Okay,' he said, 'let him have it. But not the clothes. The Defence may want to have them re-tested.'

'Defence? What Defence?' said Gordon. 'We have to catch the buggers first!'

Caton didn't need reminding.

When Kate answered her mobile she was beyond exasperation.

'Tom! At last. Where the hell have you been?'

Each day closer to their wedding day her stress levels seemed to escalate. He decided to let silence do the talking.

'Okay,' she said, 'I'm sorry. But it's that bloody woman again. She knows I'm trying to plan a wedding. I think she's doing this on purpose.'

'Whoa,' he said. 'Slow down, Kate. What woman, doing what?'

'Helen! That's who. Bloody Helen.'

'What has she done?'

'She only texted me to say that her partner is whisking her off to Paris for two days, and would we have Harry come and stay. Texted me, for God's sake!'

'Calm down, Kate,' he said, feeling anything but calm himself.

How could Helen have been so stupid? Or was Kate right; was she being vindictive? Was this jealousy rearing its ugly head? Don't kid yourself, he told himself. Harry might want the two of you to get back together, but not Helen.

'Why can't her mother have Harry?' he asked.

'That's what I said. Because she's in the Algarve, apparently. She's not stupid, is she?'

'When is she proposing to drop him off?' he asked.

Her laugh was hollow, and full of irony.

'That's the best bit. She isn't going to drop him off because neither of us is at home. She wants you to pick him up.'

'Oh, for God's sake!' he said. 'This is a murder inquiry. Murderers don't take time out to give you a breather.'

'Well, I can't go,' she said. 'My car's being serviced and they rang half an hour ago to say it needs new disc brakes.'

He took a deep breath.

'Where and when?'

'Ten minutes ago. Manchester Airport. Terminal Three Departures.'

Caton cursed. He looked at his watch.

'Tell her I'll be twenty minutes.'

'On your way back you can pop into the Trafford Centre and pick up your wedding outfit, your best man's and the ushers',' she told him. 'I'll pick up my car as soon as it's ready and meet you at home.'

She ended the call before he had a chance to object.

Helen, shifting from foot to foot, waited impatiently by the passport control gates. Harry was sitting beside her, head bowed, arms folded, on a cabin case that barely supported his weight. Roger – at least Caton assumed it was him – stood with his back to them, staring at the departure boards. She spotted him and came to meet him. Harry leapt to his feet and hurried after her.

'Tom! Thank God,' she said. 'They called our flight five minutes ago.'

No apology, no explanation. She hugged her son and pushed him towards his father.

'Be good, Harry. I'll ring you tonight. We'll bring you a present from Paris.'

Behind her, Roger picked up the case.

'Helen!' he shouted. 'For God's sake! They're going to close the gate.'

She turned to go, then stopped and looked over her shoulder.

'I'm sorry, Tom,' she said. 'I know the timing stinks. If I could have found someone else to have him…'

You could have chosen not to go, he was tempted to say. Harry gripped his hand tightly.

'Just go, Helen,' he said. 'Have a good time. Harry will be fine.'

She ran the thirty metres to her partner. He seized her by the arm and hurried her towards the passport control. While she fumbled for the boarding cards, he turned and glanced over his shoulder at Caton and Harry. It was the first time that he and Caton had met. Caton took an instant dislike. He had no idea why. The man was tall, lithe, dark-haired with a boyish head of curly black hair. Aside from the curls, he could have been a carbon copy of Caton himself. But when he smiled at Harry and waved, there was something insincere about it. More than that, it felt creepy.

Caton shook his head and turned to go. Now who was being jealous? And the wedding only days away.

He delivered the suits and Harry to Kate, who was waiting at the apartment, and agreed to meet up with them that evening. Kate was going to take Harry to see The Borrower, and then the three of them were going to meet up for a meal.

'I wouldn't mind seeing that myself,' he told her.

'It's up to you,' she said. 'You can't keep working flat-out like this. You're entitled to a break.'

They both knew that wasn't true. The flipside of not having to work weekends or shifts was, as Gordon loved to say, that when the shit hit the fan, the fan had to keep going until the mess was all cleaned up.

Three hours later, he parked up and made his way to The Orient Food Hall. He found them in Frankie and Benny's.

'We've already ordered,' Kate told him. 'There was a mad rush as soon as the film ended. If we'd waited, we'd never have got a table.'

'It's fine,' he said. 'Okay, Harry?'

Head down, his son appeared not to have heard. He was busy playing with his Nintendo.

'*Professor Layton and the Miracle Mask,*' said Kate.

Caton had no idea what she was talking about.

The waiter appeared. He'd brought a 6oz hamburger topped with pepper jack cheese, bacon and mayo, on a toasted sesame bun, with mayo and barbecue sauce, served with lettuce and tomato, house fries and tomato-chilli relish on the side, and a plate of barbecued tiger prawns served on a bed of mixed leaves tossed with sweet chilli dressing, cucumber, tomatoes, red onion and half a lemon on the side. It didn't take a detective to know whose was whose.

'Put it away, Harry,' said Caton. 'Your burger's here.'

The reluctance with which he did so struck Caton as completely out of character. He put it down to him missing his mother.

'Are you dining, sir?' said the waiter.

'I'll have the New Yorker,' he replied. 'Hold the sauce.'

The waiter's biro hovered in mid-air.

'You don't require the sauce, sir?'

'That's right, I don't want the sauce.'

'Very good, sir.'

The biro descended.

'And to drink?'

'I'm driving. Just table water, thank you.'

'Very good, sir.'

As the waiter departed, Kate picked up the menu.

'New Yorker,' she read. 'Calzone, full to the brim with spicy pepperoni, ham, bacon, mushrooms and mozzarella. All topped with Mama's rich Neapolitan tomato and herb sauce. Why no sauce?'

'Because I have no idea how long it'll take, and if you two have both finished, I don't want to sit here eating it on my own. This way we can take it with us.'

'Now you've made me feel guilty.'

'Don't be daft. I'll be able to have a glass of wine with it at home. Now eat up before it gets cold.'

'How was the film?' said Caton.

Kate had finished her meal. Harry had hardly spoken since Caton joined them. It had been Harry's choice to eat here, and his decision to order the burger, but he had taken just two bites out of it, and now sat there sipping his Coke disconsolately.

'It was good, wasn't it?' Kate prompted.

Harry shrugged his shoulders.

'Okay, I s'pose,' he said.

'What did you think of the goblins, the wargs and the shapeshifters?' said Caton, dredging up what little he remembered from having read the book decades ago.

Another shrug.

'My favourite was definitely Gollum,' said Kate, trying harder. 'And that magic ring.'

'From what I remember, it all but enslaved Gollum, and nearly destroyed him,' said Caton.

'I was thinking of the invisibility powers it bestowed,' said Kate.

Still no response. Caton decided on a fresh approach and stole one of Harry's chips instead. He dipped it into the relish and made a point of enjoying it. Where Harry would normally have protested vigorously, instead he pushed the plate towards his father and sucked harder on his straw.

'What's the matter, Harry?' said Caton.

'Nothing.'

'Your Mum will be back before you know it.'

Another shrug. Caton decided to change tack.

'How are you getting on with Roger?' he said.

Harry pushed the bottle of Coke away, and sat back with his arms folded.

Kate placed a hand on Caton's arm. The message was obvious. Let him be.

The waiter arrived with his calzone and placed it in front of him.

'Would you like some black pepper, sir?'

'No thanks,' Caton replied. 'But I'm afraid we're leaving. Could you wrap this to go?'

The waiter had been asked this many times and had perfected his response.

'I'm really sorry, sir, but we don't do takeaways, and we are not permitted to wrap food that has been served. It's down to European legislation, sir. Food hygiene. I'm sorry.'

His manner was neither embarrassed nor obsequious. It was a simple statement of fact. There was no point in arguing. If anything, the young man deserved to be commended.

'I understand,' said Caton. 'It's fine.'

He waited until the waiter had left, then reached into the inner breast pocket of his jacket and took out a folded plastic evidence bag.

'Tom!' said Kate. 'You can't do that.'

'Watch me,' he said.

Harry looked up from the Nintendo he had sneakily opened in his lap and gazed with admiration as his father opened the bag, deftly slid the calzone inside and sealed it up.

'What's that writing on the label?' said Harry.

'It's a chain of evidence record,' Caton told him.

Harry giggled. 'In case the waiter catches you?' he said.

Caton slid the bag across the table in Kate's direction.

'You've got another thing coming,' she said. 'I'm not putting that in my bag.'

'Come on, Kate,' he said. 'It's breathable, leak proof, tear and puncture resistant, and the closure is really strong.'

'This is a Ted Baker Cumari bag,' she told him. 'Finest leather, with printed cotton lining, and expensive. It's not a lunch box.'

'Go on, Kate,' said Harry, pulling at her sleeve. 'It'll be fun.'

She looked at each of them in turn, with their identical sit-up-and-beg male puppy dog expressions, and relented.

'Alright,' she said. 'But if this splits, it's going to cost you, big time.'

They had just stepped out of the lift when his BlackBerry rang faintly. He could barely hear it.

'Come on, Harry,' said Kate, taking his hand and leading him towards the door to their apartment.

'I'm sorry,' Caton called after them.

She raised her hand in a "whatever" gesture, inserted the key and shepherded Harry inside.

'You're not going to believe this!' Gordon sounded excited. 'We've got another one. A partial. In a semi-detached in Swinton.'

'Partially dead?' said Caton.

'No, he's dead alright. But they didn't get to finish the job. Disturbed by his wife arriving home with the kids.'

'Are they alright?' said Caton, trying not to picture the scene.

'They're fine. The perps legged it out the back and through the gardens.'

'So what am I not going to believe?'

'The victim. He's only a PCSO!'

A Police and Community Support Officer. A civilian member of staff, serving as a non-warranted officer. Similar uniform, blue cap badge and shoulder flashes, without the same powers of arrest. None of that was going to matter. As far as the press, the public and his colleagues were concerned, this was the murder of a member of the police service, with all that entailed. The trouble was that if he had been up to the same things as the rest of the victims, sympathy was going to turn to anger. Malfeasance in public office wasn't going to figure in the gutter press headlines. They were going to have a field day.

'The good news,' his deputy was saying, 'is that the perps have missed a trick. One that's going to blow this case wide open.'

'Save it, Gordon,' he said wearily. 'Just give me the address.'

Kate was standing in the hallway.

'Don't say anything,' she said. She held out the evidence bag. 'Here, you'll need this.'

He took it and turned to go.

'You do know we're getting married on Saturday?' she said.

Chapter 30

A youth standing on the footbridge just before the Moorside and Hazlehurst Road junction with the East Lancs Road caught Caton's attention. You could never be too careful. There were idiots who played Russian roulette with other people's lives. Who thought it clever to lob a brick or half a paving slab over the side and let fate determine what happened next. He was a fraction late in seeing the lights change and had to brake sharply. The evidence bag slid forward and fell from the passenger seat into the footwell. He let it lie.

When the lights changed, he turned left into Moorside Road and then left into Wardley Business Park. He stopped just short of the BOC building and parked up. He selected Manchester Radio, and leaned across to pick up the evidence bag. He straightened up and broke the seal on the bag.

The aroma of pepperoni and bacon set the juices flowing at the back of his mouth. He hadn't eaten for over seven hours. The crime scene was just two streets away. Gordon was on the case. The victim wasn't going anywhere. He took a bite and turned up the volume. Adele was singing about chasing pavements, even when they led nowhere. He knew how she felt.

It was a typical three-bed semi, with the addition of a glazed porch and a conservatory out back. The sort of extras that came with overtime. The sort that had appeared in their thousands during Maggie Thatcher's miners' strike. Before his time. There was an alarm box too, above the box-room window. Much good it had done him. Caton was surprised to see a mortuary van parked up behind the scenes of crime vehicle. Someone had been quick off the mark.

Gordon Holmes stepped out through the kitchen doorway, facing away from him. He stared into the back garden for a moment, then turned, saw Caton and walked towards him down the block-paved drive.

'You took your time,' he said.

'You took your time, *sir*,' Caton replied. 'Anyway, you said you were tired of playing second fiddle.'

Gordon's eyes widened. 'You mean you want me to take over Janus?'

'Don't get ahead of yourself, Detective Inspector. I'm talking about you leading on this one, not the whole caboodle. And don't sulk. You'll have plenty of opportunity when I go on my honeymoon.'

'Not to mention paternity leave,' Holmes replied.

They had to move back a few yards to let a SOCO past.

'Give me the headlines,' said Caton.

'Brian Shepherd. Twenty-nine years old. Married for eight years. Two children. A boy aged six, a girl aged four. They're with their grandparents. Their mother's with them, and so is DS Stuart, until we get a family liaison officer sorted.'

'She's not going to appreciate being stereotyped into the babysitting role.'

'For once that wasn't my decision. She volunteered.'

'Sorry, Gordon,' said Caton.

His deputy grinned. 'No need to apologise. If she hadn't, I would have asked her.'

Caton shook his head. 'You're incorrigible.'

Holmes grinned again. 'Thank you, boss.'

'When did they find him?'

'An hour and a half ago.'

'And you've only just called me?'

'I called you four times. Texted twice. Left a message on your landline at home.' He sounded hurt.

Caton pulled out his BlackBerry. The battery symbol told him that he had no power.

'You should at least be using your Airwave radio as a backup,' said Holmes.

Caton didn't need reminding.

'Mea culpa,' he said.

Holmes looked puzzled.

'My bad,' Caton tried again.

'Gottcha,' said Holmes. 'Look at you, using urban slang.'

'Shakespeare, actually,' said Caton. 'Have you got a time of death?'

'No, but we've got a window for it. He arrived home from work at six forty-five p.m., checked his emails, ate a microwave lasagne, had a mug of tea and settled down to work on his computer. He died at sometime between seven thirty p.m. and eight p.m. when his wife found him.'

'How can you be so precise?'

Holmes took him by the arm and led him towards the house.

'Come on, boss,' he said. 'I'll show you.'

They eased their way down the hall past several scenes of crime officers, then had to wait by the door leading into the kitchen for one of them to finish dusting an overturned chair for prints. Caton was frustrated that he had arrived this far into the investigation, but he could hardly blame Gordon for cracking on without him.

'He's through here,' said Holmes.

They followed the walkway past a circular black-granite table on which lay an empty dinner plate smeared with a reddish brown stain, a fork and a plain white mug containing the dregs of a milky tea. Holmes gestured towards the sink where a crumpled foil food container sat on the draining board. Gordon led the way into what Caton assumed would be a utility room, but turned out to be a small study.

This was a boxy airless room, without a window. A desk occupied the whole of the facing wall. On the left of the desk was a horizontal file store unit holding three black ring binders. In the centre was a Samsung 18-inch monitor. On the right an Epson printer-copier, with a small black broadband modem blinking away on top of it. Yellow post-it notes with scribbled biro messages were stuck to the plastic borders of the screen. On the right-hand wall was a two-foot-by-twenty-inches photographic canvas print of a smiling family group. Mother, father and two young children, a boy and a girl. On the left-hand wall was a Simpsons Family planner calendar. Beside it, a framed photograph of the man in the family portrait, apparently taken on the day he had completed his five-week training course as a PCSO.

The man in question lay slumped forward across the desk. He was still wearing the black fleece and black cargo pants that he had worn on duty. The back of his head was matted with blood. His hands were either side of the shattered keyboard. Only the fingers of the left hand had been subjected to the same treatment as the other victims. His right hand appeared untouched, the index finger intact.

'They dragged the computer tower out from under the desk,' said Holmes, 'ripped out the hard drive and smashed the rest. Then they must have started on his hands. Heard his missus open the front door and went out through the kitchen and over the gardens.'

'Did she see them?'

'No, but she heard the door slam. She thought he must have gone out back, but then she saw him in here. Freaked out, shoved the kids into the front room and rang 999.'

'Did they take anything?'

'Just the mouse. That's where we got lucky.'

'Lucky?'

'This computer wasn't his only access to the Internet. He had a tablet with Web access too. He must have been using it while he was eating. We found it on one of the kitchen chairs. He replied to two emails at six forty-five p.m. and six forty-six p.m. precisely. Probably while his lasagne was in the microwave. His Web history shows he was browsing away right up until seven thirty. I guess that's when he came in here.'

'And his wife arrived home at eight p.m.?'

'Exactly. Both the paramedic, who got here first, and Dr Tompkins, concur.'

Caton backed out of the room and stood in the kitchen watching the SOCOs work away.

'You said this one was going to blow the case wide open. I take it you're referring to the tablet?'

Holmes smiled. It was the careful smile he used at times like this when a full-on grin would hardly be appropriate.

'He only synchronised it with his PC on a regular basis, and used it to do his trolling. We've got all his contacts, files and Web activity going back to the last time he must have cleared his Internet history, six months ago.'

'Where is it now?'

'Jack Benson's got it. He's making sure they've got every physical trace they can from it, then it's all ours.'

Caton knew that Gordon was right. This was the break they had been hoping for. But time was still of the essence. For all those potential victims still out there, for the bereaved and to save his wedding day. Maybe even his marriage.

'Tell Mr Benson to hurry it up,' he said. 'Then get it over to Douggie Wallace.'

'What are you going to do, boss?'

'I'm going back to the Incident Room. I want to be there when it arrives. You can manage here?'

'No problem. Carter's heading up the door-to-doors, and like I say, DS Stuart's with the wife and kids.'

Gordon followed him down the hallway and walked with him to the car, where Caton proceeded to strip off his Tyvek suit and place it in a polythene bag in the boot.

'Just one thing, boss,' said Holmes. '*My bad*. Are you sure that was Shakespeare?'

Caton paused, one hand on the roof of the car. 'I'm sure,' he said. 'You'll find it in Sonnet 12: "Your love and pity doth the impression fill, which vulgar scandal stamp'd upon my brow; for what care I who calls me well or ill, so you o'er-green *my bad*, my good allow?"'

Holmes placed a gloved hand over his heart.

'I didn't know you cared,' he said.

A SOCO who had witnessed the exchange watched dumbfounded as Caton climbed into the car and his deputy strode back up the drive with a spring in his step.

Gordon Holmes clocked the expression on his face.

As the SOCO drew level with him, he paused, looked him in the eyes and said grimly, 'It doesn't mean we don't care, son. Quite the opposite. Sadly, one day you'll come to understand.'

Chapter 31

'It's all here.'

Douggie Wallace swivelled the screen so that Caton had a better view.

'His emails and a full history of his trolling on five different sites. Plus his exchanges with other trolls on *flammatory.com*.'

'Full history?' said Caton, remembering what Holmes had said.

'Well no, but for the past six months.'

'What if the relevant posts were made before that time?'

'That might not be a problem. He may have deleted his Web history and his emails, but there's a good chance that DS Soames' team can recover them. It'll mean contacting his Internet service provider, though. That will take a bit longer.'

'We don't have longer,' said Caton. 'In the meantime, I want you to identify people trolled by more than one of our murder victims.'

'I'd already started with the first two,' Wallace replied. 'Using the list Adam Davis gave us, and by factoring in your latest victim's, which was *bomburr#1*.' He saw the expression on Caton's face and added, 'Bombur was a fat, stupid Middle Earth dwarf in The Hobbit.' As though that explained everything.

'What about Miles-Cowper?' Caton asked.

Wallace turned back to the desk and scrolled down the screen with his mouse.

'Here you are,' he said. 'Thanks to Brian Shepherd's tablet I was able to work it out through a process of elimination.'

The cursor had stopped at a post with the hash tag *herbert#wally*.

'I was about to add it into the equation. I think we'll be looking at dozens of potential victims these four had been trolling.'

Caton read the post. Sent at seven twenty-eight p.m. today. It was to a social media site set up as a memorial for a nineteen-year-old British serviceman killed by a roadside bomb in Afghanistan. It wasn't just disrespectful, it was sick. Sick enough to anger me, he reflected, and I never knew him. What must his family and brothers-in-arms be feeling?

'There's a way we can speed this up,' he said. 'You start by listing those names, and I'll get Adam Davis brought back here. He can tell us which ones he thinks were the most vulnerable. To whom they did the most damage. Whose family and friends were most likely to have been outraged.'

'Enough to want to kill someone?'

'Enough to maim and kill four people, and counting.'

Caton made the call. Adam Davis was on remand in Manchester Prison. It would take at least an hour and a half to process the paperwork and have him brought back to the Incident Room. Longer at this time of night. Ged was preparing the room to cope with yet another flood of information to process from the latest crime scene. With half his team at the crime scene, there were only a handful left, all beavering away.

Caton decided to clear some of the mountain of paperwork that had piled up over the past four days.

Before he had a chance to reach his desk, the doors swung open and DCS Gates burst into the room. Heads turned.

'DCI Caton,' she said. 'A word.'

She closed her door and pointed to a chair by the table in the window. She sat opposite him.

'You didn't have to come down for me, Ma'am,' he said. 'I'd have found my way up.'

She grimaced. 'Oh yes I did. To make sure you didn't try to give me the slip.'

Caton smiled disarmingly. 'Now why on earth would I want to do that, Ma'am?'

She loosened the top button of her blouse, folded her hands in her lap and leaned back in her chair.

'Let's cut the crap, shall we, Tom? A Police Community Support Officer! Please tell me it was another case of mistaken identity. Like Coreishi?'

'I can't do that I'm afraid, Helen,' he said. 'It wasn't.'

'Shit!'

She folded one arm across her chest and used it to support the other as she cradled her forehead in the palm of her hand. It was times like this when Caton didn't envy her the rank. They couldn't pay him enough to compensate for the aggravation that came with it.

'At least he wasn't Assistant Chief Constable, or the Police and Crime Commissioner,' he said.

She looked up and let her arm drop.

'It might have been better if he was.'

Caton knew that she was thinking of Martin Hadfield, just as he had been. It was only a matter of time before he burst into the room, ranting and raving about the image of the Force, whilst really concerned about his own position.

'Shepherd is part of the wider picture,' he reminded

her. 'That's what the media will be focusing on. Four dead. How many more to come? Who's going to be next?'

'And I'm supposed to find that reassuring?'

'We're closing in,' he said. 'They slipped up this time. We've got his tablet computer, and we know who they were targeting.'

'How many?' she said, grasping at straws.

'A few dozen,' he admitted.

She raised both hands in exasperation.

'But I've got Adam Davis coming in to help us narrow them down,' he said hurriedly. 'I'm confident we'll know where to look before the day's out.'

'And while you're looking, your predators are out there doing…'

She looked weary. For the first time, despite the make-up, he was aware of the lines on her forehead, the wrinkles around her eyes and the shadowy half-moons beneath them.

'Remind me, when is your wedding?' she said.

'Next Saturday.'

She was the second person on the guest list who seemed to have forgotten. It didn't bode well.

'Are you sure you should be heading up this investigation?'

'Are you saying you don't think I'm up to it, Ma'am?'

He knew it was stupid thing to say. It had just slipped out. Proved how much stress he was under. That she was right.

'For God's sake, Tom!'

She pushed her chair back and turned to look out of the window, beyond the Fujitsu building, towards the BT telecommunications mast in Heaton Park. Composing herself. Choosing her words carefully. She turned slowly.

'You know very well, Tom, that I don't doubt your ability for a moment. But just because I'm single, it doesn't mean that I can't appreciate how much stress preparing for a wedding can bring. Even if you have been living together. More so in that event, I would think.'

He began to respond, but she held up her hand as though stopping the traffic in the middle of rush hour.

'And before you get on your high horse, it's you and Kate that I'm thinking about here, not this investigation. I know you'll do your best regardless, right down to the wire. Working through the night to chase it down. But is that fair? On you, or on her?'

He had been asking himself the same thing. The trouble with cases like this, with serial killings, was that they became personal. Each death ratcheted up the pressure to prevent the next, until it became the only thing that mattered in your life.

'Gordon Holmes is up to this,' she was saying. 'You mentored him. And DCI Bookham's armed robbery case has been adjourned for a month because the judge had a heart attack. He can give Gordon a hand. Officially it would still be your case. You can pick it up again as soon as you get back from your honeymoon.'

'Everything you're saying,' he said, 'I know it's right. But this is a complex case. It'll take DI Holmes forty-eight hours to bring DCI Bookham up to speed. That's a distraction he can't afford. Please, Ma'am, give me till Friday.'

She placed her hands on the back of the chair, letting it take her weight.

'You can Ma'am me all you like,' she said, 'but it doesn't change the facts. 'You're running out of time.'

'Friday,' he said. He hoped it didn't sound like pleading.

She rocked the chair back and forth. Stopped. Gritted her teeth.

'Friday. And don't make me regret it.'

Before he could thank her, the door burst open. Red-faced, ACC Hadfield charged into the room, saw Caton and stopped in his tracks.

'DCI Caton was just leaving, Martin,' Helen Gates announced, meeting Caton's gaze and inclining her head towards the door. 'Urgent. Breaking news. I'll bring you up to speed.'

Caton was on his feet and out of the door before Hadfield could gather his wits.

'And I'm sending Ambrose Bookham over regardless,' she called after him. 'Just in case.'

Chapter 32

'Ambrose Bookham!' exclaimed Holmes.

'What have you got against DCI Bookham?' said Caton. He was tempted to add, "apart from the fact that he's black," but that wouldn't have been fair. Gordon seemed to have mellowed over the past couple of years.

'Nothing. He's a good detective. And before you ask, I think he got his promotion on merit.'

'So what's the problem?'

'We don't need him. We don't need anyone.'

Caton knew that wasn't the issue. It showed in his deputy's face.

'DCI Gates has given me till Friday,' he said. 'I'd have had to hand it over to you by then anyway. I'm getting married the following day, remember? You don't need to worry. She's agreed that you'll head up Janus. Mr Bookham is just an extra pair of hands.'

'Head up Janus? That's a good one!' said DC Hulme from behind his computer screen.

They turned and stared at him. Furious that he had been listening in. Furious with themselves for discussing it in front of him.

'Head? Janus?' he said, peering around the side of his monitor. 'Janus.' He wiggled his hands in the air for added emphasis. 'Two heads looking in opposite directions?'

Gordon Holmes approached the desk and put his face close to Jimmy Hulme's.

'Anus,' he said. 'One head. Up its own. Yours!'

He had no need for gestures.

The hapless detective constable subsided into his seat. Nobody laughed.

'Right, boss,' said Gordon Holmes, calm as a cucumber. 'I suppose you want an update?'

They retreated to Caton's cubbyhole. Not that any of this was confidential. It simply made it easier to concentrate, and for the others to get on with their work.

'Apart from the tablet,' Holmes reported, 'there's not a lot that's new. We did have one sighting of the perps that confirms our suspicions. An elderly woman in one of the properties that backs on to the victim's house, three doors down. She was washing a pot in the sink. Saw two figures run across her lawn and climb over the dividing fence.'

'How tall was the fence?'

'Three foot. You could've stepped over it. She reckons the taller of the two was female. The shorter one male.'

'How could she tell?'

'The way they moved.'

'Ages?'

'She's no idea. Reckons they must have been young because of how they got over that fence. But then anything under sixty is probably young to her.'

'What time was this?'

'Eight p.m. She knows because Coronation Street had just finished.'

'And that's it?'

'Except for the forensics. I've no doubt they simply confirm what we've already got. Two sets of nice footprints on one of the lawns, though. They'd had a sprinkler on it to bed in some fertilizer.'

'I had them put the helicopter up as soon I heard, but it was hopeless. There were just too many people out and about.'

There was a hesitant knock on the partition. Ged appeared in the space that served as a doorway.

'Adam Davis is downstairs with his escort, sir,' she said. 'They want to know where you want him.'

'Don't tempt me,' muttered Holmes.

Caton stood.

'Ask them to bring him up here.'

'Are you sure that's it?' said Caton.

Adam Davis nodded his head.

He looked washed-out, and defeated. His face was ashen, his eyes sunken in their sockets, his cheeks hollow. The chair dwarfed him. It was as though in less than twenty-four hours he had shrunk in height and weight.

'Just these four?'

'I think so. I can't be sure. These are the only ones I heard about.'

They stared at the names on the screen.

'What the hell were you thinking?' said Gordon Holmes. He meant it to be rhetorical, but Davis answered anyway.

'I wasn't.' His voice was choked, and there were tears in his eyes.

'Bit late for that,' said Holmes. 'Save it for the jury.'

He walked over to the doors and returned with the two G4S escorts who had been kicking their heels in the corridor. They waited while the handcuff was unlocked from his chair and secured around the wrist of one of the escorts. Caton signed the Prisoner Escort Record and handed it back.

'Now get him out of here,' said Holmes.

Everyone in the room watched in silence as he was

led, head down, across the room and out into the corridor.

'I can't understand why he kept on doing it, once he found out the effect it was having,' said Holmes when the doors had closed behind them.

'It became an obsession,' said Caton. 'Not being able to stop even when you know it's harming you, or others; that's a definition of addiction. He's well aware of what he's done now he has to live in the real world instead of a digital one.'

'You reckon?' said Holmes.

'The PER has him down as a prisoner at risk.'

'Do us all a favour if he topped himself,' said Holmes.

'Not if he'd done it before he gave us these names,' observed Douggie Wallace.

They turned their attention to the screen. Wallace clicked on each of the names in turn, bringing up the page of media snippets he had compiled.

Jarmaine Cordell. Twelve years old. Flung from his mountain bike by a hit-and-run driver in Hodge Hill, Birmingham. Dead on arrival. According to his family, school and the police, he was an innocent victim. Lively, kind, intelligent. A bright future ahead of him. The *flammatory.com* trolls had claimed on his social media tribute site that he was a drugs courier. That the killing was deliberate. A gang-on-gang reprisal. The responses were passionate, heartfelt, gut-wrenching. That simply encouraged the trolls to make wilder, more hateful accusations that included his mother and sisters. Some of the responses were dark, and threatening.

Gemma Ravene. Essex girl. Living in Braintree. Former Page Three idol, turned soap actress and model. Doctored images were posted on various sites claiming that she was becoming obese. She started dieting obsessively. Then they claimed she was being treated for anorexia. She had a breakdown. Lost her job and her modelling contracts. A successful career blighted. Became addicted to drugs. Two accidental overdoses. All in the space of eight months.

Marvin Makinson. Sheffield-born British Olympian. Accused of drug taking. Trolls started the ball rolling and kept it fuelled. No evidence to support it, but mud sticks. His major sponsors did not renew their contract. Unable to find new sponsors while the allegations are being investigated. Affects his training regime. Is dropped from the team for the World and European Games. Furious responses from friends, fans and family in the media, and on Internet social media.

Ayesha Elissa Amroush. A fifteen-year-old schoolgirl. Trafford, Greater Manchester. Her identity stolen by one of the trolls and used by all of them to troll others, including fellow students at her school. Protested her innocence. Became a victim of bullying and hate campaigns. Committed suicide.

'If we have to identify and interview everyone who responded to the trolling in support of any of these four, it's going to take forever,' said Holmes gloomily.

'And if we don't, and someone we missed turns out to be one of the perpetrators?' said Caton.

They all knew the answer to that. You only had to look at the Yorkshire Ripper fiasco and its aftermath.

'It doesn't mean we can't prioritise,' he added.

'My money's on numbers one and four,' said Holmes.

'Because they both died?' said Wallace.

Caton nodded thoughtfully. 'And because they are both relatively close to the crime scenes.'

'Sheffield is a lot nearer than Birmingham,' Wallace pointed out.

'You'd have to be mad to kill someone because he lost his sponsorship,' said Holmes.

They both turned to look at him.

He thought about it, and raised his hands in surrender.

'Fair enough,' he said. 'Killing four people. Maiming them like that. They're mad.'

'Let's hope the jury decide otherwise,' said Caton. 'Then they'll be looking at a whole-life order, with no parole.'

Holmes rubbed his chin. It was his turn to say it.

'We have to find them first.'

They left Wallace to make a list of the more extreme respondents to the posts left by the trolls, with their real names where they were known. Too many, Caton was aware, were using pseudonyms, like the trolls themselves. But it was unlikely to take as long to reveal their true identities. In the meantime, they had agreed to visit the closest relatives of each of the four names Davis had come up with.

Gordon Holmes was going to continue to run things here in the Incident Room, and bring DCI Bookham up to speed as soon as he arrived. DS Stuart was already contacting Gemma Ravene's parents by phone. Not ideal, but it meant she'd get a feel for it, and a list of names. If necessary she'd be down there on the first shuttle out of Manchester Airport in the morning.

DS Carter was doing the same in relation to Jarmaine Cordell, the hit-and-run victim from Birmingham. Caton had started with that one, but a quick call to Birmingham CID had convinced him to let Nick Carter run with it.

'I think you're barking up the wrong tree,' said the

DI who had been the senior investigating officer. 'Lovely family. Devout Christians. Not a wicked bone among them. We got the bastard who did it. Twenty-year-old boy racer in a stolen Beamer, off his skull on pear cider. Meant nobody really took the comments made by those sickos seriously.'

'That's not what some of those responses suggest,' said Caton.

'I can see that, but we looked into them. The threatening ones. Didn't want any escalation. They were all posted by a bunch of his schoolmates. Didn't even bother to hide their identities. Too young to do anything about it. No way any of them could have tracked your victims down either, let alone do what was done to them. Just mouthing off, that's all.'

So he had decided to let Carter follow it up, just to make sure. In exchange he'd taken on Marvin Makinson, the Olympic cyclist. At worst, he'd only have a forty-mile trip over the Pennines and through the Snake Pass on the A57. It was a pleasant drive on a good day, providing you didn't get stuck behind a couple of tankers. He gathered them together.

'There's not much more we can do till the morning,' he told them. 'DC Holmes will hold the fort, and Mr Wallace has agreed to work through the night and come in tomorrow afternoon. I want the rest of you to go home and get some sleep, ready for an early start.'

He looked at his watch as they trooped out. It was already half past one in the morning. He sometimes wondered if it was worth sending them home. It wasn't easy to sleep with your brain full of images and possibilities. But if you could just snatch a few hours, sometimes the subconscious made sense of something your conscious mind had missed. And in his case, taking Kate breakfast in bed and spending half an hour with Harry might soften the blow. Mend a bridge or two.

And pigs might fly!

Chapter 33

Ged came to meet him as soon as he entered the Incident Room. How she managed to look this fresh on five hours sleep he had no idea.

'Mr Makinson isn't at home; he's here in Manchester. At the velodrome.'

'That's brilliant,' he said. It was just a mile to the National Cycling Centre; seventy-eight miles less than travelling to Sheffield and back. 'Do you know when he's due there?'

'He arrived an hour ago.'

He looked at his watch.

'Presumably that's how he made the Olympics,' she said. 'Early starts, long days.'

'I thought that was swimmers?'

'Would you like me to get Mrs Amroush on the phone?' she said. 'You wanted to see her too?'

It was why he had asked for Ged back. Not only was she efficient, she was always ahead of the game. In another existence she'd have made a great detective.

'Thanks, Ged. Better apologise for the early call. Tell her it's nothing to worry about.'

Stupid thing to say, he chided himself. She'd lost her daughter in the worst possible circumstances. What could there possibly be left for her to worry about?

His phone rang.

'Mrs Amroush, sir,' said Ged.

There was no one on the end of the phone. In the background he could hear the sound of a wireless. Tuned in to Manchester Radio. He heard a door closing, Alan Beswick's uncompromising Lancashire accent suddenly cut off. The sound of footsteps on a wooden floor. The phone picked up.

'Hello?'

'Mrs Amroush?'

'Yes, I'm sorry. The radio was on. I went to…'

Her voice was hesitant. Wondering what this was about.

'I'm Detective Inspector Tom Caton. Greater Manchester Police.'

'The lady said.'

'I'm sorry to ring you this early.'

'It isn't early. Not for me.'

He could imagine. How many sleepless nights since her daughter had died? Tossing and turning, waiting for the light to creep round the edges of the curtains.

'I'd like to come and see you,' he said. 'Today if possible.'

'Any time,' she replied.

'Later this morning, then. I'll give you a ring to check it's still convenient.'

'It will be. Just come.'

She sounded weary of it all. Hadn't even asked why he wanted to see her.

'Thank you, Mrs Amroush,' he said.

'On second thoughts,' she said, 'ring. I'll put the kettle on.'

Caton turned left by the Etihad Stadium, drove past Gordon's beloved McDonald's restaurant and swung left into the car park. He was surprised by the number of cars here this early, and how few of them had cycle racks on the roof. Presumably there was some kind of storage for the regular users. It would have to be pretty secure from what he remembered of the cost of competition bikes. Chris Hoy's, for example. What had the papers said? Fifteen thousand pounds, and he could lift it with one finger.

He climbed out of the car and stood for a moment by the railings separating the car park from Chorlton Valley and the Phillips Park cemetery. In the dip, where the battle between the gangs had begun two years earlier, steam rose where the morning sun warmed the dew still clinging to the grass. It felt as though there was nowhere left in this city that did not stir a sad, or a violent memory. More often than not it was the impact on those left to mourn that he remembered. The ripples of loss and sadness that violence left in its wake.

But then, he reminded himself as he turned and walked towards the gleaming silver carapace of the national cycling centre, this city had brought him so much pleasure and happiness. So many friends. So many good memories. In five days time, a mile to the south, in Gorton Monastery, there would another. One to crown them all. Unless everything went pear-shaped, and Kate crowned him instead.

It was like standing in the belly of a whale. A beautiful, surreal whale. Above his head arched the silver ribs of the roof. The steeply banked yellow sweep of wooden track was hugged by undulating tiered seating. A wide blue safety apron, edged by open tubular fencing, flowed down into the central pit in which he stood.

The last time he had been here was for the finals of the keirin at the Commonwealth Games. The noise had been deafening. The shouting and chanting, the bell, the sound of the wheels on the track. Today it was very different. Just the hum of the bikes, shouted instructions, muted conversation. Less than a dozen spectators were dotted around the stands. Seven cyclists in file skimmed the track. At least a dozen other riders waited their turn down here in the pit. Close by, a group of school children were riding in a tight circle following the instructions of a coach. There was a gentle vibration beneath his feet as the riders on the track sped by.

'Which one is Mr Makinson?' he asked.

'That's Marvin,' replied the steward, pointing to a lone figure thirty metres away, hugging the thin black line nearest the apron.

In the time that it took for Caton to register his presence he had flashed past, the pack, riding high on the blue line above him, following in his wake.

'Is he always here early?' said Caton.

'Crack of dawn,' the man replied. 'Always is.'

'That means an early start over the tops,' Caton reflected.

It wasn't one that he would have relished, particularly in the winter months with the Woodhead and Snake Passes closed by snow, and the M62 beset by freezing sleet, high winds and fog.

The steward shook his head, one eye on the cyclists.

'He shares a flat right here in Sportcity. He uses it when he's training and competing. Most of the British squad have one.'

'I thought he'd been dropped from the squad.'

'No. He was never dropped from the squad, just from competing till those nasty rumours were cleared up.'

'And were they?'

The steward turned to look at him. Assessing how much he could or should share. His admiration for and loyalty to Makinson were evident in his tone and the expression on his face.

'Of course they were. There was never any doubt about it, but it did shake him. That's why they asked him to step down.'

'How badly did he take it?'

'Very. First he was angry, then depressed. Then he shook himself out of it. Mainly by coming down here and taking it out on the track. He's worked twice as hard as before, and his times have come down. I reckon you're looking at a World and Olympic champion next time round. Funny, isn't it?'

'How do you mean?'

'Those false allegations had the opposite effect. They brought him everyone's sympathy and the motivation he needed to be the best. You couldn't make it up.'

Caton looked at his watch.

'How much longer will he be?'

The steward pointed to a digital counter displaying times and laps on the table in front of them.

'He's got another five laps,' he said. 'I'll bring him over when he comes in.'

When Makinson's fixed wheel drive had finally stopped turning, the steward went to meet him on the apron. The rider glanced across at Caton, removed his helmet, shook his head and wheeled his bike towards him, unhappy with having his routine so rudely interrupted.

He was bigger close up than he had seemed on the track. Twenty-three years of age, five foot eleven, pushing ninety kilos, solid muscle. Especially his calves and thighs. It was almost as though something had been stuffed inside the blue and white Lycra body suit to achieve this unnatural effect. He didn't fit either of the descriptions they had so far.

'Got to warm down,' was all he said as he drew level. His face dripped with sweat.

Caton followed him further into the pits where the rider placed his bike on a hanger, wiped his face and hands with a towel and walked across to a set of rollers on which stood another bike. He mounted and began to pedal furiously.

'He won't be long,' said the steward, having picked up on Caton's growing impatience.

'How long is not long?'

The steward shrugged. 'Five minutes tops. Come on, I'll get you a drink.'

It was seven minutes before Marvin Makinson finally sat down opposite Caton, clutching an isotonic replacement fluid bottle.

'What's this all about?' he said.

Caton explained. He kept the detail to a minimum. When he'd finished, Makinson laughed.

'So you think I might have decided to take my revenge on those stupid bastards by hunting them down and killing them?'

'That's not what I said,' Caton told him.

'Not in so many words, but it's what you're wondering.'

'Alright,' said Caton. 'Did you?'

'No.'

There was a long pause while Caton studied Makinson's face. There were no tells. He had maintained eye contact with ease. There was no dilation of the pupils, no fidgeting, the sweat was honest, not borne of fear. He was cooperating freely. Not trying too hard to assert his honesty.

'Was there a time when you thought about it? When you might have talked about doing just that? Even if you didn't mean it?'

'Thought about it? Yes. Who wouldn't? I never

talked about it, though.'

'Not even a tweet? You do tweet?'

'Course I do. I'm on Facebook, too. But no. I might have slagged them off, but that's all.'

'Did any of your fellow tweeters or your fans talk about getting back at them? Or worse, make threats?'

He had to think about that. Eventually, he shook his head.

'No, I don't think so. There were some angry reactions, but most them said I should just ignore it. That the truth would come out. Which it did.'

'Do you have a partner?' said Caton.

He raised his eyebrows and took a swig from the bottle. It didn't look like an evasion. He was thirsty.

'Not at the moment,' he replied. 'I don't have time.'

'I understand you share a flat?'

He nodded. 'Jake Marshall. He's from Bournemouth. We've been sharing for the past three years.'

'How did he take it? The allegations, your being dropped?'

Makinson shrugged. 'He knew I was innocent. He said to hang on in there. It would soon blow over. He was right.'

'What about your parents?'

'They're in Sheffield. It's where I stay when I'm not here, or training and competing abroad.'

'Brothers or sisters?'

'Melanie, my sister. She's training to be a doctor at Bart's in London.'

Caton flipped through his notebook as though checking facts. In reality there was no need; he knew the questions he had planned by heart. But it served to emphasise the gravity of the situation.

'I'd like you to confirm where you were on the following dates. Yesterday evening between seven p.m. and eight thirty p.m.?'

Makinson looked surprised. As though it was a pointless question. The sort of reaction an innocent man might have. Or a practised liar.

'I was in the flat watching a training video. I was in bed for nine o'clock. Always am when I'm training.'

'Between eleven p.m. last Monday evening, and twelve thirty a.m. on Tuesday morning?'

'Asleep in bed.'

'In the flat?'

'Yes.'

'Can Mr Marshall vouch for that?'

For the first time he looked uncomfortable.

'No. He's away at a pro-cycling training camp on the Costa Blanca. I only got back myself on Monday morning. On the roads and in the mountains,' he explained. 'Change of scenery, change of routine, lots of stamina and strength work. When I get too old for this I might tackle the Tour De France.'

'So that would be where you were last Friday, and on Sunday evening?' said Caton.

A smile crept across his face. 'I was still in the air late Sunday evening.'

Caton made a note and flipped the notebook closed.

There was little doubt in his mind that Makinson was in the clear, but it would still be necessary to corroborate his story. The CPS would require it, because the defence would seek out and exploit every gap, however insignificant. Those angry reactions he'd mentioned from fans would have to be checked out too.

'Can you let me have the details?' he said. 'And I'll need your Twitter and Facebook account information.'

Makinson picked up his helmet and got to his feet.

'Is that it?' he said.

'Actually no, it isn't,' said Caton.

He ignored the cyclist's exaggerated intake of breath and waited for him to sit down again.

'I'd appreciate it, Mr Makinson,' he said, 'if you would let me know in advance if you intend to leave the city over the next few days.'

Then he stood up.

'Thank you for your time,' he said. And good luck with the training.'

Caton smiled to himself as walked down the steps that led from the central zone, under the track, to the reception area. He knew it had been petty, forcing him to sit down again. It was more the way Gordon Holmes might have behaved. But he had to admit, it did feel good. Sometimes in an investigation you needed small victories. Sometimes it was all you had to keep you going.

Chapter 34

Marguerite Amroush lived alone. The house was a red-brick terrace with a tiny front garden, where Rusholme met Longsight; it was familiar territory for Caton. Three streets away was Longsight police station, whose Major Incident Room had been home to him and his team for five hectic years. As he alarmed the door of his Octavia he noticed the net curtains twitch in the front room of the house. The door opened before he had a chance to knock.

A woman in her late thirties stood in the doorway. She was tall and slim. The first thing he noticed about her was her hair. The colour of jet, it was thick, long and silky. Her eyes were the kind that poets talked of drowning in. Almond-shaped, with rich chocolate-brown centres. Her nose was pronounced, her lips full and unadorned. She wore a sleeveless white shift dress that emphasised her olive skin. He would have described her as beautiful but for one thing. Those eyes that should have radiated warmth and life, were weary, soulless, beyond despair.

'Mr Caton?' she said. 'Come in.'

He followed her into a large open-plan space with stairs directly in front of him. The dividing wall between the hall and the front room of the house had been removed, as had the wall between the front and rear rooms. At the far end he could see the kitchen and a breakfast table, and beyond it a half-flagged garden.

Marguerite Amroush walked to the centre of the room and turned. Her back was towards the fireplace. Despite her height, this room seemed to dwarf her. She gestured towards the sofa.

'Please sit down. As I promised, the kettle has boiled. Would you like tea or coffee? Or I have green tea?'

'Green tea would be perfect,' he told her.

She was less than a minute, during which time he went over the questions he intended to ask. Others would present themselves, they always did, but bitter experience had taught him that it was essential to be prepared. It was something they had drummed into him at the very first session at Bruche, the then North West police training school.

'Here you are, Mr Caton.'

She placed the tray on a nest of tables next to the sofa. Beside the cup and saucer was a plate with four plain Digestive biscuits.

'I'm sorry I don't have any other biscuits to offer you,' she said. 'When you're buying for one…'

He understood. It was how he had been in the decade and a half before he met Kate. Meals for one. The same packets of biscuits. The same packet of cereal. The shop assistant at Tesco Express could have had it packed and waiting for him every Saturday morning.

'This is fine,' he reassured her.

She went to pick up her cup and saucer from the kitchen, and sat in an armchair diagonally opposite him.

'Thank you for seeing me at such short notice, Mrs Amroush,' he began. 'Is it alright to call you Mrs Amroush?'

'Everyone does,' she replied. 'Not that I've ever been married. I never corrected them.' She looked directly at him. 'For the sake of my daughter, you understand?'

'Of course.'

She blew gently across the surface of her tea and sipped it noiselessly.

'I'm here regarding a number of unexplained deaths that we are investigating,' he said.

She looked at him across the rim of her cup.

'The ones on the television, and in the papers?'

'Yes.'

She nodded. 'I thought so.' She took another sip.

Caton could tell that she was thinking. That she hadn't finished. He waited.

'These deaths. Were they the ones that targeted Ayesha?' she said.

'We believe so.'

'And now someone has targeted them?'

'That appears to be the case.'

He had no idea why he was using the standard political response when a simple yes would have sufficed. Habit probably. This woman deserved better. He waited for her to tell him that she was glad. That they deserved it. But she simply sighed and took another sip.

'I thought you would want to hear it from me,' he said.

She looked up. 'Of course, thank you.' Her eyes searched his face. 'And,' she said, 'to find out if I had anything to do with their deaths.'

He was tempted to deny it vigorously. To tell her that it was obvious that she was not the kind of person who would do such a thing. His training had taught him otherwise. It required him to keep an open mind.

'Well, I didn't,' she replied. 'And I don't know who did.'

She kept eye contact, willing him to see the truth in

hers. It proved impossible. There were none of the telltale flickers of emotion there. If it was true that the eyes were the windows to the soul – and in Caton's experience that was often but not always true – then her soul was atrophied. Wasted away by grief.

'I believe you,' he said.

To hell with the manual. He didn't believe that she had the emotional strength to do what had been done, or to commission it.

'Thank you,' she replied. She put her cup and saucer down. 'Would you like to see Ayesha's room?'

Instinct and experience told him that it would be a shrine. Scarcely touched since the day the girl died. Tidied of course. Cuddly toys lined up on the pillows. Photo frames on the dressing table and the window sill. Her favourite dress on a hanger over the wardrobe door. He had studied the file before he set out. He knew how Ayesha had died. Three times the lethal dose of Ecstasy, washed down with half a bottle of vodka. It must have been a terrible death. Not at all what she must have expected. She was unconscious but still alive when her mother found her. They gave her shots of adrenaline, administered CPR and rushed her straight to St Mary's less than a mile away. She was dead on arrival. There was nothing to be gained from taking her mother through that all over again.

'That won't be necessary,' he said. 'But I would like to ask you a few more questions.'

She placed her cup on the tray, stood up and walked over to the window. She looked out through the net curtains with vacant eyes. Then she turned to look at him, her face in shadow.

'Go ahead,' she said.

'Ayesha's father. When did you last have contact with him?'

'He left when Ayesha was three years old. That was

fourteen years ago. I have not seen or heard from him since.'

'Were you working at the time?'

'No, Mr Caton. Call me old fashioned, but I wanted to give my time to Ayesha, at least until she started primary school.'

'So you would have had to claim additional benefits?'

'Yes.'

'Didn't the Child Support Agency try to track him down?'

He sensed that she was smiling.

'They found him almost immediately, in Salford. But he denied parentage, even though his name was on the birth certificate.'

'What did they do about that?'

'They told him they would presume parentage and require him to pay maintenance, or he could take a DNA test.'

'And?'

'He disappeared again. This time they couldn't find him.'

'He didn't come to the funeral?'

'No.'

'Or send a card or flowers?

She came and sat down on the chair again.

'Perhaps he's dead. I hope he is.'

It was said without bitterness.

'Because of how he treated you?'

She shook her head. 'No. So that he doesn't have to suffer the way that I am suffering.'

Caton still needed to find the father. There could be no loose ends. But if the father hadn't accepted his responsibility, why would he feel the need to avenge his daughter's death? Or was that it? Because he'd denied that he was her father, had he felt that much more guilt? It didn't seem likely. To have showed no interest in her at all for the first fifteen years of her life, and to then experience sufficient guilt and remorse to want to kill, again and again.

'What is Ayesha's father's name?' he said.

She covered her mouth with her right hand. It was an instinctive action. As though it would shield her from having to say the words.

'Please, Mrs Amroush,' he said. 'I can always ask the CSA.'

He was unable to decipher her reply, muffled as it was.

'I'm sorry?' he said. 'I didn't catch that.'

Reluctantly she removed her hand and cradled it with the other.

'Ricky Rainhill.'

This time she spat it out.

'Was that *Richard* Rainhill?' he asked.

'No. Ricky. He said that's what it said on his birth certificate. He used to tell everyone his father was a Rick Nelson fan.'

Caton vaguely remembered the TV reports of the singer's death in a plane crash north of Dallas, when he himself was in his teens. If it was true that was Ayesha's father's given name, it should have been relatively easy for the CSA to track him down. There can't have been too many Ricky Rainhills with a National Insurance Number, National Health Service Number and driving licence. This can only have meant that he had dropped out of sight. Possibly changed his name. Or moved abroad. Worst-case scenario, she was right. He was dead, and his body had not yet been found.

'I'll also need a list of the names of all of her friends and relatives,' he said.

'When Ayesha died she didn't have any friends.'

He had read some of the vile and abusive posts the trolls had made in her name. He was not surprised that her fellow students had turned against her. Only that when she had protested her innocence, her friends had been unable to provide the support that might have saved her. But then teenage girls were fragile beings. Hypersensitive to criticism and social exclusion. It was what made bullying pernicious and dangerous. In this case, lethal.

'I understand,' he said. 'But before those wicked posts appeared she must have had some friends? Good friends?'

'She did. They came to the funeral service. They were full of kind words and remorse. I nearly told them it was too late for that. But I couldn't, Mr Caton. I couldn't. Ayesha wouldn't have wanted that.'

'You'll let me have their names?'

'I can, but I'll need to check on some of them before I do.'

'And your relatives?'

'I don't have any. My parents are dead. I have no brothers and sisters. My mother's family live in Algeria. We never communicate, never see each other. It's complicated.'

Algeria. He was aware that blood feuds were not uncommon in the Middle East and Africa. He couldn't simply take her word for it.

'Nevertheless, I would appreciate the details. Including their addresses, if you have them.'

She nodded.

He handed her a card with his office number and an email address for the Major Incident Room.

'Can you email them to me today, as soon as possible?'

She took the card, studied it for a moment and placed it on the nest of tables.

'Of course,' she said.

She stood up and walked ahead of him to the front door. She opened it and stood aside to let him pass. He turned on the doorstep.

'Thank you, Mrs Amroush,' he said.

'Thank you, Mr Caton,' she replied.

'There's nothing to thank me for,' he said, surprised that she would think so.

'For not patronising me,' she said. 'For not talking about closure.'

There was nothing he could say to that. He nodded once, turned and walked to the gate.

'You see,' she called after him, 'there isn't any closure. There never will be.'

Chapter 35

While he waited for the list to come through, Caton went straight to the Regional Cyber Crimes Unit. Jenny Soames had texted to say that she had some news for him. Before he had time to knock, the door swung open. A young woman, facing into the room, was in the process of leaving. He had to step backwards and put out an arm to avoid her bumping into him. She froze at the contact, turned and then stepped back into the room.

'I'm sorry,' she said. 'I didn't see you there.'

'You'd have to have eyes in the back of your head,' said Caton, smiling.

Of mixed ethnicity, possible white African-Caribbean, she was head and shoulders taller than DS Soames. Slimmer, but with an athletic build. She wore a black sweat-wicking jersey tracksuit and matching black Adidas trainers; the serious kind.

'This is DCI Caton,' said Jenny Soames. 'Tom, this is Corrie Hoyland. She's been helping us out. One of those private consultants I told you about.'

The woman's hands remained firmly by her side. Her face was oval, and her jet-black hair had been layer cut to just below her eyes to accentuate the shape. He thought he detected a flash of recognition in them.

'Have we met?' he asked.

'No,' she replied, 'I don't think so.'

Her voice was mellow Mancunian.

'She probably saw you on tele,' joked Jenny Soames. 'You've been on a lot lately.'

Corrie Hoyland turned to face her.

'Let me know how it goes.'

'You bet. And I'll holler if I need you.'

Caton stepped back into the corridor.

'Nice to have met you,' he said.

She smiled politely as she passed. 'You too.'

Caton entered the office and closed the door behind him.

'Helping with my investigation?' he said.

Soames shook her head. 'No. Something unrelated.'

It was clear that she didn't want to elaborate. He wasn't bothered. It was none of his business. He was grateful that she had cut corners to help him.

'You said you had some news for me?' he said, sitting down in the chair he had occupied before.

'I have. Although I hope I haven't raised your hopes too high. I'm not sure that it's a breakthrough, but it is something you need to know about.'

'Fair enough.'

'Lee Bottomley, your first victim. He was into child pornography as well as trolling?'

He nodded. 'You referred it to the Child Exploitation and Online Protection Unit to look into.'

'Well, they got back to me. It seems he was part of a wide network. One that wasn't on their radar. Thanks to you, it is now.'

Caton's heart sank. It was something he had feared. Another potential raft of suspects. In a murky world where identities were obsessively guarded. It was a complication for which he hadn't time. But it was one he couldn't afford to ignore.

'How wide is this network?'

She swivelled back to her desk and clicked on an icon.

'Very.'

A map of the world appeared on the screen. The continents were outlined by bold blue lines. Thinner lines marked individual countries. Within a score of countries black dots were pulsing.

'These are the ones they've isolated so far,' she said. 'This one was Bottomley.'

She moved the mouse over one of four dots in Greater Manchester. Immediately a series of curved lines appeared, linking the dot with a dozen others, across four continents.

'Those are the contacts they know he made with other members of this network.'

She moved the mouse to the bottom of the map and clicked a small icon in the shape of a spider's web. Instantly all of the dots were joined by lines that criss-crossed the globe. Some of the dots had multiple contacts and appeared as hubs. Others had just a few contacts. She moved her mouse around the screen, hovering over some of the dots.

'These are major players,' she said. 'The glue that holds the network together. Initiators, early adopters. These other ones are outliers, satellites if you like. Bottomley was somewhere in between.'

'What kind of child exploitation porn are we talking about?' he said.

She grimaced. 'The usual, if there is such a thing. Photographs, videos. Some of them of children posing, or more accurately posed, naked. Others of sexual acts. Man on boy, boy on man, boy on boy.'

She turned to look at him.

'You don't need the details, do you?'

'No.'

'Good, because just having to say them makes my skin crawl.'

For Caton's part it never failed to provoke feelings of anger far greater than any that he felt where murder was involved. Rape and child abuse were the two crimes that had that effect. Probably because they preyed on a particular form of vulnerability, robbed the victims of their innocence and self-esteem, and left them to bear the consequences for the remainder of their lives.

'Was Bottomley involved in posting images himself?'

She shook her head. 'No. It was the first thing they looked for, knowing the reason for your interest. He was a voyeur, plain and simple.'

Neither plain nor simple, Caton reflected. But at least it eliminated one particular motive.

'But he did forward images that others had uploaded,' she said, pulling the rug from under his feet.

That might explain Bottomley's murder, but he couldn't see the connection with the other three.

'Can you ask CEOPS to let me have the identities of the others that Bottomley had contact with?' he said. 'Starting with those other three in Greater Manchester?'

'Of course. But don't pin your hopes on them being able to identify the kids whose images he forwarded. That could take months, years; sometimes they never find out who they were. Poor little things.'

Chapter 36

As soon as Caton entered the Incident Room, Ged came to meet him.

'There's a message from DS Carter,' she told him. 'He hasn't any leads so far, but he has a list of names he's going to interview. It'll mean him staying down there overnight at the very least. There's a copy of the message on your desk.'

'I'll need a copy of that list of names too,' he said.

'He's emailed that directly to you.'

'DS Stuart was compiling a list too, from Gemma Ravene's parents.'

'She's done that. That's also on your desk.'

'Good,' he said. 'Mrs Amroush is supposed to be emailing hers anytime now. I want you to create a single file for them. I'm going to try and have them all fingerprinted, and DNA tested.'

She tried to disguise her surprise, but there was no fooling him.

'I know,' he said. 'Getting the Fourth Floor to agree is going to be a challenge, but I don't think I have a choice; and neither do they.'

He made to move away, but she stepped closer and lowered her voice.

'They're already expecting you up there,' she whispered. 'Before you talk to them, you'd better have a look at today's first edition of the MEN. There's a copy on your desk.'

Caton swore. It didn't matter who heard; everyone in the office must have seen it by now. This explained the lack of eye contact when he came in. It was the second time it had happened in the space of a week. He read it with mounting astonishment, and anger.

Keyboard Killers Got it Wrong! By Larry Hymer.
Manchester student Imran Coreishi, whose mutilated body was discovered in the early hours of Tuesday morning in the Hulme house he shared with three other students, was killed in error. I can reveal that the police believe the real target of the killers was a fellow male student living in the house, who had been using Mr Coreishi's computer without his knowledge, and who returned to find him murdered.

Gripping the paper, he stormed out of the room.

Helen Gates was out. Unfortunately, Martin Hadfield was in.

'Calm down, Caton,' he said. 'I believe you. There is no way you would have been so stupid as to leak this to the press. But someone did.'

'I haven't got time for an internal investigation,' said Caton.

'No, but Professional Standards Branch have,' the Assistant Chief Constable replied.

'And do you think having them crawl all over my investigation is going to help me catch these killers?'

'*Sir*,' said Hadfield pointedly.

'And do you think having them crawl all over my investigation is going to help me catch these killers, *sir*?' Caton replied.

The two of them had been standing face-to-face across the desk like a pair of rutting stags. Hadfield sat down and folded his arms.

'Not getting to the bottom of this,' he said, 'could jeopardise your entire investigation. It could undermine whatever case you end up taking to the CPS. It could even finish your career. Do you want to risk that?'

Caton took a couple of deep breaths. Hadfield loved a confrontation, especially when he outranked his opponent. Being sucked into his power play was a waste of time and energy.

'At this moment,' he said, 'my primary concern is to prevent another murder. This article leads the killers straight to Adam Davis.'

Hadfield steepled his fingers.

'I thought there were two male students in that house aside from the victim?'

'There were. But only one of them was there when the body was found. Larry Hymer named that student at the time.'

Caton waited. The cogs in Hadfield's brain were turning more slowly since his promotion.

'So all the killers have to do is check the papers?'

'All they have to do is go online.'

Hadfield thought about the implications.

'He's not our responsibility,' he said. 'I don't want any resources tied up on this. Tell him to keep his head down and watch his back.'

It was a stupid thing to say. More so given the way the victims had died. Beaten over the head, from behind.

'And I know what you're thinking,' the ACC continued. 'I don't want you using this Davis as bait. The Chief Constable is getting enough grief over your investigation from the media and the Police and Crime Commissioner. The Chief won't be able to keep her away from you much longer.'

Caton wasn't worried about that. Charlotte Mason, the new PCC, was intelligent and streetwise. Nothing like her short-lived predecessor, Charles Grey. If anything, he was prepared to bet that she would be willing to support his strategy first, and worry about the political fallout later.

'I'd be happy to meet with her, if that would help?' he said.

It was obvious that Hadfield shared his opinion of her. There were telltale traces of that familiar purple flush as he sat upright, unfolded his arms and placed his hands a little too heavily on the desk.

'That won't be necessary,' he said. 'And don't even think of contacting her behind our backs.'

Caton smiled disarmingly. 'I wouldn't dream of it, sir,' he said.

'Is that it?' said Hadfield, pushing back his chair and standing up.

It wasn't. There was still the little of matter of all those fingerprint and DNA tests. There was no way Caton was going to run that by him. Better to wait until Detective Chief Superintendent Gates was free. Helen would moan about the cost and the flack, but in the end she would agree.

The first thing Caton did on leaving Hadfield's office was ring Adam Davis on the new mobile number he had provided as a condition of his bail.

'Have you seen today's Manchester Evening News?' he asked.

'No, why?' the student replied.

Caton told him.

'Shit!' said Davis.

He'd made the connection a damn sight faster than Hadfield, but then he had more at stake.

'I'm sorry, Adam,' said Caton. 'I have no idea how this got out. I'm afraid you are going to have to keep a low profile until we catch them.'

His reaction took Caton completely by surprise.

'No sweat,' he said.

'Adam,' said Caton, 'you do understand what this means?'

'Of course I do. But it isn't going to be a problem. I've been sent down from uni. So I'm shortly going to stay with some friends in Australia, until it all blows over.'

'Where are you at the moment?' Caton asked.

'When?'

'Right now.'

'I'm in The Sally. That's the…'

'Salutation,' said Caton. 'On Higher Chatham Street.'

'That's right.' He sounded surprised.

'Well stay there. I'll be with you in about ten minutes.'

'Why?'

'If you're not there when I arrive, I'll find you and break your legs,' said Caton. 'And before you ask, this call is not being recorded for training purposes.'

He knew it was entirely out of character. Something Gordon Holmes might have said, not him. But he felt as though it was all getting away from him. There were too many expectations and interventions over which he had no control. Hadfield, Gates, Hyman, Harry's mother Helen, and even Kate. Nothing made him angrier than feeling powerless. He stomped out of the building and out to the car park.

Under other circumstances he would have looked forward to a visit to The Salutation Hotel and Pub. In his time at the university it had been one of a handful of virtually untouched Victorian pubs. Sitting in the middle of a wasteland created by the demolition of three blocks of terraced houses, it had been the favoured retreat of students, lecturers and teachers from the local high schools. No doubt it's gone the way of all the others, he told himself. A poncey glass and stainless steel wine bar, with sports screens everywhere. He gripped the wheel tighter and switched on Manchester Radio. Just to hear a friendly voice. Becky Want was introducing a song from the soundtrack of the film *Anna and the King*.

'Tweet me,' she said, 'if this isn't the most relaxing music that you have ever heard.'

Gentle chords of piano and violin began to wash over him. Asian pipes provided a haunting counterpoint. The tension leached from his neck and shoulders. He relaxed his fingers and began to breathe slowly and rhythmically.

As he turned into Cambridge Street, the music ended.

'Wasn't that beautiful?' said Becky. 'Who'd have thought that track is called The Execution. It was used for the scene in which Lady Tuptim, the king's favourite concubine, and her lover Balat, are beheaded in front of the entire court. Ironic or what?'

From the outside, The Salutation Hotel and Pub was just as he remembered it. Solidly square, and confident. The ground-floor Victorian windows nestled by golden sandstone, those on the upper storey by red brick. Black picnic tables stood behind a wooden fence where the barbecues and music gigs were held. He had heard that the Manchester Metropolitan University had bought it. He hoped they hadn't messed with it.

They hadn't. Rich-red leather Chesterfield seating complemented the original patterned quarry tiled floor. There was the long black-ebony bar topped with mahogany, and the beer glass rack suspended on polished brass columns. The old bookcase crammed with books, the wooden plate racks, framed photographs, the ancient wall clock with the brass surround and gas-style lamps suspended from the ceiling. All still here. But not Adam Davis.

He walked through into the games room. There were two young women playing darts, and a third lining up a shot on the pool table, watched by a pair of young men. As he turned to go, the toilet door opened and Adam Davis emerged. Caton gestured to Davis to follow him. He led the way out of the pub to his car, where he held open the front passenger door.

'Get in,' he said.

Davis did so without a word. Caton sat in the driver's seat and locked the doors.

'You're not going anywhere,' he said.

'But…' the student began to protest.

'You're on bail. One of the conditions of which is that you don't leave the area, let alone the country. Now I'm going to have to ask you for your passport.'

His face fell.

'It's at my parents' house.'

'No problem. I'll arrange for a neighbourhood police officer to pick it up.'

'But I didn't do anything.'

'You committed several criminal offences, Adam, and withheld evidence.'

'I came in to see you of my own volition.'

You can always tell a university student, Caton reflected. Intelligent enough to choose the best word, but lacking the common sense needed to think about the possible consequences of a stupid action.

'Eventually,' he said. 'When you realised that forensics would place you all over that computer keyboard.'

'It wasn't like that.'

'I don't care,' Caton told him. 'Break your bail, and I'll have you in front of a judge and locked up on remand before you know what day it is.'

The young man's face paled. His confidence had evaporated. He looked almost as pathetic as he had done the first time Caton saw him, in the kitchen of that house in Hulme.

'But I can't stay here,' he protested weakly. 'Not after what that reporter's done.'

'What do you mean, here?' said Caton. 'I thought you were staying at your girlfriend's house in Bolton?'

He turned his head to avoid Caton's eyes and stared out of the window.

'She isn't my girlfriend. Not any more.'

Caton wasn't surprised. Not after what he'd done.

'So where are you staying?'

'I'm squatting with a mate who's on my course.' He pulled a face. '*Was* on my course.'

'Where?'

'Weston Hall. It's a student Hall on Charles Street.'

'By the original Manchester Conference Centre and Days Hotel?'

He nodded his head.

Caton tried to picture it in his mind. It was a busy area at the heart the city centre university complex, with UMIST, MMU and Man Uni buildings in close proximity, as well as the Conference Centre. There would be people coming and going at all hours. That had its pluses and minuses. More witnesses, but easier to blend in. Less likely to be noticed. There was also the Mancunian Way and the A34 to factor in. Fast exit routes on the doorstep.

'Who else knows that's where you're staying?' he asked.

Puzzled by the question, Davis turned to look at him.

'Nobody. Apart for the other seven in the flat.'

'Seven?'

'It's a flat with shared facilities,' he explained.

'Eight en suite single study bedrooms, shared lounge, kitchen and dining areas.'

That's better, thought Caton, there's safety in numbers. It also helped him to decide. He didn't care what Hadfield had said, he was going to watch this young man's back. If it led to the killers, so much the better. And there was no telling how much they might know about him. If he went to stay with his parents, that might make him even more vulnerable.

'In my view you'll be as safe there as anywhere,' Caton told him. 'What's more, providing you do exactly as you're told, I'll be looking out for you. Have you got your mobile phone with you?'

He reached into his pocket and pulled out a smartphone, much flashier than Caton's.

'I assume it has GPS?'

'It has everything. Just like my other one. Haven't you finished with it yet?'

'It's evidence. You'll get it back, eventually.'

Caton inserted his key and started the engine.

'Where are you taking me?' said the student nervously.

'To Central Park,' he replied. 'Don't worry, you're not under arrest.'

Chapter 37

Douggie Wallace plugged Adam Davis' mobile into a USB socket on his computer, pulled up the location-based Web service on his PC and downloaded the software to the phone.

'Here you go,' he said, handing the phone back.

'Keep it on your person at all times,' Caton told him. 'And we can use our PCs, tablets and Wi-Fi enabled phones to track you. We'll know exactly where you are, how fast you're travelling, even your altitude. Useful if you happen to be in an apartment block.'

'This is how parents track their kids,' the student complained.

'Would you prefer an electronic tag?'

From the look on his face it was evident that he wouldn't.

'We won't be tracking you on a continuous basis,' said Caton. 'Just at half-hourly intervals. But if you leave the city, the software will alert us with a text message. So don't.'

All this talk of messages and tracking gave him an idea.

'Did any of you on this *flammatory.com* website share your email addresses with each other?'

'Some of us,' Adam Davis replied.

'And you didn't think to share this with me before now?'

'It didn't occur to me. Anyway, we used a cipher for the personal stuff.'

'You encrypted it using an algorithm?' said Wallace.

'That's right.'

'Have you any idea how much time we'd have saved if you'd given us that key?'

'Sorry.'

He didn't look exactly crestfallen. Caton suspected that he had been trying not to incriminate himself any more than he had to.

'Give it to him now,' he said.

Wallace watched like a hawk as the student typed in several lines of code.

To Caton it was gibberish, which he supposed was the whole point. He understood the principle, but neither the practice nor the theory.

'So,' he said when Davis had finished, 'anyone who was a member of your little network would have access to that key and could decipher your personal information, like email addresses?'

'Only if we decided it was okay to give it to them.' He sounded affronted that he might have been considered careless.

'And how did you decide that it was okay?'

He had to think about that.

'Well, if they'd joined in. Entered into the spirit of things. Made enough posts.'

'Incriminated themselves,' said Caton.

'If you want to put it that way.'

'And who did you share your email address with?'

'On *flammatory.com*?'

'Yes.'

'There were only two people. But I didn't give them my real name, none of us did. One of them I knew as *archangelgabriel7thheaven* and another who signed himself *herbert#wally*.'

'Miles-Cowper,' said Wallace. 'The archangel one we've plotted in Los Angeles.'

'Why only two, Adam?' asked Caton.

He shrugged. 'Because they were the only ones who asked. Apart from a loony in Lebanon I wouldn't have trusted with my hamster.'

'You've got a hamster?'

He looked embarrassed. 'Not now, when I was a kid.'

Caton found it interesting that with everything Davis had done, and the tragedy his stupidity had triggered, he still didn't place himself in the same league as the troll from Lebanon. He turned his attention to Douggie Wallace.

'Check Miles-Cowper's mailbox,' he said. 'I need a list, and details of any emails from any *flammatory.com* users.'

Half an hour later, Adam Davis had gone. DS Carter had dropped him off on Charles Street and watched as he entered Weston Hall, before returning. Caton was at his desk when Douggie Wallace came to tell him the list was ready.

It was obvious that Spencer Miles-Cowper was something of a maven. A people collector. It was no surprise because he'd been one of the ones who had appeared as a hub in the *flammatory* network. Among the many email addresses he had collected were those of all of the victims, and a number of the other trolls dotted around the world.

'If you exclude the victims, how many are you left with?' Caton asked.

'About forty.'

'Are you able to check with their Web hosts and domain registrars?'

The crime analyst sat back in his seat.

'They won't give details without a warrant. Have we got due cause for a mass sweep like that?'

'Not yet,' Caton admitted.

Wallace smiled. 'Then we do what the perpetrators probably did with your victims' email addresses. We use Reverse email finder.'

'How long will that take?'

'Less than a minute per email address.'

Caton looked at the list of addresses.

'Can you find out where these emails were sent from, as well as who sent them?'

'That's the easy part. I'll show you.'

He selected one of Miles-Cowper's emails, right clicked on the address and homed in on the *Received from* section. Then he copied the permitted sender details; three pairs of numbers followed by one group of three numbers, each separated by a dot. Then he opened a website on his menu bar that included a Google outline map of the world.

'This is what's called a trace route tool,' he said.

He pasted the numbers into the search box and clicked *Host Trace*. Twenty seconds later, a series of linked bold lines appeared on the map. The first linked California to New York; the second New York to Paris; the third Paris to London; the fourth London to Walsall; the fifth Walsall to Preston; and the sixth Preston to Manchester.

'There you go,' he said. 'California is where the host is for his email address. The final one, Manchester, is the sender's location; in this case, your victim Miles-Cowper. All of the others are intermediaries.'

'Can you pin it down to an actual address?' Caton asked.

'No. But that's where the Reverse email finder

comes in. If the sender uses any social networks or other public sources, there's a good chance we can trace them. I'll show you.'

He exited the trace route website and selected another site where he was given the opportunity to search by name, email, phone, username or address. Into this one he pasted the email address Miles-Cowper had been using, and clicked *Search*. Fifteen seconds later, a screen appeared. *Match Found*.

Caton leaned forward in amazement. There was a photograph of Spencer Miles-Cowper, accompanied by the following information: *Gender Male; Number of Online Profiles 6; Shopping Sites 3.* The user was invited to pay just five dollars ninety-five cents to register and receive a detailed summary including his full name and presence, age and date of birth, other email addresses, photos, social network pages, blogs, family members, neighbourhood details, and spouse or partner, if any.

'So much for data protection,' he said.

'If you freely engage with any social network, or register with any website or agency, privacy flies out of the window,' Wallace told him. 'You can limit how much gets sucked up and spewed out, but you can't stop it all. Would you like to see your profile?'

'No, I wouldn't!' he exclaimed.

'I check mine regularly. Best to know what others know about you in my view. And if you think about it, it's not much different from having your name and address in the telephone directory.'

Caton didn't agree. This felt far more invasive. But then it was the price you paid for being a social animal in the twenty-first century. More to the point, at this moment in time it was a gift for Operation Janus.

'Right,' he said, 'I want you to use that trace route tool to find the senders' locations. Then focus on any that are definitely UK-based, and use the Reverse email finder to get their details. Let me know as soon as you've got them. I'll be at my desk.'

He had barely sat down when Gordon Holmes appeared.

'Boss,' he said. 'Bookham's here.'

'Why are you whispering?' said Caton.

His deputy looked flustered.

'Because I didn't think you'd want it broadcast.'

Caton gestured to the only other seat in his cubicle and waited for Holmes to sit down.

'Look, Gordon,' he said, 'DCI Bookham has been seconded in because we're investigating four murders, and we are short-handed. Not because we're floundering.'

Holmes raised both eyebrows. 'Is that what Hadfield told you?'

'*Mr* Hadfield. And it doesn't matter what he thinks, it's what I think that counts. Okay?'

Holmes rubbed his chin. 'Okay.'

He didn't sound convinced, but it didn't matter. Just so long as he was onside.

'I'm the senior investigating officer, and you're still my deputy. Has DCI Bookham given you any reason to think otherwise?'

'No, I haven't,' came the reply, before Holmes had time to open his mouth.

Caton stood and held out his hand as DCI Bookham appeared from behind the screen. At six foot two and fourteen stone, they should have seen the most senior black officer on the force coming.

'Ambrose,' Caton said. 'It's good to have you on board.'

The detective smiled broadly and shook his hand firmly.

'So I gather. It's good to see you, Tom.'

Gordon Holmes stood and offered his seat.

'No thanks, Gordon,' he said amicably. 'You stay there. Your office manager is fixing me up with a desk.' He turned to Caton. 'She gave me this to give you, Tom.'

It was a list of names. Some of them with addresses.

'Something about a Mrs Amroush?'

'The mother of one of the victims,' Caton told him. 'These are her daughter's friends and family.'

He glanced at it and then handed it to his deputy.

'We'll need to interview as many of these as we can, Gordon,' he said. 'Starting with those who live in Manchester, and who were closest to her. And ask Ged to put a copy on my desk.'

'Will do,' said Holmes.

Ambrose stepped aside so that he could squeeze past.

'Sit down, Ambrose,' said Caton. 'I'll bring you up to speed.'

The two of them were standing by the progress boards when Douggie Wallace came to tell Caton he was ready.

'Ambrose,' said Caton, 'this is Douggie Wallace, our Crime Analyst and Intelligence Officer. He also does the digital collation. Douggie, this is DCI Bookham.'

They exchanged nods.

'All done, sir,' said Wallace.

It wasn't like Douggie to show emotion, but Caton sensed a distinct air of excitement in his voice.

They gathered around his desk.

'I managed to get all of the senders' locations,' he told them. 'But when it came to details, some of them were distinctly thin. Most importantly, those in Greater Manchester were pretty full-on. I wouldn't have too much trouble stealing their identities. Not that I'd dream of it.'

He was really warming to his subject. Parading his talent for the new DCI.

'Get on with it, Douggie,' he said.

Chastened, Wallace sat down and pulled up a screen with a list of email addresses.

'I'll let you have the details for all of them, sir,' he said. 'But one stood out straight away, even before I'd begun the search. I'll show you why.'

He clicked on a file, and a landscape table appeared. Down the left-hand side were all of the email addresses. Columns to their right were headed with dates for the past two months. Ticks indicated on which days individual email addresses had sent emails to Spencer Miles-Cowper, or received them from him. Caton immediately spotted what had attracted his attention.

'This one,' said Caton. 'Calling himself *Mithril666*?'

'Herself,' said Wallace. 'Mithril is a female troll. From RuneScape.'

Caton shook his head. 'You've lost me.'

'The World of WarCraft? Mithril is a metal, dark blue in colour. Stronger than black.'

'You have hidden depths,' said DCI Bookham.

Wallace grinned. 'It's a hobby.'

'Why this one?' said Bookham.

'There are,' Caton told him, 'no emails from that address until a month before Miles-Cowper was murdered, and they ceased just six days before he died. Almost as though she knew he was about to die.'

'If it *was* a she,' said Bookham.

'It is,' said Wallace.

He quickly minimised the table and exposed the original list of email addresses. His cursor hovered over *Mithril666*. He paused theatrically, and then left clicked.

Caton stared in amazement. He didn't need to read the name. The photograph was good enough.

Chapter 38

'Get me Mrs Amroush on the phone,' he said.

While he waited for Ged to put her through, he looked at the list of names Gordon had placed on his desk. Since the cursory glance he had given it first time around something had been nagging his brain. Now that he'd seen the photograph, he knew what it was.

'Mrs Amroush for you, sir,' said Ged.

He picked up.

'Mrs Amroush,' he said. 'I'm sorry to bother you, but this is really important. On the list of names you sent me there is one I'd like to know a little more about.'

'Which one?' She sounded as weary as he remembered.

'All you've written is Corrie.'

'That's right,' she said. 'Corrie, as in Coronation Street. That's how I remembered it.'

'Who is this Corrie, Mrs Amroush?'

She seemed to hesitate.

'I have no idea.'

'How did you come by this name?'

'Once or twice,' she said, 'I'd hear Ayesha talking on her mobile phone. When I asked her who it was, she'd say Corrie.'

'Did you ask who this Corrie was?'

'Yes, I did.'

'And what did she reply?'

'"Just a friend, Mum." That's what she'd say. "She's just a friend."'

'How long had Ayesha known this Corrie, Mrs Amroush?'

'I don't know. A while. It was last spring I think I first heard them talking.'

'She never brought her back to the house?'

'No.'

'Did she ever tell you that she was going to meet her?'

'I really don't recall, Mr Caton.'

It was obvious that she was tiring of the conversation.

'Who did you think this Corrie was, Mrs Amroush?'

'A school friend, I suppose. I don't know.'

'Just one last question,' he said. 'Have you ever heard the name Hoyland?'

'No.'

'Your daughter never mentioned anyone of that name?'

'No. I'm sorry, Mr Caton.'

He heard her sigh.

'I haven't been much use, have I?' she said.

'Far from it,' he reassured her. 'There is one last thing, though. One of my officers will be bringing a photograph I would like you to take a look at. I need to know if you've seen this person with your daughter, or her friends. Or at the funeral, perhaps. Can you do that for me?'

'Of course,' she said.

'I promise I'll keep you informed,' he said.

'Thank you, Mr Caton.'

It sounded more like *whatever*.

He wasn't surprised, or offended. Nothing he did

would bring back her daughter. She had been right. There would never be any closure. Neither for her, nor for the rest of the bereaved. Especially the parents. The conclusion of this investigation would remove any ambiguity or uncertainty about why their loved one had died. But that would include their knowing the part their son had played in ruining other people's lives, and causing Ayesha to take her own. On top of their grief and sense of loss would come the burden of guilt, and shame. He knew that Kate would disagree, but he believed that sometimes it was better not to know.

'Corrie Hoyland?' said Jenny Soames as she finished typing something on the screen. 'What about her?'

'Everything,' said Caton. 'What she does. What she's been doing here. Anything she's told you about her private life.'

She pushed her chair back from the desk and gave him her full attention.

'What's this about, Tom?'

'Operation Janus.'

She looked surprised.

'You want to employ her on your investigation?'

'No. She's a suspect.'

Now she looked startled.

'Tell me this is a joke. Please?'

'Sorry,' he said. 'It isn't. So tell me, what does she do, and what has she been helping you with?'

Her face had paled.

'She's an independent computer and mobile phone forensic examiner. She covers virtually everything, but her specialisms are...'

She paused, swivelled round to her computer and brought up Corrie Hyland's professional website. She scrolled down to the relevant section and sat back so that Caton could see. It read:

IT forensic investigation, forensic imaging, data recovery, digital analysis, electronic discovery, indecent image discovery, email discovery, fraud investigation, litigation support, and computer forensic expert witness testimony.

'She's better qualified and more experienced than I am,' Soames told him. 'In a way, I've been using her as a mentor.'

'Did you involve her in anything to do with my investigation?'

'No! Absolutely not. In fact, I haven't seen her since you were last here, so there's no way she could have known how I was helping you.'

Caton wasn't so sure about that. After all, if she was a computer expert perhaps there was a way she could have hacked into Soames' computers.

'I know what you're thinking,' she said, 'and you can forget it. She doesn't have any of our passwords, and she didn't work directly on any of our hardware.'

'So what was she doing here?'

'She was just advising us on new systems and software we could use with regard to corporate fraud. She was Criminal Records Office cleared, and heavily vetted. They found nothing that would prevent her from working with us.'

He could hear her preparing her defence for when the internal investigation began.

'I can't believe she's had access to our work. I'll have to report it. See if anything's been compromised. Christ! This is a disaster.'

'Not necessarily. Most of us separate our professional and private lives. She probably does too.'

'I hope so.'

'Speaking of which, did she give you any clues as to her private life?'

'No.'

'She never spoke of a husband, or a partner?'

'No.'

A slight flush appeared on her neck.

'However?' said Caton.

'Well…' She sounded embarrassed. The red blotches on her neck confirmed it. 'I think she was planning to hit on me.'

'Think?'

'She didn't actually say anything, or do anything. It's hard to put into words. It's just the way she started behaving.'

'For example?'

She shifted uneasily in her chair.

'Well, getting inside my personal space. Leaning over me when I was on the computer so that her hair and her body brushed mine. And there was a change in the tone of her voice. It softened. And she was more relaxed, jokey. And complimentary, about my hairstyle, my clothes. That sort of thing.'

It sounded like full-on flirting to Caton.

'So how did you respond?'

Her hazel eyes locked onto his. He could tell that she was trying to gauge what he expected her reply to be.

'I'm not a lesbian,' she replied. 'Though it's funny how many people assume that I am.'

'I'm not one of those people,' he said. 'I learned a long time ago not to make assumptions, and certainly not to stereotype.'

'I know,' she said. 'Your reputation precedes you. But you'd be surprised how many are, especially in this job. Anyway, her gaydar was way off. I started dropping hints about my husband and three children. She backed off.'

'Backed off?'

'Physically, by putting distance between us. Emotionally, by becoming purely professional again. Not all at once, though. It was a subtle withdrawal.'

'Do you think she was really hitting on you, or was she trying to get close enough to get you to drop your guard? So she could get inside your systems?'

She had to think about it.

'I'm not sure. If it was all an act it was a bloody good one. Are you sure she's involved?'

'I'm certain she is. What I need is proof.'

She shook her chestnut curls as though dispelling a troublesome spirit, and sat bolt upright.

'How can I help you?' she said.

Caton brought her up to speed.

'So what I really need is to have sight of all of her emails, and her mobile phone records if possible.'

Soames smiled. 'That's no problem. Since last summer we no longer need a search warrant. You just need to get the Chief Constable to agree.'

Caton remembered the furore the government's decision had caused from civil liberties groups. Personally he was ambivalent about it. He was uncomfortable with the speed with which the England was becoming a surveillance society and privacy was being eroded, but on the other hand, he recognised the protection it afforded ordinary law-abiding citizens from crime and terrorism.

'I'll go back and get it straight away,' he said.

'It's not going to be easy mind,' she warned him. 'Hoyland's going to have the best anti-virus and anti-hacking software you can get.' She smiled. 'But then she's been showing me how to get round it. How ironic is that?'

Chapter 39

Caton was on his way back to Central Park when his phone rang. He put it on speakerphone. It was Mrs Amroush.

'Mr Caton,' she said. 'After we finished our conversation I decided to give some of Ayesha's school friends a call. They're at college now, but I managed to speak to a few of them.'

She paused to check that he was listening.

'Go on,' he said.

'I asked them if they knew anything about this Corrie person you were asking me about.'

'Yes?'

'Well, one of them said it was someone Ayesha met through a scheme they had at school. To encourage girls to think about going to university.'

'Mrs Amroush,' he said, 'I'm in the car. I'm going to pull over. Can you give me a minute?'

'Of course, Mr Caton.'

He waited until he reached the next bus stop, pulled in and parked up as far from the shelter as possible.

'Thank you,' he said. 'You were saying about a scheme at school?'

'That's right. They were each given a mentor and a work placement. Ayesha was always into computers. Ever since she was a child. She could do anything with them. It was her favourite subject.'

She was beginning to reminisce, to go off at a tangent. He couldn't risk her becoming too emotional to tell him what she knew.

'Ayesha's mentor was called Corrie?' he said.

'Mentor. Yes, that's what Ellie said.'

'Ellie?'

'Ayesha's friend. She said she thought Ayesha had a crush on this Corrie.'

'What made her think that?'

'The way she acted when she was asked about her. The way she always wore her prettiest things when she was going to see her, or was on her work placement.'

'How often was that?'

There was a long pause.

'When she met with her? I'm don't know for certain. Once a fortnight, I think. I am sure that Ayesha's school will be able to tell you.'

'And the work placement?'

'One week last Easter, and two weeks in the summer. I remember, because I used to make up a packed lunch for her.'

'Was there anything else, Mrs Amroush?'

'No, Mr Caton.'

She sounded disappointed. As though she felt she had let him down.

'You have no idea,' he told her, 'how helpful you have been. Thank you very much, Mrs Amroush.'

That last piece of information was enough to convince both Helen Gates and the Chief Constable. Caton gave DS Soames the go-ahead. Fifty minutes later, she came back to him.

'I knew it was going to be difficult,' she said. 'I've been able to track her posts on *flammatory.com*, but she's deleted all of her search history, and all of her emails other than those that were work related.'

'That sounds like something a guilty person would do,' he said.

'Maybe, but it's also good housekeeping practice. I tend to do it myself. Anyway, that's only circumstantial.'

'Are you going to be able to retrieve them?'

'Probably not, except for any she's deleted within the past twenty-four hours. I've sent an urgent request to her email host.'

'What about her mobile phone?'

'I'm working through the most recent calls sent and received, and any associated texts. That's why I've rung you.'

Caton felt a tiny adrenaline rush.

'Go on,' he said.

'There's one number which appears infrequently, but several times on each of the dates you gave me relating to the murders. Most of them must have involved live voice conversations which I can't retrieve, but there were a few that were text messages. All of them short, and looking like arrangements or instructions. There was just such an exchange today.'

'What does it say?'

'Hoyland texted *Still there?* The other number replied *Yes. Not moved.* She replied with one word: *Tonight.* The reply came back: *Tonite?* She replied *Yes!* Then nothing.'

'Who does that other number belong to?' he said.

'Pay-as-you-go. Can't tell you who the owner is, but at least you can put a trace on it. On hers too. Incidentally, she hasn't deleted her contacts on her emails. I've copied it and sent it to Douggie Wallace. I thought maybe if he checked it with the list of the suspects' friends and family, you might strike lucky.'

It took Wallace less than ten minutes to come up with a match.

'Anthony Woodsted,' he said. 'He's down on DS Carter's list as an uncle of Jarmaine Cordell, that lad from Birmingham who was killed by a hit-and-run driver, and then labelled as a drug runner by the trolls.'

'And he's also in Corrie Hoyland's email contacts folder?' said Caton.

Wallace showed him.

'Here you are. It just says Jarmaine. But that's too much of a coincidence, surely? And you'll never guess where he lives. Here in Manchester. Barlow Moor.'

Caton went straight to Carter's desk.

'Have you interviewed Anthony Woodsted yet?' he said.

His DS looked surprised.

'Anthony Woodsted? Oh right, he's one of Cordell's uncles, isn't he? Not yet, boss, why?'

'Why not?'

Caton's tone alerted Carter that there was something seriously amiss. He looked flustered.

'I'm sorry, sir,' he said. 'I just haven't got round to it. I've been busy writing up the interviews I did in Birmingham. Like the DI down there said, there didn't seem to be anything to it. Just a load of mouthing off. And this Woodsted wasn't one of the ones who'd been making threats. I was going to see him and the rest of his family tomorrow.'

'It didn't occur to you their living in Manchester made them more likely to be of interest?'

Some of the other detectives were tuning in. Carter lowered his voice.

'Has something come up, sir?'

Caton didn't believe in showing up members of his team in public.

'Follow me,' he said.

In the relative privacy of his makeshift office he repeated what DS Soames had told him and Douggie Wallace had discovered. He did not need to spell out the implications.

'I'm sorry, sir,' said the detective sergeant. 'I don't know what else to say.'

Caton decided not to press it. Carter was a good DS. One who rarely made mistakes, let alone schoolboy errors like this one. He looked sufficient chastened and embarrassed. It wasn't something he'd forget in a hurry.

'Get over there now,' Caton told him. 'Make it look like it's just part of the routine interviews you've been doing. Talk to other members of the family while you're there, so it looks like he's just one of the many you're seeing.'

'What if he's not there?'

'Do your bit with them, then ask casually if they know where he is. Then get back here as quick as you can.'

Forty minutes later, Carter was back.

'Anthony Woodsted went out early this morning,' he said, 'and he hasn't been home since. I spoke with his mum and dad, his younger brother and two sisters. I was careful not to rouse their suspicions, like you told me. I said it didn't matter about Anthony. I'd catch up with him again.'

'Where did they think he was?' said Caton.

'At college. They said he often doesn't come home till late. Goes round to his mates. Typical nineteen year old. I rang the college. He hasn't been in today. Not only that, his attendance in recent weeks has been rubbish.'

'Well done, Nick,' said Caton. 'Go and join the others.'

Carter grinned and shot off like a Labrador puppy.

Carrot and stick. That was the method his aunt had always used when she was bringing him up. Basic psychology. It rarely failed.

He gathered his core team in the Incident Room and brought them up to date.

'So there you have it,' he said. 'Any questions?'

'How old is this Corrie Hoyland?' asked DI Holmes.

'Thirty-six, according to her professional profile,' Caton told him.

'And Ayesha Amroush was what, fifteen? Doesn't that make Hoyland a paedophile?'

'Not necessarily,' said DI Bookham. 'It depends on what her motives were, what their relationship was and how that played out in practice.'

'According to a study by Boise State University in 2011,' said DS Hulme, 'sixty per cent of the heterosexual women they interviewed were sexually attracted to other women; half had fantasies about other women, and almost half had kissed another woman. It gets worse as they get older, apparently.'

'Not surprising with blokes like you around,' said one of his colleagues.

Caton waited for the laughter to die down.

'Right now,' he said, 'none of that is relevant. It could give us revenge as a motive, and even go some way to explaining what all the experts described as the personal nature of the attacks. Especially the anger and rage at least one of the perpetrators displayed.'

'You've met her, boss,' said DS Stuart. 'Did she give you that impression? You know, that she was capable of something like that?'

Caton thought about it.

'When do they ever?' he said.

There were murmurs of agreement.

'Okay,' he began. 'Operation Gateway. And before anyone asks, yes, we have done a risk assessment.'

It was met with serious faces. Caton hadn't intended it as a joke. He knew they were all thinking of those two female officers lost in the line of duty.

'So, I don't care what you're wearing,' he said. 'I want everyone on the street to put a stab vest on underneath.'

He ignored the muted groans.

'And I don't want any heroes. Or any disproportionate use of force. I know these murders were horrific, but we're talking about a blunt instrument and a knife having been used. Not guns. And in case I forget, no mobiles. Everyone check your Airwave radios, and use your earphones. I don't want any squawks giving you away.'

He checked the list he had made on his new tablet.

'We have three priorities at this moment in time,' he said. 'The first is to prevent any more deaths; the second is to make sure we get the evidence we need to make an arrest, and to gather that evidence in a manner that will secure a conviction; the third is to discover the identity of the other perpetrator.'

'I agree,' said Ambrose Bookham.

Gordon Holmes gave him a look that could kill.

'So do I,' he said.

Bookham cast him a sideways glance and silently mouthed the word *sorry*.

Everyone saw it, and despite the DCI's good intentions it only served to increase Gordon's discomfort.

'This is what we're going to do,' said Caton. 'Thanks to DS Soames, we have under surveillance both the mobile numbers we think they're using. Hoyland's is showing up as being at or very close to her home. DS Stuart, I want you to go to Hoyland's address and set up surveillance on it. Take a DC with you. Stay out of sight, and just report any activity. People coming or going, lights on or off. You know the score.'

'What happens if she leaves the house, sir?' she asked.

'Then one of you follows her. Preferably you; she's less likely to be spooked by a woman. The DC can stay and watch the house on foot if she drives off in her car.'

He turned to Douggie Wallace.

'Where is Adam Davis?'

'In The Salutation Pub and Hotel. I've just checked.'

'Right,' said Caton. 'DC Hulme, I want you to get down to The Salutation and keep an eye on Adam Davis. You're the only one who looks young enough to get away with loitering in a predominantly student hang-out. Plus, he's never met you. Don't let him know who you are, and if you spot either of the suspects make sure they don't spot you. And don't go burying your head in one of those reference books they've got there.'

Cue more laughter.

'If Davis leaves, follow him at a discreet distance. You can track him on your phone. That goes for all of us, and those sat in the cars can also use their tablet. You've also got photos of both targets on your tablets, and the make and registration number of target A's car. Mr Wallace will talk you through it at the end of this briefing. DS Carter, I want you and DC Jackson to check the house where Imran Coreishi was murdered. The perpetrators have no reason to suspect that Adam

Davis is not still living there. Get rid of the crime scene tape, switch a couple of lights on and set up surveillance. The landings on one of those two tower blocks will give you a 360-degree view.'

'What about the place where Davis is actually living at the moment?' said Gordon Holmes.

'We've no reason to suspect that they know he is living there,' Caton replied. 'But I've arranged for the Safe Return Team to set up surveillance on it. If there's anything suspicious, they'll contact me straight away.'

He looked at their faces. They were focused. Really up for it.

'Any questions?'

'What if Hoyland doesn't leave the house?' asked DS Stuart. 'What if nothing happens tonight despite those texts?'

'I've applied for a warrant to search her apartment. If nothing goes down tonight, DI Holmes will make his way there with a search team. If she's there, he'll arrest her on suspicion. That will be enough to get her fingerprints and DNA swab. If it was her that left her prints all over the crime scenes, we're home and dry.'

'Do we have enough for a warrant?' said Holmes. 'It's all still a bit circumstantial, isn't it?'

'We know that she was trolling as *Mithril666* to get inside the *flammatory* network,' Caton replied. 'We also know that she had regular contact with one of the victims, Miles-Cowper. It's thin, but it should be enough. Especially given the context.'

'What would you like me to do, Tom?' said Ambrose Bookham.

'Coordinate from here in the Silver Command Suite. For the purpose of this operation you and I are joint Silver Commanders. DCS Gates will be Gold Command in the Headquarters Suite. DI Holmes has completed the relevant Command courses, so he will be Bronze Commander on the ground.'

From the nods around the room he knew it met with popular approval. Everyone knew that it was time his deputy had some of the limelight.

'Any more questions?'

There were none. They just wanted to get on with it. Like hounds straining at the leash.

Chapter 40

'Try him again,' said Caton.

They were parked up in a white BMX SUV on double yellow lines outside the vault of the former Grants Arms pub, halfway between The Salutation and Adam Davis' student house in Hulme. To a passer-by, the only evidence to suggest that the four large men on-board were not drug barons was the plethora of visual displays and Comm's equipment.

In the back, Holmes muttered something inaudible. Beside him, the duty officer keeping the log strained to hear, wondering if it needed to be recorded. There was a loggist attached to each of the commands. When the operation was over, every thought expressed and every decision and action made would be examined to the nth degree. If anything went wrong, the powers that be would know exactly who to blame. Thirty seconds passed, and Holmes leaned forward.

'It's no good,' he said. 'He's not answering.'

'Try texting,' Caton suggested.

It seemed to take forever.

'What's the problem?' said Caton, twisting around in his seat.

'I don't do texting,' Holmes grumbled.

Caton pulled his BlackBerry from one of his inside pockets.

'I'll do it.'

He kept it short and to the point.

Ring me! Now!

A minute later his phone rang. He put it on speakerphone so that everyone could hear.

'Adam!' he said. 'Where the hell are you?'

'In The Sally, like you told me,' the student replied.

His speech was suspiciously slurred. But then he had been there most of the day.

'Why didn't you keep your phone on like I told you?' he said.

'I did.'

'So why didn't you answer it?'

'I didn't recognise the number, did I?'

Caton had to concede that he had a point.

'And,' Davis continued, 'I thought it would be suspicious if I was on the phone all the time.'

Another good point, but for the fact that that was what most people his age seemed to spend most of their time doing.

'Well, next time you get a call from that number, answer it. It'll be my deputy, DI Holmes.'

'Right-o.'

He sounded far more cheerful than the circumstances warranted.

'How much have you had to drink?'

'Lost count,' he said. 'But I'm not drunk.'

'Well, stop right now,' Caton told him.

'Won't that seem even more suspicious?'

'Bloody students,' muttered Gordon Holmes.

'Switch to something non-alcoholic then,' said Caton. 'Now pay attention.'

'Right-o.'

'One of my officers is on his way to you right now. He may already be there. You're not to try and spot that officer, or approach anyone you assume to be him, or her. Do you understand, Adam?'

'Yes, but…'

'But nothing. That officer is there to make sure that you come to no harm, inside or outside that pub. It is in your own interest to do nothing to compromise that officer. Do you understand?'

'Yes.'

'Good. When it's time for you to head back to Weston Hall, I'll let you know. We'll be with you every step of the way. Do you understand?'

'Yes.'

'Are you with anyone?'

'Not really. I'm watching the darts team practise.'

'Your flatmates at Weston House, do you know where they'll be this evening?'

'Most of them have gone to a gig in Fallowfield. Won't be home till late.'

'Right. Well, you stay there until you hear from me or DI Holmes. On no account go to the loos on your own or leave alone, or go home. Just stay there. Do you understand?'

'Alright,' he said. 'I'll do exactly what you say.'

Suddenly, he sounded totally different. More like he'd been when he'd come in to confess his part in the affair. As though the bravado had all been an act and reality had finally dawned.

He wasn't the only one for whom reality had dawned.

DCS Helen Gates came through loud and clear.

'This is Gold Command,' she said. 'I don't like this. The subject seems highly vulnerable and totally unreliable. I think the warrant to search with regard to Target A should be exercised immediately.'

'I urge caution, Gold Command,' said Caton. 'We don't know that Target A is at home. If Target A is at home and is detained, that of itself will not prevent

Target B from being a continuing threat to the subject. If, on the other hand, Target A is not apprehended, we are still left with the need to protect the subject.'

'I agree, Gold Command,' said Ambrose Bookham in his capacity as Silver Command One.

'Me too,' muttered Gordon Holmes.

There was a long silence. Caton held his breath. When the decision came, her voice had a steely resolve that Caton had always admired, except when it was directed at him.

'Gold Command,' she said. 'I want an immediate status report on the surveillance of Target A's address.'

DS Stuart replied almost immediately.

'Lima One. There has been no sign of life since surveillance began. There is a single light in the hall. What appears to be a single light behind the blinds in the living room. No on-street parking is permitted outside the apartments. The underground car park, which is where we understand Target A's car is kept, has a keypad panel on the barriers.'

More silence while they waited for Helen Gates' reaction.

'Silver Command One,' she said at last. 'Status report on the mobile phone devices belonging to both targets.'

They could hear conversation in the background between Douggie Wallace and Ambrose Bookham.

Bookham replied, 'Silver Command One. Signal belonging to Target A remains live and immobile in the vicinity of this target's home address. Target B's signal appears to be in or close to the location of our subject.'

'The Salutation,' said Gordon Holmes. 'We need to let DC Hulme know.'

'Go on then,' said Caton.

Holmes leant forward.

'Bronze Command,' he said. 'Lima Two, status report.'

There was a wait. They knew that Hulme would be getting his mobile out and putting it to his ear. Pretending to be using that. Nothing was more of a giveaway than being seen talking to yourself.

'Lima Two,' he said in whisper. 'Have visual on subject. No change. Target B has just entered. Seems nervous. Looking round. Walking towards...'

He stopped speaking, but they could hear him breathing. Seconds later, he started again.

'Stood by my table to see into the room where the subject is. Walked to the bar. Trying to get served.'

'Bronze Command,' said Holmes. 'Report any significant change in status. Don't wait to be asked.'

'Roger that, Bronze Command,' said Lima Two.

'Silver Command Two,' said Caton immediately. 'This confirms our suspicion that both targets intend to act tonight. They have never to our knowledge acted alone. Target A will either be leaving home shortly, or is already in the vicinity. I suggest that we wait.'

'Gold Command,' came the response. 'If Target A has not emerged within fifteen minutes, execute the warrant.'

Chapter 41

DS Carter and DC Jackson parked up on the pavement outside St George's Court.

'We'll go on foot from here,' said Carter. 'More chance of spotting anyone lurking behind the hedges.'

'Should have brought a dog team with us,' said Jackson.

'You heard the boss,' said Carter. 'There's one on standby, with the Tactical Aid Team.'

'All very well,' grumbled Jackson. 'Now's when we need them.'

They walked along the deserted streets, checking parked cars and alleyways, until they reached a corner from where they could see the row of terraced houses where Imran Coreishi died. The double-fronted house was in darkness. Several of the other houses in the row had lights on here and there. Pieces of police tape were still evident in the hedge. A dog howled, provoking another to yap incessantly. A command was shouted. The yapping ceased. A door slammed, and peace descended. The only sounds came from the traffic on the roundabout behind the flats, and a plane gaining height as it cleared the airport.

'They must know he's not staying here,' said Jackson. 'That none of them are. It wouldn't take a brain surgeon. Just a quick drive by.'

'He might have been back to collect some of his

stuff,' said Carter. 'Maybe they were following him.'

'In which case, they could have killed him there and then.'

'Not if it was in broad daylight.'

'What if they found a key while they were last here? They could be waiting inside, in the dark.'

'Why would they?' said Carter. 'They weren't expecting to have to return and do it all over again.'

'We'd better check round the back,' she said.

The rear of the house was cloaked in darkness. They peered over the wooden fence. It was an oddly shaped garden. A strip of lawn, some decking, and the outline of a picnic table and covered barbecue. The path on which they stood led to the end of the fence, where it divided. To the right it ran along the backs; ahead of them it cut across a strip of open ground, between some trees, onto Chester Road.

'That's where I'd come from,' said Carter. 'A quick in, out and off.'

As they set off towards the road, they instinctively reached for their batons. Beyond and between the trees, as cars flashed by their headlights created a strobe effect, casting weird shadows across their path. They emerged on the busy carriageway. There were neither cars parked nor pedestrians foolhardy enough to brave the traffic.

'Better call it in,' said Carter, trying hard not to sound relieved.

Caton checked the street map on the second of the screens.

'No sign of them at the house, or Weston Hall,' he said. 'We know that Davis and Woodsted are both in The Salutation. If you were Corrie Hoyland, Gordon, where would you wait for Davis?'

Holmes craned forward.

'If I knew about Weston House, I suppose it would depend on which way I thought he was going to make his way back; under the Mancunian Way, or between The Sally and Oxford Road. To be honest, I wouldn't fancy either of them. Too many people about.'

'And if she thought he was going back to the house in Hulme?'

Caton could tell that Gordon was rubbing his chin by the sound of his leathery palm brushing the stubble.

'Then there's loads of possibilities. Here or hereabouts would work. Or anywhere around Boundary Lane, or Bonsall Street.'

They were still considering the implications when Ambrose Bookham broke the silence.

'Silver Command One. Target A Update. Associated licence plate recorded by ANPR cameras at Greenheys Lane Junction on Princess Parkway heading north at twenty-two seventeen hours. No further sightings.'

Caton checked the time on the head-up display.

'Three minutes ago,' he said. 'And since she didn't come up on any of the ones closer to the city centre, she must have turned off Princess Parkway somewhere between Greenheys Lane and Stretford Road. She's waiting somewhere round here for Woodsted to tell her which way Adam Davis goes when he leaves that pub. What do you propose, Gordon?'

Holmes didn't hesitate.

'Bronze Commander,' he said. 'Lima Three and Lima Four. Proceed immediately, and with caution, to the junction of Royce Road and Old Birley Road, and await instructions. Report any visual contact immediately.'

'Roger that,' DS Carter replied.

That was followed immediately by a whispered call from DC Hulme.

'Lima One. Status report. Target B is on his mobile. Responding to a call. Looking furtive. Hasn't taken his eyes off the subject.'

'Gold Commander. Thank you, Lima One.'

'She's letting him know that she's arrived,' said Caton.

'Must be using a pay-as-you-go,' Holmes observed. 'So why didn't she use that when she called to tell him tonight was the night?'

'Same reason she didn't wear gloves at the crime scenes,' said Caton. 'Reckless abandon, or a death wish.'

'You think she wants to get caught?'

Caton had no idea. He doubted if she did. Not really. But then nothing about this case was rational. He didn't have time to dwell on it. Helen Gates was on again; she was getting edgy. That was when she became even more assertive.

'Gold Command. I am sending in a second Tactical Aid Team. Bronze Command, please advise on the best location for them. I want the cordon tightened around the current location of the subject. Please deploy accordingly, Silver Command.'

Caton couldn't argue with her rationale. Now that they knew that both targets were within the box they had created, there was no excuse for putting Adam Davis at further risk. Caton was less happy with the way in which the respective roles of each command were becoming blurred. He only hoped that this decision to give Gordon Bronze Command wasn't going to backfire. Only time and the log analysis would tell.

He listened while his deputy issued his orders for each of the waiting units. He was about to order a sweep of the entire area as the box closed in on The Salutation Hotel, when Detective Constable Hulme reported in. He sounded concerned, and with good reason.

'Lima One. Subject is on the move. I repeat. On the move. Out of the door. Target B following. I am following Target B.'

'What the hell is Davis doing?' said Holmes. 'You told him to stay put.'

'Forget that,' said Caton. 'You're Bronze Commander. What are *you* going to do?'

'Bronze Command to Lima One. Status report,' said Holmes.

'Lima One,' came the sotto voce reply. 'Subject out onto Boundary Street West, left onto Cambridge Street. Target B now following, thirty metres behind. Appears to be on his mobile. Lima One crossing road and following at same distance, back in shadow.'

Caton was impressed. He tried to raise Adam Davis on his mobile phone.

'Gold Command,' said Helen Gates. 'Who the hell told the subject to leave the secure location?'

'Silver Command Two,' said Caton. 'Nobody. We have not had contact. Subject is not answering his phone.'

'Lima One. Subject turning right onto Rosamund Street West. Target B still on mobile.'

'Where the hell is he going?' muttered Holmes.

'If he turns right onto Boundary Lane,' said Caton, 'then he's leading Woodsted back towards Hulme. Either he's drunk and has forgotten he's no longer staying there, or he's got fed up with waiting and is deliberately trying to draw them out.'

'Then he's got more faith in us than I have,' said Holmes.

'Don't write that down,' said Caton to the loggist.

'Lima One, subject turning right onto Boundary Lane.'

'Hulme then,' said Caton.

'Left onto Bonsall Street. Repeat, left onto Bonsall Street.'

'He's going to get knocked down, if he doesn't throw himself off the bridge first,' said Holmes.

Caton was busy studying the satellite view of the route Davis appeared to be taking

'Lima One. Subject crossing Princess Bridge.'

'That's it!' said Caton, pointing to the map. 'The open land between Bonsall Street and Royce Road. There's just enough cover there. If she wasn't there before, she will be now. Waiting under those trees.'

'He's falling straight into their hands,' said Holmes. 'And it looks like we told him to go that way. Setting him up as bait.'

'We haven't,' said Caton, glad for once that there was a log being kept.

'Do you think anyone's going to believe that?' said Holmes. 'Bronze Commander to all units. Move in! Move in!'

To anyone not focused solely on a single violent objective, the sound of four powerful engines starting up in close proximity might well have signalled flight, but Anthony Woodsted merely increased his pace, closing the gap between himself and his prey. Behind him DC Hulme began to run.

He saw a movement in the trees flanking the road and shouted, 'Davis! Run! Run!'

Adam turned to see who was shouting, swayed for a moment, stumbled and fell. His pursuer also turned for a moment and then sprinted towards the fallen student. A white BMW roared up the street towards them. The driver used his handbrake to bring it to a screeching halt broadside across the road, less than a yard from Adam Davis. Before it came to rest, the passenger doors were opening. Anthony Woodsted broke right and disappeared into the trees, followed by DC Hulme and, hot upon his heels, Gordon Holmes.

'There! There!' yelled DS Stuart as she and Carter sped up Stretford Road.

Fifty metres ahead of them a hooded figure had emerged from a wooded path on the strip of open ground and was making for a car parked in the adjacent bus stop layby. The figure turned, frozen, like a deer in their headlights. They could tell it was woman, her face pale, yet strangely emotionless. Suddenly, she stepped into the road towards them.

'Look out!' shouted Joanne Stuart, convinced that the woman was going to throw herself in front of their car.

Nick Carter rammed his foot on the brakes. They braced themselves as the car screeched to a halt. As the bumper made contact with the woman's shins, she fell clumsily forward, her hands outstretched on the bonnet.

Anthony Woodsted sprinted between the trees, his heart pounding, his breathing laboured. He could hear the sound of his pursuer's feet slapping the path behind him. Within sight of the road, seeing blue flashing lights, he slowed momentarily. That was the moment at which DC Hulme, head tucked in, launched himself, wrapped his arms around his thighs and flung him to the ground. Woodsted's head struck the foot of a tree and he passed out.

'DC Wood would have been proud of you, Jim,' said Gordon Holmes as they followed the paramedics to the ambulance. 'Didn't know you could play rugby.'

'There's a lot about me you don't know,' the detective constable told him. 'I'm not just a pretty face.'

Holmes grinned. 'In your dreams,' he said. 'In your wildest dreams.'

Chapter 42

'They've got a solicitor each,' said Gordon Holmes. 'But it doesn't matter. They're going to plead guilty despite what their briefs are telling them. The lad can't wait to dob her in. Reckons he'll avoid a mandatory life sentence.'

'Dob her in?' said Caton. 'Whatever happened to grass her up?'

Holmes smiled a crooked smile. 'Fancied a change. I bet you didn't know Australian Immigration has a *Dob-in Service* website where members of the public can report suspected illegals?'

'That's colonials for you,' said Caton, tongue in cheek. 'CrimeStoppers is too sophisticated for them.'

He saved the file containing the Silver Commander Two report that he was working on and gave his deputy his full attention.

'If they're so eager to make your job easy, Gordon, what are you doing here?'

His deputy pulled up a tubular chair and sat down.

'Their briefs wanted a word in private with their clients. Nothing I can do about that, but I don't think it'll make them change their minds.'

'Have you got a record of them admitting their guilt?'

'Yep.'

'After you cautioned them?'

'Yep.'

'Then you're probably right. They'll be trying to put together a case for mitigation.'

'The search teams found a lump hammer and a pair of bypass secateurs,' said Holmes. 'She must have dumped them as she fled. Professor Flatman will be pleased.'

'Vindicated,' said Caton. 'Mr Flatman will feel vindicated; he is seldom pleased.'

Holmes adopted a confidential tone.

'I know why you wanted me to be the arresting officer, boss. So I'd be stuck with all the paperwork while you slope off to get married.'

Caton held up both hands and joined them at the wrists.

'It's a fair cop,' he said. He folded his arms and rocked back in his chair. 'But that wasn't the only reason, Gordon. I took on board what you said about playing second fiddle.'

Holmes began to protest, but Caton waved it aside.

'You were right. I pulled you out of another team to work on the Okowu Bello case. But for that, you'd have had a stack of other cases under your belt by now, and had the confidence to go for promotion.'

'I nearly screwed this one up,' said Holmes.

Caton shook his head. 'No you didn't. And when these two go down, the Chief will be dragging you before the Promotion Board.'

His deputy sighed. 'Have you done?' he said.

Caton was surprised. Not by Gordon's words, irreverence being second nature to him, but by his manner.

'Go on,' he said.

'Right. First off, I'm grateful to you for making me Bronze Commander on this one, although I might want to retract that statement when I'm knee-deep in reports and you're sipping Gin Fizz in the sun, on a beach, or wherever it is you're going for your honeymoon. And I'm touched that you care. Although if you ever repeat that to a third party I may just forget that you're my boss and do something we'll both regret. Secondly, I like being a part of this team. It's where I belong. I'm a team player. I'll never, ever be comfortable with the rotas and the schedules, and the targets, and the pettifogging politics, and the mind your p's and q's. I'll be happy to lead on any investigations you care to choose. If nothing else, it'll give you a bit of a rest now that you're into your forties.' He grinned. 'Have you had a look in the mirror lately?' Now he was back to his most earnest. 'But, and this is the last time I'm going to say this, I will be eternally grateful if you never, ever mention the word promotion to me again.'

He sat back and folded his arms in a classic defensive pose.

'Do you read me, boss?' he said calmly.

It was the longest personal speech he had ever heard Gordon make. He knew how hard it must have been, and how serious his deputy's intent.

'Affirmative,' he said.

Gordon nodded. 'Thank you.'

'What about…?'

'Marilyn? She's just going to have to lump it, isn't she? She's always going on about me being more assertive. Well, like I told her, you should be careful what you wish for.'

He looked at his watch and stood up.

'It's time I was getting back,' he said. 'DCI Bookham, DS Carter, DS Stuart and DCS Gates are in the Observation Room. DC Hulme is with me.'

He saw the look of surprise on Caton's face.

'Well, I thought he deserved it, the part he played.'

Perhaps Gordon was right, Caton reflected. Maybe his leadership skills were better deployed as a DI. And then Gordon surprised him again.

'I'd like you to sit in with us, boss. And don't worry, we'll do all the paperwork.'

Caton stood, took his jacket from the back of his chair and shrugged it on.

'Just make sure,' he said, 'that you find time for your best man's speech, or Kate will kill us both.'

They started with Anthony Woodsted.

'And guess what?' said Holmes, his hand on the door of the interview room. 'He's only a trainee locksmith. No wonder she was keen to hook up with him. It explains why they had no problem getting in and out.'

He opened the door and stood back to let Caton enter.

Sitting there beside his solicitor, in a white all-in-one custody suit with less allure than a bargain basement onesie, he seemed too young to be an uncle. Closer to fifteen than the nineteen years on his birth certificate. His face pinched and pale, despite his mixed-race heritage. He looked cowed, guilt-ridden, lost and defeated. It would have been easy to feel sorry for him had Caton not seen what he and Hoyland had done to their victims.

'My client,' said the solicitor, when Caton had been introduced and the tapes were running, 'is willing to tell you everything he knows, in return for…'

He was cut off midstream by Gordon Holmes' hand thrust out in front of him like a bear's paw.

'Please inform your client,' he said, 'that whilst the court may well take into account both his full cooperation with this investigation and sincere expressions of remorse, there can be no question of deals of any kind. And certainly not any requests for immunity under Section 17 of the 2005 Act.'

He leant forward and stared directly at Anthony Woodsted.

'Ms Hoyland has already admitted her part in this sorry business, Anthony. Apart from helping us and the court to understand why and how you got sucked into this sorry mess, I don't think there's anything you can tell us that will make any difference to the fact that you will both be convicted. Just do the decent thing. Save the court a lot of time and money. And hope that the judge and the jury will take that into account.'

Caton half admired this direct approach, but was concerned that Woodsted might decide that there was now little to be gained by admitting to anything. He watched the face of the solicitor to see if she was thinking much the same thing, and weighing up the risks involved in calling Gordon's bluff, if that's what it was. Anthony Woodsted saved her the trouble. e began to sob.. The sobbing

He began to sob. And then to weep. His body shook so violently that his solicitor felt impelled to envelop him with her arms.

'Switch that thing off!' she said.

Gordon Holmes let it run a little longer. After all, if this was remorse then it might be better for her client to have it on record. Finally, he stated the time, suspended the interview and switched off the tape machine.

They were all used to hard-faced young men and women, juveniles in particular, who stare you in the face with defiant eyes and swear blind they are innocent when you've caught them in the act. Then there were the ones who were scared and guilty from the outset, and worried about the way their father would react. This was different, Caton decided. Anthony Woodsted was that rarer animal, the victim offender. Gordon Holmes had been right to ask him to sit in. He needed to hear this young man's story.

It was ten minutes before they were all agreed that Anthony Woodsted was in a fit state to continue. He spent the first three minutes telling them how sorry he was. That he wished he'd never got involved with Corrie Hoyland. How ashamed he was. How his family would never forgive him. Remorse in bucketloads, all of it on tape. Caton was inclined to believe it was genuine. Then his eyes began to well up again, and he was saying that he couldn't live with the guilt of what he'd been party to. That was the point at which Caton became concerned that Woodsted would go into meltdown and leave them kicking their heels for another fifteen minutes. He was running out of time. Kate's deadline started at midnight. Less than an hour away. DC Hulme came to the rescue.

'Anthony,' he said, 'you'll feel a lot better when you've got it all off your chest. When you've helped all of us here to understand what happened to you. Can you do that?'

It was a clever move. A new voice, a friendly tone, an implied recognition that Anthony Woodsted was himself a victim. Caton was impressed.

DC Hulme nudged the box of tissues closer to the suspect. Woodsted reached out, took one and dabbed at his eyes. He screwed it up and let it drop onto the tabletop. His solicitor leaned in to whisper in his ear. He pulled away, prising her hand from around his shoulders. Slowly he looked up.

'I'll try,' he said.

Chapter 43

'The first time I saw her was at Ayesha's funeral,' he said. 'I didn't know who she was, she just stood out. You know. With being white, and buff.'

'Good looking,' said DC Hulme, assuming they needed a translator.

One look from Gordon Holmes convinced him otherwise.

'Sorry,' he said. 'Carry on, Anthony.'

The young man studied his nails. Caton could see that they were bitten to the core. Even the cuticles were red raw. At last he continued, his voice wavering. Each time he was overwhelmed by the pain of remembering, they waited patiently for him to recover.

'The church was packed. They was even on the grass and the pavement outside. I was near the back with some of the other kids who were at school with Ayesha. We was a few years ahead of her, so we was near the back. So was...' He faltered as he said her name. 'Corrie. She was at the back too, on the other side. She was crying. That's what I remember. A beautiful white woman crying over a dead black girl. And she not even family.'

He looked at his fingers again and then hid his hands under his arms, hugging himself as he did so.

'Next time was at Jarmaine's funeral. That was

packed full too. I was down the front, with being family, innit?'

He looked up. Holmes and Hulme nodded their understanding.

'Didn't see her in the church, but she was there at the crematorium. I saw her as we was coming out. She didn't do the meet and greet bit after. You know, with Jarmaine's mum and dad? Just stood off, on the edge of the car park, and watched. I thought it odd her being there. An' she didn't do no crying this time. Just watched. Hard faced. Must've been about three weeks later she turned up. Outside my work in the Arndale. Like it was a coincidence.'

He looked down at the tabletop. When he spoke next it was almost whispered, as though he was talking to himself.

'Must 'ave been following me. Bitch.'

He shook his head and looked up again.

'Said how she'd recognised me from the funerals. Asked did I want to go for a coffee. We sat in Costa and talked. About Ayesha. She seemed to know more about her than I did. Then she asked me about Jarmaine. I talked, and she listened. Then I asked her why she was at his funeral if she didn't even know him. She said did I know that the wicked people who drove Ayesha to kill herself were the same ones who'd posted all those filthy lies about Jarmaine? I was shocked. I said I didn't. She got us another couple of coffees. Then she told me about this *flammatory* network where they picked their victims and then hunted them like animals. Then, when they'd killed or maimed them, they moved on to some other poor sods.'

His hands were out from under his armpits now. He had them clenched on the table in front of him. Caton could see that whatever shame or remorse he might be carrying, the anger and hatred that had motivated him was still there.

'She said she'd begun to identify them. To track them down. Would I like to see?'

'So you went back to hers?' said DC Hulme, unable to contain himself.

Gordon Hulme's left hand snaked beneath the table, found Hulme's thigh and squeezed hard. To his credit the young DC managed to stifle a yelp. Woodsted didn't seem to notice.

'Not then, not straight away,' he replied. 'It was about two days later. A weekend. Saturday, I think. In the afternoon. She showed me what she'd been doing. The website, the network. The names and details she'd managed to get. She even had photographs of them and where they lived. It was incredible.'

He paused again, staring into the middle distance. Each time he did it, Caton could imagine him piecing the story together. The way she had snared him. Sucked him in. Brought him to this.

'She said would I like to stay for dinner? She'd get some takeaways in. So I did. She got Chinese and some beers. I couldn't believe my luck.'

He paused, and shook his head again.

'Stupid, or what?'

He looked directly at Gordon Holmes. His eyes were wet.

'Me, and this beautiful, sexy, older woman. What was I thinking?'

They all knew the answer, but wisely no one told him. He swallowed and carried on. It came in a rush, as though he needed to get it over with, to get through it as quickly as possible.

'Turned out she had some weed and some coke. We smoked a couple of joints. Snorted a line of snow each. Then she started coming on to me. Then…'

His head dropped. Tears began to land on the tabletop like the first warning of a shower. He reached for a tissue, dabbed his eyes and then the table. There was no sign that he was going to finish the sentence.

'You made love?' said Gordon Holmes.

It was neatly put, Caton thought. Love, not sex. His deputy was staying onside. Empathising with the suspect's predicament rather than reflecting the harsh reality back at him.

Woodsted nodded his head.

'Then, after, she told me they were still at it. Ruining other people's lives. Other kids. Killing them with their evil lies. She wanted to know did I want to help her catch them?'

He looked up and appealed directly to his interrogators.

'Course I did. You would, wouldn't you?'

'Catch them, yes,' said Holmes calmly. 'Not murder them, Anthony.'

The young man gripped the edge of the table and leaned forward. His voice was stronger now, but pleading.

'I didn't know that was what she was going to do, did I? I just thought she was going to do, you know, a citizen's arrest.'

'With a hammer, and a pair of pruners?' said Holmes, having decided it was time to get real.

'I didn't know she had them, did I?' he replied desperately. 'Not that first time. You've got to believe me!'

'Maybe you didn't,' said Holmes. 'Not the first time. But what about all the others?'

Caton excused himself at that point. He had heard all that he needed to. He knew the whys and the wherefores. Anthony Woodsted was going to implicate them both with chapter and verse.

In the office he was greeted with the news that the search teams had also found the missing computer mouses, or was that mice? No sign of the severed fingers, though. They had a stack of files and Internet search history that confirmed what Woodsted had just been telling them. There were also the surveillance photographs that she had taken of the victims and their homes. He wasn't into American sporting terms, but there was one that he thought fitted perfectly. Slam dunk.

He spent the next half hour finishing his report and sorting his in-tray into things that could wait until he returned from their honeymoon, and those that someone, probably Ged, Gordon or possibly DI Bookham, would have to deal with. Then he texted Kate to let her know that he was on his way. There was a missed call on his phone. A number he didn't recognise. He decided it could wait.

He was shrugging on his jacket when Gordon Holmes arrived back with DC Hulme in tow. Those of the team that were still there gathered round to hear how the interviews had gone.

'He's given us chapter and verse,' he said. Then he gave a scowl that was a fair impression of a gargoyle. 'Hoyland, on the other hand, has changed her mind. She's going to plead not guilty on account of the fact that she was not of sound mind, given that she was acting under the influence of medication.'

There were groans and expressions of disbelief.

'The thing I don't get,' said DS Carter, 'is how did someone like her turn into a serial killer overnight, whatever the motive?'

'We found a stack of prescription drugs in her apartment,' said DS Stuart. 'Some to help her quit smoking, some that are antidepressants. There was also one that is used to treat bipolar disorder.'

'We're not going to let some smart-arsed barrister blame it all on the drugs?' said Holmes.

DC Hulme raised a hand as though he'd suddenly discovered the wisdom of waiting to asked.

'Recent studies in the States,' he said, 'including by the Federal Drugs Agency, have established a link between such drugs and violent acts, including mass killings.'

This time he knew he had their attention.

'The worst were drugs used for smoking cessation, then antidepressants, then psychotropic drugs. She'll know that. All she had to do was Google it. And lo and behold, her medicine cupboard just happens to hold all three. She's got a full house. Maybe she intended to use it as a defence all along.'

'But she's admitted it,' said Holmes.

'Only that she killed them. Not that she was in full possession of her faculties when she did so, or even when she carried out all that planning.'

'So her mitigation,' said DI Bookham, 'will be that she was under the influence of drugs. His will be that he was acting under duress, from her. At this rate they'll both end up suing the doctor who prescribed those drugs.'

'Bollocks!' said Gordon Holmes.

It wasn't exactly how Caton would have put it, but he couldn't agree more.

'Don't worry,' he reassured them, 'the jury will see through that. Especially when they know how much planning was involved, and over what period of time. And how effectively she was doing her work, including for the regional e-crime hub.'

That was going to be an unfortunate source of embarrassment for the force. He was just glad that he wouldn't be around to deal with it when the press found out. He had a feeling it would land on ACC

Hadfield's desk. The thought made him smile.

'We're all going to the pub after work tomorrow, boss,' said Holmes. 'I hope you can tear yourself away from shining your shoes and ironing your shirt to join us? We can make it a double. Celebrate Janus, and make it your stag-do since we've missed out on that.'

There was a chorus of approval.

'Nemesis would have been more appropriate,' said DC Hulme.

They all turned to look at him.

'Instead of Janus. I'm just saying it's a pity the computer didn't come up with Nemesis, Goddess of revenge, balance, righteous indignation and retribution. That would have about covered it.'

'Look, DC Hulme,' said Holmes, 'fair enough, you've done well, but don't push your luck. Okay?' He turned to Caton. 'How about it, boss?'

'I'll have to see,' Caton replied. 'I'm not sure it's a good idea, the night before the wedding. Maybe just a couple of pints. I'll let you know.'

He headed for the door.

'You mean the future Mrs Caton will let *you* know, boss,' Gordon called after him.

He turned and was greeted by a mass of grinning faces and downturned thumbs.

'In your dreams, Gordon,' he said. 'You don't call me boss for nothing.'

A chorus of laughter and ribald comments followed him all the way down the corridor and out into the atrium.

Chapter 44

Kate was in bed. In the light spilling in from the lounge he could see her rich auburn hair spread out like a halo around her. The otherwise angelic effect was ruined by a sleep mask that he had never seen before. As he began to undress, she rolled over onto her side and pulled his pillow over her head. Oh well, he reflected, at least one of us is going to get a good night's sleep.

The next morning, regardless of her beauty sleep, Kate was a bag of nerves. It was not like her at all, Caton reflected, but then six months into her pregnancy and the wedding just a day away, it was hardly surprising.

'Right,' she said. 'Order of the day. As soon as you've finished your breakfast, over to the Trafford Centre and pick up the wedding suits. Check the sizes before you come away. And make sure everything's there. Jacket, trousers, waistcoats, cravats.'

'I'm not a complete idiot,' he said in what he thought was a genial tone.

'You're a man,' she said, as though that was worse than an idiot. 'Then get straight back here. Get your dress shirt out of its box and hang it with your shirt. If it's creased, iron it. Then buff your shoes. You don't need to polish them, they're patent. And put the socks you're wearing with them. I placed them inside the shirt box so you wouldn't forget. Then make sure you've got your cufflinks and your handkerchief. I don't want you scrabbling around for those at the last minute.'

Caton nodded and shovelled in a spoonful of Shredded Wheat.

'Tom! Are you listening?' she said.

'Mmmm,' he mumbled, spraying milk-soaked shreds of wheat onto the table.

'Now look what you've done!'

She stormed off and returned with a dishcloth, which she threw down in front of him. As he mopped up the tiny offending puddle of gloop, she picked up where she'd left off.

'Then check your suitcase. Make sure you've packed everything you need. There's a list on the fridge. And check you've got our passports, tickets, accommodation vouchers, E11s and whatever else it is we need for wherever it is we're going. Where is that by the way?'

'Nice try,' he said.

He finished his orange and cranberry juice, and stood up.

'Is that it then?' he said.

'No! It's not. Then you can ring round the florist, the photographer, video woman, cars and hotel, and make sure that none of them have forgotten us.'

'What will you be doing while I'm doing all this, darling?' he asked.

'Don't you darling me,' she said. 'I've been left arranging all this while you've been enjoying yourself with your precious team.'

She saw the look on his face and held up her hands in partial submission.

'Okay. I know you didn't have choice. And I know it must have been horrible. But just think how it's been for me.'

'I know,' he said. 'And I'm sorry. I didn't mean it.'

'Well, for your information,' she said, 'I'll be at Maureen's. She's going to have to let a couple of darts out on my dress.' She patted her stomach. 'Nobody told junior to stop growing till after the wedding.'

He walked over, stood behind her and wrapped his arms around her. He placed his hands on her stomach.

'I love you very much,' he said.

She rested her head on his shoulder.

'I love you too,' she said. 'I'm sorry I've been such a cow.'

'Don't be daft,' he said. 'Anyway, I like cows.'

She giggled and tried to squirm free. They both felt the baby kick. She stopped squirming and relaxed.

'Did you feel that?' she said. 'He can hear us you know. He knows it's us. Perhaps he's trying to tell us something.'

'Maybe he's trying to get some sleep,' Caton whispered, 'and he wants us to quieten down.'

She giggled again, and then eased herself free of him.

'You'd best get dressed,' she said. 'You've a lot to do.'

It was midday by the time Caton had finished everything on Kate's list. She was having a last-minute pamper session with her chief bridesmaid. He was making himself a coffee prior to settling down with the latest series of Borgen. His mobile phone rang. It was the same number as last night's missed call. He still didn't recognise it. He switched off the kettle and took the call.

'Hello,' he said. 'Who is this please?'

'Tom, is that you? It's Sarah. Sarah Weston.'

'Sarah. It's great to hear from you,' he said. 'How are you doing over there at CEOPS?'

It was the first time they had spoken since she took promotion and was put in charge of the Child Exploitation and Online Protection Service. He missed her, and felt guilty that he had not been in touch to see how she was doing.

'Fine, Tom. Why didn't you return my call last night?'

There was an edge to her voice. Not at all what he'd expected. He wasn't sure exactly what he expected. Best wishes for the wedding at least. But then she'd be there. She'd been invited.

'Because it was late,' he said. 'And because we'd just charged two serial murderers, and I didn't realise it was you, or I would have done. You know that.'

'That's why I rang,' she said. 'Jenny Soames sent over some files that had been found on a hard disk belonging to one of your victims, a Lee Bottomley?'

'That's right. They didn't have any bearing on our case as it turns out.'

'Maybe not,' she said. 'But we've had a look at the hard drive. He had a list of contacts, all with pseudonyms. All part of what looks like a paedophile ring. At the very least they've been swapping illegal images. At worst, some of them may be creating those images, and God knows what else.'

'I understand that, Sarah,' he said, 'but...'

She interrupted him. 'We've being systematically tracking down the ISPs for each to identify them and get their addresses. We've also been checking them against our burgeoning list of suspects. The address of one of his contacts, in Standish, belongs to a Helen Malone. I'm afraid it's your Helen, Tom. Harry's mother.'

Caton felt the blood rushing from his face. He took a deep breath.

'Is one of the names on your list a Roger Hardman?' he said.

She didn't reply immediately. He had to ask again.

'Is he on your list, Sarah?'

'Yes, he is,' she reluctantly replied. 'How do you know that?'

'What name is he using online, Sarah?'

'Come on, Tom, you know I can't tell you that. Now, you tell me how come you know that name?'

'Because he's Helen's boyfriend.'

'Christ! Tom, this is a mess.'

'Mess doesn't come close. This is my son we're talking about.' He took a deep breath. 'Now, are you going to give me his pseudonym, or do I have to beat it out of him?'

She told him.

'Promise me you're not going to do anything stupid,' she said. 'Tom? Tom? Are you still there?'

Just as he was about to give up she answered.

'Hi, Helen Malone.'

She still didn't get it. The importance of not giving her name. Innocent Helen. Now look where it had got her.

'Helen,' he said abruptly. 'Is Roger there?'

'Tom. Is that you?' she said.

'Is he there Helen?'

'No he's in the Lakes. Why?'

'Does he have a lap top, or a computer in the house?'

'Yes, he's got a laptop. He's taken in with him.'

'Does he ever use your computer?'

'When he's here, why? What's this all about Tom?'

'Listen carefully Helen. I want you to go to your PC right now. Can you do that for me?'

'Yes but...'

'Please Helen, just do as I ask, and I promise I'll explain.'

'Alright,' she said. 'But you're freaking me out here Tom.'

He waited impatiently, watching the second hand on his wristwatch.

'Right,' she said. 'I'm here. What is it you want me to do?'

'On your desktop, go to search all programmes and files. Tell me when you've done that.'

'Okay. I've done that.'

'Type in boyband#21.'

'Boy Band?'

'Hash twenty one. All lower case. No spaces.'

He heard her fingers fly over the keys. There was a gasp.

'Wow!'

'What have you got?'

'There are loads of folders. Maybe twenty, thirty of them.'

'Click on the first one.'

'Tom. Should we be doing this? What's Roger going to say?'

'They're on your computer Helen. Just do it.'

'It's asking for a password.'

'Do you know his password?'

'I know the one he uses to go on his iPad, and his mobile phone.'

'Try that.'

'It still wants a password.'

He tried to concentrate. 'Try boyband#21 again,' he said.

'It says incorrect password.'

Caton cursed.

'What's going on Tom. What is this all about?'

'Helen, is Harry there?'

'No, he's in the Lakes, with Roger.'

Caton clenched his fists, the knuckles white as he

fought back the urge yell at her.

'You let him take Harry on his own!?'

'Not exactly. Something came up at work. I'm joining them tomorrow.'

He took a breath, and counted to three.

'Where are they staying?'

'Tom, you're frightening me,' she said.

'Does Harry have his phone with him?'

'Yes, but I think he's run out of credit. It's a Pay as You Go, and I haven't had time to top it up.'

'Have you got Roger's mobile number?'

'Yes.'

'Tell me.'

She did. Her voice was wavering. When she finished she said. 'Tom, what's going on?'

He could tell that she was putting it all together. It was only a matter of time before she lost it completely. Became hysterical.

'I'll tell you when I get back,' he said.

'Tom....Tom...'

He ended the call.

Chapter 45

He tried to ring Kate, but her phone was switched off, and he had no idea where she had gone for her pamper. It wasn't as though he could leave a message. What the hell would he say anyway? He decided to just ask her to ring him back. It was urgent. Then he tried her hairdresser, but she had no idea either. The note on their kitchen wall diary simply said *Pamper!! Yea!* In desperation he rang Gordon Holmes and filled him in.

'Bloody hell!' said Gordon. 'What are you going to do, Tom?'

'Go up there, grab Harry and get back here as soon as possible.'

'What about the wedding? Kate's going to go ballistic.'

'Do you think I don't know that? But I can't risk leaving Harry up there with that pervert Hardman.'

'I can see that. But if you don't know where they're staying, how are you going to find them?'

'That's where you come in, Gordon. I've got Hardman's mobile number. I want you to get Douggie Wallace to organise a trace on it.'

'Hang on a minute,' said his deputy. 'Strictly speaking this isn't our case. Shouldn't…'

'Harry is my son, so this is my case,' said Caton, though he knew that Gordon was right. 'Added to which, he was a contact of Lee Bottomley's, and he *is* a part of our case. You can say we need to trace him to find out if there's more to Janus than meets the eye.'

He could hear Gordon sucking his teeth at the other end. He imagined him rubbing his chin too.

'Go on then,' Gordon said at last. 'Keep your BlackBerry on hands-free.'

'Thanks, Gordon,' said a relieved Caton. 'And one more thing. I want you to wait half an hour and then try Kate's mobile number. If she doesn't respond, try her again every half hour until you get through. If you haven't reached her by three o'clock, try our home number.'

'What do you want me to tell her?'

'That Harry's in trouble in the Lakes. That I've gone up there to bring him back. She's not to worry, I've sorted everything for the wedding, and I'll be back before she knows it.'

Gordon sounded sceptical. 'You do realise she's going to ring you as soon as she gets my message?'

'Tell her my phone is patched through to our tracking centre. I won't be able to take any of her calls. That's why you're ringing her.'

'She's not going to like it.'

'I'll just have to deal with that when I get back.'

'Rather you than me, Tom,' said Gordon. 'Rather you than me.'

'I really owe you,' said Caton.

'I'll remind you,' said his deputy. 'Just make sure you don't do anything stupid when you get there.'

His mobile was on Bluetooth. Helen had started ringing him incessantly as soon as he'd set off. He was twenty-five miles up the motorway, just passing Preston, when he finally gave in and answered. She was hysterical.

'Calm down,' he said. 'I can't understand a word you're saying.'

He heard her panting, and then taking deep breaths and breathing out long and hard. Like someone at the end of a four-minute mile.

'I worked out his password,' she said. 'It was his favourite pop group. It was awful, Tom. All these vile photos. And there were videos too. I couldn't bring myself to look at them.'

'Of children?' he said.

'Mainly boys. Young boys. Oh, Tom!'

He could almost feel her pain.

'Did you recognise any of the children?'

'Harry wasn't in any of the ones I looked at. But there are hundreds of them.'

Caton's momentary sense of relief was immediately replaced by one of guilt as he thought about all of those other parents whose children had been abused, despoiled, some of them disappearing forever, even murdered, just to satisfy the perverted lust of men and women worse than animals. And just because Harry wasn't in the photographs, it didn't mean…

'I rang him,' she said. 'I told him to bring Harry straight back home.'

Caton silently cursed.

'Did you tell him you'd seen them?'

'Christ no! How stupid do you think I am?'

He was tempted to tell her. Ringing him like that. What was he supposed to think?

'What he did say?'

'He asked me what the matter was. I said I needed Harry to come back, it was urgent.'

'What did he say to that?'

'He asked me what was so urgent.'

'Then what?'

'He cut me off. Tom, you've got to do something!'

'I am,' he said. 'I'll call you when I've got Harry.'

'Tom, wait!' she cried. 'Harry's phone. It's got a Google tracker App on it. I put it on when I gave him the phone. I know where he is, Tom.'

'I thought you said he was out of credit? That you couldn't ring him?'

'Yes, but his battery's fine.'

'So where is he?'

'In Grange. Down by the estuary. But I don't understand. It looks like he's actually in the bay itself!'

He gripped the wheel tighter.

'Calm down, Helen,' he said. 'Look at the map. Tell me, is he moving?'

He held his breath as he waited for her to reply.

'Yes.'

'In which direction?'

'East. No, sort of south-east.'

He tried to picture it in his mind.

'That means they're heading towards the other bank. South of Silverdale?'

'Yes.'

He experienced an overwhelming sense of relief.

'Listen carefully, Helen,' he said. 'You can calm down. It means that they're doing the Morecombe Bay Walk. They are crossing the estuary on a guided walk. I've done it myself. Harry will be perfectly fine.'

'Are you sure?' she said.

He could hear some of the tension going from her voice.

'I'm sure,' he told her. 'Now, you're just going to have to try to calm down and trust me. I'll ring as soon as I have Harry.'

'I'll try,' she said. 'And, Tom, I'm sorry.'

'It's alright,' he told her. 'It's not your fault.'

'Take care,' she said. 'And, Tom, promise me, when you find them you won't do anything silly?'

He saw the sign for Forton Services, took the slip road and parked beneath the iconic 1960s hexagonal concrete tower. He stopped long enough to download the Google Tracking Pro App and register an account linking his phone to Harry's tracker. After an anxious wait, the icon marker showing the position of Harry's phone appeared. They had travelled some six and a half miles, he estimated, and were now just two and a half miles away from journey's end, on Hest Bank. Since they were travelling at a little under two miles an hour, he would arrive ahead of them, with plenty of time to spare. Reassured, he started the engine and set off.

Almost immediately his phone rang. This time it was Kate. He didn't dare answer it. It was bad enough driving fast on a stretch where he knew the Lancashire motorway patrols were always on the hunt, without the distraction of an irate fiancée with whom it would be impossible to reason. Not today of all days. He gritted his teeth and ignored it. And the next one, and the next one. After six attempts, she gave up.

With one eye on the icon moving across the map on the screen and the other on the road ahead, he raced north. By the time he reached the Carnforth turn-off, Harry and Roger Hardman were still some way off the traditional landing point. He tried to remember the day that he'd done the charity walk for Derian House Children's Hospice. It was with the Queen's Guide, Cedric Robinson. For centuries people had been crossing the bay when the tide was out. A vast, empty wilderness of mud and sand where the sunlight gleamed on isolated pools of water. It could be stunningly beautiful. No surprise, then, that thousands of people a year were tempted to make the crossing. Those with local knowledge crossed alone. The wise did so led by the Queen's Guide.

"When the tide turns," he'd told them, "it does so with ferocious speed. The first rush of water fills the empty channels and gullies, and then the tidal bore, moving faster than a galloping horse, roars in, taking with it everything in its path. These sands are forever shifting under the force of the tides, such that even I have to check and plan the routes before I take a party across."

He had paused for a moment while they waded one by one across a gully filled with water two feet deep. When they were all on the other side, he had gathered them round and waved his arm and staff dramatically across the sweep of the bay.

"If that were not bad enough, there is quicksand here that will suck you down and hold you fast. Men, women and children, horses and carts, even cars have ventured onto these sands and never been seen again."

Including the twenty-three Chinese cockle pickers, abandoned by their gang masters, who had perished there eight years ago, Caton reflected. He pushed the thought from his mind and pressed down a little harder on the accelerator.

As he approached the motorway turn-off, he checked the map on his mobile again. To his surprise, he realised that they had changed direction. Instead of heading for Hest Bank, they were now moving east, towards the shore just north of Bolton-Le-Sands. It made no sense. That was not one of the normal destinations for the guided walks. It also meant that there was every chance he would miss them. It also meant pressing on to the next motorway exit, which his GPS informed him was four miles away. He threw all caution to the wind and pushed the pedal to the floor. As he did so, his phone rang. It was Douggie Wallace.

'We've tried to reach you several times,' he said, 'but your phone's been engaged. We had a location for Roger Hardman's phone.'

'What do you mean, you *had* a location?' said Caton.

'Exactly that. I mean they warned us that it wasn't going to be anywhere near as accurate as it usually is. Not with the reception up there and the distance between the masts. But it's odd. His phone stopped moving for a while, and then we lost it completely.'

'Where was it at the time you lost it?'

'Well, that's the other thing. It looks like it was in the middle of the Morecombe Bay estuary.'

'How long ago was this? When you lost the signal?'

'Half an hour ago.'

It made sense to Caton. Hardman must have ditched it as soon as he'd finished talking to Helen. Presumably he wasn't aware that Harry had his own phone with him. And certainly not that he had a tracker on it.

'They're crossing the bay,' he said. 'Get onto the local police for me. Carnforth will be the nearest. Ask them to meet me.' He magnified the map and tried to compute their most likely landfall. 'There's a caravan site by the shore of Crag Bank Lane. Get them to meet me there.'

'What am I supposed to tell them, sir?' Wallace sounded distinctly uncomfortable.

'Just tell them that there is a male suspect we need to interview, accompanied by a seven-year-old boy. We believe the boy to be at risk.'

'Do you want me to tell them you're his father, sir?'

'No, Douggie. Just tell them it's imperative that they detain them until I get there.'

Three minutes later, he exited the motorway and sped towards the A6. His GPS told him that he had exactly one point two miles to go. Approaching Carnforth, he saw the flash of a speed camera in his rear-view mirror. Undaunted, he raced on. At a roundabout on the southern outskirts the GPS told him to turn right into Longfield Drive. As he did so, a marked police car pulled out of a lane behind him and began to follow. Good old Douggie, he thought.

A glance at the tracker suggested that Harry had not moved since he last checked. He knew there could be a delay in real-time reporting and didn't let it faze him.

As he turned right onto Crag Bank Lane, the patrol car turned on its blues and twos. Taking the siren and flashing lights as an encouragement to speed up, he did so.

They hurtled past stone terraced houses, white lime-washed cottages and then out into open countryside, between lush green hedges and dry stone walls. So fast, that despite the GPS warning he almost overshot the left turn by the sign for the caravan site, opposite a small residential home. He vaguely discerned the screech of brakes and squeal of the tyres as the police car followed him onto the narrow lane that led down to the shore.

In the yard of the farmhouse stood an empty police car, its doors wide open. Caton skidded to a halt and leaped out of his car. He looked around, desperately seeking the missing officers. Behind him, as the second patrol car pulled up, the siren died away like a strangled cat. The officer in the passenger seat climbed out.

'Who the hell do you think you are?' he said brusquely. 'Lewis Hamilton?'

Caton pulled his warrant card from his pocket and flashed it at him.

'I haven't got time for this,' he said. 'Where are your colleagues?'

The policeman looked confused.

'What the hell are you talking about?' he said.

His partner got out of the car.

'Jack,' he said. 'Switch your radio on. There's a little lad out in the bay on his own, and the tide's coming in.'

Chapter 46

His heart pounding in his chest, Caton raced around the farm buildings and out onto the shore. There were a dozen or so people from the caravan site standing there, looking out into the bay. There was policewoman beside them. She turned as he approached.

'That boy, he's my son,' he shouted.

'You're DCI Caton?' she said. 'They didn't tell us he was your lad.'

'Never mind that,' he told her. 'Where is he?'

She pointed due west.

'Out there. About half a mile. That's my colleague down there.'

Caton could see another officer in a high-visibility blouson, approximately two hundred and fifty yards away, staring out into the bay. Caton followed his gaze and imagined that he could see something small and dark in the late afternoon sun.

'Why the hell isn't he doing something?' he said. 'Why is he just standing there?'

'Because that's as close as he could safely get. Don't worry, sir, I've called the coastguard.'

But Caton had flung off his jacket and was already running.

'There's a Bay Search and Rescue craft on its way,' she shouted after him. 'They've told us on no account to go out there ourselves.'

Caton raced across the flat smooth sand with one thought in mind. He had only recently discovered that Harry existed. That he had a son. He was not going to lose him now. There was a fresh wind that cooled his face and urged him on. He kept his sights on the officer ahead of him, who was waving his arms and shouting encouragement out into the bay.

The composition of the sand began to change. It was becoming darker, heavier, slowly sapping his strength. As he grew level with the policeman, he turned and stared at Caton with amazement.

'What the hell are you doing?' he said.

'That's my son,' said Caton as he charged past him.

'Oh shit!' said the policeman, who hesitated for a moment and then began to follow him.

It was immediately apparent to Caton why the officer had been unwillingly to proceed. He was confronted by a deep, wide channel. A tidal tributary that fed fresh water into the bay and filled with seawater when the tide came in. There was already water in the bottom, and it was impossible to tell how deep it might be. He slid down the slippery slope into the water. It came up to his chest. The sudden cold almost took his breath away. Half walking, half swimming, he reached the other side, clawed his way to the top of the bank and began to run. Behind him, he could hear the policeman cursing.

Caton could now see Harry. Not clearly. Still little more than a dot against the vast expanse of sand and water. But he knew that it was him.

'Harry!' he shouted. 'It's me, Tom! Hold on, Harry! I'm coming!'

He thought he heard a faint reply, but it could just as easily have been a trick of the wind, or the sound of the policeman falling further behind him. Now there was another sound. More menacing. The sound of water flowing fast over the ridges of sand and along the gullies and channels. A steady, unrelenting rush that terrified and spurred him on.

Every step became an effort. His chest heaved and his throat burned. He had thought himself fit despite the lost weeks away from the Y Club. But this was something else. Like a treadmill set on the steepest incline. Just as he began to think that he would have to stop, he heard it clearly above the hastening tide. The sound of his son's voice.

'Daddy! Daddy!'

He raised his head and saw his son a hundred yards away. He was standing in a gully, waving his arms.

Caton waved back, and shouted with all the power that he could muster.

'Harry, hold on, I'm coming!'

Eyes fixed on his son, he raised his pace, immediately lost his footing and plunged head first into a channel of rapidly flowing water. The current held him fast and carried him towards the north-east shore. Desperately he scrabbled to get a hold on the banks as he was swept along. One hand sunk into clay-like sand that sucked it in and gripped him momentarily. Long enough for him to plunge his other hand into the bank. His body swung sideways until it lay parallel with the rushing water.

'Hang on!' came a shout.

A long dark shadow passed over him. He realised it was the patrolman leaping the channel. Panting heavily, the officer knelt on the bank, reached down and gripped Caton's arms. As he pulled, Caton's feet found the bottom of the channel. Slowly but surely he was dragged to safety.

'Thank you,' he gasped.

'Matt Wilkey,' said his companion, collapsing on

the sand. 'You're welcome.'

Across the vast expanse of the bay they heard a siren sound. The first of eight blasts.

'That's the high tide warning,' said the policeman. 'Two hours twenty minutes to go. I'm afraid it also means that the tidal bore is on its way.'

Close to exhaustion, Caton pushed himself to his feet and turned in panic. How far had the sea carried him? Where was Harry? He was amazed to find that the water had carried him only twenty yards further away. Leaving his colleague flat on his back, chest heaving, he set off at a sprint.

His supply of adrenaline exhausted, the sprint became a jog and then a stumbling walk. He could see Harry clearly now, just yards away. A cold hand clutched his heart as he realised that his son was not standing in a gully. He was buried waist deep in the ochre-coloured sand.

'It's alright, Harry,' he said. 'I'm here now. It's going to be alright.'

Harry reached out with his arms. As he did so, he began to sink further into the quicksand.

'Don't move, son!' shouted Caton. 'Don't move.'

With each step he took, circles of sand two feet in diameter wobbled like jelly beneath his feet. Sinister bubbles of water appeared on the peripheries. With less than two metres to go, the rippling surface suddenly liquefied, and his right foot sank up to the shin. His leg was gripped as though hidden hands were drawing him down. He shifted his weight to his left foot and tried to pull his trapped leg free. The left foot became ensnared. The harder he struggled, the deeper it sank, until he was unable to move either of them.

He lifted his head and found Harry looking at him with wide, hopeful eyes. He realised with pride that despite everything his son believed that his father was going to save him. Caton hoped that the fear and panic he was feeling was not reflected in his own eyes.

'Don't move! Either of you.'

Matt Wilkey lumbered up. He tested the surface gingerly one foot at a time, found the edge of the sand several metres to Caton's left and stopped. He knelt down on his haunches and caught his breath for a moment.

'Right,' he said. 'What's the lad's name?'

'Harry,' father and son replied in tandem.

'Okay, Harry,' he said, 'don't move. Just stay still and you'll be alright. Do you understand?'

'Yes, sir,' said Harry.

'It's Matt,' he replied. 'Now, Dad, do exactly as I tell you, okay?'

'Okay,' said Caton, reassured by the certainty in this man's voice.

'I'm going to lie down here, with my arm outstretched,' said the policeman. 'I want you to lie back as far as you can, with your arms outstretched, not behind, but to the side, flat on the surface. Do you understand?'

'Yes,' said Caton.

It didn't feel right surrendering the whole of his body to this treacherous surface, but what choice did he have? Cautiously he extended his arms sideways and let his body fall slowly back. The quicksand strengthened its grip on his legs, like strong elastic. When he was back as far as he could go, he felt a hand grip his left wrist.

'Right,' said Matt. 'Now wriggle your right foot in small strong circles. You'll feel water seep into the spaces you create. As you feel the grip lessen, pull your leg towards you.'

Caton did as he was told. To his surprise, his leg began to free itself.

'Now the other leg,' said Matt. 'Quickly. Now press your back and arms against the surface, and wriggle backwards.'

As Caton followed the instructions, his companion pulled his arm towards him. In less than a minute he was free, and lying exhausted beside his rescuer.

'Now for your son Harry,' said Matt.

By now the water that had inundated the channels and gullies was flowing across the highest surfaces. Already it was several inches deep. Tom saw the look of panic on his son's face, mirroring his own.

'Listen, Harry,' said Matt. 'Don't worry, we're going to get you out of there.'

'The water,' said Harry. For the first time there was a tremor in his voice. 'What about the water?'

Caton had never felt so impotent in his entire life. Nor had he experienced such a painful sense of impending loss.

'The water's good,' said Matt. 'It's going to loosen the sand and make it easier to pull you out. All you've got to do is follow my instructions. Just like your dad did. Okay?'

'Okay,' said Harry with a brave smile.

'Right then. Your dad and I are going to come around behind you. We're going to lie down on the sand just like your dad did. When I tell you, I want you to lean back as far as you can, with your arms behind you. Your dad is going to grab hold of you. Then I'll tell you to start wriggling. Okay?'

He was having to shout now over the sound of the wind and a distant roar.

'Okay,' came the plaintive reply.

Caton crawled on his stomach ahead of his companion, alert to every shift and ripple of the sand beneath him.

'Lie back now, Harry!' shouted Matt.

Caton wriggled forward until he could hook his hands beneath his son's outstretched arms. He heaved himself closer against the resistance of the hands holding his own ankles until they lay there, father and son, cheek to cheek. He was alarmed by how cold Harry's face felt.

'Now wriggle, Harry! Wriggle!' shouted the policeman.

Caton held the little body tight as it fought to free itself.

'Come on, Harry,' he urged. 'You can do it.'

He felt his own legs being pulled from behind, and a wave of relief as first his son's waist and then his hips appeared. He reached down, gripped the belt around the sodden trousers and heaved. There was a soft sucking noise, and Harry's legs and feet were liberated from the quicksand's deadly grip. The two of them were dragged through the water for several metres until Matt Wilkey judged it safe for them to kneel and then stand.

Harry threw his arms around Caton's neck and clung on tight. Caton wrapped his arms around him, hugged him close and looked around. They were now surrounded by water that came midway up their shins. There were several sandbanks visible above the surface, but it was obvious that they would never be able to find their way safely back to the shore. The strengthening wind hastened the current tugging at their feet. Worse still there was an ominous steady roar that Caton suspected must be the bore bearing down on them ahead of the turning tide. When it hit them, Caton realised, the force would sweep them from their feet and into one of the hidden channels, and then...

There was another, deeper, steady roar, like the sound of an aircraft, growing louder by the second.

'That's the Bay Search and Rescue airboat,' Matt Wilkey told them. 'I said it'd be alright, didn't I?'

Caton heard the catch in his voice as he said it; a subtext that warned him they were far from safe.

'Look,' shouted Harry excitedly as he pointed north-west across the bay.

The sun dipped below the horizon. In the blood-orange afterglow Caton saw the outline of an unfamiliar craft powering towards them. Preceding it, a torch-like beam of white light bobbed up and down. As the boat came closer he could see that it was skimming the surface of the sea, chasing a long crested wave with a white peak that seemed to roll ahead of it.

'That's the bore,' said the policeman quietly.

It was touch and go, Caton realised, which would reach them first. The rescue boat or the bore. Matt Wilkey knew it too. He moved to stand behind them, and wrapped his arms bear-like around the father and son. Somewhere faraway there was a new sound. The faint chop, chop of a helicopter. Too far, too late. At least, Caton reflected, when it did arrive there was an outside chance that its searchlight and heat-seeking equipment might pinpoint their bodies for the airboat as they were swept away. He squeezed Harry tight, felt his son's thin arms tighten around his neck and began silently to pray.

Chapter 47

The bore was close upon them. Less than fifty metres away. Had he not seen cars carried off by lesser currents, Caton would have found it difficult to comprehend that something two foot in height could have the power to drag them from their feet. But the sea was already around their knees, and their foothold precarious. He felt Matt bend his knees, and did the same to brace himself against the impact.

In unison they shouted to attract the attention of the crew. Their cries were drowned by the noise of the bore, the wind and the rescue craft. The searchlight veered drunkenly from left to right, seeking them in vain. With the lead wave less than twenty metres away the beam slid across them momentarily, lighting up as it did so the silver stripes of the policeman's yellow blouson, and then swung back, blinding them with its brightness. There was a sound like a seaplane taking off. The rescue craft changed direction, accelerated forward, surfed over the bore and hove to beside them. The noise of the engine and the propeller-like fan above them was deafening.

Hands reached out to grab them.

'Give me the boy!' yelled a voice.

Harry clung fast. Caton prised one of his son's arms loose and felt him torn from him. Strong arms gripped Caton and hauled his upper body roughly across the flat metal side of the boat.

The bore struck. As the boat rocked violently Caton felt Matt's arms slipping from around his legs as the current pulled him away. He twisted sideways, frantically clutching the neck of the policeman's blouson as he was carried past. The force of the tugging water and the weight of his colleague threatened to tear Caton's arm from its socket. The boat dipped. Matt's head disappeared beneath the water and remerged. Caton felt a rope being secured beneath his arms. He was hauled inch by inch further onto to the boat. More hands reached out and gripped Matt.

'You can let go!' someone shouted in Caton's ear. 'We've got him!'

Travelling at over forty miles an hour the rescue craft skimmed the waves. Within three minutes they were on the shore. Without a single piece of equipment beneath the hull, the airboat carried them right up the beach close to the crowd of watchers.

The three of them were wrapped in silver foil blankets and hurried towards the ambulances, and a paramedic car that stood in the yard beside Matt Wilkey's patrol car. Tom and Harry were taken to one ambulance, Matt to the other.

'I owe you, Tom!' shouted Matt.

'I think you'll find I still owe you,' Caton replied.

The policeman managed a weary grin.

'Let's say we're equal,' he said.

Not by a long chalk, reflected Caton as they helped him up the ambulance steps.

Harry lay on the treatment bench. He looked frail and cold, and scared. He was shivering despite the fact that his wet clothes were in a heap on the gurney and he was swaddled in a blanket. Caton knelt beside him and took his hand.

'It's alright, Harry,' he said. 'You're safe now. You're going to be fine.'

'He is too,' said the paramedic attending him. 'He's a strong lad. His heart's fine, he's breathing well, his blood pressure's better than mine and despite appearances, his body temperature is in the safe zone. He ought to be in shock, but he's not.' He looked down at Caton. 'To be honest,' he said, 'I'm more worried about you. You need to get on that gurney so we can have a good look at you.'

As Caton rose, Harry gripped his hand tighter.

'Don't go, Dad,' he said.

'I'm not going anywhere, son,' he said. 'Not now, not ever.'

He slumped onto the stretcher trolley, only now aware of how exhausted he really was. And cold. Bitterly cold. He held his hands in front of his face. They were bloodless. The nails had a bluish tinge. He shivered.

'Where's Roger?' said his son.

Caton felt it like a jolt of electricity. He had forgotten all about Hardman. The man who had placed his son in jeopardy and then abandoned him to save his own skin. Now here was Harry asking for him without a hint of resentment.

'He left you out there, Harry,' he said.

'He said he was going for help,' his son protested. 'He was going to come back.'

'Is that the guy who was walking with the lad across the bay?' asked the policewoman standing by the open ambulance doors, with her ear to his Airwave radio.

'That's him,' said Caton.

'Seems we've picked him up,' she said. 'The

helicopter that came out for you three spotted him up by Giant's Seat. Making for Carnforth Station. We had a welcoming party waiting for him. They want to know what you want them to do with him.'

'Tell them to bring him here,' said Caton.

She moved away from the doors, deep in conversation, only to return seconds later.

'They want to know on what grounds they can hold him,' she said.

Caton ran through the options. There was no way that he or they could arrest him with anything to do with the images on Helen's computer. Not without Sarah Weston's say-so. Nor did he want his son to know about them, always assuming that he didn't already know. He pushed that disturbing thought from his head. There was an alternative. One that in his panic and selfish flight Hardman had unwittingly provided.

'Tell them child neglect and abandonment, in that he has wilfully placed in danger the life of a child in his care.'

The officer looked uncertain.

'Children and Young Person's Act 1933,' he said. 'Just tell them.'

She nodded and walked out of sight, head bent to the radio mike.

'Roger was going for help, Tom,' said Harry. He said it without conviction, as though seeking reassurance.

Caton looked across at his son. He lay on his side, staring back at him. His bright brown eyes like saucers in that pale, wan face. So young. So innocent. It would have been so easy to lie. To tell him what he wanted to hear. The words caught in Caton's throat as he said them.

'No, he wasn't, Harry,' he said as gently as he could. 'No, he wasn't.'

He saw the shock in his son's expression slowly change to disappointment. Harry turned onto his back, tugged the blanket tight to his neck and closed his eyes.

Welcome to the real world, son, Caton reflected ruefully. Lesson one. Trust no one.

'He's here,' said the policewoman.

Caton sat up gingerly and swung his legs over the side of the gurney. As he stood, the paramedic took his arm.

'Where do you think you're going?' he said.

'Something I've got to do,' he said. 'Don't worry, it'll only take a moment.'

The policewoman took his arm and steadied him as he climbed down the steps onto the yard. He turned and saw another police car parked by the gates. It was the one that had followed him from Carnforth. The same officer who had confronted him stood beside the rear passenger door. His colleague, by the driver's door. They both wore their Hi-Vis jackets. Through the rear window, in shadow, he could see the back of Hardman's head.

As Caton approached the car, the officer on the passenger side opened the rear door and gestured for the occupant to get out. Hardman stood, and as he turned saw Caton coming towards him. He stood rooted to the spot. Shock turned to fear as Caton got closer. He cowed away.

'I didn't touch him,' he said. 'You've got to believe me. I didn't touch him.'

Confused, the officers looked at each other.

Hardman looked around him wildly, turned and ran. As the driver of the police car moved to head him off, Hardman swerved away, lost his footing and crashed into the drystone wall beside the gate. He pushed with his hands against the top of the wall and clawed himself up, dislodging stones in the process. He half turned to find Caton standing there. Back to the wall, he had nowhere to run.

'I swear I never touched him!' he shouted.

Caton shifted his weight to the rear of his right foot, pivoted around his left and hit him hard on the point of his jaw with a perfect hook.

Hardman's head flew back and his body slid down the wall.

As Caton stepped towards the body, he felt his arms being pinioned from behind.

'That's enough, sir,' said a firm voice with a distinct Cumbrian accent.

Strong arms restrained him. He was too exhausted to resist. He watched as the second officer helped Hardman into a sitting position. He appeared groggy, but not so confused that he couldn't recognise Caton.

'I want him charged,' he said. 'You saw him attack me.'

The officer holding Caton shook his head.

'We saw him attempting to apprehend you, sir. Saw him defending himself. You were the one with the slab of stone in your hand.'

'I didn't see…' Caton began, but the policeman released his grip, took him by the arm, led him a few yards away and lowered his voice.

'You're lucky you didn't break his jaw, or smash his head open on that wall,' he said. 'As it is, all he'll have is a bump and a nasty headache. You'll have to give us a statement. Nothing too explicit. Just how you tried to apprehend him after he abandoned your son. How he resisted. How you used such force as you considered appropriate in the circumstances. That's all. Leave the rest to us.'

Caton knew that he had lost it. That had they not appeared when they did, he might have killed him.

That he could no longer regard himself as immune from the feelings and temptations he had so despised in those officers who failed to live up to their attestation '...*to serve the Queen in the office of constable, with fairness, integrity, diligence and impartiality'*. On the other hand, a voice in his head urged, surely these were extenuating circumstances? There was such a thing as reasonable force. And perhaps Hardman *had* being holding one of the stones and *was* about to hit him with it? After all, he was too wound up to have noticed.

'I hit him,' he said. 'Nothing can change that. I realise that I don't have to mention it explicitly in my statement, but if he does, then I'm going to admit to it. I don't have a choice.'

The officer shook his head. 'If you're sure,' he said.

'I am,' Caton told him wearily. 'Can we make it quick? I need to be with my son, ring his mother and then I've a wedding to get to.'

Caton stood with his phone in his hand outside Accident and Emergency at the Royal Lancaster Infirmary, in a tracksuit lent to him by one of the police officers. Helen had finally calmed down when she knew that Harry was fine. That the hospital had given him the all-clear and that he would be leaving shortly with Tom. The same could not be said for Sarah Weston.

'Have you the faintest idea how difficult you've made this for us?' she said.

'Calm down, Sarah,' he urged. 'Cumbria police are holding him for putting Harry's life in danger, and then leaving him to his fate. Nobody's mentioned Internet pornography or paedophilia. Helen hasn't done anything with those files on her computer. If you get your skates on, you can send someone up here to arrest him on suspicion, seize the computers and charge him when you're ready. They'll hold him till someone gets here. So, no damage done. I've just pushed him up your wish list, that's all.'

'That's all! What about his one phone call? What if he uses it to alert the others in their dirty little network?'

'If he was going to do that, he would have done it already.'

There was silence on the other end. Caton cursed himself. He'd forgotten he hadn't told her that Helen had given the game away.

Her voice was charged with suspicion. 'If he didn't know why you were there, why would he warn them? Come to that, why did he run away?'

'Because he's a coward. Because he was trying to save his own skin.'

He could tell she wasn't buying it.

'Come on,' he said. 'The state he's in right now he'll probably plead as soon as you start to question him.'

He heard her sigh and knew that he had won. Or at best, got a reprieve until next time they met.

Now all he had to worry about was Kate.

Not for the first time, she surprised him.

'Don't be silly,' she said. 'You had no choice. Harry's your son. What were you supposed to do? Leave him up there with that pervert while we swanned off to wherever it is we're swanning off to?'

Caton was staggered, and mightily relieved.

'I thought you'd go ballistic,' he said.

'I did,' she replied. 'Poor Gordon, I hope he gets over it. Then I calmed down. You can thank Sarah Weston for that. She made me realise that all that mattered to me was that you, and Harry, got back safe.'

'I love you, Kate Webb,' he said. 'You are truly amazing.'

'I love you too,' she said. 'But my patience is wearing thin. So get yourself back here now. And remember, you're sleeping at Gordon's tonight. He's collected all of your stuff, and our suitcases. Don't let him forget the rings tomorrow.'

'I won't,' he said.

'And don't be late in the morning. Or I'll make you wish you'd drowned in Morecombe Bay.'

It was gone midnight when Caton arrived at Gordon's house. Marilyn, his wife, fussed over Caton like a mother hen. She showed a good deal less compassion for her husband, who was trying to sober up after the celebration-cum-stag-do he had been reluctant to leave. Caton drank a mug of steaming coffee. His deputy nursed a cup of black coffee.

'You missed a blinding do, Tom,' said Gordon.

'Don't rub it in,' Caton replied.

Gordon studied the two paracetamol tablets nestling in the palm of his plate-sized hand.

'Is Hardman going to press charges?' he said.

'I don't think so,' Caton told him. 'I don't know what they said to him in the car on the way to the hospital. Frankly, I don't want to know. But he hasn't mentioned it since.'

'Bloody good job too.'

Gordon tossed the pills into his mouth, grimaced, took a mouthful of coffee and swallowed.

'About your best man's speech,' said Caton.

'What about it?'

'There will be ladies present, not to mention a priest.'

Gordon grinned, and then winced at the pain that simple movement had prompted.

'Soul of discretion me,' he said. 'Your secrets are safe.'

'I don't have any.'

'I know, but they don't know that, do they?'

Now Caton was genuinely worried.

'Promise me,' he said, 'that you're not going to make things up about me just to get a laugh?'

'Come on, Tom. What is a best man supposed to say when the groom is whiter than white?'

'Given the multi-ethnic composition of the guests, not that for a start.'

'Okay. Boring as hell.'

'Certainly not that.'

Gordon drained the dregs of his coffee, rose from the table and stood there, swaying unsteadily.

'I'm off to bed, boss,' he said. 'You'll just have to wait and see.'

Marilyn let them both sleep through, leaving them just enough time to have a shower, a full English breakfast, and slip into their wedding suits. Caton had slept like a log. Standing there, looking at himself in the mirror, he marvelled at how half decent he looked. It was difficult to believe that the horrendous experience he had been through had taken place just sixteen hours before.

'Tom, the car's here!' shouted Marilyn from the hallway.

He adjusted his corsage, flicked his hand through his hair to create the ruffled effect that Kate claimed she found so appealing, and smiled back at his reflection.

'Here we go,' he said.

Life was never going to be the same again. Caton was glad of it.

He could have done without his team slipping white Tyvek protective all-in-ones over their wedding outfits and holding batons out to create a triumphal arch as they left the church, but in all other respects the wedding had exceeded their expectations. Father Brendan had even seemed comfortable with Kate's burgeoning bump. To cap it all, Helen had turned up with Harry. Kate had persuaded them to come to the reception too. At this very moment Harry was deep in animated conversation with Caton's aunt. He appeared happy and relaxed despite hs ordeal. The only obstacle that Caton could see now was the speech that his deputy was about to make.

Gordon stood to hearty applause and portentous cheers. In a parody of Dixon of Dock Green, in *The Blue Lamp,* the epitome of the good old English copper, he placed his hands behind his back, bent his knees, and straightened up again.

'Evening, all!' he began, prompting laughter. He checked his watch. 'Beg pardon. *Afternoon*, all.'

'He seems very confident,' whispered Kate.

'That's what I'm afraid of,' said Caton, nurturing the fixed grin characteristic of bridegrooms at such times.

'What to say of Tom?' Gordon continued.

He waved away the numerous, and less than flattering, suggestions from the guests.

'Let's just say, that opposites attract.' Cue more laughter. 'Let us consider the evidence.' He counted the points off on the fingers of his hand. 'Kate is beautiful, intelligent, charming, sensitive, entertaining, a delight to be with.' He paused dramatically and stared at Caton, then back at the audience. 'Quod Erat Demonstrandum,' he said. 'The Prosecution rests!'

Kate beamed, and Caton found himself joining in the applause.

'And let's face it,' said Gordon, turning to Kate. 'Who could possibly resist a woman who climbs onto the roof of Manchester Town Hall to attract your attention?'

The room erupted.

Kate leaned against Caton.

'He's doing us proud,' she said. 'Now you can relax and think about our honeymoon.'

Her hand found the inside of his thigh and stroked it sensuously. 'Where is it we're going exactly?'

Caton placed his hand over hers, stared into those fathomless green eyes, and smiled.

'That would would be telling,' he said.

The Author

Bill Rogers has written eight crime thriller novels to date – all of them based in and around the City of Manchester. His first novel, *The Cleansing*, received the ePublishing Consortium Writers Award 2011, was shortlisted for the Long Barn Books Debut Novel Award, and was in the Amazon Kindle 100 Bestsellers for over two hundred days. His fourth novel, *A Trace of Blood*, reached the semi-final of the Amazon Breakthrough Novel Award in 2009.

Bill has also written *Breakfast at Katsouris*, an anthology of short crime stories, and a novel for teens, young adults and adults called *The Cave*. He lives in Greater Manchester, where he has spent his entire adult life.

www.billrogers.co.uk
www.catonbooks.com

If you have enjoyed
BACKWASH
why not try the other novels in the series:

In order

The Cleansing
The Head Case
The Tiger's Cave
A Fatal Intervention
A Trace of Blood
Bluebell Hollow
The Frozen Contract

All of these books are available as paperbacks from
bookshops or on Amazon, and as ebooks on Amazon
Kindle, Smashwords, Nook, Kobu, Apple and most
other platforms.

THE CLEANSING

The novel that first introduced DCI Tom Caton. Christmas approaches. A killer dressed as a clown haunts the streets of Manchester. For him the city's miraculous regeneration had unacceptable consequences. This is the reckoning. DCI Tom Caton enlists the help of forensic profiler Kate Webb, placing her in mortal danger. The trail leads from the site of the old mass cholera graves, through Moss Side, the Gay Village, the penthouse opulence of canal-side apartment blocks, and the bustling Christmas Market, to the Victorian Gothic grandeur of the Town Hall. Time is running out: for Tom, for Kate... and for the city.

Awarded ePublishing Consortium Writers Award 2011

Shortlisted for the Long Barn Books
Debut Novel Award

THE HEAD CASE
*SOMETHING IS ROTTEN IN THE CORRIDORS
OF POWER*

Roger Standing CBE, Head of Harmony High Academy and the Prime Minister's Special Adviser for Education, is dead. DCI Tom Caton is not short of suspects. But if this is a simple mugging, then why are MI5 ransacking Standing's apartment and disrupting the investigation? And why are the widow and her son taking the news so calmly?

THE TIGER'S CAVE

A lorry full of Chinese illegal immigrants arrives in Hull. Twenty-four hours later, their bodies are discovered close to the M62 motorway; but a young man and a girl are missing, and still at risk. Supported by the Serious and Organised Crime Agency, Caton must travel to China to pick up the trail. But he knows the solution is closer to home – in Manchester's Chinatown – and time is running out.

TWELVE BODIES, NO MOTIVE, THE HUNT IS ON. A COLD CASE IS ABOUT TO GET HOT

A FATAL INTERVENTION

A SUCCESSFUL BARRISTER, A WRONGFUL ACCUSATION, A MYSTERIOUS DISAPPEARANCE

It is the last thing that Rob Thornton expects. When he finds his life turned upside down he sets out on the trail of Anjelita Covas, his accuser. Haunted by her tragic history and sudden disappearance, Rob turns detective in London's underworld. A series of rhyming messages arrive, each signalling a murder. Rob must find Anjelita and face a dark truth.

DEEP BENEATH THE CITY OF MANCHESTER LIES A HEART OF DARKNESS

A TRACE OF BLOOD

Niamh Caton and Tom Caton. Two people with a
common ancestry, separated by three thousand miles
and an ocean. Each of them in a city named
Manchester. Neither aware that the other exists. Until a
sequence of sudden and inexplicable deaths throws
them together in a desperate race to catch a killer,
before he catches them.

Amazon Breakthrough Novel Award
2009 Semi-Finalist

BLUEBELL HOLLOW

DCI Tom Caton's world is rocked when he learns that
he has a son by a former lover. Then the first of the
bodies is discovered at the Cutacre Open Cast Mine.
The victims appear to have addiction in common.
Suspects include a Premiership footballer, a barrister
and just about everyone at the Oasis Rehab Clinic in
leafy Cheshire. As Caton digs deeper, his world begins
to fall apart.

THE FROZEN CONTRACT

When Premiership star Sunday Okowu Bello is found
dead, DCI Tom Caton knows that this case is going to
be anything but straightforward. As he digs deeper, he
finds himself drawn into a bewildering nexus of
gambling cartels, security firms, the victim's Nigerian
sponsors, Far Right extremists, and Far Eastern and
Russian syndicates jostling for ownership of the club.
When a second body floats to the surface of the
Manchester Ship Canal, he knows that
the killing has only just begun.

also...

THE CAVE

A TEST OF COURAGE IN A RACE AGAINST TIME

A group of teenagers from a Manchester inner city academy set off for an adventure holiday in the Pennine Hills. Two days later, tragedy strikes. Deep below the ground, the six survivors struggle to stay alive until help arrives. The stories they tell about themselves will change their lives forever.

A rite of passage/coming of age novel, for teenagers, young adults and adults. *The Cave* explores themes that affect the lives of young people in the modern multicultural city. Think *The Cave* by Plato, meets *The Canterbury Tales*, and a far more hopeful *Lord of the Flies*.

and...

BREAKFAST AT KATSOURIS
An anthology of three short stories and a novella. A Caton's Quickies imprint of Caton Books

Breakfast at Katsouris – Adapted, as a short story, from *A Trace of Blood*

The Wren Boy – Adapted, as a ghost story, from *A Trace of Blood*

To Die For – A Christmas tale

The Readers – A new novella exploring the fragile barrier that separates the modern serial crime novelist from the serial killer

Printed in Great Britain
by Amazon